DEATH BY MOONLIGHT

Also by Virginia Dyer Vogt:

THE STONE STEPS

A novel of love, betrayal, and death in a
nineteenth-century New Jersey town.

"Underneath that pretty surface,
terrible things happened."

DEATH BY MOONLIGHT

by

Virginia Dyer Vogt

Lucky Publishers
Morristown, New Jersey

Printed in the United States of America

ACKNOWLEDGEMENTS

My heartfelt thanks to the following:

David Mitros, former Morris County archivist and author of many authoritative books printed under the auspices of the Morris County Heritage Commission. Many thanks for reading the manuscript and for invaluable insight on the history of slavery in New Jersey.

Mary McMahon, archivist of the North Jersey History Center and the Morristown and Morris Township Library, for aid in research and making available pictures and artifacts from the library archives.

The Honorable Kenneth C. MacKenzie, retired Judge of the Superior Court of New Jersey, for the inspiration of his fascinating public program on the Sayre case, presented in the actual courtroom in which Antoine Le Blanc was tried.

Ward Vogt Designs for photography and artwork.

Presbyterian Church on the Green and Jo Potter, church secretary, for help in locating the Sayre gravesite.

Adam Smith of the Morris County Clerk's Office for providing copies of slave birth certificates.

Tiffany Palisi and Barbara Burrell for reading the manuscript and providing insightful comments on plot and characters.

And to Lee Vogt, the most intelligent and perceptive reader I know, for being unceasingly generous with his time, support, and encouragement.

For my loves:

Emma and Mollie
Marlee and Michael

DEATH BY MOONLIGHT

To sleep – perchance to dream.
Ay, there's the rub!
For in that sleep of death what dreams may come . . .
Must give us pause –

William Shakespeare, *Hamlet*, Act iii

Author's Note

Death By Moonlight is a contemporary novel, but the horrific crime that drives the present-day plot is based on a gruesome event that actually occurred in nineteenth-century Morristown, New Jersey. The historical characters and their actions are authentic to the extensive public records that survive from that time. Some of this documentation has been reinterpreted, but not beyond what the evidence supports.

Morristown's most infamous crime has never been forgotten, and retellings of the long-ago murders and their aftermath frequently appear in a wide variety of publications and other media. Many of these stories feature a young girl named Phebe, whose restless ghost (according to local legend) inhabited the place of her brutal death, a much-renovated eighteenth-century farmhouse, until its demolition in 2007.

Most of the settings, scenes, and locations in and around both historical and contemporary Morristown are genuine, although some are altered to suit plot requirements. Sunnyside, the refuge for battered women, does not, and never did, exist.

All the characters and their actions in the contemporary portion of my story are fictional and have no relation to any living persons.

Virginia Vogt
Morristown, New Jersey

PART I

In the drowsy dark cave of the mind
Dreams build their nest with fragments
Dropped from day's caravan.

Rabindranath Tagore
Indian mystic and poet

Chapter One

Following the faint wisp of music, she stepped off the wide Victorian porch into the dappled shade of mature oak trees trimmed high. The neat yard was dominated by a large formal flower garden, divided into beds by paths of old brick. The greens of striped hosta, white-tipped ivy, and old-fashioned ferns were broken at strategic intervals by wrought-iron urns overflowing with late-season bloom of pink and red impatiens.

Her senses had become highly acute, and she noted the trick of perspective used by a long-gone master gardener to make the space seem deeper than it was – the subtle diminution of the central path's width as it wound its way toward the back of the garden. She stepped onto the path, releasing the spicy fragrance of thyme growing between the bricks.

The garden ended at an eight-foot stone wall made of a distinctive purple-and-white native rock called puddingstone, its contrasting tones softened by the dim light. This wall butted up against a less decorative concrete boundary. Between the two walls was a wide crack where the concrete had broken down. Before she could think about it, she pushed through the gap, tearing her diaphanous silk skirt.

What she saw when she emerged on the other side of the

wall would have surprised the thousands of people who passed within hailing distance of this spot every day. Only a single long block from the main street of this old New Jersey town was a deep, wild ravine. The bank where she stood plunged downward toward the deep shadows at the ravine's bottom. She could hear the soft burble of moving water, intermingling with the plaintive piano melody that hung in the air. Grasping at saplings to control her descent, she started down the steep incline.

At the ravine's bottom, growing next to the stream, was a huge oak whose enormous canopy reached far above the top of the bank. She loosened her grip on a small branch and half-ran, half-fell toward this giant tree, coming to rest against its striated bark. Lulled by the soft rush of the stream and the faint scurrying of small animals, her rapid breathing eased into a slower, deeper pattern, and her eyelids closed.

Soon she was roused by the music, louder now, and by an odd, tangy smell. When she opened her eyes, her attention was immediately drawn to the opposite side of the stream. A large grove of flowering fruit trees grew there, perhaps apple, or cherry, white-and-pink blossoms sparkling against the blue sky. The understory of the grove was made up of masses of red roses, almost iridescent in their intensity.

The sick-sweet odor in the air became more insistent, filling her nose and drifting deep inside her. The odor seemed to increase her already keen visual acuity, and she spotted something beneath the rose bushes. She quickly crossed the water, teetering on carefully placed stepping stones, and headed toward the blood-red roses.

There it was – the thing that had caught her attention. Poking out from the thorny thicket, splayed onto the path, was a human hand. The hand lay still as marble, palm upward, surrounded by a faint fluorescence, fading to nothingness beyond the slender wrist. She extended her foot and prodded the edge of the hand. It felt heavy and lifeless through the sole of her ballet flat.

She knelt down, bringing her eyes near ground level, inches from the hand. The yellowish color and smooth skin texture gave it the bloodless look of a Halloween prop. The hand displayed ragged nails and rough calluses, yet was small and graceful. A recent cut, blood-tinged and swollen, marked the fleshy part of the hand below the thumb.

She reached out and barely brushed the hand with her forefinger. At her touch, the hand trembled. She shot up from her knees, but she was too slow. Quick as a frog's tongue, the hand closed on her left ankle. A stinging, electric vibration flowed through her body. She kicked repeatedly at the hand with her other foot until it loosened its grip, pitching her backward.

She pushed herself to her feet and ran from the grove, her feet slipping into the stream as she lurched across the stepping stones. Breathing heavily and grasping frantically at branches, she pulled herself up the bank and stumbled through the space between the stone and concrete walls.

Chapter 2

A pair of women taking out trash heard the sound of footsteps coming from the back of Sonja Hildebrant's garden.

"Do you hear that, Emma?"

The other woman responded nervously. "Be careful, Mollie. The paper mentioned a homeless man in this neighborhood." Both women focused uncertainly on the rustling sounds, putting their hands above their eyes to block out glare.

The young woman emerged from the shadows. In her haste, she tripped on a broken brick on the garden path and fell forward. One of the women hung back, but the other one was at the girl's side in an instant, assessing the situation. "Take it easy, honey. I'm a nurse. I don't think you've broken any bones. You're Anya Gregory, from the Theatre – you just spoke at Sonja's meeting. What are you doing out here in the garden?"

"I saw a hand," Anya blurted.

The woman raised her eyebrows. "A man?" She turned and called over her shoulder. "Mollie. Call 911. Right away." She turned back to Anya. "You saw a man? Did he hurt you?"

The concern of the woman brought Anya back to reality. She now saw clearly what had happened – what had been waiting to happen from the moment she arrived at Sonja Hildebrant's meticulously restored Victorian home. She spoke urgently to the woman called Emma, grasping her hand. "Wait. Don't call anyone."

"It's all right, Anya," said Emma, soothingly. "Just tell me what happened. There was a man? Where was this?"

The second woman, Mollie, ran up, still holding her cell phone. "Is she hurt?"

"I think she's okay, but she's a bit of a mess."

Anya spoke quickly. "I'm not hurt. I just tripped on a brick." She let go of the woman's hand and stood up, still hoping to minimize the situation.

Emma looked doubtful. "You're pretty banged up. You've got some nasty scratches on your arms."

The two women exchanged looks above Anya's head. "The police are on their way," Mollie said.

Anya saw that there was no escaping an escalation of the incident. If she hadn't panicked and caught the attention of the two women, she could have quietly slipped out of the garden and walked home. But it was too late. She let the two women lead her into Sonja Hildebrant's kitchen.

The news of the soiled and disheveled young woman had spread among the group that had stayed behind to help after the meeting. As they watched Anya being gently deposited in a chair at the kitchen table, the front door bell rang. A uniformed policeman and a powerfully built young man in neat khaki slacks and a button-down shirt entered the room. While the policeman took out a notebook, the younger man ran a professional eye over the scene: a drop-dead-gorgeous young woman with a dirt-streaked face and fresh scratches on her arms and bare legs; several determined pants-suited women fussing around her, offering tea and sympathy; an expensively groomed older woman in a pale gray silk suit, brandishing a dampened tea towel. Other people milled around the kitchen doorway, murmuring to one another.

He'd have to get rid of the crowd. But first he took the tea towel from the woman in gray silk. He knelt down and gently held the extraordinary girl's small chin as he dabbed at a streak of dirt on her cheek. He watched as her grass-green eyes focused on him, wide open. He spoke quietly, only to her. "I'm Detective Mitchell. Are you hurt? Do you need an ambulance?"

Anya lowered her gaze. "No. It's just scratches." He noticed how her dark, curved lashes cast a violet shadow across the top of her cheekbones.

The detective, still on one knee, wanted to see the color of her eyes up close again, so he could remember it. "What's your name?" he asked.

She looked up, as he had hoped. "Anya Gregory."

"Anya Gregory," he repeated, listening to the sound of her name in his own voice.

The uniformed officer with the pad and pencil broke in. "What's this about a man in the woods, miss?" he asked.

The detective, younger than the officer by at least two decades, stood up. "Let's clear this room first, Reilly."

The two women who had found Anya were reluctant to leave, feeling somewhat proprietary. But their hostess took charge. "All right, people. Let's move out of here so the police can do their job," Sonja Hildebrant ordered. The room emptied quickly.

Someone had put a cup of tea in front of the girl, and the detective moved it closer to her. Her small hands reached toward the cup. He noted she wore no ring. "Drink your tea, Miss Gregory. Then just tell us what happened, in your own words. Take your time."

Anya searched for a way to close the matter quickly. She recounted how she'd gone outside for some air and walked to the back of the garden. The part about ducking between the walls was harder to explain.

"So you decided to squeeze through a crack in a wall and run down into a gully, the way you're dressed?" the uniformed officer asked skeptically.

She hesitated. "I didn't really decide. I just did it."

The detective broke in. "Never mind that right now. What happened then?"

"I went down the bank and into the ravine. I leaned against a big tree there. I saw something across the stream, near some flowering trees, underneath the red roses. When I crossed the stepping stones I saw . . . a person's hand."

"Someone heard you say this guy grabbed you?" the officer asked. "Could be the homeless guy," he commented, looking at the detective.

"The hand grabbed my ankle," Anya answered carefully.

Detective Mitchell turned to his companion. "Get some manpower here, Reilly. Whoever's around the station plus call in a couple of units."

While the officer used his cell phone, the detective turned back to the girl. "Okay, Miss Gregory. Was it your impression that the person who grabbed you was sick or injured? Did he mean to hurt you or try to come after you?"

"I ran. Nobody followed me."

"As soon as the other officers get here, they're going to take a good look in this ravine."

"Can I go home?"

Mitchell sensed her great need to get away. "Do you want to go to the emergency room? Have somebody take a look at those scratches? I can take you."

"Oh, no. I'm fine." She tried to smile reassuringly. "I'd really just like to get home."

"I'll take you home, then," Mitchell declared.

Before Anya could answer, a resonant voice with a slight Scottish accent spoke from the open kitchen doorway. She recognized the speaker from the meeting; he had a precisely trimmed reddish beard and close-cropped hair and was as burnished and expensively styled as Sonja herself. "I'm Dr. Bennett, a friend of Anya's. I can see her home. I'm headed right past her place."

The detective looked disappointed. "Miss Gregory?"

"Yes. If Dr. Bennett could drop me, that would be easiest," Anya replied, grateful to the man who had volunteered to get her away from the policemen.

Detective Mitchell stood up. "All right. Go home and get cleaned up. We'll do a thorough search, and I'll get back to you."

Once she was settled in the front seat of Sebastian Bennett's dark blue Mercedes, Anya felt at a keen disadvantage. She looked sideways at Bennett's even profile. She didn't know him well; he ran Sunnyside, the home for battered women that was Sonja Hildebrant's major philanthropic endeavor. Bennett was often with Sonja at the South Street Theatre, where Anya worked, but she'd never really spoken to him. To break the silence, she cleared her throat and said, "I hope I'm not getting your car seat dirty, Dr. Bennett."

He turned his head to look at her before he spoke. "Please, Anya. Don't be formal. Call me Sebastian. And I'm concerned about you, not my car. My upholstery will survive. It's leather." His firm mouth broke into a small smile.

"Please don't worry about me. I'm embarrassed enough about the whole thing."

"Don't be embarrassed," he replied, lifting his neat, dark brows. "You're obviously a free spirit. Willing to follow your nose where it leads you."

"I'm not sure why I followed my nose. I just hope there isn't a big thing made of it. I don't want it to detract from my program at the Theatre."

"I'm sure it won't, Anya. Sonja will put an end to any discussion if it should come up." He looked amused at the thought of someone broaching a subject after Sonja signaled it out of bounds.

She replied more optimistically than she felt. "I hope you're right."

Silence fell between them again, although Anya could feel him glancing at her. She was glad when he pulled up in front of the Ralston Club. She reached for the door, but the automatic lock was engaged. Bennett sat for a moment, apparently thinking. Then he turned toward her. "Anya. You can count on me to minimize the afternoon's events to anyone who asks. But I'm worried that your experience may have some adverse after-effects. If you want to discuss it, I'm always available to you."

"Dr. Bennett. Sebastian. I just took a tumble. I don't need a psychiatrist," she said, more sharply than she had intended.

Bennett raised an eyebrow, still watching her. "I don't necessarily mean professionally, Anya. If you ever just want to talk to a friend, let me know." His dark eyes were wide with concern, and she felt comforted.

Bennett got out of the car and came around to assist her. He walked her up the front stairs of the Ralston Club, holding her arm and shielding her disheveled appearance from passersby, staying with her until they reached the stairway that led to the club's rented rooms above. Before letting her go, he took her hand. "Don't worry about Sonja. She has complete faith in you and your program."

He watched her slim dancer's legs ascend the carpeted steps all the way to the top before he turned to go.

Chapter 3

The Ralston Club was built in 1838, in the Greek Revival style of the day, with graceful columns supporting a wide front veranda. The mansion was then the centerpiece of the extensive estate of a prominent New York architect. Few people knew that the three-story structure had been picked up and moved several blocks to its present location in 1885. Today the mansion floated in a sea of later-built, beautifully restored Victorian homes, comprising a historic district that extended north toward Morristown's town square, known as "the Green."

The old house had been purchased by a local neighborhood association in 1968 to prevent high-density residential development. It was quickly renovated and repurposed as a private club. A large pool was installed on the overgrown back acres, and swim memberships were offered, providing much-needed operating capital. Additional revenue was derived from the large, elegant dining room and a popular bar, and from the rental of small apartments on the second and third floors, mostly to professionals on temporary assignment or house hunters staying in town for short periods.

Unsurprisingly, Sonja Hildebrant, an enthusiastic historic preservationist, had been most generous in her support of the

13

Ralston Club. She often put Theatre guests up at the Ralston, and it was where she had settled Anya after hiring her.

* * * * *

After leaving Sebastian Bennett, Anya unlocked the door to her apartment, desperate to shower away the bits of grass and twigs from the afternoon's unplanned adventure. Her cell phone rang as she was pulling off her ruined skirt. Anya knew it would be her mother, who called her around this time most days. Anya did not mind these frequent calls, knowing that her striking out on her own had been hard on her elderly parents.

"Hi, Mom."

"Hello, Anya. How are you?" Her mother's slight Russian inflection had never quite disappeared after more than thirty years in America. Her father's accent was heavier, probably because he spent most of his spare time with an aging group of fellow Russian ex-pats at a social club in downtown Ithaca.

"I'm okay, Mom," Anya replied a bit too quickly.

Her mother was hoping for another enthusiastic report on Anya's job and her new life in Morristown. But Anya's voice set off an alarm. She was always on guard when it came to her only child. Despite a small flutter in her stomach, she spoke calmly. "What has happened, Anya?"

Anya hesitated, but she wasn't in the habit of concealing information from her parents. "I had one of my things."

"You're not hurt, Anya?" her mother asked quickly.

"No, no, I'm fine, but the police were called." Anya briefly related her descent into the ravine and the incident at the bottom, minimizing the detail.

Anya's mother asked quickly. "Did the thing you saw in that place touch you?"

"I'm not sure." She didn't want to further alarm her mother.

"Did you make contact? Tell me, Anya."

14

Anya paused for a few beats before she replied. "Yes."

Her mother was holding her hand over the old-fashioned house phone, muffling the sound, but Anya could discern the anxious tone of the conversation between her parents. Then her father came on the line. "Anya. Your mother has told me what happened."

"Daddy. Please don't worry."

"You are gone from home to live for the first time, Anya."

"I know, Daddy. But I haven't had a problem in a long time. And everything's going so well here."

"Listen, Anya. I will call Celia and Dr. Lubov. They will know what to do. Celia will come there."

"Daddy, Aunt Celia doesn't need to come. I'm doing fine."

"Celia can always come to you. Dr. Lubov says."

"I know. But I don't need anybody. Tell Mom I'll call her back tomorrow. Don't worry."

"We love you, Anya."

"I know, Daddy. I love you."

She put down her cell phone and went straight to her small bathroom to shower and disinfect her scratches. Afterward, she tried to decide whether to make a sandwich or just have a glass of wine and go to bed, putting the disastrous afternoon behind her. She was surprised by a tentative knock on the door. Usually people were not allowed upstairs to the rented rooms unless they were with a boarding guest.

"Who is it?"

"Peter."

Peter Thayer could talk himself into anywhere. Last week Anya saw him get a table in a packed restaurant by casually taking a Bible from his briefcase while chatting up the head waitress.

"I'm not dressed," Anya said through the door.

"Put on something and we'll get an early dinner."

Anya glanced at the clock. She wanted the day to be over,

but it was barely evening. She didn't feel like getting dressed again. "I don't want dinner, Peter. Thanks anyway."

"You should eat, Anya. Come down."

He was so persistent. "Wait downstairs, Peter."

Anya ran a brush through her long, still-damp hair and secured it at the back of her neck. She pulled on skinny black pants and a ballet-neck tunic with long sleeves, covering the scratches on her arms. Her image in the mirror betrayed little of the afternoon's incident.

Peter Thayer was waiting for her, sitting in a vintage red velvet sofa at the foot of the stairs. He was a big man with boyish dimples and dark brown eyes. His longish chestnut-colored hair was carefully cut so that it would casually fall forward on his forehead and curl engagingly around his ears. She had been introduced to Peter by Sonja Hildebrant during her first week in Morristown and had seen him several times. Sonja treated Thayer affectionately, like a slightly dim son who needed to be encouraged to find a better class of playmate.

Before Anya could say a word Thayer put his arm around her and led her toward the book-lined bar off the main hallway. The retrofitted bar was the mansion's former library. Its shelves reflected the eclectic literary tastes of the many occupants who had lived in the old house. Ralston Club members could borrow volumes on the honor system, and they were encouraged to add worthy books of their own to the collection.

After seating Anya at one of the bar's small bistro-style tables, Thayer hurried off to order drinks. Anya was distractedly looking at books in the dim light when she recognized the woman sitting at the next table – Jillian Tremont, Dr. Bennett's colleague, who also had been at Sonja Hildebrant's meeting. Her heart sank as the attractive blonde spotted her.

"It's Anya Gregory, yes?" the woman asked, turning her chair to engage Anya. Anya could tell immediately that Tremont had been drinking. She had the kind of look that people get when they've overshot their happy place and are on an inevitable flight path to morose intoxication. "Don't worry," the woman continued, slurring her words slightly. "I'm not going to ask you about what happened this afternoon."

"Thanks," Anya said quickly. "It's been a long day." She felt obliged to continue the conversation with Tremont. "You know, I didn't know anything about Sunnyside until the meeting today. Congratulations on being part of such a big success," she offered.

Tremont lifted her drink and finished it off. "Thank you, Anya." She dropped her lazy smile, her eyes narrowing. "That's more acclaim than I've had in two years from some people." Then there was a flurry as Thayer returned with drinks. Tremont cocked her head flirtatiously at him. "Look who's here with Anya. Sunnyside's handsome preacher guy." The blonde woman laughed, too loudly. "I can't blame you, Peter. Anya's gorgeous."

"Hello, Jillian. Are you waiting for someone?" Anya could tell Thayer was annoyed by Tremont's drink-induced familiarity.

"I was supposed to meet Sebastian. But it appears he's been summoned by Queen Sonja." She laughed again, this time without humor, reaching for her empty glass. "Maybe I should have another one of these," she said, looking up at Thayer.

"Jill, you know Dr. Bennett couldn't run Sunnyside without you," he replied, ignoring the proffered glass.

Tremont put her glass down, disappointed. "Don't worry about me, Peter. I always get my man in the end."

Thayer picked up his and Anya's drinks. "We've got to go. Our table's ready."

Before they could move off, Tremont placed her slim hand with its long, French-manicured fingernails on Anya's arm. "You be careful, Anya," she said, suddenly sober.

Anya couldn't think of what to say. Thayer guided her out of the bar. Once they were by themselves in the hall, he moved in. "I came as soon as I heard," he said, leaning his head down, so close his warm breath tickled her ear.

She quickly moved away from him. "What did you hear?" She hated to think the news of the afternoon had got out so fast, although she knew Thayer was always among the first to hear everything. His position at Sunnyside involved offering spiritual counseling to clients who were interested in that sort of thing. His vague ministerial identity, plus his friendly-puppy demeanor, gave him an inside track on town gossip.

Thayer saw he had overplayed his first card and backed off. "I just heard that you had a bit of a shock earlier," he replied easily.

"Who have you been talking to, Peter?" she demanded, not mollified.

"I happened to run into Sonja. She was worried and planned to check on you later. I said I'd like to do that."

"What did you hear?" she asked again, still irritated.

"Well, it doesn't matter, does it?" he countered. "You tell me what you want me to know. Come on. Let's have dinner."

As they paused at the archway to the dining room, Anya spotted Sebastian Bennett and Sonja Hildebrant at a corner table near one of the fireplaces. Sonja had changed her gray silk pantsuit for a full, flowered skirt and a cream-colored wrap-style blouse. Bennett was leaning toward her, speaking attentively as he refilled her wine glass. She dipped her head to one side, smiling up at him, then briefly put her hand on Bennett's when he set the wine bottle back on its stand.

Anya took Thayer's arm and pulled back. She simply could not face Bennett and Hildebrant tonight. "Peter, I don't want dinner. I just want to go back to my room and get some rest."

Thayer had been hoping to extend his concerned-friend role into at least dinner, and maybe more. He'd been hoping for much more since the moment he'd met Anya. Now he saw he wasn't going to be able to spend the evening with her, and he was bitterly disappointed. But he kept his game face on and escorted her away from the dining room.

"Are you all right, Anya? We can go somewhere else, just get coffee and dessert, or a brandy," he suggested, without much hope.

"No, thanks, Peter."

He had no choice but to concede defeat for the moment. At the bottom of the staircase he took her hand. "Listen, Anya. I'll leave my cell phone on all night. You can call me no matter what time it is." Anya let him kiss her lightly on the corner of her mouth before she went up. His hair smelled like sun-warmed wheat with a hint of chocolate.

Sonja Hildebrant had spotted Anya at the dining room threshold. She and Sebastian Bennett had been talking about what had happened to Anya after her meeting. She knew, both instinctively and from Bennett's conversation with Anya, that the last thing the young woman needed tonight was further attention. So she pretended not to notice Anya and Peter Thayer, who was hovering around her like a bee on clover.

Poor Peter. He was so obviously smitten by Anya. And why not? Anya was the most extraordinary little thing. Sonja thought back to their first encounter. She'd been in her office at the South Street Theatre when she looked up to see Anya framed in the doorway, balancing her laptop, her violin, and a basket of shiny apples and dark purple Concord grapes.

Long smoky-black hair flowing from a deep widow's peak. A small heart-shaped face with high cheekbones. Tilted, almond-shaped green eyes. Sonja, well traveled, had postulated a central Asian ancestry, perhaps with a touch of Tatar from the deep past.

Anya had shyly set the basket of fruit on Sonja's neat desk. "From home," she'd said – the first words between them. The young woman had a quirky, crooked half-smile that appeared at intervals for no apparent reason, perhaps in response to something going on inside her head. It had been lunchtime, and Sonja had countered the fruit offering with a wedge of French bleu cheese and imported biscuits from her small under-counter refrigerator.

After their impromptu lunch, Anya had presented her vision for a series of performances that she had obviously been working on for a long time. Her small, tight dancer's body was in constant motion as she described a wild fusion of music, dance, art, color, and sound. At the center of this abstract but emotionally powerful performance, providing both focus and anchor, was Anya and her violin.

Sonja Hildebrant, the only child of a very wealthy family, had followed in her late parents' philanthropic footsteps. She was very good at what she did. She understood that people who can buy anything often find themselves looking for something more meaningful in their lives. Sonja used the Theatre to attract and cultivate moneyed individuals with cultural interests or pretensions – she didn't care which. Once they were hooked, Sonja could nudge them toward her more serious charitable enterprises, like Sunnyside, her refuge for battered women.

After Anya finished her informal presentation that first afternoon, Sonja had known instantly that this was what she was looking for – a new creative sensation that would enhance the South Street Theatre's reputation for push-the-envelope artistic experiences. Where had this stunning young woman come from? Sonja wasn't really interested in details and had provided few when she convinced the board to hire Anya as visiting creative director.

She had booked the young woman into the Ralston Club and given her a few weeks to settle in before inviting her to this afternoon's meeting to kick off publicity for Anya's series, "Inside the Mirror." And Anya's effect on her audience was everything Sonja knew it would be. In less than ten minutes, Anya had successfully locked in the support of Sonja's most important contributors and volunteers.

After Sebastian Bennett's presentation, Sonja had spoken briefly with Anya, congratulating her on the successful initial marketing of her program. The young woman seemed fine. A little sleepy, maybe, but then Sebastian's program had run long.

The next thing she knew, a bruised and dazed Anya was being escorted into her kitchen.

Sebastian had advised letting the incident pass without further comment. And so she would.

Chapter 4

Anya felt guilty about stranding Peter, but she was relieved to get into her pajamas and climb in bed. She was exhausted and sure she'd fall to sleep immediately. Instead she found herself cycling through the huge collection of music on her iPod. She turned to the classics and then went unhesitatingly to Beethoven's Piano Sonata #14 in C-sharp minor, "Quasi una fantasia" – *The Moonlight Sonata*. Anya had always thought the first movement of this exquisite composition was one of the most intimate works ever written for piano.

Propped up by several pillows, she listened to the halting rhythms and rushing crescendos with her eyes closed. She gave herself over to the haunting melody, hitting the iPod's repeat arrow many times, restarting the first movement and wondering what in Beethoven's life could have produced a piece of such lonely, desperate yearning.

The room darkened. She felt cold; her fingers were icy. She got under the covers, pulled the comforter up to her neck, and fell asleep.

* * * * *

After awhile she awoke. It was a fine, soft-lit morning. A wood thrush's four-line song wafted through the tiny window above her head. She listened to the sound of carpenter bees working the wooden window frame, internalizing their excited buzzing. She put her hand on her abdomen, feeling the blood singing in her veins there, surging with new life.

She got up, and through the tiny window she could see the landscape glowing with early-morning colors. A cross-timbered fence was covered with a profusion of blood-red roses still drinking in the dew. The penumbra of the rising sun shimmered in tones of yellow, peach and orange-red.

She dressed quickly and left her room, pausing at a larger window on the landing that looked toward the woods. The joyful morning colors collapsed into muddy tones of brown. Her stomach turned in upon itself. He was out there. She couldn't see him but she knew.

Where there had been a tiny flame of hope a moment ago, all was now dark foreboding. She had pretended to herself that he had gone, maybe north, maybe west, but gone for good, without her. Long ago, in a different time and faraway place, his forefathers had been everything; here he was nothing, less than nothing, all his time on earth.

But she must break from him; break a lifetime of too-close bonds. They must go their separate ways. Yet, she was all he had ever had, and he would not go without a price. She must make him see, make him go.

Her bare feet made no noise going down two flights of stairs. Those in the kitchen looked up, startled, when she spoke. I am sick, she said, as she ran across the room, her head lowered.

Once she was behind the shed she vomited the scant contents of her stomach and heaved drily several more times. Then, hidden from the view of those in the kitchen, she ran toward the tree line.

He was there, his body blending into the deep-blue shadows.

He pulled her down to lie with him. She did not resist, but submitted passively to his great need for her, expressed in the only way he knew.

Afterward he pulled roughly at her swollen abdomen. Whose? Whose? She let him think as he would. She told him that their entwined lives were over. There was nothing he could do. He must keep running.

His anger was white-hot, but he knew they had reached the end. He swore vengeance, and she trembled to hear it. She watched while he took a small knife from his tattered shirt and wiped the blade clean on his pants. He made two small cuts in the shape of a cross just below his thumb. Then he took her small hand and put his lips to it before marking her in the same way. The wounds bled and he mingled his lifeblood with hers.

They got up. He held her face in his hands, pressing tightly until she thought her head might burst. He released her suddenly, and she ran back to the house. She had created a small space for herself, for her plan, but now she must act quickly.

The scene shifted. The sky was now black outside the small window. Clouds hid the moon and stars, deepening the night. He came up the stairs without bothering to muffle his step. There was no need, no one but her to hear. He was on the landing below her now, making the sharp turn to the short flight of stairs that led to her. He ducked under the low ceiling and came into view, revealing his ready, false smile.

He went to the bed and picked up her cloth case. She rose and turned away from him to take up her cloak that was hanging on a rough peg over the bed.

The blow paralyzed her. A reflexive tremble traveled in waves through her limbs, making them jerk spasmodically. Her soul was suspended in time and space for what seemed an eternity; then came massive collapse. As she began to fall, he pushed her toward the bed. She lay there, her eyes open but motionless, the pupils black. Not much blood issued from her head wound, a cleft so deep it self-sealed with swollen brain matter. Then something was thrown over her, and the light was gone.

She was alone in the darkness, drifting – drifting toward a distant, featureless horizon. A volume of bright red foam rushed from her lungs into her nose and mouth, issuing forth onto the bed. A scarlet curtain rose in front of her still-open eyes, and she came to rest in a darker-than-dark place.

Chapter 5

Anya's scream was muffled by the Ralston Club's nineteenth-century heavy doors and thick walls. She felt encased in blood, swimming in it, choked by it. She couldn't breathe under the heavy covering that lay over her. When her eyes finally flew open, she saw that what she thought was blood was hot sweat. Her silk pajamas stuck to her skin. She threw off the comforter and began to breathe easier, but she was soon clammy and trembling with cold. She got back under the bedclothes and pulled the comforter up.

She could tell by the thin light coming into the room through the old, rippled glass panes that it was very early morning. Her heart slowed and she lay still for some time. Finally the day brightened, pushing the shadows back. She put her feet over the edge of the bed, wrapped the quilt tightly around her, and made for the bathroom. She threw up into the toilet. After resting a minute she got up from her knees, turned the shower on full power, and climbed in.

After showering she made tea and picked up her cell phone. When her mother answered she blurted, "Mom. I don't want it to start again," her voice quavering.

After listening, she said, "Don't fret, Anya. You have people

27

who love you, who are ready to help you always. I will call Aunt Ceci now."

"Thanks, Mom. Call Aunt Ceci. I love you."

She dressed and left for the Theatre.

Despite the nightmare and her rough morning, she managed to make calls, go to a marketing meeting, and draft a contract for a dance troupe with which she was collaborating. At the meeting, it made her nervous to see how much the Theatre was counting on her performance series to anchor its spring season.

Later in the morning, Sebastian Bennett appeared in the doorway to her office. It was unusual to see Bennett at the Theatre during the day. He had residential quarters at Sunnyside, but from what Anya had heard, he spent many nights at Sonja's home. He had never before made it down the hall to her office. She immediately suspected that Sonja Hildebrant had dispatched him to check on her.

"Hello, Anya."

"Hi, Dr. Bennett," she said, forcing a small smile.

"Sebastian, please."

"Sebastian," she echoed. She watched uneasily as he moved smoothly around her office, taking note of things without seeming rude. He was elegantly dressed as always; a crisp inch or so of white cuff showed under the rust-colored cashmere jacket, punctuated by gold cufflinks.

Anya used big sheets of foamboard to keep track of the major sections of her performance series, and these were placed along all sides of the room. Anya's storyboards did not indicate specific musical scores, dance numbers, or sets in a way that would make sense to the casual observer. Instead, they were filled with intricate swirls of color, musical notation written in a rainbow of hues, bright rhythmic lines dancing across the white background. She liked to use foamboard because it was lightweight and could be continuously rearranged, cut, and pasted with ease. She had created dozens of these in different sizes.

They looked more like abstract paintings of great energy than plans for a stage performance.

Bennett stopped in front of one of the larger boards. "Your work style is as unique as you are, Anya. You're synesthetic, aren't you?" he asked without looking at her.

"Well, I've always sort of mixed up my sense of things," she equivocated. He waited for more. She began again. "Yes. I see color when I hear music, and I have idiosyncrasies involving other senses."

When she was young, Anya was puzzled when people didn't understand why she studied and composed music with colored pens. She also heard music when stimulated visually by art or natural beauty. For Anya, music was never without emotional content, whether it was inside her head or from an outside source. The slightest snatch of melody or run of notes entered her ear as sound but reached her brain as pure feeling, infused with brilliant color and movement. Early in her musical life, after a perceptive teacher discovered her crossed senses, she became part of a long-term scientific study. A neurologist interested in non-typical cross-brain connections had written up her case in a leading psychiatric journal.

Dr. Bennett came closer to her desk, his brilliant blue eyes watching her carefully now. "You'd been thoroughly checked for brain lesions, of course?"

"Long ago. It's just a little cross-wiring," she said, trying for a light note.

"Good." He let a little time elapse. "Do you play other instruments besides violin?"

"Some keyboard."

"Really?" He sounded pleased. "Perhaps we can play together some time. Maybe some works for four hands – Schubert, Brahms?"

She smiled. "That degree of difficulty would be a stretch for me. I'm mostly strings."

"I'm guessing you are being modest about your abilities," he smiled. "And I suspect you enjoy a very interesting inner life, Anya Gregory."

Interesting, maybe, thought Anya. But enjoy is not a word I would have chosen.

After Bennett left, she spent the next hour hard at work on her storyboards until her cell phone rang.

"Anya Gregory?" Her name seemed to roll off the tongue of the caller, whose voice, rushed and intense, she immediately recognized.

"Yes. Is this the detective . . . ?"

"Detective Mitchell." He was pleased she recognized his voice but didn't like the wariness he detected in hers. She said nothing else, sensing he wanted something. He postponed getting down to business. "How are you?" he asked.

"Fine." She waited again.

Ball back in his court. "I'm glad to hear that." Mitchell cleared his throat. "I'm working on my report on the incident at Sonja Hildebrant's house." Still no reaction. "I thought you might be interested in what we found," he pressed.

"What did you find?"

Her directness was disconcerting. "I need to talk to you. There's something I want to show you. I'm near the Theatre now. I could stop by."

"I'm sorry. I have a million things to do. I'm expecting some people and I have a meeting with the development office," she said quickly.

"This is something that can't be put off. It has to do with how I write my report about yesterday," he countered firmly, dropping a hint of an implied threat.

She'd have to see him. "I could meet you for a short time around one. But not here at the Theatre. And please not at the police station."

He thought for a moment. "How about meeting me at Macculloch Hall? The museum. It's only two blocks from the Theatre. Someone there will let me use an office. I'll pick up lunch."

She appreciated his understanding about not wanting to be seen with the police. "Okay. I'll see you then."

"I'll have the person at the desk watch for you. Her name's Florence. Ask for me."

Anya hung up before he did.

Ten minutes before 1:00 Anya left the Theatre, crossed South Street and headed down Miller Road. She immediately passed between two impressive stone landmarks: the Morristown Library and St. Peter's Episcopal Church with its soaring carillon bell tower.

Two blocks later she turned onto Macculloch Avenue and spotted the museum. A historical marker in front of the old brick mansion told her it had been constructed in 1810 by George Macculloch, a Scots immigrant who built a canal that once traversed the northern part of New Jersey, connecting the Delaware and Hudson Rivers. More than a century after that, a Morristown ex-mayor bought the old mansion, filled it with antiques and artwork, and left it to the town as a period museum in 1953.

She approached a large front door sheltered beneath a high portico supported by four 25-foot columns. Inside was an elegant foyer that stretched all the way to the back of the mansion. Hanging from the ceiling of the second floor over an exposed stairway was a huge, brilliant crystal chandelier.

The front desk was at the left of the door, allowing visitors an unimpeded first glimpse of the interior and the amazing chandelier. Behind the desk, a silver-haired woman lowered her red-framed reading glasses, taking in head-to-toe details of the younger woman. "You are Anya Gregory," she stated with certainty.

"Yes. You're Florence?"

"I am, indeed. Detective Mitchell is already here. Come."

The woman pirouetted gracefully and led the way up the winding staircase to the upper hall of the second floor. There, to the
left, a closed door led to another wing of the mansion. Florence
opened the door and gestured for Anya to go in ahead of her.
"Don't mind the clutter back here. It's where we plan exhibits."

"I won't be here long," Anya said, her voice sounding curt,
although she hadn't meant it to.

The woman entered a room along the hallway without
knocking. The walls held drawings by the famous twentieth-cen-
tury political cartoonist Thomas Nast that were not currently
on display in the galleries. Sitting at a work table that had been
hastily cleared of reference books and catalogs was Detective
Mitchell. Florence's blue eyes fell on the broad-shouldered
young man. "Detective, here's your Miss Gregory."

He absentmindedly mumbled "Yeah. Thanks, Flo," without
looking at the woman, who turned and left the room with an
enigmatic smile on her face. Then he was on his feet, holding
his hand out to Anya, watching her green eyes. He used his
powerful handshake to maneuver her into the seat opposite him
at the table.

The detective opened a large brown bag and started pulling
out paper plates and napkins, wrapped sandwiches, packages
of chips, a container of pickles, and several cans of soft drinks.
"I took you for a chicken person, but I also have vegetarian,"
he said.

Anya was vaguely amused despite herself. "Do you cater on
the side?" she asked.

Mitchell was pleased to have elicited a light-hearted remark.
"I'm a cop. I know every deli and donut shop in town." He
passed her a sandwich.

She busied herself pouring diet soda into a plastic glass.
While they ate, he asked her some small-talk questions about
what she was working on at the Theatre. She wasn't hungry but
ate a few bites while he finished his sandwich quickly.

She accepted black coffee and sipped it while he cleared away the lunch things. Then he carefully stacked several manila files onto the table in front of him. "So, Anya Gregory. Is it all right to call you Anya?"

"Okay."

"We need to talk about yesterday."

Anya shifted in her chair. "I can't tell you any more than I already have."

He ignored her comment. "I don't usually join police searches. But there was something about yesterday's situation that made me curious." He got no response from Anya and pressed on. "So I went with the officers. We found your trail down the side of the gully. Followed it to the big tree you mentioned. But to make a long story short, we didn't see signs of anyone else but you."

Anya spoke carefully. "People said something about a homeless man. I'm sure someone like that would have run away."

"Ah, yes. The homeless man. The homeless are always among us," he mused. "There are homeless women, too. Some people don't think about that much."

"Morristown doesn't seem the kind of place to have much of a homeless population."

"That's a reasonable but uninformed observation. You'd be surprised. Our local address-impaired population keeps out of sight for the most part. They don't want trouble. When it's really cold, though, they'll get an urge to catch up on their reading. They sleep at the library tables and monopolize the washrooms. The police have to pick them up and take them to shelters."

"Libraries are public places, of course," she commented mildly. She shifted in her chair. "Do you have everything you need for your report?"

"Not so fast, please, Anya. We didn't find anybody, homeless or not, down there. But I did come across this." He slid his hand into his jacket pocket. Reaching across the table, he picked up

Anya's small hand, turned it over and dropped something into her open palm. She looked down and saw a corroded charm of some sort on a broken chain. It lay there in her hand, its surface an iridescent, mottled black. There was a small, now-empty setting near its center. "Is this yours?" the detective asked.

"Of course not." Anya abruptly dropped the chain on the table. She pulled her hand back and put it in her lap, surreptitiously scrubbing her burning palm back and forth on her skirt under the table.

"I didn't think so. It's obviously been on the ground for a long time. Probably decades." He picked up the chain and dangled the necklace in front of her. "It was near the big tree you mentioned."

She reached for her purse. "Listen. I'm going to have to run. I've got a lot to do this afternoon."

The detective made no move to get up. "I need to ask you something first, Anya. When I was poking around in that gully, I thought about everything you told me. A running stream. Stepping stones. Apple trees in blossom. Red roses. Wheel tracks."

Anya sat very still. "I was upset. Maybe I didn't remember the details right."

"The devil is in the details, Anya."

She lifted her eyes to take a good look at him for the first time. The muscular, sculpted body she remembered. That had been obvious in his powerful presence in Sonja Hildebrant's kitchen. Now she noticed his blue eyes, no hybrid color in them at all, just clear, blue eyes under short, spiked black hair. But his mouth – she shifted her gaze, not wanting him to see her looking at it. How had she not noticed the thin scar slightly to the left of the center of his mouth, tracing the narrow upper lip? A congenital cleft palate, long repaired? It was the only flaw in an otherwise perfect face.

She focused on what he was saying. "The thing is, Anya,

34

there's no water down in that ravine. Maybe some run-off in the spring, but not now. No stepping stones. And fruit trees blossom in the spring. Everything is dark and overgrown down there. There are no roses. And there's sure no wheel tracks. The only tracks I noticed beside yours were made by some kind of large canine – probably coyote."

He paused and put down his notes. "I don't think anybody but you has been in the bottom of that gully for years. To tell you the truth, I didn't even know it was there, and I've lived here most of my life."

Anya responded carefully. "Listen, detective. I'm sorry the police got involved. I wasn't hurt and I don't want to pursue the matter. I realize I cost you and your officers some time and trouble. I hope you'll forgive me and pass on my apology." Anya picked up her purse. "Thanks for lunch."

He spoke quickly to hold her. "I did a little digging." He picked up another file and settled back in his chair. He opened the file briskly. "You're from Ithaca, New York," he stated.

She sat back down.

"I gave the police in Ithaca a call. Someone passed on the name of a retired detective who knew your case. He says he came in contact with you at fairly regular intervals through the years." He shuffled papers and began to read from several faxed clippings: *Missing Girl Found in Woods. Young Woman Follows Music; Rescued After Fall into Well. Student Hears Screams Behind Wall.* He put the clippings down. "That was all you, wasn't it?"

He now faced a furious Anya, green eyes slanted and shining. "I was a kid. My record was expunged."

"Why expunged, Anya?"

"Those incidents were not police matters. An explanation was found."

"What explanation?"

Anya got up. She reached over and roughly pushed his stack of papers at him. He grabbed them as they slid off the table into his lap. "You shouldn't have done this," she said, her voice tight around the lump in her throat.

Mitchell got up and moved around the table. "Hold on. I followed a hunch, that's all. I found an old cop willing to fax me some clippings."

"That's it for me at the Theatre if this gets out."

"Listen, will you? If I hadn't – well, taken an interest in you, I probably would have written a report chalking up the entire incident to an unknown vagrant. I wouldn't have gone into the gully. I wouldn't have made any phone calls. I'm not even on official duty now."

Anya was incredulous. "You're not on duty? You got me here under false pretenses?"

"I just wanted to understand what's up with you. Listen, I'll officially close this case as soon as I get back to the station today. This is the last you'll hear of it."

Anya turned and started toward the door.

He was in front of her in an instant. "You're like a cat," she said, startled.

Holding the door closed, the detective spoke fast. "Anya, let's start over. I could care less about your wild teenage years."

Anya looked at him. "But won't you always wonder about those reports? And about yesterday?"

"It doesn't matter. You can tell me whatever you want."

"I'm telling you to leave me alone."

"Shit." Detective Mitchell hit the doorframe with his fist as she pulled the door open. It made her jump. She kept moving, going out of the room and down the curved staircase. Florence, at the front desk, raised her eyebrows as Anya rushed past her desk and pulled open the heavy door.

A few minutes later Detective Mitchell strode down the staircase, his face stiff and flushed.

"How'd that work out for you, detective?" Florence asked, her blue eyes peering over the reading glasses.

"Shut up, Flo," he replied, tossing the remains of the lunch into the trash container behind her desk.

Florence smiled and went on with the tasks at hand.

Chapter 6

The next morning Anya arrived at the Theatre in a loose dress, which she slipped off to reveal ballet leotards and warm-ups. She wanted to run through a dance sequence to check its length and to work on a passage orchestrated for strings. She left her office with her violin under her arm and her iPod hanging on a cord around her neck.

Anita Taylor from the Theatre's development office was backstage when Anya entered from the wings. Anita wore a name tag on her suit jacket and was speaking to a small group of older men and women. Several of Taylor's charges smiled at the pretty young woman with the long black hair and purple tights. She was apparently singing along with whatever was playing on the iPod, oblivious to her surroundings. When one of the group laughingly asked if Anya had escaped from *A Midsummer's Night Dream*, Anita Taylor did not smile.

Anya remained on the stage until she was satisfied that the juxtaposition of the experimental dance and the classical string sonata would work. On the way back she passed the open door of the Theatre's development office. She paused when she heard an angry voice.

"Who does she think she is?" exploded Anita Taylor, pushing

her mousy brown hair away from an angry face. "She roams around the Theatre in tights and then she's on stage when I want to use it for my presentation. Doesn't she look at the schedules?"

Anya listened as the young office assistant replied mildly from behind her desk. "Anya's doing her job. Music's her job. Tights are her work clothes."

An older woman standing by the filing cabinet chimed in. "You should have brought your donors into the Theatre with Anya on stage. They would have gotten a kick out of seeing 'art in progress.' Soften 'em up for your sales pitch."

Anita Taylor wheeled on them both. "You both think she can do no wrong. If it weren't for this development office, Ms. Gregory wouldn't be doing her job here at all, because the Theatre wouldn't be able to pay her. Her crazy program costs a lot more than individual artists. But that didn't stop Queen Sonja and the board from falling in love with her, did it?" Without waiting for an answer, she turned her back on them to go into her private office. "Your salaries have to be paid, too. Don't forget that."

The pair shuffled papers on their desks, exchanging looks.

Anya moved on to her office. She was sitting at her desk trying to decide whether to talk to Taylor about her unintentional gaffe when she heard the faint scratching again. She had been hearing the noise, and occasional bumping sounds, for weeks. Several times she had thought of reporting it to the front office but hadn't done so. With everything else that was on her mind, the sounds were more than she was willing to ignore. They seemed to be coming from the back wall of her office. She banged on the wall with a book. The banging was answered by the distinct sound of a cat's meow.

There were, in theory, no rooms beyond this wall; hers was the last office along the west side of the building. Looking closer, however, she noticed a faint outline around the tall bookcase that was centered on the back wall. She slowly nudged the heavy bookcase aside and saw clear signs of a plastered-over doorway.

She left her office and strode through the lobby, out the front door, and into a narrow alley that ran along the side of the Theatre. She passed her office window and then turned the corner to the back of the Theatre. Here she found an overgrown hedge bordering a thin strip of ground, unkempt and strewn with typical urban waste – plastic water bottles, wrappers, cigarette butts. On the back wall of this wing of the Theatre was a boarded-up window, the frame rotting.

As she reached the obvious conclusion that the wall in her office was not the back wall of the building after all, she heard the cat again. She tentatively pushed on the dirty boards. They swung in the window frame surprisingly easily, and a big calico cat shot out of the window. She involuntarily gave a startled curse.

Tentatively, she pushed on the loose wood panel again and inched her head over the frame to have a look. A woman's voice, heavily overlain with a forced-soprano, childlike cadence, spoke impatiently. "Hey, girl. You gone and scared the cat, banging on the wall like that."

Anya considered running away, and the owner of the voice sensed it. "Wait a minute, girl. I'm coming out. I ain't gonna hurt you."

Anya saw a muscular brown leg thrust itself over the windowsill, followed by its mate, and then a large woman gently lowered herself to the ground.

"My god, who are you?" Anya demanded, backing off.

"Hold onto your knickers, honey." The woman turned to face her, adjusting several layers of odd white apparel, although it was her face that caught Anya's attention. The reddest of red lipstick on the wide mouth. A full complement of dramatic eye makeup, penciled dark brows carefully arched. All on a canvas of pale pancake makeup spread thickly from hairline to neck.

On the woman's head was a platinum-blonde wig, side-parted, turned under in an outdated pageboy style. A pair of large white sunglasses was perched on the top of her head.

The white halter dress was bare, and for warmth the woman had draped a white pleated wool skirt around her shoulders. Her arms were big and meaty, walnut-brown, many shades darker than the pale face makeup.

Anya looked in the window of the hidden room again. She could see a narrow space of no more than six feet running the width of this wing of the Theatre. There was a small mattress lying on a pallet supported by old books; a board with nails holding what must be the woman's wardrobe, most of it white or at least was at one time; several stacked egg crates holding toiletry and household items. A good-sized cracked mirror was tacked to one of the green-streaked, mildewed plaster walls. Near the center of the wall behind the narrow mattress was a blank doorway, or what had been a doorway before it was plastered over in Anya's office.

"You're living in there?" Anya asked incredulously.

"Not everybody can live at the Ralston Club," the woman said archly.

"But are you supposed to be in there?" Anya asked, quite stupidly she thought, as she heard her own words.

The large woman jumped on it. "Oh, sure. The Theatre welcomed me with flowers and a big chocolate cake when I moved in."

"Who are you?" Anya asked.

"I'm Marilyn Monroe, as if you didn't know."

"The movie star?" Anya put together the platinum hair and the dress, vaguely in the style of the one Monroe had worn for the famous sidewalk-air-vent-blowing, skirts-flying publicity shot.

"That's right. Everyone thinks I passed, but I didn't. It was just a Kennedy cover-up. Those boys could fix anything. I'm just fine. I'm back with Joe. I'm waiting here for him."

"Joe?"

"Joe DiMaggio, of course." She looked impatient at Anya's question.

"Joe DiMaggio is dead." Anya wished she hadn't made the comment the moment it passed her lips.

The woman spat. "That's bullshit. Joe's gonna meet me here. He's the love of my life. Miller was too skinny for me. And too damn smart for his own good. All the others, they didn't mean nothing. Joe's coming for me soon."

Not wanting to follow this line of conversation further, Anya asked, "How long have you been living here?"

"Who cares? You're going to rat me out anyways. They'll have this place boarded up by nightfall. Then I'll have to go down by the tracks. It's dangerous there for an attractive woman, if you know what I mean."

"I'm told there's a shelter."

"More dangerous there."

Anya glanced inside the dark room again. "This must have been a big storage closet."

"So what? Doing nobody no good before I come. Followed the cat in. Cleared the place out and set it up real nice." The woman in the blonde wig, sensing that Anya had committed a fairly good chunk of time without bolting, pressed her advantage. "Look, honey. I know your name. It's Annie, or something like that, and you're the big new star here. I read the papers. Listen, Annie. We're both artists. Pretend you never saw me."

"Do you smoke or cook in there?"

"Nah. I promise." Marilyn quickly reached out and took Anya's pale hand into her own, surprisingly clean, black one. When Anya didn't flinch, she sensed a further advantage. "Then it's a deal between us stars," Marilyn smiled, slyly. "We're buddies, right? You won't be sorry, girlfriend."

Anya closed her eyes and put her hand to her head, where

she felt a tension headache threatening. "You know what, Marilyn? I've had it for today. You do what you want. I'm going home."

Marilyn smiled broadly. The thick makeup cracked a little around her lips. "See you around, Annie." She climbed back over the windowsill.

Chapter 7

It was 4:00 before Anya finally got back to the Ralston Club. She opened the door to her room and went straight to her laptop to check her emails. Celia's was on top.

> Hi Baby – I'm putting a few things in order here and will be with you tomorrow. Don't fuss. This will pass. Jimmy's coming, and we'll figure things out as always.
>
> Love, Aunt Ceci

There was another message, typically brief.

> Cya kid – J

Celia Ormand was not really Anya's aunt. Celia was working for Dr. Yuri Lubov at Cornell Medical Center when Anya was first taken there as a young girl. Whenever tests were done, or when Anya was to meet a new doctor, it was always Celia who explained everything, walked her along the confusing hallways, and held her hand while she drifted off in Dr. James Lang's sleep lab. Somewhere along the way, Celia had become "Aunt

Ceci" and Dr. Lang just "Jimmy." Over many years, through all the bad dreams, Jimmy and Aunt Ceci had kept her safe.

* * * * *

The next day after lunch her cell phone rang. "Hi, kid. Front door."

Anya recognized Jimmy's deep voice. "Jimmy! I'll be right out." More relieved to hear a voice from home than she'd like to admit, Anya hurried down the hall to the lobby and out the front door of the Theatre. There they were by the large free-standing Theatre marquee: Jimmy raising an invisible baton in a dramatic imitation of Leonard Bernstein and Aunt Ceci, chin up, holding a graceful ballet pose.

Jimmy hung back while the red-haired woman opened her arms to Anya. "Aunt Ceci. It's so great to see you," Anya said, peeking from behind the tall, slim woman. "You, too, Jimmy."

Celia Ormand took charge. "Let's go, baby. Our car's right over there. Jimmy's already got his stuff stashed in a hotel down the street."

They walked the few steps to a black van with New York plates parked illegally in front of the Theatre. Jimmy cut across heavy South Street traffic to go east. The Radisson Hotel was just a few blocks down, and Jimmy parked near the hotel's side entrance. Their rooms were at the end of a blind hallway at the back, remote from hotel bustle.

Jimmy unlocked the first door, a suite with a pleasant sitting area, a small kitchenette with a tiny refrigerator, and a big desk where he had set up his laptop. "Sofa bed for me," he said as they walked through to the other room. There, a queen size bed took up center space but still left lots of room for a series of hard-sided cases that were piled up under the window.

Anya eyes welled up and she couldn't stop an unexpected sob.

"Something I said?" Jimmy asked, turning to look at her.

The woman put her arm around Anya. "Why the tears, baby?" Celia asked, wiping them away from Anya's eyes with a tissue.

"Because you are both so great to come. I'm so sorry I had to ask. At home it was one thing, just going to the Center, but now you've had to bring all this stuff with you and leave your work."

Jimmy put his feet up on the desk. "Hey, Anya. It's nothing. Everything's portable these days."

Celia leaned close to Anya. "Listen, honey. You're our favorite work. You came out of nowhere all those years ago with your special qualities, pointing the way for Dr. Lubov. He got his genius award partly because of you."

Anya stopped crying and smiled at Celia. "Stop it, Aunt Ceci. I hardly register on the scale of Dr. Lubov's science stuff."

"Well, maybe I'm exaggerating a bit." The older woman made a face. "But you do matter. Most of Dr. Lubov's work is theoretical. You're real. You hold the promise of hard evidence in an important area of his work. He's always been interested in you, ever since you were a little girl. You know that."

Anya hastened to assure Celia of her appreciation of Dr. Lubov's efforts on her behalf. "I'm grateful to him. I don't know what I would have done if he hadn't reassured me and everyone else I wasn't crazy."

Anya had seen Yuri Lubov often during the years she spent time in the laboratories at Cornell. He was a razor-thin man with neatly trimmed beard and mustache; a remote man who lived mostly within his intellect, she suspected. He had the unbroken concentration of a grizzly bear intently watching the river at the beginning of the salmon run. When she was older, Anya sometimes felt like one of those bright pink fish swimming upstream. Lubov never said much; once or twice he'd awkwardly patted her head. For some reason she remembered his hand lingering in her hair.

Jimmy broke in. "Enough of this Great Dr. Lubov stuff. Let's hear what's going on." He set his small digital recorder.

Celia kicked off her high maroon-red heels and threw her oriental-style tapestry jacket on the bed. She ran her hands through her perfectly straight, auburn hair. "Right, Jimmy. Okay, Anya. Shoot. What's happened?"

"I should have been able to read the signs. But I never can. And now I've put my job in jeopardy."

"Just tell us, Anya."

"I was invited to talk about my program to a group of important people. At my new boss's house," she began. "I did well, I think, and afterwards there was lunch." Anya thought back to Sonja's impeccably restored Victorian home and its beautifully decorated period rooms. The mahogany dining room table had held a rich spread of tiny sandwiches and other finger foods arranged on silver platters, including an extensive array of fancy sweets for dessert.

"I ate too many desserts," Anya blurted, then giggled at the fake-surprised looks on Jimmy's and Celia's faces.

"Your sweet tooth is legendary throughout the civilized world," Jimmy declared. "What happened after lunch?"

"I went into the parlor to listen to Dr. Bennett talk about an addition to a women's shelter. He had an easel with drawings. Lots of budget talk and graphs and time lines." Anya explained how Dr. Bennett's presentation had set off a bout of post-lunch drowsies. It was warm in the room. The comfortable, over-stuffed chair she had chosen faced a large bay window. Outside, a sharp breeze roiled the limbs of a large maple tree, and the swaying branches cast flickering silhouettes on the semi-transparent silk curtains. She had tried not to watch, but the rhythmic movement was irresistible.

"You fell asleep?" Celia asked.

"Yes. The next thing I remember was sensing movement all

around me. I looked up and Dr. Bennett had finished his presentation. My heart was pounding, and I was hoping no one had noticed my little nod-off." She made a face.

Celia frowned. "What happened next?"

"I started to gather up empty tea cups to cover my grogginess. Sonja Hildebrant came over to compliment me on my talk. She told me not to worry about the dishes, that they had committees for everything. But I already had a handful, so I took them to the kitchen. As I was putting the cups on the counter, I heard music – just a snatch of a melody. It was familiar, but the notes kept fading in and out. At first I thought the sound was being piped into the kitchen through speakers, but then it seemed to be coming from outdoors, sort of floating through the open screen door. So I followed it outside, into the garden, and then through a hole in the wall."

"Maybe we should call you Alice," Jimmy quipped.

"When did you first notice inconsistencies, Anya?" Celia asked.

"It was like always. Nothing I did seemed odd in the slightest until I saw the look on the faces of the women in the garden later."

"But thinking back now?"

"When I first heard the music. It was beautiful and it seemed to call to me; so sad and plaintive." Suddenly Anya stood up. "I just remembered. Before I went to sleep last night, I found the music. It's Beethoven. First movement of *The Moonlight Sonata*."

"And you followed it outside and went straight for the ravine?"

"The music came from that direction and I went through the garden wall as soon as I could."

"When did you notice enhanced senses?"

"It started in the garden. I noticed so much detail. Then at the bottom of the ravine, there was this enormous old tree. The tree felt alive in a weird way, almost breathing. I leaned against it and may have slept again. When I opened my eyes, everything was vibrating and shimmering; the colors were glowing from within, vivid and unreal. And the smells were wonderful. Pinks and greens and soft grays. Sweet red roses and new grass and recent rain; even the soil smelled sweet – fertile and rich."

Anya paused, recalling the pleasure she'd felt. Then her face clouded. "But after I crossed over the stream, everything changed. The colors were all muddy. The red roses were mottled with black and purple spots, like bruises, or Japanese beetle damage. I smelled animals and mold and something else. Something sour and astringent – the smell of fear. I walked straight to . . . a human hand." Anya shivered. "I let the police think it might have been the homeless man they'd been looking for."

"You made contact with it?"

"Yes. It was like electricity."

Celia moved on. "Talk about your experience with the necklace this detective found. You had a reaction to that. You actually held it, right?"

"The detective put it in my hand on purpose. It was just a piece of old junk, but I didn't want to touch it, and he could see that. He used it to keep me there a bit longer. He enjoyed upsetting me."

Jimmy smiled. "Maybe. But guys with sudden crushes do dumb things. Describe the necklace, Anya."

Anya closed her eyes and her breathing slowed. It was a long moment before she spoke. "The necklace was so pretty. A delicate cross with floral etching, silver. There was a small green stone at the center, an emerald, I think."

Anya opened her eyes. Celia and Jimmy were staring at her. "What, Aunt Ceci?" she asked, puzzled.

Jimmy looked down at his notes. "You told us a minute ago the necklace was broken and tarnished."

"That's right."

"Well, just now you described it as in mint condition, and in detail."

Anya put her hand to her mouth. "Oh, my god. I'm remembering the necklace I saw near the hand. I forgot all about it until now."

Jimmy raised his eyebrows. "We may need to get that necklace."

Celia saw Anya was upset. "Why don't we just take things one step at a time, baby? We've made a good start. We're all together again, and that's good. Isn't it, Jimmy?"

Jimmy took his cue. "I'll tell you what I want to do. Get my gear unpacked and then have a nice drink followed by a good meal."

"Do you have to go back to work, Anya?" Celia asked.

"Yes."

"So Jimmy works here while I drop you off at the Theatre and then check a few things out. We meet for dinner later. Where, Anya?"

"Not the Ralston. The dining room's temporarily closed. The plaster fell or something. There was a sign up this morning."

Jimmy said, "The bartender pretty much dissed the food here at the hotel."

Celia wrinkled her nose at Anya. "Leave everything to me."

Chapter 8

After Celia returned to the hotel, she and Jimmy sat in his suite sipping large coffees and listening to the digital recording of Anya's voice. Celia was the first to speak. "Anya thought moving away from Ithaca would make her less vulnerable. But this incident has all the bells and whistles – initial aura, enhanced sense perception, induced dreaming, possible temporal displacement."

"You and Lubov discouraged her from leaving Ithaca," Jimmy offered bluntly.

"She'd been doing so well. We didn't want her to stumble and risk a setback."

"She might stumble, but she doesn't have to fall."

"You're so glib, Jimmy."

"Lubov tried to scare her into staying."

Celia was annoyed. "That's a gross exaggeration. Yuri just wants Anya to be safe. We all want that. That's why we're here."

"Lubov has never considered Anya as a young woman entitled to a life of her own. She's his personal science project. The gift that just keeps on giving, year after year, incident after incident. *That's* why we're here."

"That's ridiculous. I'm here because I love Anya and want

53

to help her. If you didn't want to come, you should have said so," Celia shot back.

"Of course I'm fond of Anya, too, after all these years. But I want her to succeed on her own."

Celia continued to defend Lubov. "You misinterpret everything Yuri does. Yuri's not good with people. Everybody knows that."

"Ah, yes. And you handle the human side of the equation. Keeping the subjects calm and pliable."

"People like Anya provide insight into what Yuri's been looking for his entire career."

Jimmy got up, sorry he'd started this old argument, but he couldn't stop. "Sure. Nothing's too small or too big for the great Lubov. From the inside of Anya's sweet little brain to the secrets of the universe."

"You've worked with Yuri all these years. You must think he's onto something."

"That's not why I've stayed around." He looked at Celia.

"Oh, Jimmy. Why do you do this?" She moved to his side of the room and took his hand. "Come on. We're alone together in a hotel room. Why are we fighting?"

Celia had little time for Jimmy when she was busy with Lubov's requirements. That was the way it had always been. But when the opportunity arose or when Celia had a need, Jimmy was her choice. Despite the bitterness of their arguments, Celia could leave off in mid-sentence and suddenly come at him with immediate and intense desire. And despite the misery of their long emotional standoff, Jimmy never said no.

For a long time the arrangement had worked. Excellent sex with a stunning redhead with minimal commitment required. What's not to like, he used to ask himself. But things change. He watched both of them get older and pass up certain life options. She wouldn't see that she invested most of her time and energy on a completely self-involved, giant intellect with no more than a superficial need for anyone else in his life, including Celia. He hadn't realized how much these facts would hurt him until he wanted more from her.

But now Celia was in his arms, all tension between them forgotten. She teased him by holding her body away while kissing him expertly, then moving tight against him. As he responded, she laughed with anticipation. There was no talking. This wasn't a seduction on either side. She wanted what he was so willing to give.

Most of their clothing was shed quickly. He pulled her toward the bedroom. She followed his lead, giving him the great gift of her huge, generous, untroubled smile – the smile he rarely saw outside of sex.

They made it last and enjoyed every second of it. Afterwards, they pulled away from each other to shower and meet Anya for dinner.

After dressing, Celia called Jimmy and suggested a drink in the hotel bar before picking up Anya. Seated in a comfortable booth, they were careful to keep the talk light, both wanting to hang on to their post-sex high and put the earlier rift behind them. At 7:00 they drove the van to the Ralston Club and found Anya waiting for them on the long porch.

As the three of them walked toward the van, they startled a large woman wearing a blonde wig and bizarre makeup, dressed in white, sitting on the curb. "Oh, hello, Marilyn." Anya said, startled to see her odd neighbor here, exposed to the disapproving eyes of this upscale neighborhood.

"Hello, Annie," said the woman in her little-girl Marilyn voice, raising her fifties-style Hollywood sunglasses, as if she had run into Anya by chance while shopping on Rodeo Drive.

Anya tried to think of something else to say and ended up awkwardly introducing Marilyn to Celia and Jimmy. Marilyn accepted the introduction regally. "I'm pleased to meet you both, I'm sure," she said, brushing leaf residue from her skirt and then solemnly holding out her hand to each in turn. She turned back to Anya. "I don't have time to chat, Annie. I have a date. With you-know-who," she finished coquettishly, pulling her sunglasses down over her eyes and turning dramatically. She strode off in the direction of town.

Jimmy raised his eyebrows at Anya.

"Someone who hangs around the Theatre. Homeless. I keep thinking I should call some agency about her," Anya responded.

Celia laughed. "You make the darnedest friends, baby."

The Red Rose Restaurant, or "the Rose" as it was often called, sat close to the road on South Street, not far from the Radisson Hotel and about a half-mile from the Morristown Green. Celia had noticed it when she and Jimmy first got into town, and she had stopped there after dropping off Anya at the Theatre to see if it might do for dinner. An attractive middle-aged woman at the podium who wore a name tag that read *Maureen* had advised reservations; it was Friday, the Ralston dining room was down again, and the Rose was a favorite backup, she'd said.

Maureen and Richard Sullivan had bought the restaurant, then called Phebe's, a number of years ago and transformed it from a staid local eatery into a trendy meeting place. Dinner from a fairly extensive menu was served in the early evening. Later the place became a popular singles hangout, where people of all ages sought, among the ubiquitous bar jerks, someone acceptable enough to hook up with and not feel completely humiliated in the sober light of the next day.

After parking in the lot at the back of the restaurant, the three of them walked around to the double doors in front. Inside, Celia approached the young woman who was standing behind a lighted podium, looking closely at a seating chart with penciled-in table assignments. "Good evening. I made reservations earlier. Celia Ormand."

"Thank you. Just a minute, please," The girl replied, her voice soft and breathy. She was small in stature, and the tight top she was wearing accentuated her generous breasts. Her shy, uncertain air contrasted with her sophisticated eye makeup and suggested a precocious, too-beautiful-for-her-own-good child dressed up in her older sister's clothes and cosmetics. She seemed nervous, her blue eyes darting from the chart to an adjacent private dining room. Her delicate hands pushed back the long, wispy blonde curls that framed her face.

The woman who had taken Celia's reservation earlier, Maureen Sullivan herself, was leading a group into the private dining room. Anya could see Sonja Hildebrant and Sebastian Bennett moving among the group, making sure everyone was comfortable. Anita Taylor from the development office was there. Anya surmised that the people at the table were likely an important group of potential donors who were being carefully cultivated. As she watched, Dr. Bennett straightened up, looked out into the foyer and winked pleasantly in the direction of the podium.

The young girl at the podium tightened her grip on the seating chart, her hands visibly trembling. She had the biggest eyes Anya had ever seen. And the color, a pure topaz, was very unusual. The blue dinner-plate irises seemed to float on pools of white milk. Maureen had returned from the private dining room and come around behind the girl where she couldn't be seen, watching her, perhaps giving her time to work things out on her own.

The door of the restaurant opened behind them, and two couples came in together. Right on the couples' heels was Peter Thayer, alone, looking vaguely ecclesiastical in a black shirt and slacks. The girl at the podium looked up. The seating chart fell from her small hands to the floor, and she turned to bolt.

Maureen was at her side immediately. She stood close to the girl and spoke to her quietly. "You're doing fine, Lily. Everything's going to be all right." The older woman addressed Celia.

"I forgot to put your name on the chart and that confused Lily. But there's room for everyone. Your name's Ormand, right?" she said, recognizing Celia.

"You've got a good memory, Maureen."

Maureen Sullivan took charge. "Let's get this sorted out, Lily. Peter, are you eating in the bar? Go seat yourself. You're a big boy."

Thayer had been staring at the tall, elegant man near Anya, who looked thoroughly western except for something subtly Asian about his eyes. He tried to figure out whom the man was with. He's nearer to the redhead's age, Thayer thought, but he was standing very close to Anya. Jimmy saw Thayer looking at him, and something annoyed him about the dramatic black clothing and the way he was watching Anya but pretending not to see her. Jimmy casually put his arm around Anya. She looked up at him and smiled, and he saw the other man's face darken. "Take your time, Lily," Jimmy said. "We're in no hurry, are we, Anya?" He smiled in Thayer's direction, still holding Anya lightly.

Thayer turned nonchalantly toward Anya as if he had just spotted her. "Hello, Anya," he said expansively, dimples flashing. "How are you? I'll call you later." He ignored Anya's companions as he moved off toward the bar.

Maureen sent Lily to seat the party of four and turned her attention to Anya's group. "Thanks for understanding. Lily's been a little under the weather, but she's a good kid. She's learning the ropes." When Lily returned she seemed back in control. She picked up three menus. Anya noticed her small, delicate hands, with a tracing of blue veins under the white skin. She was wearing a collection of silver rings with different pastel stones.

"Follow me, please." Lily spoke very seriously and led them to a nice corner table.

They ordered a bottle of white wine from a fairly large wine list and asked the waiter to put a second one on ice. While they were looking over the menu, a sandy-haired man with a thin moustache came up to their table.

"Good evening, folks. I'm Richard Sullivan. I own the place." Sullivan turned toward Anya. "My wife Maureen just told me we had a star in the house. Now I recognize you. Anya Gregory." Sullivan turned and pointed out a row of spotlighted posters near the small bar. One of them was a dramatic publicity shot of Anya standing in front of a large, ornate mirror, part of her arm and back seemingly on the other side of the glass. She was wearing a green dress cut for maximum effect, holding her violin. "Maureen and I go to a lot of the performances at the South Street Theatre. What's this 'magic mirror' thing on your poster all about?"

Anya smiled. "My show is called 'Inside the Mirror.' I hope you and your wife will come. If you're open to all kinds of music and dance and don't mind seeing things put together in surprising ways, you might like it."

"Just so I'll be seeing you in that green dress," Sullivan laughed, looking like he wanted to sit down with them. But his wife Maureen signaled from behind the bar. He frowned. "I've got to go. My bar manager took off on me last week. No notice. Just hired him, too. You never know about people. Maureen's helping out in here at the front bar until I can get someone else." His pleasant smile reappeared. "Listen, folks. The wine's on me. See you at the Theatre, Anya."

After Sullivan went off, Maureen came by their table and asked if Anya would sign her poster before she left. "Here's a Sharpie. Richard will be thrilled."

The food at the Rose was very acceptable, if not gourmet, and the wine was good enough, too. While they were looking at the dessert menu, a pleasant-looking man in a sports jacket who was seated by himself at a nearby table got up and sauntered self-consciously toward their table. "I just want to say a quick hello. I'm the Sullivans' business partner, Mark West. Maureen asked me to tell you if you ever need anything, a special party or celebration, or if you need a good table at the last minute, you can call me directly. We like to keep everyone at the Theatre happy."

Anya took the business card he proffered. "Thank you, Mark. We've enjoyed our dinner very much. And this is such an interesting building."

West lit up, smiling warmly at Anya. "I love this place. The Red Rose Restaurant is not only my job, it's my hobby. I get teased about that a lot." He smiled shyly, as if he had revealed too much about himself. "I'm almost always around here someplace. That's my regular table, over in the corner." He stood there awkwardly for a second or two, then said, "Order dessert. Everything's fresh from the Swiss Chalet in town." He bowed slightly, a nervous gesture, and went back to his table.

While Celia tried to talk Jimmy into the tiramisu so she could share it, Anya excused herself. She walked over to the bar area and looked at the posters and notices hanging on the wall there. She signed her poster with a flourish, using the broad point of the Sharpie. Maureen, behind the bar, winked at her. Then she started off down the hall that advertised a route to the restrooms.

Along the hallway there were several doors, most of them unmarked and closed. One of the doors, however, was slightly open, enough to reveal a small lounge area, perhaps a private retreat for the Sullivans when they needed a few moments of respite during business hours. As she got closer Anya could hear someone crying. She paused and glanced through the door's opening. Inside, the young restaurant hostess Lily was sobbing, her face in her hands, blonde curls spilling on either side of her head. Richard Sullivan was hovering over the girl, attempting to comfort her.

Something about the tableau halted Anya in her tracks. She

drew back out of sight and watched while Sullivan took Lily's white-blonde head between his large hands and made her look at him. He talked to her steadily, murmuring low. He put his arms around her, his back to the door. As Lily laid her head against his chest, Anya could still see her through the partially open door. Her eyes were round and innocent, like a child's, but they seemed haunted by things that had little to do with the usual misfortunes of children. She didn't blink and kept looking at Anya, making no attempt to hide the raw helplessness in her eyes or indicate Anya's presence to Sullivan. Finally Lily dropped her gaze and Anya was able to move on.

She found the ladies' room. There was only one other woman using the facilities, and she was soon alone. Anya surmised that there were lots of restrooms in a place like this, which was broken up into many customer spaces because of the structural layout of the old building. It was after she left the ladies' room that Anya noticed a faint strain of music wafting through the hallway. It made her uneasy, and she began to hurry.

She reached the end of the hall. But rather than proceed to the dining room where Celia and Jimmy waited, she turned in the opposite direction. She soon found herself near the center of the building, where the old structure was most compromised by decades of retrofitting. A jumble of odd-shaped rooms with offset doorways led from one to another with no discernible traffic pattern. She saw a small dining room set for a future buffet and passed a room with a huge TV screen tuned to a football game. She walked faster, trying to lose the melody line that was becoming louder.

After passing the relatively well-lighted sports bar, she stumbled into a space that was very dark, even for a bar. The only light was from candles on the tables and a mirrored-ball ceiling fixture that revolved slowly, throwing a pattern of diamond-like facets on the ceiling and walls. The shock of the sudden darkness made her lose her balance. She grabbed the end of the bar to steady herself.

Someone was instantly at her elbow. "Look out there, little lady," said a husky voice very near her ear. "Come and sit down. What are you drinking?" Anya felt an insistent pressure on her elbow, steering her toward one of the dark booths. For a few seconds she was mesmerized by the jewel-like light patterns sweeping the room but illuminating little. She pulled her arm away brusquely and left the way she'd come in.

She sensed she was near the back of the restaurant now, beyond the customer area. An old staircase led up to a second floor. She climbed the stairs and came to a landing. There were several small rooms along the corridor, perhaps originally bedrooms. The music was more discernible here.

Off the second-floor landing was a small door made of wood cracked with age and uneven with many coats of paint. She put her hand on the door, and it opened at her touch, no longer fitting its frame. The space beyond revealed short headroom and narrow unpainted steps, worn and black. Here the music was louder still, and jumbled, hectic. Without hesitating, she climbed the old staircase.

When Jimmy and Celia finally found Anya, after a frantic search of the premises assisted by Mark West, she was sitting just inside a small room at the top of the old building, in an unfinished attic space crammed with ancient detritus. West helped them bring Anya down. At the bottom of the steps he quickly cleared a small group of onlookers who had followed them as they hurried through the various bar spaces looking for Anya when she hadn't returned to the table.

West let them out the private back door of the restaurant. When they were in the car, Celia put her soft wool shawl around Anya's trembling shoulders and held her close. "It's time we got to work, baby," she said.

Chapter 9

Back at the hotel, Celia got Anya into a pair of her own elegant lounging pajamas, which were a size or two too big. Scrubbed of attic dust and without makeup, Anya looked like the child who had spent so many hours in Jimmy's sleep lab in Ithaca.

"Are you ready?" Celia asked. Anya raised her eyebrows, a reluctant affirmative. "Tonight we're just going to get a reading on what's in your mind. Jimmy will monitor you as you dream. Afterward we'll wake you, and you can tell us what you're dreaming. You've done this hundreds of times."

"I was hoping . . ."

Celia saw the feeling-sorry-for-herself look on Anya's face. She cut her off, adopting a stern tone. "Anya, I am aware of your hope that you would outgrow your sensitivity. But you have been taught – by me, your parents, by Dr. Lubov – that what you have is a gift to be valued."

Anya looked contrite and Celia softened her tone. "Just remember, Anya. There are a fair number of people who have dreams that suggest an unexplained knowledge of the past. But your experience is so much more specific. And your dreams are subject to self-guidance and resolution. And that's just what we're going to do. You'll be fine, baby."

Jimmy tried to lighten Celia's lecture. "Lubov thinks you hold the universe in your head, Anya. You have only to close your eyes to touch eternity."

He made Anya smile, just a little. "I've learned to live with the oddities. But I'm afraid I'll never have the life I want. I need to work hard at the Theatre without distraction and without people thinking I'm crazy."

Celia adopted Jimmy's tone. "Honey, they'll just think you're a little eccentric. Eccentricity is the birthright of creativity. Right, Jimmy?"

Jimmy turned to Anya. "Getting sleepy, kid?"

After Jimmy had carefully placed a headband arrangement of probes just above her forehead, Anya lay back on the big bed. Celia dimmed the lights, patted Anya's hand and followed Jimmy into the adjoining room. Anya's brain signals would be relayed wirelessly to the monitors in the next room. To while away the time, Jimmy picked up a book, and Celia settled on the pullout couch.

Jimmy kept one eye on the monitors, watching Anya quickly pass through a restless pre-sleep state into light sleep. Soon long, shallow delta brainwaves indicated she was entering deep sleep, and her body was relaxed and at rest. But within an hour her brain waves shortened, the troughs of the waves moving closer together and getting steeper, indicating the onset of the night's first period of REM, the dream phase of sleep, characterized by the rapid eye movements that give it its acronym. For the next twenty minutes Anya's eyes moved as if she was watching a movie inside her head, a private production presented by her brain as it processed the day's experiences and thoughts, related them to the trillions of memories already recorded in her cortex, and created an infinity of new neural connections.

When the REM period began to pass off, Jimmy woke Anya gently. She reported an obviously anxiety-driven dream: She was on stage in a huge hall, the lead dancer in a production called "Pins and Needles." But she found herself dressed in an incredibly tight, diamond-spangled dress and a blonde wig. She could barely move, let alone dance, afraid that the dress would split and expose her. She sang Happy Birthday to a young Jack Kennedy, acknowledging in dream code her new acquaintance, the self-proclaimed Marilyn Monroe. Jimmy smiled at her dream report and sent her back to sleep. At several intervals during the night, Jimmy or Celia waked her and recorded the scenes and snippets of other dreams.

It was early morning when Anya finished what turned out to be her last REM period of the night, when the most vivid dreams occur. Jimmy woke her. She began to speak groggily, with her eyes still closed, re-playing the dream in her mind before she forgot it. "I'm above the ground somehow, in a black sky, flying. A black night with no lights anywhere. It's misty and wet. Below I see people walking in the dark in small groups or alone, joining together, breaking apart, almost like a dance. There are others lurking about, hiding, watching, doing secret things."

Then she was silent, and Jimmy thought she might have fallen back to sleep, but she picked up the dream as if it were still in progress. "The black has lifted. It's dawn, I think. I can see. More people are on the street below, moving about, doing ordinary things. There are horses and cattle on the street. Everything seems normal, but something has happened in the night."

Anya put her hands over her eyes, talking faster, trying not to forget details. "Suddenly I'm falling so fast my breath is taken away. I'm on the ground on a dirt road. There are a few houses. I see wooden wheels. There's a big animal standing by a fence across the road, watching me. It has terrible human eyes. I'm afraid of the animal and turn away. People around me are looking at some clothing. They're excited and afraid at the same time. I look across the dirt road and see a house, close to the road. Two people are standing near the front door dressed in old fashioned clothes. They're motioning to me. They're smiling. The others run across the street toward the house. I don't want to go. I'm screaming Don't go. Don't look. But no one hears me. I hide myself under a blanket."

Anya stopped speaking. Jimmy waited a minute or two before prompting her. "Anything more, Anya?"

Her eyes were still closed. "Yes. Something pulls me from my hiding place. I'm flying through an open gate, past the animal, past the house and barn, down into a deep ravine. There's an apple orchard there, and roses everywhere. Red roses. I crouch under a big tree watching the back of the house and barn. I'm waiting for something. It's dark and rainy. I'm sickened by the smell of the roses. My heart is exploding and I want to run but I can't. I can't move." She opened her eyes. "That's the end. That's when I lost the dream."

"Good dream, kid."

She settled back into the pillows, and then sat up abruptly. "Wait. There was something else. The people by the house, calling to me. It was Maureen and Richard Sullivan, from the Red Rose Restaurant."

They knew she would not sleep again. A half-hour later, in the pre-dawn chill, Jimmy took her back to the Ralston Club. When he returned to the hotel, the early morning light was just breaking in the west. Celia was waiting for him, dressed in jeans, a denim shirt and sneakers.

"So? Off on a morning jaunt?" Jimmy asked, puzzled.

"Anya's dream, Jimmy. It didn't suggest anything to you?"

Jimmy was cautious. "I found it interesting that she dreamed in an earlier timeframe. But that's not uncommon. Something she read or saw on TV."

"And seeing the Sullivans in her dream?"

"Anya had a fairly traumatic experience in their restaurant

66

last night. That's the basis of the dream right there. Dreams scramble bits and pieces of the day and play them back in weird scenarios – Dreaming For Dummies."

"Look at your notes. The last part of the dream, about being in a place by a big tree with roses all around?"

"The same again. She's combining a lot of powerful events from the last few days."

Celia got up. "Put your sneakers on. I want to check something." While Jimmy changed, she studied a local street map that was stretched out on the desk.

It was quiet and deserted when Jimmy pulled into the Red Rose Restaurant's parking lot. There was a Citibank a few hundred yards east of the restaurant and a small strip of shops to the west. It was too early for much activity on either side.

They got out of the car in the still-warm September air and walked to the back of the parking lot toward a chain link fence. Behind the fence was a foot or two of level land; beyond that the ground disappeared from view. The abruptness of the drop-off was likely due to the development of the modern businesses along South Street – to create level parking, huge amounts of fill had been trucked in, altering and making much steeper what had formerly been a more natural declination.

Celia and Jimmy slipped through a broken section of the fence and began to walk along the narrow border toward the east. Below them, they were surprised to see an extensive area of dense, overgrown bottomland. They continued carefully along the ledge, stretches of which were being eroded from underneath, undermining good-sized trees.

After a hundred yards or so, the incline moderated. They skidded down the bank into the ravine, where a jumble of fallen trees and thick vegetation obscured the spongy ground. Once at the bottom, they continued to walk east, following the course of the bank above them.

Then the bank veered south, and almost immediately they

came to a small grove of extraordinary trees – long-lived maple, oak, and beech – old growth that had somehow escaped the denuding of the landscape for firewood and charcoal-making in earlier times. The trees had reached maximum size here, soaking up spring run-off, surviving and thriving.

Standing in the grove of trees, Celia and Jimmy looked up. There was a wall made of purple and white stone far above them. "As I thought," said Celia. "The Rose Restaurant and the Hildebrant woman's house back up to the same space. Anya has had intense reactions in both places. This ravine has become meaningful to her."

They retraced their steps and returned to the Rose's parking lot. Celia was excited. "I need to find the local history museum."

"I need a nap."

"You sleep. This is my job."

"Don't get excited, Celia. This is just something going on in Anya's head that got attached to the places she's been to recently. That's how these things usually resolve."

"There's been more than that in Anya's years with Yuri."

"Lots of sleep lab time, lots of dreams and a few maybes. But no real proof of anything."

"Jimmy, please. Could we get on the same page? Don't be negative."

"I'm not negative about the possibilities, Celia, just about the chances of proving anything. I've spent years chasing dreams, in more ways than one."

They drove back to the hotel.

Chapter 10

After leaving Jimmy, Celia showered and changed her clothes. She went down to the lobby and looked at the rack of local interest literature. There were several museums: Washington's Headquarters; Acorn Hall, home of the county historical society; the Morris Museum of Arts and Sciences; Macculloch Hall. Since Anya had mentioned the latter, and it was closest, Celia chose to go there. She drove the short distance to Macculloch Avenue and parked on the street near the big brick structure.

Seated at the welcome desk was a silver-haired woman who looked up from her paperwork and asked if she could help.

"Hi. Yes, I hope so. I'm looking for historical information."

"Morristown is the crossroads of the American Revolution. George Washington spent two winters here. We've got the real deal if you like history."

"Washington's Headquarters?"

"On the other side of town. Washington stayed there while his men hunkered down in the snow at Jockey Hollow or practiced drills on the Green."

"The Green?"

"The town square. We call it the Green today. It dates to the early 1700s. Have you seen our Green? It's a nice peaceful place to eat your lunch. South Street leads right there. Of course, a lot of streets lead to the Green."

"What about South Street in the other direction? That's the part of town I'm interested in."

"Have you recently moved to Morristown? Or just visiting?"

"Visiting."

"I hope you enjoy your stay. We're working hard to make Morristown a Destination Vacation for history buffs. Heritage Tourism. It's the latest marketing concept. Where are you staying?"

"At the Radisson." Wanting to move the conversation along, Celia hurried on. "I had dinner at the Red Rose Restaurant last night. It's a very old building, isn't it?"

"Dates back to well before the Revolutionary War – 1749, I believe. Did you like the food?"

"Very good. Is the Red Rose Restaurant an old tavern, perhaps?"

"It's the old Sayre homestead, but it's been an inn or restaurant of one kind or another for almost a hundred years now." The woman leaned forward and lowered her voice a bit. Florence was always glad to offer an interesting historical tidbit. "The Sayre farmhouse was the scene of a terrible crime."

Celia sensed the woman's eagerness and put a lot of energy into her question. "Really? What happened?"

"Judge Samuel Sayre and his wife were murdered there in 1833. And their servant girl Phebe."

"A triple murder? Was the killer caught?"

"The sheriff and his posse found him the next day near Newark, trying to leave the country. He'd been working for the Sayres. He was tried and hanged quickly. Not like today. He was the last person to be hanged on the Morristown Green, as a matter of fact."

"That wasn't a good day to have a peaceful lunch on the

Green, I expect."

"Not peaceful, maybe. But the spectators had a great time. Thousands showed up from all over the county. They brought the kids and picnic lunches and made a day of it. Venders made a fortune selling souvenirs."

"I'll bet it would be the same today if we still executed people out in the open," Celia observed. "You'd get a pretty big crowd."

"No doubt. Human nature being what it is. After the hanging, doctors dissected the body and performed electrical experiments on it. They managed to make the killer's legs jerk and his eyes roll. His skin was tanned and made into souvenirs."

"Good lord. That sounds like justice with a great big dash of vengeance. Do you have any books or newspaper accounts I can read about the case?"

"I think I can help you there." Florence went to the phone and dialed a programmed number. "Marlee? Hi, dear. I'm here with a woman who wants to know more about the Sayre murders. I'm sending her over. Her name is . . . ?" She paused for Celia to fill in the blank, passed the name on, and hung up the phone. "The Morristown Library's on the corner of South Street and Miller Road. Just ask for Marlee Quinn in the local history department. She has a big file on the murders."

"Thank you so much, Florence."

"You're so welcome, Celia," said Florence, her blue eyes crinkling in a smile. "Welcome to Morristown. And remember, George Washington really did sleep here."

Celia drove the two blocks to the library, across the street from the South Street Theatre. After inquiring, she took the elevator to the lower floor where the local archives were housed, and there she found Florence's librarian friend waiting for her. Quinn, a young woman with long blonde hair, had spread out several oversized folders on one of the tables.

After introducing herself, Celia got right to the point. "So what's this about a triple murder in Morristown, Marlee?"

"It was May 11, 1833. Judge Samuel Sayre, his wife Sarah, and Phebe, a servant, were killed during the night. The bodies were discovered in the morning. Luckily, Judge Sayre's daughters were away. The murderer was a hired hand named Antoine Le Blanc, a French immigrant who couldn't speak English. He'd only been with the family for two weeks. He went into town for a drink on a Saturday night, came back to the farmhouse, and clubbed the Sayres to death in their barn. Then he went up to the attic and took an axe to Phebe. He stole everything he could carry, saddled up the judge's best horse, and was on his way to catch a boat back to where he came from when the sheriff caught up with him."

"Did he confess?"

"Not at the trial. Just before he was hanged, there was a written confession released to the papers. The jury brought in a guilty verdict in minutes. If you're really interested in the case, we have the contemporaneous day-to-day report of the trial. It ran in the local newspaper and was printed as a pamphlet for sale at the hanging, along with the confession."

"I am really interested."

"Then make yourself comfortable." Quinn pulled out a chair for Celia.

The librarian indicated the manila files and several microfilm cannisters on the table. She took a cream-colored pamphlet, now darkened and spotted with age, out of an acid-free folder.

S.P. HULL'S REPORT OF
THE TRIAL AND CONVICTION
OF ANTOINE LE BLANC,
FOR THE MURDER OF THE SAYRE FAMILY,
AT MORRISTOWN, N.J. ON THE NIGHT OF
THE ELEVENTH OF MAY, 1833.

The cover of the pamphlet was a sketch of a thuggish-looking man with straight hair, long sideburns, and a bulbous pug nose. Next to the sketch was a statement from the local sheriff declaring that it was a "correct likeness" of the convicted killer Antoine Le Blanc.

Celia said good-bye to Marlee Quinn two hours later. She gathered up her notes and headed back to the Radisson. Jimmy was working on a glass of scotch and offered her a drink.

"I'll have wine. Did you nap? I've had quite an afternoon."

"I slept. I had a cheese plate sent up, if you're hungry."

"Bless you. I'm starving. Jimmy, listen. In 1833 a spectacular murder was committed in the house that's now the Red Rose Restaurant on South Street."

Jimmy's reaction was cautious. "That's interesting."

"The killer was caught and the murder trial was a local sensation. Everyone in the county followed it. The trial record was published in the newspapers."

Jimmy offered no comment, and Celia let his silence hang there a moment. Then she sat forward on the desk chair. "Jimmy, I've looked at old maps, and I think the time and setting of Anya's flying dream is 1833 South Street." Celia shuffled through her notes before Jimmy could respond. "Anya indicated that the old house in her dream was the Red Rose Restaurant by putting the Sullivans there. She saw wheels of some kind. There was a carriage repair shop opposite the murder scene in 1833. And Anya reported seeing clothing. The trial record says the killer dropped some of his loot as he was struggling with the stolen horse while getting away, including a bundle of clothes."

Jimmy put his feet up. "Vague, but go on."

"Anya mentioned an animal watching her. One of the most important witnesses spoke of a white-faced ox guarding the alley to the farmhouse. That's not vague, is it?"

Jimmy didn't reply.

Celia pushed her papers aside and looked straight at Jimmy.

"And Anya's death nightmare? Was that vague?" She took a short breath. "I think Anya's first dream was the death of the serving girl Phebe. It happened in the attic of the farmhouse. And that's where we found Anya last night at the Red Rose Restaurant," she finished triumphantly.

"Could Anya have heard the details of these murders since she came to Morristown?" Jimmy asked.

"I can't imagine she knew and didn't mention it to us."

"She may have seen something unconsciously. There easily could have been an article in a newspaper or magazine. Something she saw while she was doing job research."

"Granted. I'll have to check."

Jimmy stood up. "Don't jump to the conclusion that Anya spontaneously dreamed her way to these old murders, Celia."

"But this is Anya's pattern."

"Her pattern is that she dreams of awful things. And she can't stop dreaming until she dreams the end of the story. Until she does that, she can be drawn to a certain physical location and find herself in an embarrassing situation. In some cases she's put herself in danger. Then we help her finish her dream, and she moves on."

"You and Yuri have done far more than that for Anya. If Anya had to deal with these dreams on her own, who knows what may have happened? Yuri's ideas have given her an explanation for the phenomenon."

"Except that the explanation is unproved."

"I know what you think, Jimmy. You think it's just twitchy neurons working overtime in Anya's brain. A supercharged creativity gene making connections where there are none."

"And Yuri thinks Anya is swimming in a vast sea of dark energy and tiny dimensions that give her access to the past," Jimmy rejoined. "Which explanation is most likely?"

Celia's eyes became almost luminous. "Every year Yuri's ideas seem less unlikely. His work is validated by every new discovery made. Dark matter and energy and extra dimensions are now mainstream scientific thinking."

"Well, Yuri may be one of those grand masters of the universe, but the rest of us have to stick to the accepted laws of scientific proof on good old Earth."

"Let's not argue anymore, Jimmy. Let's just let it go for now."

He shrugged. "Then you'll have to continue to put up with my boring insistence on scientific interpretation of observable evidence."

"Let's just do what we came to do, Jimmy. To help Anya. Deal?" She walked over to Jimmy and put her arms around him in an attempt to cut off further bickering.

"If it's what Anya wants." His voice was carefully neutral, but he reached out and stroked her arm.

"Do you actually think she chooses this, Jimmy? Do you think she wants to wander into ditches and old attics chasing musical clues?"

He gave Celia what she wanted to hear. "No. Of course not. So tonight Anya will stop watching her dream and start to direct it."

Chapter 11

Celia and Jimmy waited in the Ralston Club's bar for Anya to finish work. When she arrived, they took their drinks up to her small suite. They gathered around a glass-topped table in the sitting area.

Celia asked Anya if she had ever heard of the Sayre case. Had she read something about a triple murder in Morristown? Anya said she couldn't remember ever having heard of the case. She told Anya the broad outline of the 1833 crime and its aftermath, omitting details. When she finished, Anya got up and began to pace. "So you think this is what is affecting me?"

Celia answered quickly, without including Jimmy. "I do, baby. All paths lead to the Red Rose Restaurant. The big difference between this case and most of your other episodes is that this time your dream subject matter is fully documented in the public record. It makes it easier to get you where you need to go."

"You mean guided dreaming?" Anya asked.

Celia looked toward Jimmy to do his part.

"It'll be like old times, Anya," he offered "You're still the best lucid dreamer I've ever had in my lab."

Anya bowed to the inevitable, wondering how she was going

77

to find the energy to direct her dreams at night and work during the day.

Celia, relieved, leaned forward. "Anya, we could use that necklace. You had a very odd reaction to it. If your description was accurate, it could be a physical link to the past, a human artifact – a relatively rare happenstance. Do you think you could get it from that detective?"

"Knowing Detective Mitchell, he's going to want a good explanation, if not a pound of flesh, before he even considers it. I hate to ask him for anything. We're not on the best of terms. Although he did close the police report on the incident at Sonja Hildebrant's, as he promised."

"Call him. I'll come with you," Jimmy replied.

Anya dialed the number for Morristown Police Headquarters and asked for Detective Mitchell. He picked up quickly. "Mitchell. Who's this?"

"Detective Mitchell, this is Anya Gregory. About the . . . incident last week at Sonja Hildebrant's home."

There were several beats of silence before Mitchell replied. "Are you all right?" He never expected her to call him about anything.

"Yes, of course. I was just wondering if you still have the old necklace you found."

"Could be."

She let his annoying comment go. "I'm wondering if you would give, or loan it, to me?"

Mitchell angled for advantage. "I can't just hand it over to you. It might be evidence. Why don't we meet somewhere and talk about it? What about the Red Rose Restaurant on South Street? That's close for both of us. Do you know it?"

No way that's happening, thought Anya. "Not there," she hastily said.

"What about Le Campagna? Italian eats on Elm. I'll pick you up. Name the time."

Anya knew he'd get worked up like this. "Wait, Detective Mitchell. I don't want to put you to a lot of trouble."

"It's no trouble. We both have to eat. And you can tell me why you want the necklace."

Jimmy had scribbled a note on a pad and passed it to her.

She spoke carefully. "There are some things you should know about me. It's complicated. Could you meet me in the bar at the Radisson at 7:00 tonight?"

"I'll be there." Mitchell hung up and went to the locker room to shave and change into a fresh shirt.

Detective Mitchell arrived at the Radisson bar at 7:00 sharp. His eyes swept the room and quickly spotted Anya sitting with a tall, good-looking man in a secluded booth. Mitchell was instantly angry both with her and himself. He should have known that dinner with Anya alone had never been in the offing.

Jimmy, facing the door, saw the detective arrive and observed the younger man's face turn from neutral and guarded, which Jimmy assumed was his signature expression, to an angry scowl. At least it was a genuine reaction, unlike the phony friendliness of that jealous friend of Anya's at the Red Rose Restaurant.

Jimmy got up and walked to the entrance. "You must be Detective Mitchell." Before he could continue, Mitchell interrupted him. "And you're Dr. James Patton Lang from Cornell University."

Jimmy was surprised – he never used his middle name – but recovered quickly. "That's me." He put his hand out. "I know you weren't expecting a third party, but Anya felt it was best for me to come."

"No problem, Lang." Mitchell swallowed his anger but barely touched the hand Jimmy offered.

The detective's reaction both amused Jimmy and induced a sense of sympathy for him. "I'm Jim. Just follow me and be a good listener."

Mitchell hesitated, wanting to walk out on the two of them.

But in the end he followed Jimmy's back through the bar. "Two's company, Anya," he said by way of greeting her. She looked tremendous in a green sweater with some kind of low knotted neckline.

"As I said on the phone, Detective Mitchell, it's a complicated story. I need help telling it," Anya replied stiffly.

"So shoot. I'm all ears." Mitchell slid into the booth across from Anya.

Jimmy remained standing. "Let's get you a drink first."

"I'll have a Corona. I'll get it."

"Stay here with Anya. I'll get it."

Mitchell looked across at her. "You could have got the necklace out of me easier without the extra company."

"You weren't going to give it to me without extracting a price for it."

"Do you think I was going to make you sleep with me to get it?"

"You didn't mind putting pressure on me the other day."

Mitchell rolled his eyes. "I can't believe how bad that got screwed up. You misunderstood everything."

"Sure I did. Do you always go after the women you meet on the job?"

"I never have before."

"You used your job to intimidate me. That's the worst thing you can do – use power to get what you want."

"How many times do I have to say I'm sorry? It was wrong, and it obviously didn't work."

"Would it have been right if it had worked?"

He threw up his thick arms in frustration. "My god, Anya. How sorry do I have to be?" She noticed a small blood-red shaving nick right at the tip of the scar that ran down his lip to his mouth. For some reason it blunted her anger and stopped her from continuing the essentially silly exchange.

Jimmy arrived carrying the Corona with its lime wedge and

put it in front of Mitchell. "You two hitting it off?" he asked, observing the color in their faces. "C'mon, kids. Play nice."

"Jimmy, shut up," Anya said, exasperated with both of them. There was silence while Mitchell half-drained his beer.

Mitchell turned to Anya. "So why do you want an old broken necklace? Does it have anything to do with your further adventures at the Red Rose Restaurant the other night?"

Anya narrowed her eyes. "How do you know about that?"

"The Rose is popular with off-duty policemen."

"And so you invited me to meet you there to see what I'd say?"

"That's what detectives do."

Jimmy broke in. "Please, please, you two. Let's move on, Detective Mitchell."

"This is off-duty. Call me Mitch."

"Okay. Mitch. Anya would like to borrow the necklace because it might help her solve a problem she has."

"I'm listening."

Jimmy paused to select the best words. "Anya has a peculiar gift. She doesn't always see it that way, but it's true. Anya is what you might call a talented dreamer."

"What does that mean? Everybody dreams, right?" Mitchell fiddled with his nearly empty beer bottle."

"Nearly everybody. Dreaming is an essential function for human beings. We don't know for certain why that's so. Maybe to integrate the day's experiences and save them to memory, or to provide insight into our emotions, or something else. We just don't know. Whatever they are, dreams begin at a cellular level in the brain, induced by chemicals. They alter the entire physiology of a person's body while they're occurring."

Mitchell looked at Jimmy over his glass. "Your bio says you're some kind of sleep scientist, right?"

"Well, yes. I'm a neurobiologist. And Anya has been dreaming for me in my sleep lab for nearly ten years."

"Why is she such a great dreamer?" Mitchell asked, gesturing in Anya's direction without looking at her.

"Anya sometimes seems to get dreams imposed on her. More significantly, some of them appear to come from somewhere else, outside her brain. 'Appear' is the working hypothesis. Nothing has been proved." He looked at Mitchell. "Do you ever get earworms?"

"What in god's name are you talking about?"

"Do you ever get a song or a melody in your head and you can't get it out? You keep hearing it over and over?"

"Sure. Usually it's some lame television commercial."

"Anya's dreams are like that. Something gets in her brain and it won't go away. Instead of just whistling an annoying tune, however, she keeps revisiting the dream, repeating it, trying to finish it. A brainworm. She can't get rid of it. She has to keep dreaming until she ends it."

Mitchell looked at Anya for the first time since Jimmy had started speaking. "You said something about chasing some kind of music that day at the Hildebrant woman's house."

"It often starts that way," Anya answered. "The music tries to take me somewhere."

"Down into a gully?"

Anya thought she heard sarcasm. "I told you it was complicated."

Jimmy broke in. "The significant thing is that once Anya starts one of these episodic dreams, she has to finish it. The story has to end, unlike regular dreams."

Mitchell was thinking. "Do you mean Anya wasn't hallucinating the stream and the roses, not to mention a bloody human hand, but dreaming them?" He turned to Anya. "Did you know that when you let the police spend hours in a damp hole looking for a hobo?"

Anya answered carefully. "At the time these things happen, I could swear that everything is real. I can touch and feel and see and smell all these things. Even now it's real to me. It doesn't matter that you tell me there are no roses or orchards there. It's still real."

"Please don't tell me this is a ghost thing," Mitchell said.

"Try and credit me with a little common sense even though you obviously feel this is all beneath you," Anya retorted, leaning back to maximize the distance between them. Mitchell acutely regretted his comment.

Jimmy ignored them both and went on. "Anya's dreaming is a rare phenomenon. As you have seen, it carries some physical risk. The more dangerous risk, however, is psychological. It could prove overwhelming if she had no insight into what was happening. Do you understand, Mitch?"

Mitchell really didn't, but held his tongue. "What's this got to do with the necklace?"

"Well, Mitch," said Jimmy. "That's part of how we help Anya lose her ghosts."

"Very funny, Jimmy." Anya scowled at him.

Jimmy turned toward Mitchell. "Ever heard of lucid dreaming?"

"You know you're dreaming while you're dreaming," Mitchell answered promptly.

Anya and Jimmy looked at each other. "I'm impressed," said Jimmy.

"I read a lot. My mother made me read as a kid and it stuck. I like science, as a matter of fact."

"Then you know that a fair number of people are able to become aware they are dreaming and not wake up. Lucidity, it's called. And if you follow the science, you know that a smaller number of these people can get into their dreams and actually direct what happens. It's not all that uncommon, and some people can be trained to do it."

"And all this explains why you're here in Morristown."

"Absolutely. The glamorous world of dream study. Late

nights and long hours."

"And the necklace?"

This was harder. Jimmy spoke more carefully. "Anya is special in that she dreams of other times and places, sometimes very specifically. If there is a physical item available from her dream time and place, it can bridge the past and the present and help Anya focus. It's possible such an artifact could have triggered her brainworm in the first place, or reinforced it, like I think the necklace did."

Mitchell looked at Anya. "I noticed you didn't want to handle it. I thought it was strange."

"But you made sure I had to touch it," she said, airing her resentment once again.

Mitchell didn't respond. "How does this dream treatment work?" he asked instead. "Are you wired to machines?"

Jimmy answered. "It's simpler these days. Not so many sticky-patch connections, thanks to digital telemetry and wi-fi. There's a kerchief-like arrangement that places the electrodes in the right places to measure brain activity in different parts of the brain, plus breathing, heart rate, temperature, and eye movement monitors. I can watch Anya as she goes from drowsiness to deep sleep. When her brainwaves become short and choppy, I know she's heading into REM sleep. Her muscle response shuts down and she becomes essentially paralyzed, with the exception of a few involuntary twitches. The only thing that can move is her eyes, which is why it's called REM – Rapid Eye Movement – sleep."

Mitchell broke in. "That's when you dream. The eyes move like they're following the action in a movie."

"Essentially, yes. People do dream in other sleep stages, but less frequently. REM sleep is the true midnight realm of the strange and fantastic. The sleeping brain releases substances that completely change the body chemistry. A different region of the brain takes control of all information processing. This part of the brain isn't bound by conscious rules of logic. It's free to make the craziest connections, drawing on trillions of memories and experiences, jumbling everything together with no holds barred." Jimmy sat back in the booth and grinned. "Thus the complete total weirdness of dreams."

Mitchell sat without speaking for a moment and then reached into his pocket. He placed the necklace carefully in front of Anya. Jimmy reached over and took it.

Jimmy stood up. "Thanks, Mitch. I'm going upstairs to have dinner with Celia. I suggest you two grab a quick bite. You both have to eat."

"So I pointed out to Anya," Mitchell said.

Anya was angry with Jimmy. "I don't think Detective Mitchell is interested in . . . "

"Anya, please. Throw the guy a bone. He listened to me go on for an hour. He's probably starving. And for chrissakes call him Mitch." Jimmy turned and left the bar, smiling to himself.

Chapter 12

Later that evening, while setting up his gear, Jimmy took the necklace from his pocket and put it on the bedside table. Just then Anya came into the room in a lightweight yoga outfit, ready to sleep. She immediately spotted the tarnished and broken cross. "No. Not tonight. I don't want to touch that thing tonight," she said quickly.

Jimmy was surprised. "After all the trouble we took to roll Officer Mitch for it?"

Celia hurried to Anya's side. "Don't worry about the necklace tonight, Anya." She dropped the chain in her pocket.

Jimmy let the moment pass. "Okay. 'To sleep, perchance to dream,'" he paraphrased lightly, as he had done so many times." Anya nodded, a bit grimly. Jimmy sat in a chair beside her bed and carefully set out her task. "The dream story you're working on began at Sonja Hildebrant's house. Shadows on the curtains put you into a meditative pre-sleep state, and you nodded off. Your sleeping brain became receptive, and a portal opened.

"The initial clue to your state of mind was musical, as is often the case with you. You followed this music into a ravine below Sonja's garden, experiencing considerable sensory distortion along the way. You leaned against an old tree at the bottom of

87

the ravine, where you apparently nodded off again. When you opened your eyes, you could see like an eagle and spotted a human hand lying under a rose bush across a stream. That's pretty dramatic, even for you, Anya," he smiled, then continued.

"That night you had a vivid dream depicting a scene of violent death. The day Celia and I arrived, you dreamed again after the incident at the Red Rose Restaurant. This dream story you're working on may relate to the time and location of a past event but is more likely just one of your more interesting night-time theatrical productions. It doesn't matter. Your job tonight is to find the dream again and bring it to a conclusion, so you can get it out of your head and move on.

"We've done this hundreds of times, Anya. I'll monitor you for REM. You'll let me know when you are aware you are dreaming by moving your eyes left to right. When you complete the REM period, I'll wake you to record your progress. Hopefully one or two sessions will resolve the dream's story line and break your attraction to it. And then Celia and I can go home to our boring old jobs, and you can get back to your exciting new career."

Anya spoke sleepily. "I hope so, Jimmy. You could probably use some rest."

"I don't sleep much, kid. And I never dream," he quipped.

"Everybody dreams," she smiled.

"I don't remember my dreams. Maybe I don't want to. But enough about me. Tonight you need to find your dream and also look for a dream body – some character that fits your dream in time and place – a character that can become an integral part of the action. That will give you a way to explore your dream more widely. We've done that before, lots of times."

"Okay, Jimmy. I'm ready. Wire me for action."

Tonight Jimmy was using a more elaborate array of electrodes. The cap-like gear sprouted dozens of colored diodes that fed impulses wirelessly to a central computer and monitors in the outer room.

"All right. You're ready to go. Remember, look for mirrors. And clocks. Or anything with writing on it." Odd behavior on the part of these common dream themes often triggered lucidity in the dreamer.

Anya was so conditioned to the headgear that it helped rather than hindered her descent into sleep. She immediately entered that pleasant state of drowsiness where breathing slows and the brain goes into a suspended, meditative state, interrupted by an occasional sharp contraction of the leg muscles in response to the strange but common sensation of falling that so often precedes sleep.

Anya's brainwaves began to slow as she downshifted from the last remnants of conscious wakefulness into light sleep. Fifteen minutes later, Jimmy saw long delta waves of deep sleep on his monitor. This was the sleep stage that triggered Anya's occasional but alarming episodes of sleepwalking, but now Anya slept heavily and uneventfully.

After a half-hour or so of deep sleep, Anya's brainwaves began to shorten and spike. Her heart rate quickened, and she twisted and turned restlessly. It was then that the oldest, most primitive part of Anya's brain gave an electrical signal to shut down production of the substances that enable logical thought. Different chemicals took over, and her neurons were soon pickling in the neurotransmitter acetylcholine.

Anya settled on her back, and her body sank into almost complete paralysis, her motor impulses blocked by the chemical state of her brain. The only part of Anya's body that could move were her eyes, which now twitched energetically and erratically under the thin skin of her eyelids as her brain spilled sensory fragments onto the surrealistic landscape of her dream.

Thus Anya began her voyage through a vast sea of memory, experience, thoughts, and emotions, completely unhinged from rationality and logic.

DEATH BY MOONLIGHT

*****

Anya heard men's voices coming through the open window. She got out of bed and dressed quickly for the Theatre. A small mirror hung on a wall, and something told her she should look in the mirror, but she was distracted by the sound of heavy boots and horses' hooves below her. Looking out the window she saw a wide, paved street crowded with concrete and brick buildings – a bakery, a liquor store, clothing stores, a large supermarket, apartments, and office buildings as far as she could see. She tied her long dark hair away from her face and prepared to leave for work.

She passed the mirror again. She really should look in the mirror. But first she must find the musical score she had been working on last night. The pages were scattered all around the room. Some were hanging from the open rafters like wet clothes. The pages tried to escape her, wriggling away toward the room's corners, but she managed to grasp them all, hastily stuffing them into a leather saddlebag. Noticing the mirror again, she put down the saddlebag and walked over to it.

She saw her face in the mirror, her dark hair short and curly, the way it had been when she was a child. That's strange, she thought. And she was wearing overalls. That's not right for the Theatre. She'd have to change. She looked at her watch, afraid of being late, but the watch was melting along her arm, like the timepieces in Salvadore Dali's famous painting. She momentarily accepted this oddity, but then decided to check the mirror again. The face she now saw was heavily freckled and framed with straight straw-blond hair, and the chin displayed a hint of fuzzy down – a young boy's face. Bleached-blue eyes looked out from under a battered, dirty straw hat.

Anya suddenly became aware that she was dreaming. Staying within the dream, she moved her eyeballs in a wide arc from left to right to signal Jimmy that she had become lucid.

Back in her dream, Anya looks out the window again and sees that the dreamscape has shifted. The modern road has become a narrow dirt street, lined by only a few one-and two-story wooden structures. Open farm fields stretch to the east and south. The smell of fresh manure hangs in the air. There is a great deal of shouting and hurried movement below.

Something has happened, the young boy thinks excitedly, sensing a rare break in the routine of dreary farm chores. He leaves the sleeping loft and runs down the narrow steps, almost tripping on his overalls.

Out on the street men were gathering in front of an open store front. He goes over to investigate and sees various items on shelves: a monogrammed shirt, pantaloon trousers, women's lingerie, a silver necklace, a bikini bathing suit and a green turtleneck sweater from Epstein's Department Store. I don't think I'm supposed to be shopping, Anya thinks. She is having trouble staying with her dream character, flipping back and forth in time, looking for direction. She picks up the silver necklace and leaves the shop.

Out on the street men had gathered, milling about, excited, uncertain. The things inside have been stolen, they declare, their voices clipped; their eyes flashing. Anya senses fear and dark anger. She tells her dream self to join the men, and she watches as the eager young boy joins the agitated group as it drifts toward the farmhouse across the road.

The scene shifts, and the boy is inside the farmhouse with the men. Some have armed themselves with pitchforks and shovels. He feels the dread of the sweating, cursing men. He follows along as they look in the rooms on the first floor, but then he wanders away from them.

All is still. The young boy climbs one staircase and then another to the very top of the house, a low-ceilinged place sparsely furnished with a narrow bed, a trunk, and a rough wooden table. Dust motes are drifting in the stuffy air. Over the bed is a window that looks out toward a stable built into the side of a bank. Masses of red roses are growing along the fences that line the short path. Standing in front of the stable, a familiar man and woman wave to the boy. He waves back and the two slowly dissolve into nothingness.

When Anya turns back to the room, the young boy has faded as well. The sunlight shining through the window begins to swell with brightness. The intense light separates into a spectrum of shimmering jewel tones: red, orange, yellow, green, blue, violet. Then the rainbow collapses into a single narrow blade of purest white light, stabbing the bed beneath the window with icy precision.

She looks down at the bed, apprehensive. Don't go to sleep, she tells herself. She lies down on the narrow bed on top of a blanket, stretching out on her right side with her feet hanging over the end of the bed, and promptly falls asleep.

She is roused by the sounds of men's heavy boots. she hears the men on the stairs, their guttural muttering becoming louder, and then they are in the room, looking down at her. There is a movement under her, under the blanket. She screams and rolls off the bed. One of the men pulls away the covering to reveal a woman with a hideously deformed, bloody face. The woman's eyes are open, staring. As Anya watches, the dead eyes shift and lock onto hers.

She runs from the house, down the rose-lined path toward the stable, looking for the man and woman. The ground is soft, and Anya's feet sink down into the pungent brown mass. She feels something beneath her feet and looks down to see a human hand emerging from the soil. She falls to the ground, pushing away the sticky soil, and uncovers the woman she had seen earlier, and then the man, both now corpses, smiling as if grateful to her for their release into the light.

I cannot go on. I must wake up, Anya decides. She stands in the manure-filled barnyard, reaching out to Jimmy, who is waiting on the other side of the dream. But the dream continues.

I'll run away, her dream self decides. But the dead woman's hand moves and grabs her leg, fastening onto it with a steel-like grip. Electricity jolts up her leg to her heart. She grasps her chest with both hands, convulsing.

Then she hears Jimmy's voice. "It's all right, Anya. Wake up. It's only a dream. Come on, kid."

Beneath Jimmy's deep voice she hears a weak, involuntary moaning that is apparently coming from her. Her hands are white and rigid as they clutch the front of her yoga top. Then Celia and Jimmy are lifting her into a sitting position. She can smell Celia's perfume and feel the soft warmth of Jimmy's cashmere sweater against her cheek.

"I lost my dream character and couldn't wake myself up," she mumbled, when she was able to speak.

"You're awake now, Anya," Jimmy said. "Tell us everything you remember quickly."

Anya took a drink from a glass of water proffered by Celia and talked fast, before details could fade. Then she fell peacefully into a deep dreamless sleep for the rest of the night. When she woke, Jimmy drove her to the Ralston Club.

Two hours later, in front of the Theatre, she ran into Peter Thayer. Thayer, she had come to know, was an expert at orchestrating the chance meeting. He had called several times since she'd seen him in the Red Rose Restaurant. She felt guilty for not returning his calls. Despite his intense and somewhat proprietary interest in her, Peter had been a generous, amusing and, for the most part, undemanding companion since they'd met.

"Here you are! I'd begun to think you'd gone back to New York," he enthused, dramatically reaching out to take both her hands in his. His luxurious brown hair and tanned skin was set off by a silky lavender shirt under his black jacket. He should have been an actor, Anya thought.

"Hi, Peter," she said, taking back her hands. "I'm sorry I haven't called you. Thank you for being understanding the other night when I skipped out on you."

Thayer hadn't been able to get the good-looking man he'd seen with Anya at the Rose Restaurant out of his mind. True, she hadn't been alone with him. There was the other woman, the redhead, but the man had purposely moved closer to Anya and put his arm around her when he saw Thayer watching them. It had driven him nuts. He'd gone to the Rose for a quick bite but, after seeing Anya, he had stayed too long in the bar and had too much to drink, an occasional vice that had gotten him into trouble in the past.

Now he had to act as if not hearing from Anya was inconsequential. "Don't worry about it. We're both busy people," he smiled.

Anya sensed he wasn't going to let her go until he had secured a promise of a future date, and his next words confirmed that. "Sonja is having a party to benefit Sunnyside this Saturday, Anya. Come with me. It'll be fun."

"I have guests in town."

"Oh, right. The couple I saw you with at the Rose?" he asked, probing for more information.

"They're friends from Ithaca."

"Well, Sonja would love to have them, too, I'm sure." He knew that would be okay with Sonja.

"I'll have to see what's going on," she equivocated.

Thayer had desperately wanted a commitment but took what was offered. "Great," he said with phony enthusiasm. I'll call to remind you. I'll pick you up if your friends can't go. In the meantime, want to meet for dinner tonight?"

"Can't, Peter." She started to turn toward the Theatre. "I'm tied up."

"Okay. Another time," Thayer said graciously, moving a step closer and putting his hot hand on her back. He resisted the impulse to grab her arm and pull her away from the Theatre by force. Don't be stupid, he told himself quickly. Instead he smiled a bit too brightly and walked away.

* * * * *

Jimmy knocked lightly on Celia's door. When he entered the room she was by the window, scrubbing at something with a shoe-polishing cloth. Wordlessly she handed Jimmy the necklace from Detective Mitchell. Considerable bits of it had corroded away, but it had clearly once been a delicate silver cross. Now that Celia had applied silver cleaner, traces of an etched flowery pattern were evident on its surface.

When Jimmy didn't say anything, Celia spoke. "See, Jimmy? It's beautifully designed. And it originally had some kind of setting, just as Anya described. It's quite pretty, isn't it? It's definitely old."

"Maybe Anya looked at it more closely than she realized when Mitchell put it in her hand."

"You couldn't see the etching before I cleaned it up."

"Maybe." Jimmy was non-committal.

Celia put the cross in her pocket. "Jimmy, this is all coming together. There's no doubt that Anya has found the time and place of her murder dream – the killing of Judge and Sarah Sayre and their servant Phebe in 1833 Morristown."

"Well, she's constructing a dream around an awful event, anyway," Jimmy replied. "Her dream character has taken some of the horror out of the event for her, but I didn't like the way she came out of it last night."

"I'd say she's constructing pretty accurately. I've read all about the case. Anya hasn't. Yet she's dreamed many historical details that match the crime. Listen, Jimmy. Here is exactly what happened the morning the murders were discovered according to the trial testimony." She began to read from her notes.

95

"At 6:30 a.m. on the morning of May 12, 1833, a local farmer chased a calf down the path beside Judge Sayre's farmhouse. He noticed clothing, jewelry, and other household goods scattered along the path leading out to the side road. The farmer brought everything across the road to a carriage maker's shop. He spread the clothing on a woodpile. Everything was wet from the previous night's rain.

"Some of the clothes were embroidered with initials and were obviously the property of the Sayre family. Two men were sent across the road to check on the Sayres. The men found the cattle out of their pen, roaming around in the yard.

"When they didn't get an answer after knocking, the men sent for reinforcements, and a small crowd entered the house through the back door, which was unlocked. They found the house ransacked. After milling through all the rooms and finding nobody about, they went up to the attic room where Phebe, the serving girl, slept. She was lying on her bed on her right side, underneath a buffalo rug. Her head had been cleaved with a single blow from an axe." Celia paused for effect. "Does this sound familiar?"

When Jimmy didn't comment, she continued. "After Phebe's body was found and with the Sayres missing, the men went out to the stable. The stable doors were open and one horse was gone. Somebody noticed a piece of cloth sticking out of a pile of manure in front of the stable. It turned out to be Mrs. Sayre's calico dress. They dug her out of the manure. She'd been given a fatal head bashing. Judge Sayre was found nearby. Same cause of death. Just as was seen by Anya in her dream."

"You want very much to assume that Anya's dream is coming from outside her brain."

"It's obvious. Somehow, Anya can slip into another dimension, or it slips into her. It's happened many times in her life."

"It's your favored hypothesis. But science doesn't start by assuming one hypothesis is the only possible explanation for a set of phenomena."

"How do you explain her knowing what she can't know?"

"If something is known, as this murder is, Anya can know it. She can have heard of it without remembering. She can be taking cues from those who *do* know – like you, Celia. You affirmed Anya's account of the murder scene when she first dreamed it, so it's likely she'd dream it again the same way. And you've given her subtle signs and encouragement that she is on the right track, so she picks up where she left off."

"But Jimmy, she's now added the discovery of the other bodies to her dream of Phebe."

"She knows, from you, that the Sayre crime included three victims," Jimmy said impatiently.

"The detail, Jimmy. The little things. Like the clothing. The animal across the road."

"Nothing is conclusive. Far from it." Jimmy ran his long fingers through his hair. "You need to slow down."

Celia's cell phone rang. She listened. "We know, baby. Jimmy and I were just talking." After another pause, she replied. "We'll see you after work."

Celia closed her phone and turned to Jimmy. "Anya's having a difficult afternoon. She feels sleepy and can't shake it."

"She knows she's got more dreaming to do."

"She'll walk over here later. And Jimmy. I want this is to be something interesting for Yuri, yes. But I want it to be over for Anya, too, so she can get on with her life."

Jimmy left to check to his equipment without commenting.

Anya had gotten through her planned day's work despite her overwhelming drowsiness. She kept on her feet, working at her storyboards and reviewing music. Finally she left the Theatre, heading west on South Street toward the Radisson. She passed a small bakery on the corner of an intersection. There was a selection of baked goods in a window display, and her sweet tooth wanted one. She went inside and ordered cookies, some small fruit-filled pastries, and six pieces of baklava.

As she came out of the bakery, she thought she saw someone slip around the corner, and after that, she was conscious of a feeling of being followed. When she reached the lobby of the Radisson, she went in and sat down on one of the leather chairs in a small seating area. No one came in after her.

Anya went upstairs and knocked lightly on Celia's door. The three of them passed some time watching the news on TV together, eating room service sandwiches, and drinking decaf coffee with the bakery goods Anya had brought.

Finally Anya could let herself embrace the drowsiness she'd been fighting all day. Jimmy helped her put on the wired cap, and Anya fell into an immediate deep sleep. Celia cleaned up the room while waiting for Anya's first dream period to begin.

* * * * *

Instantly Anya found the young, freckled boy in the too-big overalls. Exhausted from the early morning excitement at the farmhouse, he had gone into the woods behind the farmhouse, where his father wouldn't be likely to find him and send him back to his farm chores. The boy leaned against the trunk of a big tree in a bed of soft ferns. The raucous calls of a crow, an occasional double-tweet from a cardinal calling her mate, the intermittent sound of woodpeckers working the dead trees in the small, sunken forest – all soon receded into the background. He slumped into a more comfortable position, pulled his straw hat down over his eyes and was soon asleep.

As Anya roused from deep sleep and entered into her first period of REM sleep, her dream body – the young boy – wakes and stands up, swiping soil and bracken from the baggy overalls. He retrieves the straw hat, runs a rough hand through cropped, yellow hair, and leaves the woods, walking up through the field behind the farmhouse. As he goes higher, out of the hollow, he hears a commotion up on the street and hurries toward it.

Several men on horseback are riding in from the east, accompanying a wagon holding a wet, filthy man. A rope is strung around his shoulders and tied to his wrists, which are held in handcuffs in back of him. He keeps his head down. People line the dirt road on both sides, shaking their fists and screaming epithets as the slowly moving wagon makes its way toward town.

The dream abruptly shifts, taking Anya by surprise. She is bodiless, flying through a darkening sky, high enough to see the dirt roads below leading from all directions toward a large, uneven patch of open land. A violent wind drives her even higher. Huge thunderheads with anvil-shaped tops form, writhing with hot lightning and winds that shake the landscape.

The storm just as suddenly ceases, and she drops through the cloud cover into a sun-drenched scene with a sea of people filling the open square space. The people are laughing and talking. There are couples strolling arm-in-arm and families with children. They are eating food from carefully packed cloth-covered baskets or purchased from venders with flat wooden trays suspended from their necks. There is marching music, pipes and drums. Older children play games and run about excitedly with their friends. Anya, back in character, falls in with a group of older boys as they push through the crowd, getting closer and closer to a wooden platform near the center of the square.

A final surge brings the boy to the front of the pulsing and swaying crowd. He looks up but can't see much beyond the platform's floor, which is high above him. Anya decides to take over in order to observe from a better vantage point. She floats upward above the heads of the crowd and comes face-to-face with the terrified, miserable man. He is short, with close-cropped hair flat against his head. His countenance is pale beneath his rough, swarthy skin. There are several small cuts around his chin and upper lip where he has been clumsily shaved. The man is weeping copiously. His hands, tied in front of him, are trembling, and his body shivers as if he were standing in a winter snowstorm instead of under the warm sun at the center of a pleasant country village.

The man turns his head and looks directly at Anya, hovering in front of him. He gestures to his neck, where a great black snake is coiled. The snake's body pulsates with power, pulling its coils tighter and tighter. Suddenly a heavy boulder crashes from the sky, and the weeping man flies upward past Anya's head. There is an audible, collective intake of breath from the spectators. Anya can see the man's feet, now dangling above her, kicking spasmodically. She hears a low, hungry murmur emanating from the crowd. Minutes pass, and the man's weak, spasmodic kicking slows. When his feet are finally still, a great cheer goes up from the crowd. Anya flies away from the deafening noise and the overpowering stench of the crowd's black, palpable pleasure.

She comes to earth near two churches. At the doorway of the smaller church, a man dressed in black stands quietly, looking in the direction of the distant platform, smiling faintly. She hates his cynical face. The man turns and walks into the church.

Anya began to lose the dream. Colors broke up into pixel-like fragments. What was left – a fading, sepia-colored outline of the crowd – receded rapidly in all directions before disappearing into the atmosphere, until there was nothing.

Anya awoke easily and told her dream to Jimmy and Celia. Celia grinned broadly. "Thank god. You've reached the end of the dream. The hanging of Phebe's murderer."

"But he flew into the sky," Anya said uncertainly.

"That was because the town was trying a new method of hanging. Instead of falling through a hole in the platform, the other end of the noose was attached to a heavy piece of iron suspended by a rope pulley. Stephen Vail, who owned a local ironworks, set it up. When the iron was released, it crashed to the ground and Le Blanc flew up, just as you saw."

"It took a long time for him to . . . be still." Anya's voice was quiet and a bit shaky.

"It was a long time ago, Anya. What's important is that it's over."

Anya didn't think she'd be able to sleep again, but she easily fell into the most restful, dreamless sleep she'd had in a long time.

Chapter 13

The next morning Celia ordered orange juice and champagne, breakfast pastries, and fruit from room service. When Anya woke and came out of the bedroom, Celia almost picked her up in a congratulatory embrace. "Anya, you dreamed your dream to the end. You're finished with it. Let's have mimosas and celebrate!"

Anya laughed, running a brush through her bed hair and reaching for a cherry pastry. Jimmy poured the champagne.

Celia could not stop talking. "Baby, you did it. You dreamed the past. You were there at the discovery of the murders. You were at the killer's hanging. There are just too many points of agreement with the record for it to be a coincidence. I can't wait to tell Dr. Lubov."

Jimmy suspected that Celia had been speaking to Lubov all along, before there was anything concrete from which to draw scientific conclusions. His reams of data would have to be analyzed to find the precise location of the brain activity during each of Anya's significant dreams and the results compared to scans of normal dreaming. Would this analysis indicate activation in memory storage areas or arise from a deeper, more primitive part of the brain? Lubov looked outside the dreamer, beyond the present. Jimmy bet on internalized experience and activated memory as the source of the dream material.

After their celebratory breakfast they headed out of the hotel and strolled toward Morristown's center, sited on a plateau above the surrounding area. The relatively high elevation of Morristown had made it George Washington's "eagle's perch" during the winter of 1777, where he watched and waited for the British to come for him and his ragtag army, exhausted after battles at Trenton and Princeton. In addition to severe problems feeding and rearming the troops, a smallpox epidemic forced local churches into service as both hospitals and morgues. Yet the British failed to make a decisive move.

At the end of 1779 Washington would return to his Morristown refuge to face the coldest and snowiest winter on New Jersey record. Supply wagons were stranded, and starvation was widespread. A British plan to kidnap Washington from his headquarters in Jacob Ford's mansion was disrupted thanks only to the wretched weather. But somehow Washington and his Continental Army survived the winter, successfully defending Morristown and making plans that would result in the defeat of the British at nearby Springfield the following summer.

All that was a long time ago, and on this sunny morning the annual Morristown Fall Festival was in progress. Traffic had been stopped and dozens of tents and booths were set up. There were booths offering arts and crafts for sale and others serving food and drink. There was live music in various styles, and games for the children. Celia recognized Florence from Macculloch Hall and Florence's friend Marlee Quinn manning the Morris County Historical Society tent.

They ventured onto the Green itself, exploring the interior walkways, a double elliptical pattern that flowed traffic around flower beds, trees, and manmade features. They admired a complicated bronze fountain depicting a Revolutionary soldier bidding his family, including the dog, good-bye from horseback.

On the other side of the Green, a Civil War monument honored soldiers of another terrible war, soldiers who had been destined to never again walk the paths of this peaceful park.

Later that evening, they stopped for a light dinner and drinks at the Red Rose Restaurant. The lovely child-woman Lily was on duty at the podium. Anya could feel Lily's huge, turquoise eyes fasten on her, still searching for something. At the table Lily dropped the menu meant for Anya, and they both reached for it. "You've got such small hands," Anya said spontaneously as their fingers touched. She held Lily's white, soft hand for a moment, turning it palm up. A small collection of rings wreathed the slender fingers. Was that an old scar near her thumb? Anya shook her head to rid herself of that errant thought.

"My hand is not much smaller than yours," Lily replied, showing a tiny smile. "Try one of my rings." She slipped a slender silver band with a pink pearl from her middle finger. Anya felt odd about the request, but she accepted the ring, finding it would fit only her little finger. The young girl watched Anya dreamily until she was summoned back to the podium by the watchful Maureen.

Jimmy walked to the small bar to order drinks. While he waited he studied Anya's poster for the Theatre that she had signed with a green Sharpie. Next to it was a smaller poster holding a greatly enlarged newspaper article. When Maureen served him the drinks, he asked if he could borrow the article. "Sure. We've got the original," Maureen said as she removed it from the wall. He folded it and slipped it in his jacket pocket.

After dinner they returned to the Ralston Club, where the three of them lingered in the book-lined bar for a nightcap. Then Anya said goodnight and went up the stairs to her room, feeling better than she had in weeks. Later, while she was emptying the bag of brochures and inexpensive promotional items she had collected at the festival, she discovered Lily's ring with the pink stone nestled at the bottom.

* * * * *

The next morning Celia, up early and packed, went down to the Radisson's lobby to get her first coffee of the day. Jimmy could sleep in as long as he liked. She'd get the local newspaper and the *New York Times*, have a good read and perhaps even start the *Times* crossword puzzle.

Struggling with the oversized Sunday papers and the large coffee, she chose a comfortable leather sofa under a skylight. After glancing at the *Times* headlines, she picked up the *Morristown Daily Record*.

She felt her stomach spasm as she jolted from the depths of the sofa, her hands shaking. The coffee and the *Times* forgotten, she grabbed the *Daily Record* and raced upstairs. She knocked on Jimmy's door frantically, then knocked again immediately without waiting. Inside Jimmy struggled with the lock and opened the door a crack. "Celia, what the hell's up?" he asked, obviously having been awakened. When he saw the color of her face he quickly brought her into his room. "What's wrong?" he asked, leading her toward the sofa.

She refused to sit. Holding up the front page of the paper, she blurted out the news. "Maureen and Richard Sullivan were murdered at the Rose Restaurant last night."

PART II

Dreams which delude pass through the Ivory Gate,
Those which come true pass through the Gate of Horn.

Greek legend

Chapter 14

Owners of Local Restaurant Found Dead; Foul Play Indicated

Morristown: Richard and Maureen Sullivan, owners of the Red Rose Restaurant, a popular local eatery and bar, were found dead at the restaurant at approximately 5:00 a.m. by the morning cleaning crew. The exact causes of death have not been disclosed at this time, but both bodies showed signs of violence, according to witnesses. Autopsies will be performed and results announced when they are available, said lead detective Brian Mitchell.

The restaurant closed at its usual hour of 12:00 a.m., and all employees had left the premises by 12:30, according to the Rose's business partner, Mark West. The Sullivans' only son Andrew, who lives in New York City, was informed immediately of the deaths. No more details were available as the *Daily Record* went to press.

The Red Rose Restaurant occupies an old

farmhouse that was witness to a famous murder case in 1833, that of Judge Samuel Sayre and Sarah, his wife. A black female servant named Phebe was also killed. The murderer was Antoine Le Blanc, an immigrant farmhand who had been working at the Sayre farm. The motive was robbery, and Le Blanc was arrested, convicted, sentenced to death, and hanged on Morristown's Green.

Jimmy lowered the paper.

Celia spoke in clipped words. "Anya is going to freak out. She's going to be knocked off her feet by this. This is the kind of thing Yuri always feared."

"Wait a minute, Celia. This has nothing to do with Anya and nothing to do with what happened at that farmhouse 175 years ago." Jimmy tossed the newspaper on the rumpled sofa bed. He walked over to the agitated Celia and caught her by the arms, stopping her pacing. "You understand that, don't you?"

Celia took several deep breaths. "Ok, Jimmy. I'm all right. Let's just figure this out."

"Sit down while I get dressed."

In ten minutes Jimmy had showered and put on jeans and a black tee shirt. Strands of gleaming black hair, combed back hastily, fell onto his forehead. Sitting opposite Celia, he took up the pre-shower conversation. "Of course Anya will be shocked when she hears about this, so it's important that she understands it's just a nasty coincidence, Celia. A lot of things can happen over 175 years in any single location. Statistics prove that lightning can indeed strike twice, given enough time."

"It's terrible. Richard and Maureen Sullivan seemed like such nice people."

Jimmy repeated his point. "Just so Anya sees it for what it is."

They decided to go to the Ralston Club and intercept Anya before she saw a newspaper. Jimmy was pulling on a denim jacket when there was a knock at the hallway door. He went to the door and pulled it open, expecting the maid.

A large, uniformed policeman was standing in the hall. Next to him was Anya, wearing a police jacket over pajamas, her shoes wet and muddy.

"Are you James Lang?" the policeman asked.

"I'm Lang. Anya, what's going on?"

The policeman answered. "You tell me, Mr. Lang. I'm just making a delivery for Detective Mitchell. He's at the Rose Restaurant working a double murder," the officer said, going for shock effect.

"It's in the paper," Jimmy replied.

The officer looked disappointed. "Already?"

"A short article on the front page."

"Wait until tomorrow," the cop retorted.

Celia came to the door and brought Anya into the room, handing the uniform jacket to the officer. Anya's uncombed hair tumbled down her shoulders, damp and interwoven with small twigs and grasses. She had a dazed, puzzled look on her face, seeming not to recognize Celia or Jimmy. Jimmy stepped out into the hall with the officer and closed the door behind him.

"Where did you find her?"

The policeman was happy to share the details that had led to his extraordinary mission. "It's been a helluva morning. We were out in the Rose's parking lot looking for a murder weapon. Detective Mitchell caught sight of someone moving down in a gully behind the restaurant." The officer jerked his head in the direction of the door behind Jimmy. "Mitch recognized that one. So he told me to go get her and bring her to you and be quiet about it. Mitch – Detective Mitchell – is a friend of mine. So that's what I did."

"Thank you, officer. And thank Detective Mitchell."

"Yep. If Mitch hadn't spotted her first, she'd probably be sitting at the station or in the psych ward at Memorial. Helluva morning for that one to be out strolling." He jerked his head at the door again.

Jimmy stepped back into the room. Anya was sitting quietly, Celia hovering with a cup of tea. He addressed both of them. "What happened?"

"She had a dream," Celia answered. "I'm just trying to keep her talking before she forgets any more of it."

"Talk, Anya." He picked up a pad and pen.

Anya took several tissues from the box Celia was holding. "I was so relieved last night when I went to bed. We'd had such a happy day. The whole thing was finished without ruining my life here. But then I dreamed, Jimmy. It's as if the dream had been hanging over my bed, waiting for me. It was the dead woman. The young woman. She'd got out of the attic somehow."

"What was she doing?"

"She was leaning over me, covered in blood. She had those terrible wounds. I could see the skull depression under her matted black hair. She put her hands on me and pulled me up. Her hands looked rough and dry, but when she touched me they were soft. She started dragging me toward the door. She was frantic."

"It was you in the dream, not the young boy?"

"Oh, yes. There was no filter. It was me. She pulled me through the door. We flew over the houses and stores along South Street until we came to the Green. It looked exactly how it did yesterday at the festival, with all the people and the tents and booths. But when the woman and I came down, the people at the festival started to run toward a big wooden platform. Everyone had been happy and having a good time, but now it was different. The people's eyes, even the children's, were hard and glittery, like black diamonds. They were excited, but it was ugly and menacing, like wild animals. They wanted something terrible, knowing it was terrible but wanting it anyway.

"The people were holding little books, and they pushed each other to get near the platform. The woman was holding one of the little books, too. She picked me up so I had to look into the face of the man high above the platform. The snake was tight around his neck. His face was red and swollen. His eyes protruded from their sockets, and I could see tiny blood spots in them. The man's legs weren't tied. I thought perhaps this was done on purpose, because the man's kicking seemed to make the crowd more excited. Some of the men took out pocket watches to time how long he twisted and kicked.

"The woman pointed to the hanging man and slowly shook her head. She ripped up the little book, and the pieces were scattered to the wind. Then we flew to a little church nearby. She gestured to her bloody head wounds and held out her arm, pointing toward the church. But she was fading away, and I couldn't hear what she was saying. Then she was gone, and I was tumbling toward the earth. I was cold and wet, and I got the idea I was dreaming, but I couldn't get out of the dream.

"The next thing I remember was a policeman coming toward me saying something about Detective Mitchell. I let the policeman lead me away. I was amazed to see I was behind the Rose Restaurant."

"Did you realize you were awake then?" Celia asked.

"I wasn't really sure until you began to talk to me."

Celia looked at Jimmy over Anya's head. The fact that Anya had not been able to tell sleep from waking, dream from reality, was not good.

"All right, Anya. Just get some rest for now." Celia took Anya into the bedroom and pulled a down comforter over her. Anya fell into deep sleep immediately.

"What a mess this is, Jimmy," Celia said when she returned to the sitting room.

"She hasn't got this out of her system," he said, thinking of the possible ramifications of Anya trying to follow her dream onto the streets of Morristown in the middle of the night.

Jimmy's cell phone rang. Detective Mitchell didn't bother to identify himself. "Is she there with you?"

"Yes. She's sleeping."

"I need to talk to you privately but I'm tied up for awhile. Meet me in the garden behind Macculloch Hall in three hours. I'll slip away for a few minutes."

Jimmy left the hotel for Macculloch Hall as Anya was coming out of her deep, dreamless sleep and Celia was ordering hot soup from room service. He parked in front of the museum, which was closed, and strolled around to the back of the mansion. A well-kept lawn was encircled by an elliptical border of mature perennial flowers, mostly roses that were far into their seasonal decline but still lovely in their mature, blowzy state. A sign told Jimmy that the garden was possibly the oldest in Morris County, containing wisteria plants brought to America by George Macculloch's explorer friend Admiral Matthew Perry.

He was startled when Mitchell silently came up behind him. "Enjoying the posies?"

Jimmy turned, covering his surprise. "Actually, yes. I'm a flowers guy."

The detective led Jimmy to a brick veranda at the back of the mansion. The veranda was covered by the famed wisteria. Tall roses set along the edges of the patio shielded them from view, if anyone had been watching. Detective Mitchell took out a small notebook and turned the pages. He spoke without looking up. "She's going to have to be questioned."

"Why? The cop who brought her realized she was sleepwalking."

"The station transferred a call about a trespasser. That's why I looked over the fence and saw her down there."

Jimmy was careful. "So go ahead and report a sleepwalker picked up and released."

"Not so easy, Jim. What we think is the murder weapon was found in the gully near where she was spotted."

"A likely place to throw it, I guess," Jimmy commented, suppressing a stronger defense of Anya. "What happened at the Rose Restaurant, Mitch?" he asked. "The paper had a few paragraphs, no details."

"There'll be a lot more tomorrow. This will be huge for Morristown, more so because of the 'history repeats itself' angle. We've got our hands full."

"What's going to be in tomorrow's paper?" Jimmy persisted.

Mitchell shrugged. "Richard Sullivan, white male, age 55, knifed in the heart sometime between 1:00 and 5:00 a.m. when the body was found near the back door by the cleaning crew. Motive appears to be robbery — a locked bank box was broken into and personal items were missing from the body."

"And his wife?"

"Found inside, not far from the back door, garroted with something soft."

"And what about Anya's situation?" Jimmy asked apprehensively.

"At the moment, no juicy 'Sleepwalking Woman Found Near Murder Weapon' headline. But I'm telling you, Jim, at the very least she's a potential witness. She was found at the scene."

Jimmy interrupted. "But not until later."

"She'll be interviewed and fingerprinted. Her fingerprints will be matched against those found on the knife. And I'll be questioning her at length."

"She's not going to give you anything, Mitch," Jimmy said quickly. "She wasn't in a conscious state. She didn't even know what was happening until after your officer friend delivered her to the hotel. And her fingerprints aren't going to be on any weapon."

The detective looked grim. "There have been sleepwalking defenses before, nearly all of them rejected in court. All this chitchat about her being a world-champion dreamer can't keep her out of it. I have my job to do."

"You sound a little like Sam Spade," Jimmy said quickly, because he was nervous and not sure what to say.

"Not remotely funny, Lang."

"Sorry." Jimmy regretted the dig.

Mitchell leaned forward, toward Jimmy, and spoke intensely. "Anya needs to be at the station house tomorrow. She'll be interviewed by me and another officer. I'll try to pick someone not prone to leaking to the press for free drinks."

"Thanks, Mitch. I mean it."

"Don't forget, no matter who is involved, I'll do my job."

"Of course."

Mitchell left the garden bower abruptly. After a few minutes, Jimmy headed back to the hotel.

Chapter 15

Celia was waiting for Jimmy. The moment she heard him at his door she was in the hallway.

"What happened with Mitchell, Jimmy?"

"He's playing tough guy. Not that he has a choice. Anya has to be interviewed tomorrow. How did Anya take the news about the Sullivans?"

"I'm not sure. She was upset but pulled herself together – at least I think she's okay." Celia followed him into his suite. "Jimmy. I've spoken to Yuri. He thinks Anya is in the middle of something important."

"I've heard that before."

"He also thinks she could be in danger."

"That's a no-brainer. Sleepwalking into a ditch in the middle of the night in her nightie suggests a certain element of risk. Not to mention two dead bodies a stone's throw away."

"Yuri is concerned about Anya's well-being first, of course. But this case is phenomenal, Jimmy. Anya has dreamed things she couldn't know except through some kind of time displacement."

Jimmy hesitated, then went to the closet and retrieved the folded article from the pocket of his jacket. He spread it out and put it in front of Celia. It was a reproduction of a restaurant review from the local newspaper:

The Red Rose Restaurant:
Good Food With Just a Pinch of Murder

Morristown: In addition to good food and high spirits, Morristown's Red Rose Restaurant offers a fascinating history lesson and, according to owners Richard and Maureen Sullivan and partner Mark West, a genuine ghost.

In 1833, the Rose (as the restaurant is usually called) was a typical farmhouse, the ancestral home of respected Judge Samuel Sayre, his wife, two daughters, and various servants. On a rainy spring night in May, one of the judge's hired farmhands went into town, overindulged on the local applejack, and returned home to bludgeon the judge and his wife to death in front of their stable. The farmhand, an immigrant named Antoine Le Blanc, also took an axe to their black serving girl Phebe in her attic bedroom, leaving her body on the bed underneath a blanket.

Fortunately the Sayre daughters were away from home that murderous night. And Phebe's brother Martin had recently run away, escaping her fate.

According to local legend and confirmed by West, Phebe's ghost still roams the hallways and rooms of the old farmhouse. "There's a distinct presence, especially in the attic," says West. "There are cold breezes coming from her room, even in summer, and sometimes the attic is found in disarray."

Phebe should be resting peacefully, not wandering eternally in search of vengeance. Le Blanc left a trail of stolen articles that was discovered at dawn by a nearby farmer chasing a cow down an alley. This alerted neighbors to the theft, and the murders were soon discovered. The killer's trail was followed, and he was in custody by the end of the day. He was tried, found guilty, and sentenced to hang for his bloody misdeeds.

But Le Blanc might have gotten more than he bargained for when he dispatched the Sayres for some clothing and other household articles. After a "special" hanging that involved being catapulted upward by the dropping of a heavy chunk of iron, Le Blanc's body was given to local physicians who managed to make his eyes roll and his legs contract with electricity experiments. Then Le Blanc body was delivered to a local tanner, who turned his hide into gruesome mementos such as wallets and book covers.

So, while you're enjoying dinner at the Red Rose Restaurant, you could get more than good food and friendly service. Perhaps you'll feel the presence of the hideously murdered Phebe, her head cruelly cleft by Le Blanc's axe, hanging out in one of the Rose's popular bar spaces!

The rest of the article was food related, and Celia broke off reading. "Where did you get this?" she asked.

"It was hanging near the bar in the dining room of the Rose Restaurant. Next to Anya's poster."

Celia faced was slightly flushed. "Your theory is that Anya read it unconsciously when she signed her poster, and that's where her dreams are coming from."

Jimmy shrugged his shoulders. "Occam's Razor. The correct answer is usually what's left after eliminating the more unlikely hypotheses – almost always the simplest answer."

"Wait, Jimmy. Anya had already had her first dream before we had dinner at the Red Rose Restaurant."

"The date on the restaurant review is several months ago. It's a copy of an article printed in the newspaper; the review could have been reprinted in a local magazine as well, maybe even in a Theatre program."

"Anya said she didn't know about the case."

"It obviously didn't register consciously."

"But Anya has dreamed in more detail than that article provides."

"Maybe by suggestion. You've certainly made it clear what you were looking for. Or maybe her overheated imagination is simply filling in the blanks."

"And why didn't you show me this before?" she demanded, brandishing the article. "I've given Yuri misleading information."

Jimmy shrugged his shoulders. "I noticed it when we were there after the festival. Anya's episode appeared to be over. I didn't think it made any difference."

"How could you keep this information from me?"

"I just wanted to let Anya get back to living a normal life. Away from Lubov."

"You think Yuri is the root of all evil. You're so childish."

Jimmy sighed. "Don't think I'm not aware of that."

"I'm sick of this." Celia snapped. "You withhold information and then accuse me of jumping to conclusions. You set me up to give incorrect information to Yuri. It's your resentment of Yuri that closes your mind to what's going on right in front of you. You're so jealous of him you can't even be scientifically objective."

Celia had never before attacked Jimmy's scientific judgment; never accused him of bias or questioned his integrity, despite their many differences of opinion. She looked up at Jimmy's shocked expression and quickly apologized. "I'm sorry, Jimmy. I didn't mean that."

"Don't be sorry," he replied curtly. "It's long past the time we should have had this conversation." He indicated the chair opposite him, and she automatically sat down, nervous.

Jimmy spoke slowly and deliberately. "No matter what you claim, Celia, you are Lubov's apologist in all things. This fact colors your interpretation of events and your judgment of people and their motivations. That's the reason Lubov has always kept you out of his real work, despite your own scientific training. Not that what you do isn't essential to a man like him. You're an incredible organizer, facilitator, record-keeper. But beyond that, you're the human face of Lubov's work – you talk people into doing what Lubov wants."

Celia didn't move. Her face was flushed a shade of mauve that contrasted unfavorably with her red hair.

Jimmy continued. "And the reason you are Yuri Lubov's facilitator and apologist is because you're in love with him. You always have been. I knew that within weeks of working with you. What is so sad is that he will never return even a modicum of your devotion, no matter how smooth you make his professional life, how hard you press to further his goals, how thoroughly you manipulate people to do what he wants."

Celia struggled out of her chair and waved her hands for him to stop talking, her eyes red-rimmed. "Shut up, Jimmy. Shut up."

Jimmy didn't look at her. "Sit down, Celia. I'm not finished. It's not that I'm jealous of Lubov, as you accuse me. Or at least not about his work. Lubov has his scientific goals and I have mine; our separate objectives overlap in certain small areas. But for many years I was in love with you. You knew it. We've had an amazingly long-lived fling, when you think about it. Stupidly, I thought you might want more some day.

"But even though your relationship with Lubov is completely one-sided, I have come to realize you have little to give to anyone else. You serve him in everything and bask pitifully in his rare faint praise. You've never realized that if you hadn't shown up to take care of him, someone else would have. That's the way it works when you've been declared a genius. You expect to have your needs met. It doesn't matter who does it, just so someone is there 24-7 with no expectation of anything in return. That's you, Celia."

Celia said faintly. "I don't sleep with Yuri."

"Whatever. That used to matter to me, but it hasn't for a long time. And you're right that I'm resentful. Of all the things I resent, it's Anya's case that most rankles me. All the other interesting, promising subjects that you and Lubov have marched into my lab were treated professionally. The goals and limits of treatment were explained to them and their families. They were offered choices and were allowed to opt in or out. But Anya – she was different from the beginning. She was induced to take part in Lubov's experiments without full disclosure of other options. You became 'Aunt Ceci,' Anya's guide, her confidant, in some ways closer to her than her parents. You did this in a way that never alienated her parents, something I've never understood. You got to Anya so that Lubov could have full use of her."

When Celia spoke Jimmy could hardly hear her faint voice. "You're wrong. Wrong. You don't understand." She lifted her head and looked at him. "Why did you go along if this is what you thought?"

Her question shouldn't have been so hard to answer. What could he say? Because I was in love with you? Because Anya really is a fascinating case? Because I wanted to protect Anya from an over-zealous scientist and his devoted acolyte and her self-destructive fantasies? He didn't know which answer was true, maybe all of them, so he didn't answer. He looked over at Celia, her blue eyes dull, her body slumped. He got up and went to her, touching her arm. Celia sensed his pity and pulled away. Neither of them spoke further; there was already too much truth in the room. He left her and went down to the hotel bar.

After the confrontation with Jimmy, Celia went to her room and slept for a while, exhausted. When she awoke she ordered coffee and a sandwich from room service. Jimmy sat at the bar most of the afternoon. Eventually he went for a long walk to clear his head. When Celia heard him fumbling at his door around 10:00 p.m., she turned off her light.

Chapter 16

The next morning Celia went to the lobby for the newspapers. The *Daily Record's* banner headline read:

Red Rose Restaurant in Morristown
Scene of Double Murder

Owners Found Dead Early Yesterday;
Restaurant Hostess Missing

The story reiterated the known facts of the killings, but Celia
rushed to the section about the missing Lily Doone. A sense of
doom enveloped her as she read the few details being released.
On the evening of the killings, Lily had left the restaurant early,
not feeling well. She told several people she was going to take a
cab home, but her bed had not been slept in when she was
missed the next morning. The police had questioned restaurant
employees for leads on her whereabouts and had apparently
gotten nowhere.

Inside the paper was a long sidebar on the Sayre murders of
1833. The *Newark Star Ledger* also had extensive coverage, including pictures of some of the gruesome artifacts made out of

Le Blanc's skin from the collection of the local historical society.

Celia rushed upstairs with the papers. She was nervous about facing Jimmy after yesterday's game-changing fight. He answered her knock and formally invited her inside.

"Jimmy. Lily Doone is missing." She was glad to have something to focus on.

Jimmy scanned the newspaper stories. When he was finished he looked up at Celia's bleak face. "Lily seemed on the edge of losing it both times we saw her. I hope she just chose to take herself out of her situation."

"With Lily missing, that will ensure even more 'history repeats itself' stuff in the press. Phebe and now Lily."

"I suppose Phebe and Lily could both be characterized as 'serving girls,' if you're the sensationalist press looking for things like that," Jimmy replied carefully.

Celia had brought up a huge container of coffee for him. She handed it over. "Peace offering?" she asked, smiling up at him with an insouciance she didn't really feel, trying to break the tension between them.

"Thanks," he said shortly.

Celia had taken care to look particularly attractive this morning, wearing black pants and a form-fitting white silk blouse, make-up carefully applied. Yet she was a little too bright-eyed, giving off an aura of trying too hard.

They drank their coffee, Celia watching Jimmy surreptitiously. She finally broke the silence. "Will you accept that I have great personal affection for Anya? That I care deeply about her, beyond my work for Yuri?"

"Yes. I accept that. I also accept your criticism that I have been too unwilling to admit to you, because I was so angry, that this episode of Anya's is scientifically interesting."

"Thank you, Jimmy." She was a little relieved but had hoped he would retract what he had said about their relationship.

"Anya comes first," Jimmy reiterated. "She's in a sticky spot.

She has to talk to the police today."

"Of course Anya comes first."

Jimmy went to retrieve his files from the table, and Celia got up to get a soda. As they brushed by each other, Celia stopped him. She pulled his head down toward hers and kissed him on the lips. The kiss intensified, and he responded out of long habit. But then he moved gently but firmly away and picked up his notes.

Celia felt something shift inside her. She looked at him but could no longer hold her smile in place. She dropped her eyes and awkwardly opened her notebook. With no reference to what had just happened, she asked a question. "Have you had a chance to look at the raw data?"

Jimmy was glad to focus on the case. "I've gone over some of Anya's brain scans. Most of the data is clearly associated with internal memory. But there are a few oddities. More analysis is necessary before drawing conclusions."

"Why has Anya not been able to dream her way out of this like she always has before, Jimmy?"

"I've been thinking about that. Maybe it's because she's dreaming the wrong dream."

"What do you mean?"

"Maybe she's trying to dream the dream we want her to dream, but she needs to dream her own dream. Perhaps we tried to bring the dream episode to a close too quickly because we were eager to have it over with."

"You mean I did that," she said, acknowledging his generosity in sharing the blame. "But what can we do now?"

"She's developed a dream character. We need to give her the freedom to let that character go wherever it needs to, not just to follow a historical script. She's got to get back to her own dream."

Celia nodded, and Jimmy closed his file. "In the meantime, I'll go to the police station with Anya this morning. I don't like to step on her independence, but she was out of it the day of the murders, and Detective Mitchell is loaded for bear."

"Okay, Jimmy." She started to leave for her room, then turned uncertainly, trying once more to heal the breach between them. "Jimmy. I feel so much better knowing we're working together again for Anya's sake."

"Sure, Celia." He didn't look at her.

Chapter 17

Detective Mitchell opened his casebook. He was alone in one of the private conference rooms, away from the constant interruptions of his office, carefully checking the notes from his initial interview with Mark West. West had been the Sullivans' business partner for fifteen years, when the three of them bought the tired old tavern on South Street. They renamed it the Red Rose Restaurant for the vintage blood-red roses that still clung to life in improbable niches on the property, especially along the fence line at the top of the ravine that dropped off just behind the parking lot.

When Mitchell finally had a chance to interview Mark West on the morning the murders were discovered, he could tell the man had been crying. Under questioning, West said he had left the restaurant after all the staff had departed, leaving the Sullivans to lock up, which was customary. He claimed to have gone straight home to his townhouse a few blocks away. His live-in friend, or long-time companion, Mitchell wasn't sure which, was away on a business trip and wouldn't be able to vouch for that claim. Mitchell had let West go at that point, telling him he would want to talk to him again.

Mitchell's interviews with restaurant personnel had revealed that the Red Rose Restaurant was like any small business where people worked in close quarters. There was always plenty of gossip among the staff – who got the best tip tables, who was getting more hours, who was hooking up with whom after work. There was the usual speculation and grousing about management.

Mitchell soon discovered there was resentment of Lily Doone. A long-time waitress, a flashy, raven-haired girl named Rhonda, had been up for the hostess gig. But then Lily had arrived on the scene. No experience and a bag of nerves, but she had been given the job, a friend of Rhonda's had recounted to him. During interviews, there also had been several sly references to Richard Sullivan's relationship with Lily. Richard seemed to be Johnny-on-the-spot when it came to comforting the little blonde hostess, with lots of hands-on stuff, according to a couple of the male employees.

There was also a lot of eye rolling about Mark West. He was known as the "ghost guy," for being so fixated on the old Sayre murders. He spent a lot of time (way too much, according to employees) recounting the story in lurid detail during staff meetings. One older long-time waitress who claimed to have dated him for a short period described him as obsessed with the murders and with the old farmhouse itself. He told her he had a standing offer with the Sullivans to buy them out if they ever decided to get out of the restaurant business.

Julio Martinez was the Rose's barback, responsible for keeping the various bars of the restaurant supplied with liquor, beer, and mixers from the walkout basement delivery and storage area. Mitchell asked him if he knew anything about the sudden disappearance of Lenny Paco, the restaurant's recently hired bar manager. He wasn't surprised to see him leave, said Martinez. When Mitchell pressed him, the barback mentioned some back-and-forth between Lenny and Lily, most of it coming from Lenny's side. Lenny was always careful to make his moves when the Sullivans and West were nowhere in sight, and Lily seemed scared of Paco, Martinez claimed.

Mark West was escorted to the interview room by Officer Joan Hadley. West stood at the doorway, dressed in a plaid tie and casual jacket, not sure of what to do, his eyes on Mitchell.

Mitchell got up. "Thanks for coming in, Mark. Sit down. Coffee? Soda?"

West sat down and asked for a diet coke. "Hadley, make that two," Mitchell said. West still looked shell-shocked but was more in control than yesterday. He was what women called a nice-looking man, perhaps in his late forties, glasses, an inch or two short of average height and maybe a few pounds over ideal weight, but in relatively good shape.

"I'm sorry again for your loss, Mark. Let's see. You had a business arrangement with the Sullivans. Beside working with them, I take it you knew them well?"

"Oh, god, yes. I've been close to Maureen and Richard Sullivan since the day I met them almost twenty years ago."

"They were good people?"

"Absolutely the best. They kept to themselves outside work, but they did a lot for other people through the years."

"What about their son, Andrew? He wasn't interested in the restaurant? He's their only kid, right?"

West hesitated. "Andy was adopted. I didn't know the Sullivans when he was a kid. I met them after he started to get into trouble as a teenager."

"How much trouble?"

"Enough to get put away, if not for his parents. Maureen and Richard went through a lot to keep him out of jail. A lot of heartache and money. Maybe they should have let him take his medicine. Teach him a lesson. But they bent over backwards for him. It broke their hearts that he was so mean and ungrateful."

Mitchell had spoken with Andrew Richard Sullivan – a real prick, he'd thought. He lived in New York City, managing a cheap club in the East Village. Upon hearing of his parents' deaths, he was mostly interested in getting the Red Rose Restaurant on the market as soon as possible. It was in a prime location and desirable to developers. Banks had been scooping up properties around the Green and its main feeder streets, Andrew told Mitchell, and he expected to get top dollar. Mark West would have to agree or be able to buy Andrew out at his asking price.

"I understand the restaurant was always more to you than just an investment," Mitchell said.

West answered eagerly. "I love the Rose. I've researched the history of the place for years. Love to talk about it, too, I admit. I know people laugh at me behind my back, but I guess the Rose is both my job and my hobby." He paused, then added, "Or was."

"Did you take an active part in managing the place? Hiring and firing decisions?"

"I did the books and paid the bills and taxes. Helped with closing most nights. The Sullivans ran the bar and food operations, including personnel."

"What about Lily Doone, Mark? Some of the Rose's staff resented her being dropped in as hostess, with no experience. They seemed to think there was more to it than met the eye. Between Lily and Richard Sullivan, you know."

West's face hardened. "They don't know what they're talking about. They forget about when Richard would give some poor busboy an advance to pay his rent. Or he'd keep a single mother on the payroll even though she's missing work because of a sick kid. No, they have to make up stories about Richard, who was only trying to help."

"Sure there's nothing to it, Mark? Lily is a remarkable-looking young woman for all I'm told. Did you like her?"

"She's pretty. Very. Also vulnerable. Sure, I liked Lily. But there's nothing to those stupid comments. Both Sullivans treated her like a daughter. I don't know the whole story, but Lily came to them through that Sunnyside place out by the lake. Abused women, you know? I think it was Sonja Hildebrant, or maybe the doc out there, Dr. Bennett, who asked them to give Lily a chance. Lily had a terrible life story. The Sullivans just fell for her and wanted to help her. Maybe to make up for Andy. Andy sure didn't like it, I'll tell you."

"How do you know that?"

"I was in the office once when he was haranguing Maureen about taking in a little slut from the shelter. Very nice guy, Andy."

"Did Lily know any of the other workers at the restaurant?"

"No. She kept to herself."

"No one else took an interest in a pretty girl like that?"

"All the guys looked. But Richard and Maureen kept a pretty close eye on her."

"What about Lenny Paco?"

West shrugged. "Paco showed up when Richard happened to need a bar manager. Good references. He disappeared after some trouble in the parking lot."

"What kind of trouble?"

"He was there when someone tried to accost Lily after work one night. According to the bouncer who came to the rescue, Paco wasn't doing much to help her."

Mitchell sensed that West had something on his mind. "Look, Mark. I need you to tell me everything you can that might have some bearing on this case. Anything you're thinking. You can't help the Sullivans, but Lily's out there somewhere, and she's the kind of girl who needs all the help she can get, from what you say."

"That's just what I was thinking about, detective," he said slowly. "Lily. Lily and the history of the Rose Restaurant."

"What do you mean?"

"You know, the murder of Phebe. And now Lily."

"You're talking about the Sayres' servant who was murdered

way back when?"

"Yes. Phebe was killed in the attic of the Rose. I've been up there dozens of times, thinking what it must have been like. How terrorized she must have been."

This guy's really hung up, Mitchell thought. "I'm not getting it, Mark. Help me out. What's this got to do with Lily?"

West spoke pensively. "This sounds ridiculous to you, I'm sure. But Phebe was killed, horribly. And now I'm afraid for Lily."

Mitchell was afraid for Lily, too. Because she was missing, not because of the old murders, as West seemed to be inferring.

"You don't think that what happened to the Sullivans is connected with those other murders, do you, Mark?"

"I know that would be hard for some people to believe," he said carefully.

"Well, let's hope that Lily Doone has just dropped out of sight for reasons of her own." Mitchell thought West looked doubtful. He let him go, for now.

When he returned to his office, there was a thick envelope with a Macculloch Hall return address on his desk. On the top of a pile of scanned pages was a short note: Per your request. Hope this sheds light. Florence.

Mitchell settled back. The first article was from the *New York Times*, a biography of Dr. Yuri Alexei Lubov's life and scientific credentials written at the time of his MacArthur Grant, the so-called Genius Award given by the foundation of that name to individuals who "best demonstrate the elusive and indefinable quality of creativity in conjunction with demonstrable mastery in their chosen field," according to the piece. The money and prestige of the award was meant to free recipients from the constant grind of pursuing grants and other funding.

Lubov had been born in the waning days of Stalin's Russia and had passed through its highest-ranked scientific academies to become one of the Soviet Union's leading mathematicians and cosmologists. He was a second-generation pioneer in quantum physics. In the 1970s he left the Soviet Union to work in the U.S. and never went back. With his new scientific colleagues, he became one of the first to postulate the existence of dark matter and energy, the unseen stuff that makes up most of the universe and propels its ever-faster expansion. He also became a major player in string theory, a conjecture of modern physics that holds the promise of unifying all the forces of nature: electromagnetism, the strong force that holds particles together, the weak nuclear force of radioactive decay, and gravity.

Smart guy, Dr. Lubov, Mitchell thought. What in the hell does he have to do with Jimmy Lang's sleep lab?

The next article in the packet had run in one of the popular science magazines a few years back.

The Smartest, Least-known Man
In the Universe(s)

You've probably never heard of Dr. Yuri Alexei Lubov, but he's one of the top scientists chasing a long-elusive goal of quantum physicists – the not-so-modest sounding Theory of Everything. This theory would link all the forces of nature and take modern physics far beyond Einstein's famous $e = mc^2$.

Dr. Lubov and other physicists are working on superstring theory, the idea that the tiniest bits of matter are not particles, as accepted in what is known as the 'standard model,' but instead are infinitely tiny 'strings' of pure energy, vibrating at different rates to create all the elements that make up the known universe.

Because these strings are far too tiny to ever be seen directly, the work is pursued in mathematical terms through equations that can sprawl over hundreds of pages. And the implications of string theory are amazing. It predicts that there are seven other dimensions in addition to our perceived four-dimensional world of length-width-depth-time. Why don't we notice the extra dimensions? Because they are infinitesimally tiny. Remnants of the 'big bang' that brought the universe into being, these dimensions are thought to be rolled up on themselves, hiding among the familiar, larger dimensions, far too small to be perceived.

But there is another direction of experimentation and study, one that looks inward, into the brains of certain special people.

Dr. Lubov does not comment on this aspect of his scientific inquiry, so we solicited input for this article from a scientist who is familiar with his work. The hypothesis goes like this: During dreaming, when the conscious, logical mind chemically gives up its control of brain function, the tiny dimensions predicted by string theory come into play, at least for some ultra-sensitive people. These undetectable dimensions made of vibrating energy steal into the brain and do their mischief during sleep, when the barriers of consciousness are down.

This could be why dreams contain elaborate, detailed settings of places we've never seen, people we've never known and powerful emotions we've never experienced. This kind of dreaming – even the fantastical and surreal – theoretically could originate in places that actually exist:

other dimensions.

More intriguingly, the mathematical models of string theory discredit the instinctive 'arrow of time,' that bedrock, logical belief that events move in only one direction and then are gone forever. But if there is no favored direction for time outside our subjective feelings, one could theoretically move backwards in time, if only in that special state of sleep known as dreaming. Some physicists suspect that time itself is a delusion, and that the universe is static. As we slip randomly from tableau to tableau in our own tiny slice of the universe, our brain fills in the sensation of movement and elapsing time.

What if everything that has happened does not fade away but is stored as vibrating matter/energy that can never be destroyed, as Einstein stated in $e = mc^2$? What if the past persists in tiny parallel worlds and numberless alternate universes, perhaps as the unseen dark matter and energy that rules our universe? These hidden dimensions could be portals that make certain people, when they are rendered helpless during dreaming, susceptible to input from all that ever was.

For most of us, the human brain patches over tiny inconsistencies and contradictions caused by these hidden dimensions. But not the brains of the super-susceptible. Such people have no way to reconcile or process these contradictions except as hallucination or mental aberration.

These are the rare people who spend time dreaming in certain sleep labs. Dr. Lubov and his colleagues attempt to identify dreams that seem to enter the dreamer's consciousness from somewhere outside of their experience. Proof of this is hard to come by, but certain dreamers appear to dream premonitionally, revealing events yet to happen, or to dream about things that actually occurred in the past that they have no way of knowing. Lucid dreaming, where a dreamer becomes aware, without waking, that he or she is dreaming and can sometimes control the content and flow of the dream, is used to help such dreamers integrate powerful dream material.

You may never hear of Dr. Lubov and his wide-ranging scientific gifts again. In part, that's what the no-strings-attached MacArthur Genius Award is for. But maybe someday he will become the discoverer of a Grand Unifying Theory that explains everything, at least to those smart enough to understand it. Lubov's name will then become as recognizable as Albert Einstein's – throughout an infinite number of universes.

The next article in the packet had been printed in the same magazine, in the following month's issue. It was a stinging Letter to the Editor written on behalf of Dr. Lubov, excoriating the second part of the article on his work that had been purportedly provided by "a scientist familiar with Dr. Lubov's work." The letter called into question both the article's overly facile interpretation of this work and the magazine's right to disclose it.

Dr. Lubov obviously did not wish to advertise his interest in dreaming, thought Mitchell. Maybe Lubov the Genius thinks anything to do with dreaming is too prosaic, or too connected in the public mind to simplistic dream interpretation, and not worthy of being associated with someone of his stature.

We all have our vanities, thought Mitchell as he put the package away.

Chapter 18

Later that day Jimmy accompanied a nervous but prepared Anya to the Morristown police station. She had thought all yesterday afternoon about what she was going to tell the detective. Jimmy advised her to stick to exactly what she remembered, even if her story seemed disjointed.

As Anya and Jimmy were pushing through the door, they almost collided with Marilyn. The large white-garbed woman was being roughly escorted out of the police station by a uniformed officer. She was balancing a large paper plate that held a Danish, two donuts and a sugary bear claw. Her dark arms and legs contrasted bizarrely with the white canvas of her face.

The officer gave her a slight push in the direction of the parking lot. "You got breakfast out of us. Now hit the road, beautiful, or I'll have to take you to the shelter."

Marilyn drew herself up, struggling for a dignified pose. "Call me Miss Monroe, officer. And be careful, or I'll report you to Detective Mitchell. He likes to consult me on his cases."

"Yeah, yeah, Miss Monroe. You tell Mitch on me. That would make you a snitch, wouldn't it?"

But Marilyn had forgotten the officer. She had spied Anya, and she became alarmed. "Annie. What are you doing here?

You okay, girl?"

Anya put her hands on the homeless woman's arms and said quickly. "I'm all right, Marilyn. Don't worry. Just go home."

The black woman looked doubtful. "Remember what we said, girlfriend? We stick together. You help me and I help you."

"You *are* helping me, Marilyn." Anya said intensely. "I can't talk now. Just get home."

The heavily made-up face relaxed. "You bet, Annie. You know where to find us."

The officer stepped forward again. "Get lost, Marilyn. I mean it," he said impatiently. Then he turned to Anya. "Anya Gregory, right? You come with me. Your friend here can wait in reception."

"I'd like him to be with me."

"Detective Mitchell might not allow it."

Jimmy broke in. "Tell Detective Mitchell he can talk to Anya with me or with her lawyer."

The officer shrugged and then walked down the hallway. When he returned he said, "Detective Mitchell says he'll take the doc. Follow me."

They were escorted to one of a series of interview rooms. Mitchell was talking with another police officer, a tall, attractive blonde woman, and he let them wait a minute or so before he looked up and introduced them. "Officer Hadley, this is Anya Gregory and Dr. Lang." The blonde nodded toward them.

Mitchell turned to Anya and Jimmy. "Have a seat. Want coffee or soda?"

There were bottles of water on the scratched, worn table between them and Mitchell. They turned down the coffee. Mitchell wasted no more time on niceties. "Miss Gregory, what were you doing behind the Red Rose Restaurant yesterday morning?"

Anya poured water into a plastic cup and took a sip before answering. "I have occasional bouts of sleepwalking."

"That was a bad morning for a walkabout," commented the woman officer.

"I understand," Anya said, her voice neutral.

"How long were you in the ravine?" Mitchell asked. "What were you doing?"

"I'm sorry. I can't answer those questions because I don't know. I remember getting out of bed and putting on shoes and a jacket. And knowing I had something to do."

"What did you have to do?"

"I don't know. Just that I had to go to that place."

"Did you see anyone else on the way, or in the parking lot of the restaurant?"

"Not that I'm aware of. I usually don't remember much when I'm . . . in that state."

The woman officer frowned. "So you sleepwalked onto the scene of a major crime?" Her voice had a hard edge.

"I can only tell you what happened from my point of view."

Mitchell looked annoyed, and he turned his back toward Hadley. He addressed Anya. "Are you sure you can't remember seeing anybody behind the restaurant? This is important."

Jimmy spoke up. "I can vouch for Anya's psychological condition during these episodes. She has no recall of events upon awakening."

"I asked Anya, not you."

"I have some expertise, that's all."

"Right, Dr. Jim. I remember the Weird Dreams And The People Who Dream Them lecture," he replied.

Jimmy was hoping the tough stance was mainly for the female officer's benefit. After a few more questions, Mitchell suddenly turned to her. "Listen, Hadley. Under the circumstances I'm not going to push this much further right now. Go check on what's happening in the big room, will you?"

Officer Hadley left, her disappointment showing in the stiff way her long legs carried her out of the room.

Mitchell waited until the door closed behind her, then turned to Anya. "You read the stories in this morning's paper?"

"Yes."

"By the time you read the next news cycle you'll know why I'm not fingerprinting you right now. We have a suspect."

Jimmy was surprised at the extent of his relief at this news. "Can you say who it is?"

Mitchell shrugged. "It's already out. An undocumented immigrant who sometimes bussed tables at the Rose Restaurant. He dropped a pad of order sheets from another restaurant he works at, probably while cleaning out Richard Sullivan's pockets. We found money, likely from the Rose's strong box, and Sullivan's watch in the house where the suspect lives with about two dozen so-called cousins."

"That'll put a lot of people's minds at ease," Jimmy commented.

"It'll also goose the anti-immigrant feeling in this town."

"And what about Lily Doone?" Jimmy asked.

"Nothing," Mitchell replied. "We've got a lot of work to do there."

At the sound of Lily's name, Anya stood up abruptly, breathing rapidly and clenching her fists. "Mitch, you've got to help Lily," she blurted.

Both Jimmy and the detective were taken by surprise. Mitchell, ridiculously affected by her use of his nickname, rose instinctively, his first urge to comfort her apparent distress. But it was Jimmy who took her arm and gently eased her back into her seat. Mitchell could only speak from across the table. "Anya, we all want Lily to be safe. We're following every lead." Jimmy still had his hand on Anya's arm, and she was now leaning against him. "Do you know Lily, Anya?" Mitchell asked.

"Oh, no. Only from seeing her at the Rose Restaurant."

"You never saw her outside the restaurant?"

"No."

144

The detective got to his feet. "All right. That's it for now. I've got things to do."

Jimmy put out his hand. "Thanks for keeping Anya's bit part in this out of the papers."

Mitchell, afraid Jimmy had noticed his less-than-professional response to Anya, reasserted his toughness. "That's just for now. Until this whole thing is put to bed, everything's up for grabs," he snapped. He guided them out of the room without looking at Anya, into the capable hands of Officer Hadley.

As Jimmy and Anya were leaving, they saw a handcuffed man being led out of a windowless room by two officers. There was another man in the group, wearing a suit, talking fast in Hispanic to the prisoner. The cuffed man was young and dressed in scruffy warm ups. He looked confused and terrified. He was short and had broad cheekbones and straight, matte-black hair like many of the Central American men who lived in dilapidated housing north of town, often six or more to a room, the code-violating practice known as "stacking."

As they were leaving the station, Anya suddenly pulled back from Jimmy. "Wait." Before he could respond, she turned and headed back toward the interview room.

The door was open, and she went in. Detective Mitchell was there with the woman officer. He was packing up his files and listening impatiently to what seemed to be a complaint from Hadley. Both of them looked up in surprise when they noticed her. "Anya. Did you forget something?" Mitchell asked. She twisted her bracelet nervously, and her voice was agitated when she spoke. "He didn't do it."

"Who didn't do what, Anya?"

"The man in the handcuffs."

"What are you talking about?"

" He didn't do it. That's all."

Anya turned and ran back down the hallway, reaching Jimmy at the double doors. "Let's go, Jimmy," she said.

Chapter 19

Jimmy dropped Anya off at the Theatre and returned to the hotel, where Celia was waiting.

"How did it go, Jimmy?" she asked.

"A lot better than it could have. It seems that the Morristown Mounties may have their man. That makes for less interest in Anya."

"Who's the suspect?"

"An illegal immigrant. Anya and I saw him at the police station with a translator."

She thought a minute. "The Sayre murderer was a non-English-speaking immigrant."

"That's a not-too-amazing coincidence, given the times, then and now."

"Of course. But it might reinforce the press's comparison of the two cases."

"I hope you won't emphasize your observations to Anya."

"Of course not. But I remember what you said about Anya not dreaming the right dream."

"The right dream *for her*. She has to settle it in her own mind, not according to what you, me, or history says."

"But, Jimmy, what would make her dream something different from what she knows really happened?"

Jimmy was impatient. "Most of the time dreams are just dreams. Like cigars are usually just cigars."

"*Most* of the time, you say."

"Most likely, all of the time."

Celia backed off. "I've got to meet Marlee Quinn at the library. I'll see you later."

Celia entered the library and went immediately downstairs to the local history room. There were three people waiting for her. A lot of documents had been laid out on one of the long tables.

"Hello, Marlee. Thanks again for helping me out."

"No problem, Celia. When you called with your question, I knew just who to get in touch with." She smiled at the two men standing there. "This is Mark West and his friend Michael Williams. They're friends of mine from the Historical Society and Morristown's acknowledged experts on the Sayre murders. I've told them how interested you are in the case."

Celia acknowledged the introductions. "I've met Mark. Michael, nice to meet you."

Williams took her hand. "We're happy to share everything we have about the Sayre case."

Celia sat down next to West. "I know you were very close to Maureen and Richard Sullivan. I'm sorry for your loss, Mark."

"Thank you. Yes, everything has changed for me. At the moment I don't even have a job to go to, with the restaurant closed." West looked suddenly pale, and the younger man, Williams, offered him a bottle of water. Williams was a short, stocky man with a receding hairline, younger than West. He had gentle hands.

"Let the police do their job and then see what happens, Mark," Marlee advised.

"Are you sure you feel like talking?" asked Celia, hoping that he wouldn't take her up on her implied release.

West straightened up. "I do. I do want to talk about it. Maybe my research can shed some light on the Sullivan murders. I want to help the investigation. I'm worried."

"Worried about what?" Celia asked.

"I'm worried about Phebe."

Williams broke in hurriedly. "You mean Lily, Mark."

"Yes. Of course. Lily Doone, poor little thing."

Celia opened her notebook. "I read John Cunningham's and Donald Sinclair's book again last night. Cunningham did a great job putting murder cases like that of the Sayres into the context of their time and place."

Mark West was pleased at her perception. "Yes, he did. The discrimination and violence against foreigners and the tendency to blame them for all society's ills was especially rampant at that time. Antoine Le Blanc was not only a foreigner but also a Roman Catholic. A double whammy in 1833 Protestant America. There were thousands of attacks on Catholic churches and the ethnic groups that attended them during that time."

"Like discrimination against the Irish and Italians later," Marlee added.

"And Hispanics and Muslims today," pointed out Celia.

"And Jews throughout history. Hatred for outsiders is a depressingly common human theme," Williams concluded.

West continued. "Another common theme is the universal eagerness to wring a profit from human tragedy." He reached for a small cream-colored booklet, now darkened with age: THE TRIAL, SENTENCE AND CONFESSION OF ANTOINE LE BLANC. "The author managed to print this by the day of the hanging and sold thousands as souvenirs. Even the sheriff made a few bucks for his endorsement and signature."

As she watched West handling the booklet, it suddenly occurred to Celia that this pamphlet was what Anya had seen in the hands of the crowd at the hanging in her latest dream. And perhaps it was also the small booklet torn up by Phebe at the end of that dream. What could that mean? Celia thought, well aware she was on shaky, non-scientific "dream interpretation" grounds.

She paged through the fragile pamphlet and read aloud: "'EVERY DOCUMENT CERTIFIED AS CORRECT, BY THE PROPER PERSONS.' It's hard to argue with that degree of vagueness," she smiled. "I've read this, and also the trial report that ran in the newspaper. Apparently all the evidence supported the verdict that Le Blanc was as guilty as sin."

Williams spoke. "You understand that Le Blanc denied everything except the burglary throughout the trial?"

Celia lifted her eyebrows. "So he lied. Isn't that what criminals do? But then he confessed to everything afterward."

"There was a written confession issued by a translator, but Le Blanc refused to sign it during the trial," West replied.

Williams picked up the trial booklet. "Here's the printed confession. In it, Le Blanc reveals he had been a horrible child and worse teenager: 'Mischief was my delight and sole aim . . . My father corrected me for my faults, but I soon returned to my follies.' He ignored his parents, refused to pray, and made fun of their religion. He wouldn't study in school and was so abusive to his girlfriend that the girl's mother banished him."

"A thoroughly bad seed," Celia quipped.

Williams continued. "After assassinating his own character, Le Blanc's picture-perfect confession goes on to account for every single detail of the crime. Every fact that supported the conviction at trial was included in his complete and extremely literate narrative." Williams picked up the booklet again and read a passage. "'In his admonitions, my father had frequently and vividly portrayed to me my end, and many a time have his admonitory lessons recurred to my mind since I have arrived to the years of maturity.'" Williams mouth curved in a slight, ironic smile. "Who would have thought an illiterate farmhand could be so eloquently philosophical?"

Celia raised an eyebrow. "Michael, I take it you think there's something suspicious about Le Blanc's confession?"

"The confession is just boiler-plate, part of a set formula that people of the time expected: admission of guilt, remorse, a vivid object lesson for their children, a speedy trial followed by prompt, unequivocal punishment. Who really wrote the confession? At the time, some people questioned the newspaper that printed it because it sounded so false. The paper defended it as the gospel truth, straight from the lips of Le Blanc," Williams concluded.

West summed up. "The ritual of conviction, confession, and punishment reassured people. Ironically, it also delivered some high-octane excitement to their otherwise dull, backwater lives. It gave them permission to enjoy the hell out of a well-orchestrated public execution."

"So the confession may not be worth the paper it was printed on," Celia replied, fingering the slim pamphlet. "But still, there was an awful lot of evidence against Le Blanc. It seems like an open-and-shut case to me. Every defense loophole was closed by a parade of witnesses. There were no other suspects. Surely they got the right man, phony confession or no?"

Marlee Quinn spoke uncertainly. "It was a circumstantial case. No one saw Le Blanc do it."

"Aren't most murder cases circumstantial?" asked Celia.

"That's quite true," Williams smiled. "Murderers mostly prefer no witnesses."

West cleared his throat. "I've spent years studying this case. It's full of holes big enough to drive a fleet of trucks through."

"Are you saying you don't think Le Blanc did it?"

"I'm saying that the victims might have good reason not to rest in peace, if they require justice to do so."

"That's a big claim, Mark," Celia responded. Not quite sure of what she wanted to say next, she began tentatively. "The issue of Le Blanc's guilt has become very important to some work I'm doing. This work appears to be impacted by these old murders in a way I don't yet understand. I'd like to hear your case."

West was almost trembling with eagerness. "Most of the evidence is all there in the record you're holding, hidden in plain sight."

"Let's hear it," Celia replied.

Chapter 20

Mark West began. "I propose we stipulate that Antoine Le Blanc was guilty of burglary, since he was swimming in stolen stuff when he was captured."

"So stipulated." Celia nodded. "But that puts Le Blanc at the scene of the crime."

"Timing is everything, Celia, as you will see. What Michael and I will do is to re-examine the testimony to better understand what happened on that rainy spring night."

"I noticed that the defense counsel's questions on cross examination were not recorded. It makes the case seem much more cut-and-dried when you have only the prosecution's side of things," Celia commented.

"We also don't have the defense's summation or final arguments. But we can figure out the case for the defense from the witnesses' cross-examination responses, which *were* recorded." West paused and then began his case in earnest. "What exactly convicted Le Blanc? Obviously there was no fingerprinting, no DNA analysis. And today's rules concerning evidence – its discovery, authentication, and the chain of possession – were nonexistent then. So let's look at motive, means and opportunity.

"*Motive*: robbery and revenge. Le Blanc wanted to return to the arms of his French girlfriend, Marie, and shower her with stolen booty. And he hated Judge Sayre for treating him at best like a menial laborer working for little more than room and board; at worst like the runaway slave whom Le Blanc replaced. *Means* is a throwaway. The Sayre farmhouse was fairly bristling with lethal farm implements, including axes, picks, chisels, pitchforks, and heavy blunt instruments of all sorts. *Opportunity,* as we will see, was the sticking point. The timing had to be right to convict Le Blanc."

Celia noted the practiced performance of West's presentation. It was a passion with him. It brought him alive; he was no longer a colorless middle-aged man with a slight paunch.

She returned her attention to West's last point. "Time was a major theme of the trial. What time did Le Blanc arrive at each tavern he visited that evening? How much time did he spend drinking? When did the town clock strike and who heard it? All of Le Blanc's fellow actors in this drama seemed to have concentrated most of their attention on watching time that night."

West nodded his head. "Exactly. Le Blanc's return to the Sayre farmhouse had to be within a very small window of time in order to fit the testimony and the prosecution's narrative of the crime. Several witnesses testified that LeBlanc left Luse's tavern, the last place he visited, at precisely 9:30 p.m. Another witness, David B. West, also left Luse's at 9:30. He caught up with three friends, and they all walked together along South Street toward their homes. Eventually the friends broke away to go to homes that were nearer to town. David West continued on alone, arriving opposite the Sayre farmhouse at 10:00, just as the town clock chimed the hour. Through the front window, he saw the judge and Mrs. Sayre reading by the light of a candle in their parlor.

"Remember that all the witnesses attested that it took exactly a half hour to walk to Sayre's place from Luse's tavern. So if the Sayres were alive and well at 10:00, and Le Blanc left town

154

at 9:30 and went straight home, his story about finding an empty house and Phebe's dead body had to be a lie."

"What about the fishermen's testimony at the trial?" Celia asked.

"Ah, yes. The intrepid fishermen. Even though the night was foggy and rainy, three locals went fishing that night. They passed Sayre's farmhouse at 7:00 p.m. on their way to Post's Pond. Upon their return by the same route at 1:00 a.m., the three testified that a lamp was on at the Sayre farmhouse, and that they saw a man come to the front window and look out. The prosecution claimed it was Le Blanc. That's why many witnesses, including the sheriff, were encouraged to testify that it would have taken at least three hours to properly rob the house. This line of questioning was necessary to counter Le Blanc's story that, after discovering Phebe's recently-expired body, he was so frightened for his own life that he quickly grabbed some valuables and ran, dropping some of the stolen items in his haste. Le Blanc still being there at 1:00 a.m. shows a cold-hearted fiend in no hurry, intent on maximizing his take."

"This all sounds like a pretty tight case to me," Celia commented.

West sat back. "Except that there was another timeline. From the beginning of his interrogation, Le Blanc claimed he didn't get back to the Sayres until *11:00*, not 10:00. And it's perfectly possible that Le Blanc could have dawdled on his way home. He could have passed out in a ditch from an overdose of hard cider and brandy, awoken later, and then went home to discover the Sayres missing and Phebe dead, just as he claimed. This timeline gives the defense an hour of wiggle room."

West paused and looked at Celia for her reaction. She put down her pen. "That's all very interesting, Mark. But there was direct forensic evidence pointing to Le Blanc. A bloodstained vest. Powdery marks on his pants having to do with a barrel of plaster."

West nodded to Williams. "Michael will take you over that ground."

"The plaster was lime, extracted from local limestone by heating rocks in a kiln," Williams began. "Farmers rolled seed in it to aid germination. Lime is a fine dusty powder that clings to everything. The prosecution tried to make this lime one of the major legs of their case. They claimed that it was used by Le Blanc to cover up bloodstains in the stable, and that the incriminating white stuff got on his clothing in the process."

"Strewing white chalky stuff on something would focus attention on the spot, not disguise it," Celia commented.

"I agree," said Williams. "And there were conflicting stories by witnesses anyway. The sheriff didn't notice an overturned barrel of plaster at the scene of the murder. Later witnesses described plaster spilled in a large circle; then it seemed to be all over the place – they had to be careful not to walk in it. Remember, there were dozens of men milling about the Sayre farm that morning. And Le Blanc claimed he got lime on his clothes planting corn during the day. He also claimed he'd had a nosebleed, and that's how blood got on his vest. In fact, Sayre's carpenter was a witness to Le Blanc's nosebleed that morning."

"Didn't the defense have another idea about the blood on the vest?" Celia asked, looking through her notes.

"Upon cross-examination, the local doctor answered a question asked by the defense by stating that there was no way to distinguish human blood from the blood of animals. This question was a followup to a witness's testimony that he saw a dead chicken in the cellar near where Le Blanc slept."

Celia furrowed her brow. "I didn't really follow that point."

West took over. "On the morning the crime was discovered, after a cursory examination of the crime scene, the sheriff and his deputies took off after Le Blanc, leaving several men, ordinary citizens who were friends and neighbors of the Sayres, in charge of the house. These men stayed in Sayre's house for more than a week. If you'll remember, when Le Blanc was arrested, he was wearing clothes belonging to the judge. It was during their week-long occupation of the house that one of the men found incriminating blood- and lime-stained clothing in Le Blanc's bed, 'nicely spread beneath the quilt,' to quote him."

West put his fingertips together thoughtfully. "For years I've been thinking about those men who stayed at the Sayre house. They had no doubt that Le Blanc had butchered their distinguished neighbors. Perhaps, after a few rounds of applejack, one or more of them took clothing of Le Blanc's and rubbed lime and chicken blood on them. Maybe he carefully laid out the doctored items under Le Blanc's mattress, then later 'found' them."

"Do you think someone would do that?" Celia asked.

"Everybody in town was incensed by this unspeakable crime. A dirty, Catholic foreigner had come into their midst and brutally killed two of their finest citizens. He'd been caught on his way out of the country with stolen goods. How hard would it be for one or more of the house sitters to decide to do his part to bring the monster to justice? No one ever questioned why the killer would leave incriminating evidence folded neatly in his bed, waiting to be discovered. Le Blanc wasn't a neat kind of guy."

"True. But if the jury accepted the prosecution's assertion that Le Blanc went straight home, and the Sayres were seen alive at 10:00, Le Blanc is still the outstanding nominee in the leading role of murderer," Celia concluded.

West smiled. "That's the really interesting part of the case. As we've noted, there was a parade of witnesses talking time at the trial. Who was where when. Who heard the fateful chiming of the town clock, marking the witching hour of 10:00." West paused dramatically. "But, in all of the talk about time, only one person's testimony mattered. One person's statements made everything on the prosecution's timeline work, and without it, the entire case would have been much weaker."

Celia answered immediately: "David West."

West smiled. "Yes. David B. West. He was the witness who set the time trap for Le Blanc. He was alone when he claimed to see Judge and Mrs. Sayre sitting in their living room. The judge, he testified, was reading a newspaper by candlelight, wearing a vest but no coat. Mrs. Sayre was peacefully sitting in a chair nearby."

"He described the scene as if it were a tableau laid out in front of him," Celia observed.

"That's right. Despite the fact that it was a dark, foggy, moonless night, raining and misty, David West described the interior of the Sayre house, the Sayres' clothing, exactly what Judge Sayre was reading by the light of a candle. And there is that odd detail about a white-faced ox rubbing against the barn. A detail that embellishes the picture by showing how incredibly observant the witness was."

"Wasn't there some cross-examination about sight distances that night? Because of the weather?" Celia asked.

"Yes. 'One could not distinguish a person across the street,' a witness answered when questioned. Another witness declared you couldn't see anything beyond a few feet in the fog and rain. And, in addition to the visibility issue, the hired man who stayed with the Sayres during the week said that they read in the kitchen, not the parlor, and generally went to bed by 9:00 p.m."

"Is it really possible that David West simply lied about seeing the Sayres in their parlor at 10:00 p.m.?" asked Celia.

"That's been an interesting question in my family for the past five generations or so," West chuckled.

Celia raised her eyebrows. "David West. Mark West."

"Same family. Been in Morristown all these years," he grinned. "By now it's a less than pressing question, whether old Uncle Dave was a perjurer in the service of justice."

"So you believe Le Blanc could've been framed," Celia concluded.

"I wouldn't put it that way, but the case may have been helped along by various well-meaning citizens, including my Uncle David."

"But your uncle was the centerpiece on the cake. Without his testimony, the defense would claim that the Sayres could have been killed earlier, while Le Blanc was drinking in town. That might have changed everything."

"Maybe. But let Michael outline the headwinds that Le Blanc was facing at his trial."

Williams picked up a copy of the transcript. "You've read the trial judge's instructions to the jury?"

"Yes. Pretty strong stuff."

"I'd describe it as incendiary. Judge Ford fanned the jury's outrage by describing in gory detail the victims' hideous wounds and terrible deaths. He told the jury that they could acquit if they had reasonable doubt, but he characterized any such doubts as 'mere creations and vapours of fancy, lighter than air, nothing more than nervous affections.'

"Then the judge advocated for the death penalty. 'Worthy men may disagree,' he said, 'but death for a death was good enough for the Israelites . . . and those who disagree with the God of the Old Testament should take heed not to advance Satanic policy in giving murder a free scope.' As for any weak-kneed jurymen who might shrink from convicting a capital case on circumstantial evidence, the judge had this to say: 'Do such carpers know their own meaning? Do you wish to give a free license to murder?'"

Celia raised her eyebrows. "I guess that put the task at hand into perspective for the jury."

Williams nodded. "If the judge was prejudicial in his general instructions to the jury, he really piled on by giving them five 'considerations' to keep in mind while deliberating. First, he blessed the prosecution's version of the timeline which proved that only LeBlanc could have done it. And he endorsed the prosecutions's claim that the burglary had to have taken three hours, to fit the fishermen's testimony.

"In the judge's third point, he asks why the prisoner didn't raise the alarm when he discovered Phebe's dead body if he were innocent of the murders. But Le Blanc had answered that question quite clearly: he decided to burgle the house instead. The judge's fourth point was a false syllogism: Someone had to have done the murders. There was a burglary. Therefore, the burglar must be the murderer.

"The judge's final consideration was a blazing discourse on the depravity of the prisoner, as if he had already been convicted. What kind of wicked fiend plunders a house for hours after he kills three people? What kind of evil beast dresses in his victim's clothing? His final words to the jury were: 'Judge ye, gentlemen, the ruthlessness of such a monster.'"

"I wonder why it took the jury a whole twenty minutes to reach a verdict," Celia quipped.

West concluded the story. "Everything went into high gear after the verdict. A special hanging platform was built, with the noose attached to a big chunk of heavy iron to jerk Le Blanc upward to his death. The reverse joy ride failed to break his neck. He choked to death, gasping and kicking."

The room fell silent.

Marlee Quinn considered herself a local historian of some merit. She had always been interested in the Sayre case and how it reflected the values of a typical early nineteenth-century rural town. Twelve thousand people converged on Morristown that day in 1833 to enjoy a picnic lunch on a nice fall day and savor the illicit thrill of watching a fellow human dangle by his neck until dead.

The gruesome aftermath of this hanging – the prolonged death struggle, the experiments administered by doctors on the corpse, and the flaying and tanning of the killer's skin – crossed a line for many. Immediately after the hanging, the souvenirs made from pieces of Le Blanc's tanned hide were highly prized and proudly displayed. But the gruesome leather goods gradually disappeared from view as public sensibilities evolved.

Which is not to say there wouldn't always be those who look back on the days of public executions with fond nostalgia, thought Marlee. "An eye for an eye" might be a simplistic formula for revenge from an earlier time and place, but it remains seductive to the primitive brain still lethally alive deep within us all.

Chapter 21

Celia stood up at the library table, stretching her legs. "You two have made a very arresting case that Antoine Le Blanc may have been in the wrong place at the wrong time," she declared. "Or at least that some of the townspeople might have given Lady Justice a helping hand. But the burning question is – who else could have done the murders?"

"Remember, the defense team is only required to establish reasonable doubt," replied Williams, the lawyer. "It doesn't have to solve the crime."

"I know that, but you have been studying the case for years. Surely you've thought about who else would have been willing to murder a pair of leading citizens so brutally."

"Why are you so interested, Celia?" West asked.

"I'm involved in some interesting dream research that might touch on the case," she said, perhaps too quickly.

He jumped on her comment. "What do you mean? Someone has dreamed about the Sayre murders? That's incredibly interesting."

Celia backpedaled. "I didn't say that exactly. But people can dream of anything and everything. They dream about what they see or read, about both their friends and enemies. They have good dreams and bad dreams. They dream of the present and the future. And sometimes of the past."

"And that's what you do, Celia? Figure out why people dream what they do?" West asked.

"That's pretty close." She laughed, trying to make light of West's probing. Then she directed attention back to the case. "So, if not the Frenchman, who do you think did it?"

West let himself be directed. "There's someone I've suspected from my first work on the case."

"And that is . . . ?

"Martin."

"Martin? Judge Sayre's runaway slave?"

"Yes. It was Martin's escape that directly led to Sayre's hiring Antoine Le Blanc to replace him."

"I always thought of slavery as a southern thing."

"Shame on your history, Celia," West chided. "The original states, both south and north, were built with slave labor. Read any New Jersey historical newspaper well into the 1800s and you'll see runaway slave notices. New Jersey was the last non-southern state to relinquish slavery.

"So when was slavery abolished here?"

"The state passed a 'gradual abolition' act in 1804. Any child of a slave born after that date would be freed at the age of 21 for women and 25 for men. But slaves could still be bought and sold, and babies could be taken from their mothers and given to the Overseer of the Poor so they wouldn't have to be supported. And sometimes slaves were sold illegally to southern slave owners as they approached the age of emancipation to make a last bit of profit on them. Later a new law freed children of slaves born after 1846. But existing slaves were reclassified as 'apprentices for life' – still slaves. There were slaves in New Jersey until the Thirteenth Amendment finally settled the matter for good."

"How old were Phebe and Martin at the time of the Sayre

murders, Mark?"

"Martin was 19 years old. Phebe was 18."

"So Martin would have been free in six years if he hadn't run away. Phebe in three years."

"Obviously Martin was desperate enough about his situation not to wait and take his chances."

"When Martin ran away, why wouldn't he have just kept going? Why would he have hung around Morristown?"

"Maybe he was waiting until it was safer for him to travel. Especially if his escape had been advertised in the newspapers. There were local abolitionists who would have helped him. But there is other evidence."

"Such as?"

West saw that he had captured Celia's interest, and he leaned forward to present his case. "At the trial, Judge Sayre's daughter Mary testified that something had recently happened between her father and Martin. She said Martin was 'not so obedient as formerly.' Mary described her father ordering Martin to remove his shirt to be 'corrected.' That's what slave owners called beatings – 'correction.' The undeniable fact is that Martin's life was miserable enough for him to take the risk of running away. Maybe Martin wanted to even the score before he left town," West added, watching Celia for her reaction.

"He killed Judge Sayre for mistreating him?" Celia asked, somewhat skeptically.

"Also, there might have been more between Martin and Phebe than meets the eye," West replied, advancing his theory.

"What do you mean? Phebe was Martin's sister."

"Yes. They are listed in the county's slave birth registrations as the children of Samuel Sayre's female slave Jude."

"So they grew up as slaves in the Sayre household together?"

"They did. That was somewhat unusual. And that may have been the problem."

"What problem?"

165

"Phebe's and Martin's mother died when they were young. They probably grew up very dependent upon each other for what little comfort they could muster in their situation. Maybe, as they grew into young teenagers, this comfort was translated into something sexual. Under normal circumstances, a slave-holder wouldn't have particularly cared what went on between two slaves. But Sayre considered the pair brother and sister, even though they likely had different fathers."

"Do you really think that's a viable scenario, Mark?"

"Who knows?" West replied impatiently. "But something happened to make Sayre angry enough to beat Martin. And the next step might have been to sell him."

"Then Martin would lose Phebe, the only significant person in his life – is that what you're saying?"

West shrugged. "Whatever the truth, Martin was in a bad position. Why wait around to be beaten or sold? Running away was a huge risk, but Martin obviously decided it was his best alternative. Maybe he thought Phebe would join him."

"Could Phebe have been pregnant?" Celia mused aloud.

"What makes you say that?"

"I thought maybe I read something in the files," she said hastily.

"There's nothing to indicate that in anything I've ever seen. If that were the case, Martin might have concluded Sayre was the responsible party."

"Never mind, Mark. I must be mistaken." To get West back on task, she addressed the most obvious question. "You're not saying Martin killed Phebe, are you?"

"I think Martin could have killed Judge Sayre. And Mrs. Sayre if he couldn't avoid it. But not Phebe."

"Then, in your scenario, who murdered Phebe?"

West's forehead wrinkled. "I'd give anything to know. Especially now."

"What do you mean, especially now?"

West had a dreamy look on his face. "I don't want anything to happen to Lily."

All three looked at West. Celia asked the obvious question. "Phebe died a long time ago. What does she have to do with Lily?"

West felt their eyes on him. "Nothing, of course. It's just that Phebe was a victim, helpless, and I have similar feelings about Lily. Both of them were really still children. Neither of them was ever in a safe place."

West's eyes looked red, and Celia was afraid he might cry. She hastily thanked them both and brought the meeting to a close. West walked out of the library with her, and by the time they reached the sidewalk, he seemed to have recovered.

After getting back to the hotel, Celia went directly to Jimmy's room. She recounted what she'd heard from West and Williams.

Jimmy carefully chose his words. "I don't understand how you have gotten caught up in this thing to this extent, Celia. Whether Mark West and his friend's research is valid, or they're just run-of-the-mill conspiracy theorists – it really doesn't matter. It doesn't have anything to do with our work."

Celia's mouth turned down. "But Jimmy, Anya's dreams keep pointing away from Le Blanc as the murderer. Anya's dreaming didn't end when Le Blanc got his just deserts at the end of the rope. Phebe continues to co-opt Anya's dreams. So it somehow matters to Anya, doesn't it? And as you said yourself, that's the only criterion that counts."

"Do you understand that it's not necessary to Anya for your two buddies to figure out 'what really happened?' Anya's dreams are a product of things she's heard or sensed, plus an extremely fertile imagination. She doesn't need the 'real' ending. Anya's brain has selected these old murders as a dream language to play out some sort of confused inner storm."

"The storm in Anya's brain has seeped into her waking life,

Jimmy, and it threatens her safety and well-being. She needs some help, some guidance, and if it's based on Mark and Michael's theory, why not?"

He raised his voice, threatening the shaky cease-fire between them. "The dream belongs to Anya. Not to you, Mark West, or me. It's up to Anya to figure out where the dream has to go to relieve it of its power. Don't attempt to guide her, and above all don't suggest to Anya that Phebe must dance through her head until she dreams up an alternative culprit lurking behind the stable door."

"Of course not," Celia said quickly. "But we have to bring Anya through this."

Jimmy looked at the panic in Celia's eyes and took pity. "We'll do what we can," he said.

Chapter 22

Sebastian Bennett stopped by the door to Anya's office, watching her in silence until she sensed his presence. She looked up, a bit flustered.

"Come in, Dr. Bennett. How long have you been there? I didn't hear you."

"I didn't want to disturb you suddenly."

"That's all right. I'm not that delicate."

"Also, I like to watch how you work," he smiled.

"To each his own." She felt self-conscious as she stood in front of the large board she was marking up in colors.

"I understand why you don't like to talk about your capabilities, Anya. Most people wouldn't understand your work methods. In fact, your approach might appear quite exotic to the casual onlooker."

"You know, those case studies in the psychiatric journals tend to make more of these things than the evidence indicates. I muddle through life like everybody else," she said. "I've never thought of myself as exotic."

Bennett laughed, knowing she wanted to close the subject. "I do have a good reason to visit your den of creativity today. Sonja sent me. Did you know that the young woman who is missing from the Rose Restaurant – Lily Doone – was a resident at Sunnyside?"

"Yes. I've heard."

"Sonja wasn't sure you knew." He fingered a gold cufflink. "They say all publicity is good, Anya. But not where Sunnyside is concerned. Most people don't know about Sunnyside. Sunnyside is never publicized and its location is not disclosed."

"That's for the privacy of the residents, of course."

"Yes. But more importantly, for their safety. Men who abuse women never willingly give up their formerly complacent wives or girlfriends. They're heavily invested in the power end of the abusive relationship, and they've got everything to lose. When a woman manages to escape, the abuser is outraged and wants to get her back and punish her. It's critical to his stunted ego. The women at Sunnyside are required to pledge not to see anyone from their former lives and to inform their counselor if there's any attempt at contact from their past."

"Did you think Lily was in danger from someone in her past?"

"Not that I knew of." Bennett straightened up. "Anya, you should come out to Sunnyside and see the work that's being done there. Sonja really wants you to come."

Anya thought, I've got so much on my plate right now. To Bennett she said, "I'd like to get out there sometime."

"Good. Tomorrow there's a luncheon for key staff and volunteers, and Peter Thayer said he'd be glad to drive you out."

She resented being pulled from a general agreement into a specific commitment and tried to plead out on the basis of work. He smiled and shook his head. "It's just lunch, Anya. Peter will pick you up here."

The next day Thayer arrived at the Theatre on the dot. He was so overtly grateful about getting to spend time with her that Anya found it almost endearing. "We should have done this before," he effused. "Sunnyside is an impressive place. It's helping a lot of women. We'll have lunch and a chance to catch up."

He led her to his car, an older Toyota, and soon they rounded the Green and turned off on the main route south from Morristown. After a few picturesque country miles, Peter took a left turn onto an unnamed dirt road. The road dropped down toward a small lake. There were many cottages scattered along the shoreline, nestled among tall evergreen trees with drooping branches. Nearer the road was a much larger structure, a lodge-like building with a low, cedar-shingled roof and stone pillars supporting a wide porch.

"The buildings are mostly Craftsman style. Gustav Stickley. Stickley had his home and trade school out near Route 10," Thayer informed her.

"The lake is lovely. I'd never have guessed it was here. You can't see it from the road."

"It was a summer colony about sixty years ago. Everything was in pretty bad shape when Sonja purchased the property. The lodge was basically sound, but the cottages all had to be extensively renovated. They'd been built for summer living, no heating or insulation."

"How many women live in a cottage?"

"It depends. Some women have children. Some cottages house several women, but each has her own room. There are also some single cabins, for women new to Sunnyside, until they get adjusted to life here."

"What about those two houses under the trees, Peter?" These houses were larger and not as rustic, although they blended in well with the overall surroundings.

"The smaller one is Jillian Tremont's, and the larger one is Dr. Bennett's."

They drove slowly through the little settlement. It was bucolic and serene. Most of the children would be at day care or school, and many of the women had jobs on the premises or in town.

Anya concluded that the women who landed at Sunnyside after their individual nightmare journeys through domestic violence were among the luckier ones, and that thought prompted her next question.

"Who gets to come to Sunnyside, Peter?"

"M-m-m. That's the hard part. There are so many women in need of a safe place. Churches make referrals, of course. And the police. Sometimes a school will act on behalf of the children. Dr. Bennett and Jillian have to make the most of the available spots. Who can be helped by religious institutions, relatives, social agencies? Who has nowhere else to turn? The women here have been terrified, beaten up, some even tortured."

"Sunnyside is impressive, Peter. You should be proud to be a part of it."

Thayer spoke carefully. "I'm very grateful to Sonja. I have a background in counseling and ministering to troubled people, and she took me on."

"And where did Dr. Bennett come from?"

Thayer pulled the car into the gravel parking lot beside the lodge. "I'm not sure. But he soon became involved up to his neck in business plans, renovations, and new construction. He brought Jillian onboard to do the day-to-day running of the clinic. A lot has fallen on Jillian's shoulders lately. I sense she's not happy. She'd probably be better off leaving. But you know how people are. They keep hoping something will happen to change things."

They walked up the wide steps to a sweeping veranda and through wooden doors that were now propped open. Inside was a large, cavernous space with high, exposed-timber ceilings. When an interior door at the back of the building swung open, she could see a sleek, shiny stainless steel kitchen. Luncheon was to be served buffet style, as were all of the meals at Sunnyside, although the food today would be more celebratory than the usual fare. The tables were set formally with fresh flowers and small battery-powered lights that looked like candles.

Sonja Hildebrant was just inside the door, greeting each arrival, and Anya and Thayer took their place in the short line to receive her benediction. Sonja was wearing a certain shade of moss green with blue undertones that fascinated Anya's senses. Green was her favorite smell, and Sonja's suit made Anya experience a combination of fresh mint and fall leaves, bridging summer and autumn.

Sonja's eyes lit up when she saw them. "Anya! How nice to see you at Sunnyside. I've wanted to invite you out, but I know how busy you are with the show." She turned her attention to Thayer. "Thanks for bringing Anya, Peter."

Thayer went to the makeshift bar to fetch two glasses of wine. Anya looked around her. She recognized some of the women from the disastrous afternoon at Sonja's. In a far corner of the room she spotted Sebastian Bennett talking to an attractive blond woman. He had that way of subtly leaning forward when he spoke to people, as if he were totally available to just that person alone. Probably the psychiatrist in him, she thought. Maybe they learned it in school. The woman with whom he was speaking so attentively turned her head, laughing lightly, enjoying Bennett's attention. Anya recognized her as the officer who had been with Detective Mitchell when she went with Jimmy to be questioned at the police station.

Thayer returned with two long-stemmed glasses holding chilled white wine. "Did I mention how great you look?" he said softly. "You're always different from everybody else, but you always look just right."

She rewarded him with another smile. "Peter, the blond woman in the blue dress talking to Dr. Bennett. Do you know why she's here?"

"Joan Hadley. She's the Morristown police liaison to Sunnyside. If they get a case that needs referral to social services, Joan will evaluate it. If anyone knows how badly Sunnyside needs to expand, it's Joan. She's a great volunteer. Want to meet her?"

She didn't want to mention they'd already met. "Um, not now, Peter. I think we're meant to sit down." Sonja, Bennett, Jillian Tremont and several other people had taken seats at a long table at the front of the room. There was a graceful speech by Sonja about how important this group of volunteers was to Sunnyside and to its planned expansion.

After a delicious light luncheon, people began to circulate until dessert and coffee were set up. Several people came by their table to welcome Anya to Sunnyside, probably sent by Sonja. "Perhaps you can perform here for the residents and their children, Anya," one woman suggested. "This space would be perfect for a small, intimate fund-raiser," another woman enthused. "Maybe you and Dr. Bennett could perform together. He's a very talented pianist."

Anya's head was spinning with all these unsolicited ideas, and she was almost grateful when Bennett approached the table. "Peter, I'm going to borrow Anya for a moment," he announced. Thayer acquiesced graciously.

"I'm so glad to see you here," Bennett said as he firmly guided Anya toward the back of the hall.

"I'm really impressed with Sunnyside," Anya said truthfully. "It's such an idyllic spot."

"Most of the women who come here find Sunnyside a wonderful setting in which to heal."

"I can see that. It's only a few miles from Morristown, yet it feels as if time stops once you enter the grounds."

"I watched you come into the lodge today, Anya. You have a unique feel for time and place." Before Anya could think of how to respond, Bennett spoke again. "I'd like you to see something." He began to lead her, his hand lightly on her waist, toward the shiny modern kitchen. She thought this is what he wanted her to see, but he guided her toward a back door that led out onto the grounds of Sunnyside. Without giving her a chance to respond, he quickly headed down one of the foot-paths toward a grove of pine trees by the shore of the lake. Near the trees was a group of tiny cabins.

Anya had been following him uncertainly, and now she said, "Where are we going, Dr. Bennett?"

"I want to take advantage of your being here at Sunnyside. To help Lily Doone," he answered.

"Help Lily?" Anya repeated, confused. "Has Lily been found?"

Bennett shook his head and kept walking toward a nearby cabin, its entrance partially hidden by a huge pine tree. Anya hung back, but Bennett turned and urged her forward. "Please don't be nervous. I'm so worried about Lily. About Lily and about Sunnyside. Lily's disappearance has cast a pall over this place and is threatening to bring unwanted publicity."

"The newspapers have kept things pretty low profile about Lily's connection to Sunnyside," Anya responded.

"So far. But if she isn't found soon, that could change. We can't have that."

"Do the police keep you in the loop about what they're doing to look for Lily?"

"Detective Mitchell holds his cards pretty close to his vest." Bennett produced a key and quickly opened the cabin door and pushed it wide. "This is Lily's cabin."

"There's no police restriction on being here?" she asked quickly.

"No. The police searched the place. It would be upsetting for the other residents to see yellow police streamers, and Mitchell agreed not to do that. Lily is a sweet girl who has had a terrible life. Everybody liked her. We all want to find her and bring her back here, where she can be safe."

Bennett was visibly upset as he spoke about Lily. He had dropped the always-calm, adult-in-charge demeanor that he usually exuded and did not disguise the concern in his voice.

She felt sorry for him and didn't know quite what to say. "Dr. Bennett – Sebastian – I hope Lily will be back at Sunnyside soon."

Bennett shifted his weight. "I would feel so much better if I could believe she's alive and well, Anya. That's why I brought you here. You're so aware. You're able to sense things."

Anya was instantly uncomfortable. "I really don't have that kind of ability. Those cases you read about are almost always examples of hypersensitive individuals unconsciously picking up subtle clues." To forestall further discussion, she started to edge toward the open door.

But Bennett gently took her arm. "I know this makes you a bit nervous, Anya. I'm sorry."

He maneuvered her into the main room of the cottage, a small living area, accentuated by feminine clutter. Lily had draped colored scarves over the lamps and placed scented votive candles around the room. They moved into the tiny kitchen. On the windowsill was a ring-holder stacked with several silver rings with semi-precious stones.

Bennett saw her looking at the rings. He picked one of them up and held it out to Anya. "I was vaguely hoping if you came here to Lily's cabin, maybe touched something of hers, you could give me some reassurance. It sounds silly, I know," he added, a bit sheepishly.

"That's not what I do. I'm sorry."

Bennett immediately drew himself up and regained his usual composure. "Of course not. Thank you for indulging me. Go on back and have dessert with poor Peter. He'll be missing you. I'll be right along." He smiled broadly and gave her a friendly pat on the shoulder as he held the door for her.

She hurried back to the path. As she passed through the line of trees, she saw Jillian Tremont behind her on a parallel path. Anya watched Tremont adjust her pace so that the two of them would converge at the intersection leading back to the lodge.

She greeted Anya effusively. "Hi, Anya. I'm probably the last one to welcome you to Sunnyside. I saw you talking to Sebastian. You came with Peter Thayer? Peter must be in heaven."

Jillian was taller, blonder and prettier than Anya remembered from the night in the Ralston's bar. Anya ignored the comment about Thayer. "I'm glad to get out here to see all this. It's wonderful."

The tall woman fell in step, matching Anya's shorter stride as they walked toward the lodge. "Yes. I'm very proud of the strong start we've made. It was always my dream to work with women who don't understand that they can be as powerful as the men in their lives – and if they've made bad choices, to teach them they can get back on track and do better." Tremont's brown eyes were intense under her dark brows as she watched Anya. Then she dropped her gaze and adopted a more casual tone. "Sebastian was giving you a little tour?"

"He wanted me to see Lily Doone's cottage," Anya said.

"He's sick with worry about Lily. Did he speak to you about Lily's situation?"

Anya answered cautiously. "A little. He's also concerned about the negative effect of adverse publicity on Sunnyside."

"We're all worried about that, of course. But the most important thing is that Lily be found. We have to find out what's happened to her. Get her back. I can't say anything, of course, but Lily was in a particularly bad situation. She was very vulnerable. Did Sebastian mention any of this?"

"Just in general."

They were approaching the lodge, and Tremont stopped and put out her hand. "Well, I'm glad I had a chance to talk to you. I'm going to slip in the back way."

"See you, Jill." Anya hurried back to the lodge.

Chapter 23

Anya thought Peter Thayer might be annoyed at her having been gone so long, but he greeted her as if she were returning from a short jaunt to the ladies' room. There was a rather large selection of sweets from the dessert table waiting for her.

"Petit-fours, cheesecake, *and* canoli?" she laughed. "I'll be snoozing the afternoon away in a sugar coma." She was anxious to get back to town but felt she owed Thayer the time to drink coffee with him.

Less than an hour later they had bid their luncheon companions good-bye and were back in Morristown. As they approached the Green, they became aware of police activity. Several police vehicles were pulled up along the curb, their lights flashing. Uniformed officers were spread out along the sidewalk, alert to a growing crowd carrying large, hand-lettered signs with a variety of unfriendly messages concerning "illegals."

Thayer leaned out of the window as they snaked by the scene. "It's an anti-immigration rally," he said. "It looks like the mayor's capitalizing on the arrest of the Hispanic guy for the Rose murders."

Anya raised her eyebrows. "Is there an election coming up?"

Thayer rolled his eyes. "There's always an election coming

179

up for politicians. In the last election the mayor promised to shut down the day-labor gathering place near the train station, where contractors come to pick up workers. He's had trouble making that happen."

"Why?"

He shrugged. "Basic supply and demand. Immigrants are an integral part of the economy. They work cheap for cash – no benefits or health care. But an illegal accused of murder gives the mayor a chance to burnish his anti-immigration credentials."

When they arrived at the Theatre, Anya gathered her purse and the big box of desserts that Sonja had thrust into her hands "for the Theatre staff." Inside, she deposited the plate of sweets on the secretary's desk in the development office.

Just as she got back to her office, her cell phone rang. Detective Mitchell didn't say hello. "Look, Anya. I need your fingerprints after all."

"What?"

"I'm sorry. It has to be done. If you can get over here now, there are very few officers and no reporters around."

"I just saw them all at a demonstration on the Green."

"Yea, well, that's unfortunate. Not that it's going to change any minds in general, but the Hispanic guy we had in custody didn't do it." She didn't comment, but he was defensive. "He was found with blood on his clothes and Richard Sullivan's money and jewelry. But it's not his fingerprints on the knife."

"You'd better get that news to the crowd on the Green."

"It's being taken care of," he said shortly. "But now I have to officially eliminate your fingerprints. Just come down and get it over with. Come to the back entrance, where the cop cars park. I'll be there."

She picked up her purse impatiently and left the Theatre. She was going to accomplish nothing more today anyway. When she reached the police station parking lot, Mitchell was waiting by the door as promised. He walked her directly to the procedures room and did the fingerprinting himself, saying little. There were only a few clerks around, waiting for the end of the working day.

He wiped the ink from her hands, taking each of her delicate fingers and thoroughly but gently removing the black smudges. When he was finished, he looked at her directly for the first time. "Look. I need to know. Why did you come back to the interrogation room the other day to tell me the guy we had didn't do it? I didn't know what you were talking about. What did you mean?"

Anya looked blank. "I'm sorry. I did what?"

"You left with the doc. Two minutes later you came back into the room alone and said 'he didn't do it.' Not another word. What made you say something like that?"

"I don't know what you're talking about."

"You don't remember coming back?"

Anya didn't answer right away. Finally she said, "I had forgotten, but now I think I do remember. I'd left my scarf behind. That's why I came back. I don't think I said anything to you."

"I'm not mistaken, Anya. Officer Hadley was with me."

"I don't remember speaking to either of you. Maybe I was talking to myself." She picked up her purse. "I have to get back."

"All right, Anya," he sighed. "You drive me nuts." He let her out the back door.

Back in her office Anya soon discovered, as she had suspected, that nothing creative was going to happen the rest of the afternoon. She went to the large table and shuffled through some of her storyboards, idly rearranging them without inspiration. By 4:00 she was feeling at loose ends. She knew Celia had left early that morning on a quick trip to Ithaca to talk face-to-face with Dr. Lubov, catch up on a few things in her office, and pick up some clothes from her apartment. She planned to be back in time for the night's planned dream session.

Anya decided that a walk might help pass the time until Celia returned. She hurried back to her apartment to change clothes, slipping into black tights, a purple tunic and a pair of pink athletic shoes. With her long hair pulled back into a high ponytail held by a silver butterfly-shaped barrette, she descended the stairs of the Ralston Club and walked out onto Colles Avenue.

After strolling along several side streets in the Historic District, she turned toward South Street and started walking east, lost in thought. She soon found herself near the Radisson Hotel. Anya had never just shown up at either Jimmy's or Celia's office in Ithaca without calling first. Now, as she approached the Radisson, she hesitated. She sat down on a park bench and took out her cell phone.

"Lang." Jimmy picked up on the first ring, apparently without looking at the caller ID.

"Jimmy," she said, in a breathy voice.

"Anya. Hi, kid. What's up?" Jimmy asked.

"Jimmy. I – um – I was just calling about tonight's session." Her voice sounded slightly shaky. She wondered if he could hear it. Now that she had him on the phone, she didn't know what to say.

"What about it?" He sounded puzzled.

"I just wondered how we would approach things."

"Same as always. You snooze, I stay awake and watch you snooze. You get the good part. Are you worried about something?"

"No, of course not." She paused a second or two before continuing. "Jimmy?"

"What is it, Anya?"

"Did you hear the Hispanic man at the police station didn't kill the Sullivans after all? It wasn't his fingerprints on the knife."

"No, I hadn't heard," Jimmy answered. "Anya, where are you?"

"Well, I'm right outside the hotel, as a matter of fact."

182

"For godsakes, kid. What are you doing hanging out there? Someone will take you for a terrorist. I'll come down."

In about two minutes Jimmy came out the door, pulling on a casual leather jacket over a black tee shirt. He smiled broadly at her, shaking his head. She couldn't help but laugh. "I don't know, Jimmy. I just ended up here."

"You're probably following your stomach. You're hungry, and you didn't want to ask me to dinner because then you'd have to pay."

"Sure, Jimmy. After Peter made me eat four desserts at lunch. I'll never want to see canoli again."

"That guy." He made a face. "Oh, that's right, you went out to Sunnyside with him." They started to walk along South Street.

"I didn't want to go. I didn't want to take the time. But I found it very interesting after all."

"Don't tell me you're falling for the lusty man of the cloth?"

She made a face. "Peter's nice enough, Jimmy. He just didn't like you when he first saw you because . . ."

"Because he thought I was interested in you?" Jimmy smiled, remembering how he'd purposely put his arm around Anya at the Rose Restaurant, just to stick it to the guy who had pretended not to see her.

Anya laughed. "True. But I didn't go because Peter asked me, Jimmy. It was Sebastian Bennett. He stopped by my office and said that Sonja would like me to be there. Sort of a command performance. Funny, though. I thought Sonja seemed a little surprised to see me."

"Well, you got pastry out of it. You do have such a sweet tooth, Anya. Ever since you were a kid. Even though you always deny it."

"I do have an enormous appetite for a relatively small person," she admitted. "I guess I could eat a bite. But only if you're hungry. And I'll be glad to treat," she hastened to add.

Jimmy rolled his eyes. "Sure, Anya." He took her arm and they started to stroll toward Morristown's center. They ended up in a small Greek restaurant not far from the Green. They were shown to a quiet booth, and Jimmy ordered a scotch for himself, a cosmopolitan for her. They sipped the drinks and chose the lobster pasta from the evening's specials recited by their young server, with a bottle of white wine to drink with it. The pasta was excellent, the wine went down easy, and the non-stop, rare one-on-one conversation made the time fly.

It was after 7:00 p.m. when they left the restaurant, walking out into the twilight. "Are you chilly?" Jimmy asked, taking his jacket off to give to her.

"No, I'm fine." Anya draped a cashmere pashmina around her shoulders. Jimmy pulled it up higher, covering her exposed neck. "Thanks, Jimmy," she said, sensing he was a little embarrassed about his fussing.

They walked back to the hotel, looking for Celia's car. It wasn't there. "She's later than she thought she'd be. But she hasn't called, so she's probably on her way," Jimmy said. "Let's wait in the bar."

They slid into a booth and ordered two sambucas, which arrived with coffee beans floating on top, as Anya liked. Jimmy stretched out on his side of the booth, smiling at her.

"This has been fun, Jimmy," she said spontaneously. She immediately felt guilty.

"It has. But what's with the sudden long face?"

"I don't know. I was thinking about having to go upstairs and get to work soon. Sometimes I get so tired of it."

"You don't have to do it. No one can make you."

"But it's important to Dr. Lubov's work."

"Lubov's work extends in a hundred different directions. He's looking for the alpha and the omega of What Is. Dancing strings. Dark energy. Parallel worlds. The End of Time. Your dreams are intriguing, because you sometimes seem to tap into a portal between here and there, whatever 'there' is. Who knows? Yuri just wants to keep tabs on your inner workings and maybe on you, for some reason."

"So I'm just a low-level blip on Dr. Lubov's radar?" Anya asked. "That's it?"

Jimmy leaned over the table and took her hand. "Of course you're more than a blip," he smiled.

Anya tried to pull away her hand, suddenly feeling anxious. "I think we should have waited for Celia, Jimmy. That's the way it's always been."

Jimmy kept her hand. "Don't get upset. Things can't be the way they've always been forever, kid."

That thought frightened Anya further. "But Jimmy, what would happen to me if I didn't have Celia and you?"

"Probably nothing, Anya. Nothing you couldn't handle, anyway."

"What do you mean, Jimmy? My dreams. What would happen if the three of us didn't figure things out?"

Jimmy had ordered and now took possession of another sambuca. "You'd figure things out yourself."

Anya stirred her drink with the small, stiff straw, faster and faster, watching the little brown beans spin in the vortex. "But I get into situations."

Jimmy finished his drink. "Did you ever consider that all these years of delving so minutely into your admittedly weird dreams may have increased your sensitivity? Maybe if your episodes had been treated more like simple nightmares they might have dissipated on their own. But no. Along came Dr. Lubov with you in tow. A cute little pre-teen, all hung up on some not-so-cute dreams. I introduced you to induced dream activity, lucid dreaming, dream bodies. All the tools to enhance and spin and magnify your dreams, perhaps inadvertently giving them a life of their own. That might've been a mistake. Sometimes I'm sorry I took part in it."

Anya put down her glass. "I don't want to hear any more." Jimmy sat up at the tone of her voice and saw that she was close to tears. He left his side of the booth and came around to hers. As he slid in next to Anya, he thought he saw Celia outside the bar entrance, but he kept his full attention on Anya. He moved close to her, taking her hand again. "I'm sorry. I've had more to drink than I should have. Don't let me upset you with my babble. I'm an idiot. We were having fun. I just wanted to point out that you have a choice in this stuff."

They sat there for what seemed a long time. His eyes were brighter than usual, from the drinks or whatever he was thinking – she couldn't tell. He wiped an incipient tear from the corner of her eye. He touched her long hair where it had fallen from the barrette, then tucked it behind her ear. Finally he found his voice again. "Come on, kid. Let's order coffee. A huge black one for me and decaf for you. Celia will be back by now." He kissed her brow, and she smiled a little.

They got their coffees, plus one for Celia, then took the elevator up to Jimmy's floor. Celia was waiting for them. "Look who's here, the two of you together," she said brightly. "I'm sorry I'm late getting back. I got off later than I wanted and the traffic was terrible." She smiled at Anya. "Dr. Lubov is so excited about your recent results, baby." Then she looked at Jimmy, dropping her smile. "I take it you're okay to handle your job tonight?" she asked coldly. Jimmy didn't answer her. She got up and followed Anya into the other room, and he went into the bathroom.

After Anya was in her warm-ups and ready for sleep, Celia sat down on the side of the bed and took her hands. "Baby. I spent two hours with Dr. Lubov this afternoon. He looked at Jimmy's readouts and my notes. He wants me to tell you how important this episode might be. It could be a real breakthrough." She put her face closer to Anya's and massaged her small hands. "He says that you must finish it. You will continue to dream until you resolve the conflict. You know that, don't you, Anya?"

"Yes, Aunt Ceci," Anya murmured.

"Dr. Lubov worries about you. He doesn't want you in danger."

"I know," Anya said, gently pulling back her hands.

"You're ready then? I'll send Jimmy in."

Jimmy entered her room, ready to work, despite the alcohol. He'd washed his face, and his eyes had lost their glitter. Anya looked into their calm depths, concentrating on what he was saying.

"You want to do this, Anya?" he asked.

"I have to."

"You don't have to."

"I want to," she said, less certainly.

Jimmy sat up, his face unreadable. "All right, then. Let's get started. Tonight, when you fall asleep and pass into your first REM period, you will look for your dream body – the young boy with the blond hair and freckles, who wears floppy overalls and muddy boots. Anya, what does this young boy do all day?"

Anya's eyes were closed. "He has to work on the farm, plow the fields, feed the animals."

"What does he want to do on this day, Anya?"

"He wants to sneak away. He's working at the back of the field all by himself. No one will see."

"Go ahead, then."

* * * * *

The boy slips through his father's fields and over the livestock fence that separates him from the Sayre farm. He sees the pretty girl with the light brown hair laughing and flirting with a handsome young man in black clerical dress. The couple follows the terrain down sharply, until they are below the sight line of the farmhouse. No one can see them, except for the boy.

The man takes the young woman's hand and brings it to his mouth, kissing it. He leans over her. Her wide-brimmed hat falls from her head, hanging down her back from its tie under her chin. The handsome chestnut-haired man kisses her knowingly on the mouth. The watching boy senses that she likes this, likes pushing her mouth against the man's. The man transfers his lips to her neck, and then further down, to where her dress closes just above her breasts. She pulls back, but he just laughs, and the boy knows she is uncertain.

"What is this?" the man asks, putting his hand on her bosom where she wears a delicate silver cross set with a small stone. He fingers the necklace as an excuse to keep his hand near her bosom.

"A birthday present," she answers, putting her hand on his to keep it from wandering.

"From another man?" He was bitter, because he could afford nothing like it.

"From mother. A family piece."

"It's beautiful and it suits you, because you are beautiful." He kisses her again, lingeringly, teasingly. As he becomes aroused he gets rougher, pulling her to him and sliding his hand lower, onto her right breast.

She pushes him away. He is angry but hides it with more laughter, finally letting her go. She stands away from him, confused and hesitant about what to do or say. But she is secretly thrilled.

"Come on, Mary," he cajoles her. I'm so fond of you. I just want to touch you."

"You shouldn't even think of such things – a man of the cloth." But he understands the girl is not angry, and he moves close again. Could he see her necklace again? The green stone is so pretty. If she liked him she'd prove it by letting him have the necklace, just for a while. He'd sleep with it wrapped about his hand, his hand on his heart, dreaming of her.

She allows him to remove the necklace and its delicate chain.

The man and woman became less clear to the watching boy. They shift in and out of focus, flickering, then transparent. The woods themselves fade and start to pixilate. Anya realizes she is losing the dream and tells herself to spin like a top. She concentrates and spins in a tight circle in her mind, blocking out everything but the spinning sensation, and her dream reconstitutes.

Jimmy, sitting with Celia and watching the monitors in the next room, broke the silence. "She just had a near awakening. But she's going back into REM."

"Should we wake her now?"

"No. She must have used a trick to stay in the dream. So she must want to continue."

The boy is leaning against the counter in the shop. The counter is open to the street with a deep overhang of rough wood. He watches a man in dirty overalls swinging a heavy iron hammer at the rim of a large wheel. The boy looks across the road at the farmhouse and sees the black girl come up the alley from the back of the house. She is young and small in stature. She wears the clothes of someone much larger, with a loosely woven woolen shawl draped around her shoulders. She has on heavy shoes that had been sewn for a boy.

Her head is exposed. The boy sees her hair is kinky, like all her race, but it is luminous and soft-looking. The boy looks into her face as she crosses the street near where he is standing: black eyes, wide nose, dark complexion, full lips. She carries a small package, and when she walks by, he notices a raw cut below her thumb, slightly festering, not yet having begun the healing process. Her eyes show excitement and fear at the same time. She is breathing rapidly.

The boy spits out the piece of grass he's been idly chewing

and begins to follow the young woman. She is moving quite fast and they reach town quickly. She turns into the wide dirt road that circles the Green and follows it to the building that houses the post office. The boy watches as she lowers her head and speaks to the older white man behind the counter, keeping her eyes on the floor even when he hands her some letters and a newspaper.

The woman emerges from the post office and crosses the road to the Green. She skirts the edge of the open space, then quickly scampers over the road again. She is now standing in front of a small church on the corner, the only church in town to allow her kind within its sanctuary. The boy watches as the door to the church opens a crack. The woman glances over her shoulder and then passes silently inside.

The boy also crosses the road but heads down the alley next to the church. There are two dirty windows that offer a limited view inside. The church consists of a large room with rough wooden benches set in two rows. There is a door near the pulpit that leads into a smaller room. He brings his hands up to the window to shade his view and sees the young minister put his arms around the black woman. They talk. The woman is agitated. The man calms her with a kiss on her mouth. This is so strange that the boy is not sure he actually saw it. The minister seats the woman in the front pew. He goes to a painted wooden piano, the poor church's only treasure, sits down, and begins to play.

The boy can hear the music. He has never heard anything like it. It does not sound worshipful; it is too stimulating to the senses, unsettling. It doesn't have a slow melody, or verses, like a hymn. The music thrusts forward insistently under its own power, like a moon rising in the night sky. The playing goes on for some time, and the woman sits as still as a fawn in an open field. Finally the minister stops playing and puts his hand out. She looks up, her eyes shining. The two leave the vestry, passing into the small room behind it.

After a while the woman emerges from the church. Her face, hidden behind her rough shawl, is flushed beneath her natural color. She carries the newspaper and mail under her arm, and there is something else in her right hand. She looks at it, a piece of jewelry of some kind, and clenches her fist tightly. Now the woman moves fast, almost running along the Green, and is soon on South Street again. The boy is tired by now, and when the Green begins to fade, Anya does not resist.

Anya woke on her own and reported her dream.

Chapter 24

Early the next morning, back in her apartment, Anya sat down on her bed with her iPod and found *The Moonlight Sonata*.

Although the piece wasn't given its evocative title until after Beethoven's death, it fit the first movement of the composer's otherworldly composition perfectly. As she listened, the room filled with white light, and the walls became black sky, icy cold but passionately alive. She lay back on her bed and was lost in the yearning and hopelessness of the music's minor key. Then came the short respite of the mild-mannered second movement. After that brief interlude, the frenetic third movement crashed onto the scene, with its thousands of notes tripping over and under each other in high and low registers, rushing inexorably toward an abrupt, unsettled ending that left the listener's acutely stimulated nerves and raw emotions unresolved.

Anya tried to imagine how Beethoven's music might have affected people hearing it for the first time. It had taken even his more sophisticated musical public by storm, some critics claiming it was too powerful and unsettling for women to hear. An aspect of that perception had leached into her dream, where the boy and the woman were both deeply moved by this music.

When Anya studied music history early in her education, she

disagreed with music historians who argued that, because of his perfection of the classic music forms, Beethoven was a classical composer. She thought this was like saying Elvis Presley was a gospel singer because he was a master of the southern gospel genre.

Beethoven's music may have been conventional in form, but it was revolutionary in style and spirit, veering away from western musical tradition and blazing an altogether new path toward the future of music, never looking back. Beethoven slashed his way through the accepted forms, then lifted a veil on possibilities not yet imagined. The elder Joseph Haydn, upon hearing Beethoven's *Symphony No. 3* for the first time, had instantly known this. "Things will never be the same again," he'd prophesied, and history had proven him right.

Anya closed the music file and hurriedly dressed for work.

That same morning Celia walked to the Morristown Library again. The morning newspaper under her arm displayed the front page story:

Rose Restaurant Murders: Hostess's Ex-Husband Sought

A picture of a blond, long-haired man, handsome but common-looking, flashing a knowing, smirky smile for the camera, dominated the right hand column. Under the headline the main story continued:

> *Morristown:* Late yesterday police announced that fingerprints on a knife found behind the Red Rose Restaurant have been matched to those of Brandon F. Doone, whose last known address was in rural upstate New York. Doone, who has a record for unarmed burglary, public

disturbance, and domestic violence, is the estranged husband of the Red Rose Restaurant's missing hostess, Lily Doone.

In a related story, police have released Eduardo Suarez, who had been arrested and detained last week after police found money and personal items belonging to murder victim Richard Sullivan in Suarez's Morristown apartment. Police now conjecture that Suarez may have come upon Sullivan's body as it lay behind the restaurant and took the opportunity to rob the dead man. Suarez, an undocumented immigrant with little English, has been arraigned for theft.

Doone's motive for the killings has not been disclosed, but police are also looking for Leonard (Lenny) Paco, a former partner of Doone's, who had been employed as bartender at the Red Rose Restaurant before the murders.

Lily Doone remains missing. Brandon Doone may be armed and is considered dangerous. Anyone who has seen Doone or Paco should contact police immediately.

Mark West was waiting alone for Celia in a small study room. West's eyes were shining, and he had a half-smile on his face.

"Hi, Mark. What's up?" He had called her earlier this morning, his voice crackling with excitement, asking her to meet him, unwilling to say anything more on the phone. His manner had slightly alarmed her.

"Sit down, Celia. I have some new information to share with you. I have news about Lily Doone that sheds new light on everything, especially in view of what we talked about last time."

"I'm not sure what you mean, Mark."

"There are even more parallels than before."

"Slow down, Mark. What do you mean by 'parallels?'"

He was disappointed in her response. "Celia, it's obvious. In both the Sayre and the Rose murder cases, a non-English speaking immigrant was immediately accused of the crime. It's only because of modern forensics that the Hispanic won't be prosecuted for murder."

"We talked about that."

"But now there's more. Someone has contacted me – someone from the restaurant who used to talk to Lenny Paco before he disappeared. Paco told this person that Richard Sullivan was going to pay for fooling around with Lily."

"Your friend should have told somebody about this threat."

"At the time this person didn't think anything would come of it and doesn't see the upside of getting involved now."

"It's a cruel twist if Brandon Doone listened to a gossip-mongering bartender and killed an innocent person," Celia replied.

"That's true. But there's something else, Celia. You'll be especially interested in this. This person I've been talking to was sure Lily was pregnant."

Celia was aware of the silence in the closed library room. Several seconds went by before she asked, "Is your friend positive about this?"

"They'd bet on it."

"Did he or she tell anyone?"

"Unfortunately, yes. Lenny Paco tricked this person by pretending he knew more than he did." West shrugged. "My friend is not all that bright. But it proves Lily was involved with someone. And it wasn't Richard Sullivan."

He paused and let that information sink in before continuing. "Something else. Did you know that someone tried to abduct Lily from the restaurant a couple of weeks ago?"

"No."

"She was dragged into a car behind the restaurant after

196

work. The restaurant's bouncer happened to see her struggling in the car and managed to get her away. From her appearance the bouncer was sure she had been sexually assaulted. She denied it and didn't want the police called."

"You think it was Lily's husband?" Celia said.

"It looks like it." West tapped his pen on the wooden library table. "Paco obviously told Brandon Doone that Lily was pregnant. Paco also told him that Richard Sullivan was the offending party, since that was the common restaurant chatter."

"Lily had a chance to set the record straight by telling her husband the truth," Celia responded.

West shrugged. "Maybe she was too scared to say anything. And maybe there's another reason." He looked at Celia expectantly. Celia didn't respond.

West was annoyed to have to fill in all the answers. "Because she was protecting someone else," he said impatiently. "Does that remind you of anything, Celia? Think back 175 years."

"I don't get where you're going, Mark."

"Both Phebe and Lily were pregnant. Perhaps they were both protecting someone else."

"No one can know whether Phebe was pregnant. There's no evidence whatsoever. This talk of 'parallels' has gone way too far, Mark."

"Take it easy, Celia." West replied a bit petulantly. I'm just suggesting that the two cases ping-pong back and forth through time in some way. And it was _you_ who suggested that Phebe was pregnant. You didn't read that anywhere. I googled Dr. James Lang. You and he work with people who dream about things they have no business knowing. Like the young woman from the Theatre who ended up in the Rose's attic. I think that's what you're doing here in Morristown, and that's where you got the idea about Phebe being pregnant. From something Anya Gregory dreamed."

Celia was brought up short. She'd been far too open with

West. "Hold on, Mark. Just because Anya dreams it doesn't make it true. Almost all dreams spring from a person's experience or memory, not from a long-ago past event."

"It's your patient's dreams that tie together the Sayre and Rose murders. I'm right about that, aren't I?"

It seemed to Celia that the library shelves were receding into the shadows of the room. She sensed only the high-intensity lamps spreading warm circles of light on the dark wood of the library tables. She felt hot and glanced into the shadows as if she expected to find someone listening. "Mark, what I'm going to say is confidential. Between you and me. Do you understand?"

"Yes. Of course," he said eagerly.

"I have said more about my work than I should have. But you were there in the Rose Restaurant the night Anya Gregory ended up in the attic. You saw her state of mind." She shifted in her seat, leaning toward West.

"I don't know where I'm going with this," Celia continued. "But Anya's dreams, while triggered by the Sayre case, seem to resist the historic record. The dreams always begin and end with Phebe. It's Phebe's death that's got hold of Anya. It's Phebe who appears unwilling to accept history's verdict on her killer."

West listened to Celia raptly. He was motionless, his mouth open slightly. "Just as Michael and I have suggested. What else has Anya dreamed?" he asked, almost inaudibly.

Celia spoke, still unsure of what she was doing here with West, half-whispering in the golden puddles of light. "In Anya's dream, Phebe meets a dark man in the woods behind the Sayre farmhouse. There is a sexual encounter. He senses Phebe is pregnant and he is angry. Phebe is frightened of him. Then, in another dream Phebe meets another man she is involved with, in a church near the Green."

West was trembling slightly in his excitement. He leaned back in his chair and closed his eyes, trying to calm himself, thinking out loud. "There were two churches near the Green at that time. The Presbyterian church is still there, of course, in a later building. And there was a small Baptist church near it, on the adjacent corner of the Green. It had some kind of itinerant pastor back then."

"Mark, it's important to remember this is all just Anya's dream. But would a young girl in Phebe's situation be able to manage these relationships?"

West sat back in his chair. "History shows that despite their lack of freedom slaves were able to direct their lives in ways their owners found difficult to control. They practiced the religious rituals of their forgotten homeland, had sexual liaisons, pilfered, spied on their owners, rebelled in a variety of subtle obstructive ways, and often ran away, despite the promise of brutal punishment if they were caught. Their resourcefulness and unspoken defiance was astonishing, and it made slave owners nervous. There was often an undercurrent of fear among slave owners, a sense of being at the mercy of those you oppress."

"And sexual relationships with white men?"

"Please, Celia. Two words: Thomas Jefferson. Jefferson very likely fathered six children by his slave Sally Hemings. In fact, Sally Hemings's mother was probably fathered by Jefferson's wife's father. Black girls and women were subject to sexual attention from everywhere and anywhere – their owners, their owners' relatives and friends, fellow slaves, overseers – whoever had a need or took a fancy."

West picked up a slim green volume lying nearby. Celia could read the title: *Slave Records of Morris County, New Jersey* by David Mitros. "Here's more primary-source proof for you, Celia," West said. "After 1804, slave owners had to legally register all births to female slaves in their households. The names of the slave mothers were duly recorded in the registrations, but the fathers were rarely identified."

West opened up the green book and turned to a marked

page. "Here's an entry: *'I certify my female black wench named Phillis was delivered of a male yellow child named Bounce on the fourteenth day of March last. Israel Canfield.'* The term 'yellow' in this listing described the child as light-skinned, born to a black mother and a white or racially mixed biological father. Here's another entry: *'On May 8, 1808, a mulatto female named Brom was born of a black slave, property of Solomon Cooper.'*"

"All right. I admit I am extremely naive and ignorant of the full implications of slavery for women. Obviously, for men, black or white, sexual liaisons with female slaves were common and non-consequential."

West shrugged. "That's the history of it."

Celia was quiet for a minute before speaking. "You know, my colleague would think I am absolutely nuts and way out of bounds for sitting with you comparing events of the past with those of the present."

"But your colleague would have to agree that the major motives for murder remain distressingly similar down through the ages. It's possible for two similarly motivated crimes to occur in the same place over a period of time. So there's no harm in researching, or even speculating, about one to gain insight into the other," he said, carefully backing off his earlier eagerness that had turned Celia off.

"Put that way, even Jimmy might agree." She looked at her watch quickly. "I've said too much and I've got to get back. But, Mark . . . "

"Yes?"

"You should let the police know what your friend told you about Lily being pregnant."

Chapter 25

Anya arrived at the Radisson at 8:00 p.m. Celia answered the door to the suite. "Hi, baby. Jimmy had to go out, but he'll be back soon."

Celia put her arm around Anya and brought her inside. "This could be the night when it all comes to an end, Anya," she said, smiling enthusiastically.

Anya looked uncertain, not wanting to remind Celia that she'd said the same thing a few days ago. "Aunt Ceci, I've been thinking about all this – about everything that's happened since I came to Morristown. The episode at Sonja Hildebrant's was embarrassing and could have cost me my job at the Theatre."

"It was a disappointment for you, I know."

"And then I had the first dream. I called you and Jimmy."

"That's what you are supposed to do."

"I know. But sometimes I wonder if I just tried to tough it out . . . "

" . . . it might go away?" Celia finished Anya's sentence, pulling away from Anya. "Has it ever gone away on its own?"

"Well, you've always been there."

"Dr. Lubov has done so much for you. You have to continue to help him, Anya. And he will always see that you have the help you need."

"He didn't want me to leave home, did he?" Anya asked.

Celia got up and straightened the bed. "He feels you're safer there, honey. Near to your parents and to him and the lab."

"But dependent. On you and him. Jimmy. My parents."

"Let's not think about that now, Anya. You have been drawn into a dream. You have produced spontaneous dream material, verifiable in the historical record. Think how exciting it is."

Anya didn't respond. "You want me to find the dead woman again tonight. That means I have to *be* the dead woman. I don't think I want to do it, Aunt Ceci. Using a dream body is easy. But being Phebe is terrible."

"Anya, I spoke to Dr. Lubov for a long time yesterday. He told me that you should finish it as soon as possible."

Anya walked to the bed without responding. She switched on her iPod and turned her face to the wall.

Jimmy returned thirty minutes later. He looked surprised. "Hi, kid. I thought you weren't coming until later."

"Aunt Ceci said 8:00."

Celia smiled. "Sorry. I guess I made a mistake."

Jimmy took off his jacket and sat on Anya's bed. "Anya, are you sure you want to do this dream tonight?" You know what it could entail."

Anya put her headphones down on the side table. She went to the bar area and got a bottle of water, then returned to bed before she answered, avoiding his eyes. "I'll do it."

Jimmy felt vaguely disappointed but began to place the cap on her head. "Then you'll need to lucid-dream your way back into Phebe's life to see if you can resolve her dilemma."

Anya lay back on the pillow and closed her eyes.

"She's already on her way," Celia commented as he came out of the room and sat down to watch the monitors and wait.

* * * * *

The overcast sky had become darker all day. The mister comes into the kitchen to tell her he and the missus were ready to eat. She has already given the hired men leftovers from last night's joint, thickened with cornmeal and extended with potatoes. She had eaten quickly by herself, standing at the kitchen sink.

The mister takes off his boots and sits at the table. She serves the food, a fresh-killed roasted chicken, cornbread and greens from the garden. She hovers nearby, and finally he says what she is waiting for. "Go get my paper, girl." The mister looked forward to the news at week's end.

The young black woman reaches for her rough-spun shawl to ward off the damp, then leaves the farmhouse through the kitchen door and walks up the alley to the street. There, the day's work is coming to an end for many. Across the road at the blacksmith's, a young boy with blond hair, wearing overalls, is watching her. She puts her head down and turns toward town, moving fast. She needs as much time as possible with him to make him understand her situation and the danger to himself. Then he will help her.

She goes to the post office and gets the mister's mail, then crosses the street to the small church at the corner.

The man is waiting and locks the door once she is inside. She can't contain her fear and blurts her news. "Martin is back. He knows I am with child."

The man grasps her hand roughly. "What did you say?"

"He thinks it is the mister's."

"You are sure it is not?"

"It is not. The mister will know that. It is you. And my belly is growing. I will soon be found out. Then I will have to tell the truth."

The man speaks urgently. "Settle yourself. I promised you

will get away. There are people to help."

"You will take me to those people? It must be soon. I fear that even tomorrow I may be undone. The new man watches me. Yesterday he tried to touch me. He knows." Her face is shining with tears and a tiny hint of cunning.

His eyes show alarm. He moves to her and encloses her in his arms. When she does not leave off crying he says, "I have already made arrangements. You will go away tonight."

Her face is transformed. "Yes. Yes, thank god. How will I go?"

"It's all arranged. He had been pacing back and forth. Now he stops and leads her to the front pew, bowing to her and seating her as if she were a queen. "Sit here and rest. I will play for you. You will like that?"

"You know."

He walks to the small piano and lifts the painted cover. He removes a delicate cross on a chain that is wound around his wrist and places it on top of the piano. He begins to play the music he heard in Vienna, where he was sent by his wealthy father to escape another difficulty with a woman. If only his father had understood that his calling was music, not religion, and that banishment to this one-room, godforsaken church would not change that. The girl Mary could be his deliverance from the abject boredom and poverty of his predicament. She is ripe for the picking. But he had been tempted once again by easy prey, and he had this wretched, pathetic black girl on his hands, a disastrous obstacle to his plan's success.

This new music is the only thing that makes his miserable life bearable. Ironically, this wretch of an ignorant black girl, this girl of whom he must quickly somehow rid himself, shares his craving for the music while all the others do not understand.

From the instant the man first causes the piano's hammers to hit the taut, waiting strings, producing the first measure of bright notes, the woman is lifted out of her circumstances. Her spirit rises out of her being and hovers far above the pews. From her soul's perch, she watches the man as he caresses the ivory and black keys, his eyes closed, lost in the music. All around him the sound cascades in waves of pure color; vibrant greens, rich golds, deep purples and blues. The strings of the piano produce quivering sheets of luminous hues that wash over her, cloaking her in shimmering sound.

She wishes to float on such ecstasy forever, but after a last powerful crescendo the music fades. She is back in the hard pew, and he is coming toward her. "Meet me at the bottom of the low woods tonight. In our place," he whispers. "Be ready to travel."

"Thank you. Thank you." She takes his hand and kisses it.

He pulls away and unfastens the back door.

She cuts diagonally across the Green, clutching the silver cross tightly in her right palm.

Chapter 26

Her dream faded, and Anya awoke. It was still dark. Her hair, damp from tears, was stuck to her cheeks. She found that she was gripping the front of her pajama top, pulling them tautly against her abdomen.

"It's all right, Anya," Jimmy was saying. "You're awake now."

"*The Moonlight Sonata,* Jimmy. I've never heard it played so beautifully, so mournfully."

Celia interrupted. "Just tell us what happened."

Anya recounted everything she could remember of her dream. When she finished, Jimmy said, "Great dream recall, Anya."

"I've had enough training. And I want this to be over."

Celia was disappointed. "But you're not at the end yet, baby. Not quite."

Jimmy said shortly. "That's enough for tonight. Put on your iPod, Anya. Or just rest. It will soon be morning."

"You know what I feel like, you two?" Celia asked, pulling her straight red hair away from her face. "Hot chocolate."

"Let Anya be alone for a while, Celia," Jimmy said.

"Oh, Jimmy. Let's have hot chocolate and keep her company. I'll make it in the coffee maker."

Celia went to the service area and soon returned with three cups of hot chocolate, complete with tiny marshmallows melting on the top. She handed one of the cups to Anya. Jimmy put his down on the table, but Celia and Anya finished theirs.

A little while later Anya said, "I'm sleepy again. I think I'll doze for awhile."

Celia quickly turned to Jimmy. "You know, I think this is it. Anya really wants to finish this thing. Put the sleep cap on, Jimmy." Jimmy glanced at Anya, surprised. But she nodded at him sleepily.

After Jimmy went into the next room, Celia sat down on Anya's bed. She took a small box out of her pocket. "Here's the necklace, baby." She lifted out the broken cross with the missing stone and offered it to Anya. "Let's get this over with, right?"

Anya started to object, but found speech difficult. She took the cross, now strung on a silken black cord, and fell back on the pillow.

In the next room, Jimmy watched the monitor as Anya almost immediately slipped into **REM**.

* * * * *

The young black woman gives the mister his paper and letters and goes up to her attic room. She retrieves a small cloth valise from beneath her bed and quickly fills it with a few pieces of clothing – a long, rough skirt, much like the one she has on but somewhat cleaner. Two much-worn shirts and a pressed-wool coat for the cold and damp. Some thick stockings and a pair of boy's boots. She opens a cigar box that contains found items: buttons, a brass thimble, a small mirror that had lost some of its silvering, a shell hair ornament. She puts them in the case.

Also in the box is the dull blade of a broken dinner knife. She pushes the narrow bed silently to one side. Hunched over her knees, she wiggles the knife's dull blade into a seemingly tight seam between two end-to-end floorboards. One of the boards shifts a fraction of an inch, enough to insert the knife blade further. She carefully pries the board up, revealing a small cavity between two ceiling rafters of the room below. From the cavity she gathers up some brilliantly colored feathers; a small ceramic bowl made of baked clay, its strange painted decorations faded to dark smudges; several flat white stones with incised designs – things from the old place where her mother had came from. She could not remember what her mother had said about these things, but they had always been precious to her. She puts them in her valise, then goes back to the cavity once more.

Pushed toward the back of the space is an oilskin pouch. She loosens the leather string that holds it shut, and puts her small hand inside the pouch. Tenderly, she runs her hand across a tiny skull's small concave cheek and strokes the wispy hand bones, almost as fine as those of a bird. After securing the oilskin once again, she tucks the package carefully into a corner of the valise. She replaces the floor board and pushes the bed back.

She listens at the top of the stairs. All is quiet. The mister and missus are in the front room. The man who worked the farm during the week has left for his home, and the new man has gone to town.

She picks up her valise and cloak and moves silently on the two flights of stairs to the kitchen, then down the cellar steps. She makes her way through the walkout cellar and out of the farmhouse.

It is a dark night with no moon showing. A cold, wet fog has descended. Once out of the house, she puts on her shoes and heads away from the stable yard, following the field as it slopes toward the tree line. Here the land tumbles into a gully with a shallow stream at the bottom. She walks down the steep slope, through the wet underbrush, to a large tree by the stream. Nearby is a recently toppled tree, its upended roots making a large depression in the forest floor. She sits down to wait for him.

She steadies herself with an old slave trick taught her by her mother. She becomes motionless, unfocuses her eyes and puts all thoughts of past and future out of her mind, becoming part of the ground and trees around her. In this state she is all-powerful, able to whisk away the mist and will the moon to appear. She makes the moon grow until it is fuller than any harvest moon, shining its cold blue-white light on her. Beneath the halo of her shimmering moon, she can again hear the piano notes that earlier had filled her with such longing.

The man comes to her from the other side of the woods. He takes her arm. She discerns his anger. "Did you take something from the church today?" he demands.

She lies calmly. "No."

"A necklace?"

"Why would there be a necklace in the church?" she asks.

"Never mind now."

In the stillness they hear a sound in the direction of the farmhouse, the sound of small pebbles rattling against glass. "You stay," he says, and moves off.

She does not stay. Instead, she follows him at a distance. The man draws up at the edge of the wood and looks back, but she drops down behind a tree. The man stops. When she comes closer, she sees he is watching a small light moving toward the stable. She hears a slight scraping noise and guesses that the sound is the removal of the board that serves to keep the stable doors closed.

In the kitchen of the farmhouse, a yellow lantern light appears, getting brighter as someone inside moves to the back door. She hears the mister call into the dark, Who is it? Who's there? The mister moves out onto the porch and holds the lantern up in the direction of the stable. She hears him curse: Stable door's open. Damn Frenchman.

The mister walks carefully with the lantern in his hand. The stable doors are open wide. The mister puts down the lantern on the nearby bench. He closes the left door of the stable and is turning to the right when there is a flash of movement behind him.

As the man and the girl in the woods watch separately, out of the shadows slips a dark, powerful body. The light of the lantern gleams dully on his black shoulders as he raises his arms and brings the dull side of an axe down onto the older man's head. There is a thud and then low moaning. The moaning soon stops.

She recognizes the man in the lantern light when he turns to run back the way he had come. Neither she nor the watching man moves.

Then another figure comes to the back door, holding a candle. An older woman looks out of the open kitchen door and then comes onto the porch. Judge, where are you? she calls, looking in the direction of the stable and the faint light from the lantern.

The watching man sees his chance laid out before him. A chance to fix all his problems. The girl Mary would be his and take him out of his miserable circumstances, if he can just find the nerve to seize this opportunity in front of him. The girl wants him, he knows that well, and she would afterward need him, would turn to him in her loss. Most important, she would come to him with all her parents' property and goods. But he must be bold, bolder than he has planned. But why not? He has already accepted the need for extreme measures to rid himself of the black girl. One further step on such a bloody night would not matter. The die is cast – was cast, spectacularly, by another. The man stands up from his hiding place and hurries toward the house.

"Who's there?" cries the woman with the candle, uncertain.

The man lets himself be seen. "Mrs. Sayre. It's me, ma'am. I was out at the pond and took the shortcut back to town, hope you don't mind, Mrs. Sayre. I saw a light by your stable. And the stable doors were open. I thought something might be wrong."

"The judge heard something and went out to look. He's not answering me."

"Come. Let's take a look. I'm sure the judge is just checking the horses. I see his lantern." He smiles as he takes the candle from her. "Any word from Miss Mary?"

"She's still away. "You'll be visiting us again regular when my daughter returns?" the woman replies, not sounding especially pleased.

"I hope so." The man affects to be both embarrassed and encouraged by her question despite her tone.

The black girl at the edge of the woods watches as the pair drifts toward the stable. The man stands between the lantern and the fallen figure that lays just inside the open stable door, to shield it from view. "Mrs. Sayre. Is that the judge's coat there on the railing?" he suddenly asks.

"Where?" She turns her head to look and the man smoothly reaches down for the axe dropped by the black man. He brings it around in a wide arc and slams it against the woman's left temple as well as he can manage from a half-crouching position. The woman's hands fly to her bleeding temple. She lurches and screams but doesn't fall. He raises the instrument and gives her another blow with more leverage behind it, but it doesn't land squarely and she staggers sideways in a lopsided circle like a chicken that doesn't yet realize it has lost its head.

The man becomes sick of the sight of the stupid woman who is so hard to fell. This time his blow lands clean, the axe embedding itself in the top of the woman's scalp, and she goes down, finally quiet. The man stands there breathing heavily, exhausted. He washes his hands and face in the watering trough, wiping away the blood and brain matter. He turns back towards the woods.

The girl has watched the scene unfold as if it were a play on a stage. Her mother once had told her of a strange carnival she had attended when she was a tiny girl, when she was still with her own mother on the pretty island where the sugar cane grew. Her mother's master had let all the slaves attend this carnival, allowing them to watch the musicians and partake of special sweets. Then a crude platform had been set up, and several of the overseers acted out a story. The story was about a black slave who did not obey his master and ran away. He was caught by white men. There were whips, and switches with leather tails. White children played at being the dogs that ripped at the captured slave's body. At the end of the play, a group of slaves were forced onstage and whipped hideously for the sins of the runaway slave.

She imagines now how her mother felt. She cannot change what has happened or stop what is to happen next. Her fear is like an animal, a fierce canine living inside her body, ready to eat her entrails if she dares to move.

But when she sees the man turn in her direction, she breaks from her watching place and runs silently back through the woods to the gully where he had told her to wait. She finds her valise at the foot of the big tree and opens it. She takes out the small oilskin package first and gently nestles it at the bottom of the depression made by the toppled tree. She reaches in her pocket for the necklace and puts it in the hole, along with the feathers and stones of her mother. Using a branch, she hastily covers everything with soil. She takes her place by the tree and waits for him. The only noise is her raspy breathing and the occasional sound of a hoot owl in a pine tree nearby.

"Phebe. Phebe, something terrible has happened," he says as he drops down beside her.

"What? What has happened?" She can smell his damp, gory clothing and barely stops herself from gagging.

"Martin has killed the judge and Mrs. Sayre. People will

blame you. They will think you and Martin killed the Sayres."

She can't think. She hears some small night creatures scurrying in the dirt nearby.

"How could this happen?" She asks herself more than him.

"It's your fault," he says harshly. "Martin came back to avenge you."

She weeps. "I did wrong. I should never have let you touch me. It was the music." Then the fear returns. "You go away now and leave me here. I won't tell. I won't say nothing. I'll say Martin killed mister and missus and I heard him and ran away into the woods. Go now."

He reaches for her and pulls her closer. "No, no, Phebe. You're my special one. Come here." He begins to kiss her and caress her small body, moving close to her. He moves back and forth, pressing up against her, laughing a little. Then he pulls her under him. She holds her breath to stop from throwing up.

When it is over, he rolls off her and straightens his clothing.

She doesn't dare cry aloud, but her face is awash with silent tears. "Come on, Phebe," he laughs lightly. "That was just for good-bye to my sweet girl. Martin's crime doesn't change anything. You still need to go away. And you will," he says, still breathing hard.

She watches his false, shining eyes.

"Let's go, Phebe. It's all arranged. Where is your valise?" He finds the cloth bag and searches it, then angrily tosses it to her. "I want that necklace. I know you took it from the piano at the church." Then his manner softens, and greed gathers in the shadows of his face. "Maybe we can find some money in the house to help you on your way. When I tell the sheriff what I have seen, it will appear as if Martin stole what is missing."

"There's no need. I can get away myself."

"Come, Phebe." He half bows to her, sweeping her in front of him, forcing her to walk. They move out of the gully and through the wet field, toward the farmhouse. When they are inside, he breaks into locked drawers and cabinets, putting selected items in his pockets. "Here, Phebe. Some money for your journey." Then he pushes her toward the attic. "Now go to your room and wait. I will come when I am finished here."

No light shines through the window on the landing as she walks up the two flights of stairs to her room. The air is damp and chill at the top of the house. She shuts her eyes and sits down on the bed. The icy moon music returns to comfort her.

Soon he comes up the stairs with the lantern, now in a hurry, remembering the hired man. When he sees her sitting on the bed, he smiles a false smile, alligator teeth shining white in the dark. Are you ready? he asks. She can see dark red patches seeping up the sleeve of his right arm. His pants are already stiff with lifeblood.

"Just leave me. I won't tell." She doesn't know whether she says this aloud or not.

He had broken into the mister's liquor; the smell of brandy follows his movements about her room. "What's to tell, black girl? No one would believe you."

She turns to pick up her valise. The first blow pole-axes her, paralyzing her reflexes. A blanket hangs on the wall over the bed. She watches a fine spray of carmine droplets and some heavier clumps of grayish matter splash across the surface of the blanket, making it glisten. Then her nervous system reflexively throws off her paralysis, and her limbs jerk violently in reaction to the massive assault to her brain. She collapses forward onto the bed. With the last of her physical resources, she turns on her right side and places her hand under her head, gently, as if cradling its gross injury.

He searches the room drunkenly, looking for the necklace, pocketing the money he had given her. Her open eyes seem to follow him. He takes down the heavy buffalo skin blanket and throws it over her, to hide the eyes. Only her small feet remain visible.

After he is gone, her lungs spasmodically express a quantity of airy foam through her nose and mouth onto the bed. Wrapped in the dark cocoon of the blanket, her pain lessens and then is gone. She can see the silvery moon again, and her mind is filled with the music. The music had been her undoing. In the beginning it was the colors of the music that had caught her, led her down her path. Now, at the end, the music is her salvation. Floating on a final color-drenched piano arpeggio, she begins her final journey.

Chapter 27

The dream ended, but Anya did not experience the normal progression to shallower brain waves. Jimmy watched the deepening troughs on the monitor. He rushed into the bedroom, looking at her with a clinical eye. "Anya. Anya, are you awake?" he kept repeating, with growing alarm. When there was no response, he pulled her up in the bed. She slumped, and he supported her limp body with pillows. Among the blankets he saw the broken cross on its black cord, still entwined in her fingers. He threw it on the floor. He chafed her arms and pulled the comforter around her, but she still felt cold. Celia appeared in the doorway, looking anxious. "Get hot tea with lots of sugar," he ordered.

After Celia had gotten some sweet tea between her lips, Anya's eyes cleared and became more focused. Jimmy asked her some questions and she seemed to understand where she was and what was happening. Jimmy felt immensely relieved. He encouraged Anya to get up and move around, to work off the dream's aura.

Celia watched Anya. "Jimmy, can't you see? She's obviously been through hell with this dream and has to get it out. Let her tell it."

Jimmy's first concern was Anya, not the dream session. Ignoring Celia, he continued to talk to Anya and rub her arms.

Celia appealed to Anya. "You've come so far, baby. Tell us." Anya stared blankly for a moment, but then habit and years of training propelled her forward, and she told her dream in detail. She had experienced rape and death in her dream world, and Jimmy recognized the signs of post-traumatic stress disorder as she spoke: sweating and crying, anxiety, confusion.

Celia followed Anya's story avidly, taking her own notes. When Anya finished, she got up and paced the room, unable to contain her excitement. "This is incredible. Such detail! And consistency. This story is true, and it's coming from the past."

Anya indicated she wanted to get dressed. Jimmy led Celia out the door and into her room next door. He sat her down roughly on the sofa. "What was in the hot chocolate?" he demanded.

"For godsakes, Jimmy. It was just a valium."

"Anya has never received a sedative drug while sleeping in my lab. It would skew the chemical profile, and there's no gauging the physiological reaction when she's in a state of lucid dreaming."

"She seemed to need something to relax her, Jimmy. Who knew she would dream again?"

Jimmy took her arm and forced her to look at him. "You did. You know the optimum time for lucidity is toward morning, after there's been a period of awakening. You wanted her to dream again, so you spiked her drink and gave her the necklace."

Celia pulled away. "You don't get it, Jimmy. Either from Anya's viewpoint or from the research side of it. This episode had to be completed."

"You've passed the point where Anya is your main concern. You want this episode to be your special gift to Lubov, to show him you can still get results from Anya, even though she's clearly trying to break away," he said furiously.

"Break away? She called *us* for help, Jimmy. That doesn't sound like someone intent on breaking away."

"A lifetime of dependency has its pitfalls, Celia." He got up and walked to the window. Outside the day had broken. Deep shadows were giving way to shafts of early-morning diffused sunlight. It looked to be another golden fall day. He turned back toward Celia and spoke in measured tones. "It's long past time Anya got away from you and Lubov." He walked past her and slammed the door to her room. Celia picked up a pillow from the sofa and threw it against the door. She slumped onto the sofa.

After a short time she left her room and went downstairs, using the back staircase. She waited near a concealed service entrance where she could see the hotel lobby. She watched as Jimmy and Anya left the elevator and walked toward the doors to leave the hotel. Anya leaned heavily on Jimmy, who kept his arm around her firmly, steadying her. As they reached the entrance, Celia saw Anya look up into Jimmy's dark, brilliant eyes. He put his arm around her more tightly and smiled a certain smile she hadn't seen in a long time. Jimmy's and Anya's eyes remained on each other as they passed through the heavy doors and out onto the street.

Celia stayed in the shadows until she could no longer see them.

Chapter 28

As Jimmy drove her to the Ralston Club, Anya sensed his lingering anger. Even in her confused state she was aware that Celia and he had had a fierce argument. This was different from the general sense of uneasiness between them that she had detected almost from the moment they arrived in Morristown. Now she spoke hesitantly. "Jimmy . . . "

"Go ahead. Say whatever you want."

"I'm worried about what's happening between you and Celia. I know it's none of my business," she added hastily.

The last thing Jimmy wanted to do was to involve Anya in his and Celia's exploding personal problems. "It's your business if it worries you, Anya. But I don't know if I can provide much comfort," he replied. He saw her brow crease. "I told Celia that I don't think you need Dr. Lubov's constant care any longer. And that your intense involvement in Lubov's studies has become increasingly negative for you. Celia disagrees with me. I'm sorry you overheard our argument." He didn't mention the valium.

Anya was silent for a full minute before responding. "Jimmy, this is hard, after so many years."

"It's our problem, Celia's and mine, not yours. I don't want you to feel you have to take sides. You'll have to make your own decisions about your future some day, no matter what either of us thinks."

"What would I say to Aunt Ceci?"

"Do you want me to say something to Celia for you?"

"No. I'm a big girl now. Isn't that what you just said?"

"Yes. I guess that's my point."

When he pulled up in front of the Ralston Club, she took his hand in hers, then let it go, clearly frustrated. "Thanks, Jimmy. Please don't get out." She was up the front steps of the mansion before he had a chance to respond.

After she reached her room she put her iPod into its speaker and dialed Beethoven. She wanted anything but *The Moonlight Sonata* and selected the *Violin Sonata in A Major*. She was immediately caught up in the passion of the violins in counterpoint with the dense piano passages. The veils of muted color from the strings alternated with the bright sparks of the major piano chords. She sat listening with her eyes closed, feeling unsettled and anxious.

Above the music she heard a familiar knock on her door.

"Anya. It's Peter. I need to talk to you."

She turned the music off and opened the door. "I have to get to work, Peter."

Thayer stood there on the threshold. She saw immediately that he wasn't his usual brash self, looking to whisk her away for some private time. For a change, not every hair was perfectly in place. He looked as if he'd hurried here on a mission. She opened the door wider and let him in.

"I had an odd conversation with Sebastian Bennett this morning, and I can't get it out of my mind," he said.

She couldn't be sure whether he was overdramatizing or not. "What conversation, Peter?"

"He somehow knows that you're spending a lot of time at the Radisson with your friends," he said without preamble.

"That's none of his business. Yours either, Peter," she said quickly.

Thayer hastened to reword. "I got the sense he knows you're working with them in some way, something about dreams. He seems to know a lot about you, and I get the idea he cares about you, too."

Anya was still hearing the Beethoven music in her mind. But now the colors had collapsed and turned dark. "Everybody is at me for something. And I can't help anybody," she said, her voice rising in frustration.

Thayer continued his defensive analysis of Bennett's motivations. "Anya, I think Dr. Bennett is so upset about Lily that he's looking for any hope he can find. I suspect he talked to you about Lily at the luncheon. You were gone a long time. He's asked me if you've had any more thoughts; if you've heard anything from the police."

She focused on Thayer and spoke intensely. "Peter. Don't let yourself get pulled into this. Dr. Bennett has got it in his mind that I have some special way to help Phebe. But there's nothing I can do. Sometimes people just have to help themselves."

"You mean Lily, not Phebe," Peter said quickly.

"Lily. Yes."

Thayer was thoughtful. "My life and experience has shown me that sometimes people can't help themselves, Anya. They've learned to be helpless and afraid; they've been hurt so badly they can't move to help themselves."

"I'm sorry I sound so hard-bitten, Peter. If I could help I would. That's what you should tell Dr. Bennett, and then just leave it be."

Thayer was disappointed. "Thanks for hearing me out, Anya. Bennett wields a lot of authority when he asks me to do something. At least I can say I spoke to you."

"I can't talk about it anymore, Peter."

But Thayer went on. "Bennett knows these abuse cases. He

223

knows the husband's not done with Lily yet." After a slight pause he added, "Unless he's already got to her."

"Stop it, Peter. Shut up," she said sharply, putting her hands over her ears. She was aware of Thayer in front of her, but her eyes were behaving oddly. Thayer was shifting in and out of focus, looming close, then fading. The phenomenon made her feel disconnected with her surroundings, and her hands and feet felt leaden.

Thayer was shocked to hear her raise her voice. She wasn't looking at him, and she seemed to be having trouble breathing. Alarmed, he went to her, but she moved away. "I want to help them, but I can't. I can't even breathe," she gasped. Her legs buckled, and she grabbed for the back of the sofa. Her arm felt like a hundred-pound weight hanging from her shoulder, and her hand slid off the sofa. She went down and was still, her cheek pressed against the rose-patterned carpet.

She became aware of Thayer at her side, turning her over, putting his arm around her shoulders, lifting her head, calling her name. She remained limp as he frantically felt her neck for a pulse. Her breathing was thin and reedy; her heartbeat rapid. Thayer fumbled for his cell phone.

She opened her eyes. "No. Peter. Don't call anyone."

"I'm calling an ambulance."

"No. I don't need an ambulance. Don't call. I mean it."

He grabbed pillows from the sofa and put one under her head, another under her feet. He went to the kitchen for water. She took the glass with a shaky hand. After awhile he helped her off the floor and settled her on the sofa. "What happened, Anya?"

"I don't know what happened. But I'm fine now."

"You're sure?"

"Yes." She was thankful he had put his phone away. She just wanted to clear her head of everything. After a few minutes she tried to get up. "I need to get to the Theatre."

"Wait. Why don't you just stay put for the day? I'll stay with you. I'll bring you whatever you need."

She was on her feet. "No. I just want to get to the Theatre. I have things to do there. Things to think about. Work."

He was uncertain. "All right. But I'll take you there."

He picked up her briefcase and opened the door for her, following her out to the landing, putting his arm around her firmly as they negotiated the stairs. She seemed to be steady now, but the feel of her through her thin blouse was electrifying. Her strange aloofness stirred him unbearably. He was careful not to let her see his face, for anyone could read the raw desire in it.

They walked the few blocks to the Theatre without talking. He knew she didn't want him to go in with her, so he told her to call him if she needed anything, anything at all. Before she disappeared behind the glass doors, he couldn't resist holding her arm a moment longer so he could feel her again through her blouse. He leaned down and kissed her lightly. His lips lingered longer than he had planned, and he felt her pull away.

Anya was immensely relieved to be alone in her office. She had a pent-up desire to work without interruption, to work so hard that everything else would be kept at bay. She began by organizing her stacks of stiff storyboards on the two long tables that lined her office wall, layering on dance sequences, photos of artwork, and notes on lighting and other stagecraft. She worked swiftly, her colored pens flying, shuffling through the boards again and again.

The episode in her apartment crept into her mind. She didn't understand it. It was more an instance of blacking out, rather than fainting. It was not an anxiety attack. She could remember nothing during the time she had been unconscious, but somehow she felt she should.

As the afternoon wore on, she had trouble keeping her mind on the work. The idea that she was missing something had first presented itself in a tiny corner of her mind, and it now began to grow. She got up again, moving the boards around on the tables, shifting them back and forth, looking for something. Nothing seemed right.

She decided to take all her storyboards to the Theatre's stage. If she worked with them in the space where her production would be performed, it might help things to fall into place, she thought. She hastily loaded everything onto a long metal pushcart.

She rolled the cart through the back halls to the left stage entrance. The windowless, ornate auditorium was dark and the seats mostly invisible, except for a faint glow that came from the electronics in the sound box about halfway up the aisle. She threw the switch for a row of downlights and wheeled her cart to center stage. She lifted one of the large boards from the cart and propped it against the back of the space, under the downlights. She went back to the cart and continued until she had fifteen storyboards in sets of three strung out across the stage. Then she began to intersperse medium and smaller pieces, overlapping the larger ones.

She stepped toward the front of the stage and looked at the arrangement. "No. It's not right. Why isn't it right?" she said out loud, her voice echoing in the empty auditorium.

She began to move the boards around, first slowly and then faster and more impatiently, pushing some out of the way and stacking others. Then suddenly she was tossing them away from her, one by one. They fell on the wooden stage floor with a series of hollow thuds until they lay in a wide circle all around her. Abruptly, she threw herself down on the stage in the center of the circle.

She felt something hit her arm. It was as if someone had slammed her hard with a sharp, pointed stick, but there wasn't anyone there. She fell backward in the direction of the force. Then there was an air disturbance that made the fine hair on her arms stand up, and immediately the rail of downlights that had been the stage's only lighting exploded. The stage was plunged into darkness.

The darkened space was silent except for a faint electrical crackling from the dangling lights. She touched her arm, which had begun to sting and burn. It was wet. She got to her feet and half-staggered offstage.

She stumbled into the first dressing room, grabbed a white fluffy towel, and pressed it to her arm. Then she ran toward the exit where the big trucks transporting stage equipment and scenery were unloaded. There was no one in the loading bays, and she crept around the side of the building where there was a row of portable toilets that had been placed to accommodate construction workers. She slid through the door of the nearest toilet.

By looking through the space between the vinyl door and its frame, she could see the front of the Theatre. Sebastian Bennett and Sonja Hildebrandt were standing near Bennett's Mercedes. Sonja was annoyed, pointing to her watch. Bennett, looking rushed, shrugged his shoulders and hurriedly helped her into the car. Then Peter Thayer appeared in her line of view, moving quickly away from the Theatre.

Anya lifted the towel from where it was wrapped around her upper arm. Blood had saturated the first two layers of the thick terrycloth and was bubbling from a small, deep, black-encrusted hole. She put the towel back in place and sank further down in the small space.

PART III

All that we see or seem
Is but a dream within a dream.

Edgar Allan Poe

Chapter 29

When his phone rang, Jimmy looked at his watch. It was after 4:00 p.m. He had wanted to talk to Anya all day. He had been thinking over and over about their last conversation – about the changes in his and Celia's relationship, about the implications of Anya breaking away from a life dominated by Lubov. These things had been a long time coming and were momentous in their effect on his and Celia's future. But it was Anya he was most concerned about.

He glanced at the caller ID – an unidentified Morristown number. He hit the talk button. "James Lang."

"It's Mitchell."

"Hello, detective," he said warily.

"Is Anya with you?" Jimmy could hear Mitchell breathing rapidly.

"No. Why?"

"I'm at the South Street Theatre. An hour ago someone heard a noise and then the lights went out. By the time the maintenance guy hit the generators and the staff got into the auditorium, Anya's stuff was scattered all over the stage, but no Anya. You haven't heard from her?"

"Not since this morning."

"What about Celia Ormand?"

"I haven't seen her. Tell me what's up, Mitch."

"There's blood on the stage."

"I'm coming." Jimmy put his cell phone in his pocket, grabbed his jacket and left the room. He knocked on Celia's door hard. There was no answer. He tried again, then went to the parking lot for the van.

When he reached the Theatre, he saw several police black-and-whites at the curb. He parked the van and tried to go into the lobby. A uniformed officer blocked his entrance, but Mitchell saw him and waved him through. Theatre employees were standing around, looking worried.

"Have you found her?" Jimmy asked.

"No. You have to keep away from the crime scene."

"I'm not going to crash the scene, Mitch. What's this about blood?"

"A quantity of blood on the stage. Not a big fatal puddle, all right? Also a trail of blood going off the stage into a dressing room. Looks like she wiped the blood off there and took a couple towels with her. No more trail. She just disappears."

"What kind of wound?"

"Gunshot. Small caliber. Found a bullet on the stage and another in the ceiling."

"You're still searching for her here?"

"Please, Lang. We're crawling all over this place. I need some answers from you. You were with Anya early this morning. Who might want to hurt her? Was she worried about anything?"

Jimmy didn't know how to answer. "She was upset about Celia and me, some problems we're having, but nothing else seemed wrong."

Mitchell watched him. "You know, there's been some chatter within historical circles that your partner Celia has been open to connecting the Rose Restaurant murders with what happened there a long time ago. There are certain people in town

232

whose hobbyhorse is the Sayre murders, and Celia's been talking to them. I hope she hasn't allowed someone to get the idea
that Anya could somehow dream her way to knowing who killed
the Sullivans."

"Celia wouldn't do that. Lily Doone's husband killed Bill Sullivan, didn't he? Why would he hang around here and take a
shot at Anya?"

"It was Doone's knife that likely killed Richard Sullivan. But
Maureen Sullivan's death is different. There's information we're
sitting on. But that doesn't matter right now. I've got work to
do. You have to get out of here," he said, dismissing Jimmy.

Jimmy didn't budge. "I have to see the stage where Anya was
working."

"All right, but just for a minute." Mitchell motioned for
Jimmy to follow. He opened the doors to the auditorium, where
there was now as much light illuminating the interior as possible.
There was a white-jacketed police technician in the sound box
and two more on the stage collecting evidence samples and taking measurements.

Mitchell was stopped by an officer. "Looks like the shots were
fired from the sound box, Mitch. The angle is right. With the
downlights on, she was fully lit from above and behind. It should
have been like shooting fish in a barrel."

Jimmy walked up the stage steps and was barred at the top
from going any further. He tried to understand what he saw on
the stage. He had occasionally watched Anya work with her storyboards, carefully lining them up and precisely moving elements around. The boards were now spread in an erratic circle,
tossed randomly. It appeared to him as if Anya was desperately
trying to figure something out and had become increasingly
frantic. At the center of the circle of discarded boards was a
large, dark blotch, now mostly soaked into the floor.

Jimmy saw that there had been something wrong with Anya
before the bullet hit her. He wondered if she had even been

aware of what she was doing.

"Mitch. Have you found out what Anya did earlier today, before all this happened? Who she was with; who she talked to?"

Mitchell considered how much to tell Jimmy. "We're tracing her movements. The Ralston Club says that a local minister she sees went up to her apartment this morning around 9:00. He was up there almost an hour."

"I know who that is."

"Yeah. So do I. Anyway, they parted at the Theatre doors around 10:30."

"Then you've got to talk to Thayer about her state of mind. I don't like what I see here."

"Of course I'm doing that." Mitchell hesitated to say more, but getting Jimmy's analysis of the situation seemed more important than not revealing information about the case. "Thayer says she had a funny incident. She became upset about something and fainted for a few minutes. She came to with all vital signs okay and wouldn't let him call an ambulance. He stayed with her until she felt better and then walked her here. She seemed fine by then, he says."

Whatever Thayer told Mitchell about Anya's apparent recovery after the alleged fainting spell, he would bet that Anya's blackout experience wasn't transitory. The scattered, irrational arrangement of Anya's work on the stage suggested she was in a kind of fugue state, as if she hadn't been able to shake off her last dream session and was suspended between reality and nightmare. It explained why she hadn't shown herself or approached anyone for help since she disappeared.

Jimmy turned to Mitchell, who was watching him. "Put everything you have into finding her in a hurry. I think she may be unable to get help for herself, even if she's conscious and functioning on some level."

"What do you mean?"

"She may be hiding."

"From whoever shot her?"

"She may not even understand she's been shot."

"I don't know what you're talking about. But I'm on this," he said impatiently. "Go on and get out of here so I can get busy."

Jimmy nodded. "Call me immediately when you find her."

Chapter 30

Peter Thayer sat at a small table in the Theatre's marketing offices. To the officer watching him through a large plate glass window he looked nervous, pushing his long hair back from his forehead, adjusting his black, clerical-looking jacket.

Detective Mitchell opened the door and quickly sat down across from him. "Tell me what you were doing here at the Theatre today, Thayer. There's no show scheduled. The box office is closed."

Thayer answered quickly. "I dropped off Anya Gregory."

"That was this morning."

"Let me finish. Yes, I dropped her off earlier. But, as I told you, she'd had a fainting spell. I came back this afternoon to make sure she was okay."

"You could have called her."

The police would have a record of his phone calls. "I did call her several times. But she didn't answer. So I decided to come over and check on her."

"You're quite the mother hen, aren't you?"

Thayer ignored the comment. "I hadn't even gone into the Theatre when your officer stopped me."

"You could have been coming out of the Theatre and turned

around to make it look like you just arrived."

"But I didn't. And I've been asking what this is all about for two hours now."

"Are you still worried about Anya Gregory?"

"Yes. What am I supposed to think with you asking these questions? I'm worried to death about her. What's going on, for god's sake?"

"What inspired you to go to Anya's apartment this morning?"

"Something my boss asked me to do."

"Who's your boss?"

"Sebastian Bennett. I work part time at Sunnyside."

"Are you sure you just didn't want an excuse to see Anya? You've been watching her pretty closely, haven't you?"

"She's a friend. Dr. Bennett wanted me to ask Anya about Lily Doone. He seemed to think Anya might know something."

"Ask her what?"

"I'm not even sure. He just wanted to know if Anya had any thoughts concerning Lily."

"Why would Anya know anything about it?"

"I don't know. I don't care. She's very creative, and she senses things. At least that seemed to be the gist of it on Dr. Bennett's part."

"So you're just a friend of Anya's?"

"Listen, detective. I'll be truthful. I was – am – infatuated with her."

"You tried to see her at every opportunity? She was on your mind constantly?"

"So what? She was new in town and I was very attracted to her. Sonja Hildebrant encouraged me to see that Anya got to certain events, and so on. What's wrong with that? I'm a clergyman, but that doesn't mean I'm not interested in women."

Detective Mitchell leaned back. "I couldn't agree with you more, Thayer. What's wrong with being attracted to a really good-looking woman and going after her? Maybe I'd do the same thing." He watched Thayer. "But then I'm not married, and you are."

Thayer looked up, surprised. "That's none of your business. I'm separated and on the way to getting divorced as soon as possible."

"I take it your young wife is aware of this? And your pursuing other women?"

"She's having difficulty accepting the situation," he replied stiffly.

"Did you tell Anya about your marital status?"

"Our relationship hadn't got that far."

"Did you tell her you were an ex-priest? Or why you got out of the religion business? And your son, Thayer, how old is he? Doesn't he miss daddy when ex-Father Thayer is in another state playing games with the needy women of Sunnyside?"

Thayer looked across the table at Mitchell. "That's all none of your business. You have no legal reason to investigate me. I haven't broken the law. I was a priest. I never should have been a priest. I liked women too much and ended up having to marry one of them. I'm only too glad to be out of the priest business." He leaned back and shot a belligerent look in Mitchell's direction. "But that's my story. What's yours? You're the one with a huge, frustrated crush on Anya Gregory. I don't miss things like that."

Mitchell was infuriated at Thayer for turning the interrogation on him. "So you were only trying to help Anya, not worm your horny fraudulent ass into her bed?" he asked. "And your ministering to the needs of vulnerable women at Sunnyside has never gone beyond spiritual guidance? Like with Lily Doone?"

Thayer stood up. "Screw you, detective. I didn't have anything going with Lily Doone. Or Anya, more's the pity. You're so jealous you can hardly stand it."

Mitchell kicked the chair next to him with his foot, sending it against the wall. "Trust me, Thayer. You'll never get within shouting range of Anya again after she hears your sordid little story."

"Maybe so, maybe not," Thayer said, needling Mitchell. "But you're too hung up on Anya to help her. You should step aside and let some cop who's not so obsessed get on with the job of looking for her."

The cop observing through the window had moved to the door of the room when Mitchell kicked the chair, but Mitchell motioned him not to come in. "What makes you think Anya's missing? Or needs help?" he asked.

Thayer sat back down, nervous. "I sensed this morning she was in some kind of danger. I might be an ex-priest, but I'm still good at that sort of thing."

"You're about to be checked for gun residue, Thayer. You might want to call your wife." Mitchell got up and left the room.

Chapter 31

When Jimmy got back to the hotel, he asked the maid on the floor if she had done Celia's room yet. The maid reported Celia had been in her room a few minutes ago and had refused service. Jimmy went to Celia's room and kept knocking and calling her name until she finally opened the door.

In the many years Jimmy had known her, Celia was invariably well groomed and impeccably put together. Her polished auburn hair was always in place, either swaying in straight lengths beside her face or fastened behind her ears. Even after sex she managed to retain an air of neatly tousled, long-legged elegance.

Now she was shoeless, dressed in a wrinkled blouse that was pulled out over her skirt. Her face was almost bare of makeup, with dark circles of smeared mascara under her eyes. Her hair was lank, somehow having lost its golden gleam.

She retreated into the room, leaving the door open for him. He followed. She took a seat on the sofa, curling her legs under her, hugging a pillow.

"You've heard about Anya?" he asked, sitting down beside her.

"Her parents called. The police told them Anya has been

241

hurt and is missing." She looked at Jimmy and could tell he had no good news. She closed her eyes and tears gathered at the outer corners. "I didn't know what to say to them. I was supposed to be taking care of Anya."

"Why aren't you answering your phone?"

"I don't want to hear the worst."

"I saw the stage where Anya was working when this thing happened, Celia. There were indications that she was in some kind of walking blackout state. I've told Detective Mitchell not to expect her to show herself voluntarily. He has the entire police force looking for her. The wound isn't fatal. They'll find her."

"She's been shot, Jimmy. How could I let that happen?"

Jimmy got up. "Look, Celia. This isn't helping anyone." Alarmed at her appearance, feeling sorry for her, he took her hand. "Come on. Let's go get a cup of coffee or a drink or something. Mitchell has promised to call the minute he finds her."

She pulled her hand away. "You don't understand. Yuri has always entrusted Anya to me. I am to keep her safe at all times. He depends on me exclusively and totally to watch her and report to him. I've failed him."

"It's not about Yuri," he said harshly. "Anya is out there somewhere, and she's the only one that matters."

"She's not going to be found alive, Jimmy." The way she said it made Jimmy's legs feel slightly weak.

"Why would you say such a thing?" he demanded.

"You've refused to see what's going on from the beginning. The Sayres and Phebe were murdered. And the Sullivans and Lily are dead, too. The same thing has happened again. And Anya will pay for all of it."

Jimmy was stunned by her statement. "What does Anya have to do with any of these other people, past or present? We've talked about this kind of thinking before, Celia. It's superstitious nonsense."

She seemed not to hear him. "Anya's dreams told her what was going to happen, Jimmy. She couldn't stop it. Now they're all dead and they hate her. They want her with them. They can't wait to get their hands on her."

For the first time, Jimmy leaned over and looked into her face with a physician's eye. Her eyes were unfocused and the pupils dilated. Her hands spasmodically opened and closed. He recognized that she was in a state of hysteria.

"Okay, Celia," he said soothingly, stroking her rigid arms briskly. "Listen. We need to get you calmed down." He pulled her out of the sofa. She stood there, her arms stiffly at her sides. "Help me out, Celia. Walk." She moved her arms and put them around Jimmy, loosely first, then tighter. "Come on, Celia. Let's get you into the shower."

She let him lead her into the bathroom. He rolled up his sleeves and turned the shower on, then helped her slip out of her wrinkled clothes. She finished undressing and got into the shower, letting the water fall over her, her eyes closed. After a while she opened them and said in a tight voice, "I'm okay now."

"Good. Finish showering and get dressed."

He retreated out of the bathroom but left the door open. Ten minutes later she came out wrapped in a white hotel robe, a towel around her hair. She'd put on some lipstick and her eyes had regained their color and focus.

"There. That's better," he said, smiling at her.

"Thanks, Jimmy. I just lost it."

"Never mind. Anya's going to need you when she's found."

Celia looked toward the window, slowly unwrapping her hair. "Anya's never going to need me again." She sensed his reaction to what she'd said and turned toward him quickly. "I don't mean she's not going to be found. But she's not going to need me."

243

Jimmy tried to be comforting. "Anya will always love you for everything you've done for her."

Celia said nothing. She ran a brush through her wet hair, then expertly pulled her fingers through the red and gold strands until they fell into place around her face. She walked toward Jimmy and put her arms around him. "Love me, Jimmy," she said, opening her robe. "You've always been there for me."

He held her for a minute or two, and then she pulled his head down and kissed him, a sad and hungry kiss. He responded instantly, as he always had. But then he took her hands and made a space between them, gently closing her robe. He looked down at her, but her eyes had shifted away. "I've got nobody," she said, so softly he could hardly hear her.

"You've still got me, Celia. It's just different."

"Everything's different," she said bitterly. She went into the bedroom to get dressed. Then they took the elevator down to the hotel restaurant and ordered coffee and sandwiches. Neither of them ate.

Chapter 32

As the hours of the evening wore on, Detective Mitchell ordered the circle of the search for Anya widened. He stayed at the scene until well after midnight and then went home for a quick shower and change of clothes. His mind was still racing as he showered.

According to what Jimmy had told him, Anya was unlikely to show up voluntarily. If she had run blindly from the Theatre immediately after the attack, she could be anywhere. She could be dead behind a dumpster on the other side of town. A great shudder ran through him, and he had to lean against the shower wall. He prided himself on never letting his job get to him personally, and he'd seen plenty in his career. He'd never had a reaction like this before.

Wrapping the towel around his waist, he went into the bedroom, flipped open his cell phone, and checked in with the officers on each point of the search. Nothing. He stood there a minute and then dialed another number. A familiar, if sleepy, voice came on the other end. "Mitch? Do you know what time it is?"

"Sorry, Flo."

"You haven't found her yet?"

"No."

"Look, Mitch. I think she's okay out there. I really do. It's the damnedest thing that you met her under such circumstances. But she's counting on you now. I know you'll find her."

Mitch stood there, appalled that he'd actually called his mother in the middle of the night. He couldn't think of anything to say to cover up the fact he'd wanted – no, needed – to hear her say just what she'd said. But he didn't have to say anything. That was the way it had been between them ever since his father died when he was a small boy. "Go back to sleep, Flo," he said, closing his phone.

Feeling calmer, he grabbed his jacket, put his gun into his side holster and headed out of the house. While he was locking the front door, he heard a noise in the shadows beyond the wide Victorian veranda. He put his hand on his gun and quietly moved toward the noise. There was another rustle, and a breathy voice said, "Don't shoot me, Detective Mitchell."

He looked closer and saw a splotch of white, then a blonde wig. He ran down the stairs and around the side of the porch. "Marilyn. What the hell are you doing down there?"

The black woman stood up. "Trying to think of a way to get your attention. I was going to throw stones at your windows, like I seen on TV. But then you come out."

"What do you want? Come around here."

He led Marilyn onto the porch and into the house. She was shivering from the night air. "Sit down. Put that afghan thing around you. I'll get you some hot tea."

She sat on the sofa, arranging the afghan as if it were a fancy shawl. She wore the usual extreme makeup from forehead to chin, trimmings carefully applied. He guessed she had changed clothes and renewed her makeup in preparation for her visit to him. He was in a hurry to get back into town and regretted he'd offered her tea. But he went to the kitchen and hastily poured water over a teabag and ran it through the microwave.

She read his haste. "Listen, Detective Mitchell. I'm not out in the chill of the night on some kind of social call. I have something to ask you. Something important."

"What is it, Marilyn? I'm busy."

"What if you promise somebody – somebody who is your friend – something. And then something else happens. And then your friend is acting funny. And you know you gotta do something, but then you'll be breaking your word to your friend?"

"What in god's name are you trying to say, Marilyn?" he said impatiently. But Mitchell's detective instinct had kicked in, and he leaned closer.

"I could be in a lot of trouble, Detective Mitchell. I could lose everything I got."

What does she have to lose? he thought. She's a female bum in ludicrous clown makeup who thinks she's married to a dead baseball player. Instead he said, "Listen, Marilyn. You've never been in trouble with me. I've helped you a few times, right?"

"It's true, detective. We're friends. You always been fair with me."

"We're friends all right, and you've come all the way here in the middle of the night, so just tell me what you came to tell me. Please, Marilyn."

She was mollified but still wary. "You're my friend, detective. And the girl you like is my friend, too."

"Who's the girl I like?"

"You know who. From the Theatre."

"You mean Anya Gregory?"

"That's right. Annie. The Theatre is why she and me got to be friends. She's working on being a star, and she knows I was a big star in my day."

"Anya is your friend, Marilyn?"

"Oh, yeah. We're close. She leaves me things."

Mitchell couldn't tell where this was going, but he was going to ride with it. If only she would get to the point. "What does

Annie leave you, Marilyn?"

"Well, she nearly always leaves a nice lunch, all wrapped. Fresh. Not somebody's leftovers. How about that?"

"That is nice of her, Marilyn."

"And then when her friend came along, she left me money. You know, so I can be a good hostess. You should always be good to your guests, detective. You know that. You give me a nice blanket and something hot to drink. Your momma taught you right."

"Marilyn. This isn't a Miss Manners column. Do you know Anya – Annie – is missing? We're looking for her everywhere."

"I know that, detective," she said impatiently. That's what I'm trying to think on. My friend Annie swore me to help someone and not tell. And I did it. But now we're nervous about Annie."

"I am, too, Marilyn. That's why I've got to go find her."

"That's what I have to tell you, Detective Mitchell," Marilyn said. "Why I came here tonight. I know where Annie is, and she needs help bad."

Mitchell was on his feet. "You know where Anya is? Why didn't you tell me?"

"I *am* telling you."

"Let's go." He took the teacup from her hands, pushed the afghan aside and pulled her up from the sofa.

They were at his car in less than a minute. He jumped in and turned the key before he noticed she was still standing near the passenger door. "Jesus Christ," he groaned, jumping out of the car and running around to open the front door for her. "Get in, Marilyn."

The black woman smiled and settled in her seat. "Thank you, detective," she said sweetly. "You're a gentleman."

Mitchell got back in the driver's seat. "Which way?"

"To the Theatre, of course."

"The Theatre? We've searched there."

"Well, you don't know everything, do you?"

He brought his car to the curb at the Theatre and ran around to the passenger's side. Marilyn daintily dangled a large leg before disembarking. She started down the alleyway that ran by the side of the Theatre with some speed, urged on by Mitchell. Then she stopped. "I'll lose my place over this."

He turned her around hard. "It's too late now. You're doing the right thing, Marilyn. Just show me where she is."

Marilyn followed the building down to the back of the Theatre. She pushed against the boarded-up window. It opened, and she swung her leg over the sill. "Well, come on, then," she encouraged Mitchell, and he followed her into the hidden space.

He quickly took in the small room, lighted by a single flashlight, absorbing the extraordinary fact that Marilyn had made a neat little home for herself in a busy public place. But he was not interested in a homeless woman's resourcefulness now. He went directly to Anya, who was lying on a mattress with one arm thrown over her eyes and a long bandage-like wrapping covering her other arm from shoulder to elbow. The bandage was not soaked with blood, but there was a fair amount of fresh seepage.

"We tried to wash her up, detective. I got some 'biotic cream. We used one of my slips to make a bandage. We gave Annie some aspirin. She's not bleeding so bad now, but she's not talking anymore. She told us not to tell anyone, but I got so worried about her, I came to you. God, I hope she's not gonna be mad at me."

He ignored Marilyn as he felt Anya's face. He vaguely wondered about the "we" she kept mentioning, and then he noticed a dark-skinned figure under a lot of long black hair in the corner. He touched his hand to Anya's cold skin, and she moved. "It's Mitch. I'm going to get you out of here," he said. She pushed his hand away from her face and slapped at him, screaming, "No, no, no, no."

Mitchell turned to Marilyn. "Stay by her until I get some help."

"Sure, detective. I'm helping you, right?"

"See if you can get her settled down. And put something over her. She's freezing."

He left them and had his cell phone in his hand before he made it out the window. He summoned the rescue squad and then went to the curb to direct them. He also called Jimmy Lang.

By the time Anya had been stabilized by the emergency responders and transferred to a stretcher, Jimmy had swung his van curbside. He ran to the stretcher. Mitchell was standing nearby, giving instructions.

"How is she?" Jimmy asked, looking down at Anya's pale face half-hidden by her tangled hair, her eyes closed.

"Don't know. The gunshot's not life-threatening, but she's not talking and is really out of it. She went a little wild when I found her."

Jimmy waved his hand in front of Anya's eyes and said her name several times. He felt for her pulse. Her heartbeat was racing at nearly twice normal speed despite the fact she was still as stone. "I'll follow the ambulance."

"Ride with me. You'll need to tell the docs what's wrong with her beside being shot."

Memorial Hospital was just a few miles from downtown Morristown, and Anya was wheeled into the emergency door within ten minutes.

"This is the gunshot victim?" the waiting triage nurse inquired, pointing the way toward the automatic doors.

The resident on duty ignored Anya's primitively bandaged arm to check her vital signs first. "She looks shocky," he said while expertly hooking her up to various monitors. He elevated her feet and looked her over carefully for other trauma. Only then he checked the gunshot wound. "So how'd this happen, detective?"

"Someone took a shot at her on stage at the South Street Theatre."

"I guess they really didn't like her act," the resident quipped. Nobody laughed. "Sorry. E.R. humor," he said without sounding sorry. He partially unwrapped Anya's arm and took a quick look at the bullet site. "Where's she been? She looks traumatized. I don't see any signs, but do we need a rape kit here?"

Mitchell answered. "No, nothing like that. She ran and hid after getting winged and was just now found."

"Outdoors?"

"No, but in a damp and chilly place."

"She's still cold. She should have warmed up by now. We'll get her under and over some heat." He looked around and motioned to a nurse. "Get her core temp up quick." Mitchell and Jimmy moved out of the way.

After Anya was wrapped in a cocoon of heated blankets, the doctor removed the dirty bandage from her arm, injected a local pain killer, and probed the bullet site. "She's lucky. The bullet missed the bone and the artery, but there's significant blood loss. And there's an obvious danger of infection. What is this thing wrapped around her arm?"

"Marilyn Monroe's lingerie," Mitchell answered.

The resident raised his eyebrow and began to clean the wound, a small neat hole. Anya never blinked. The resident looked worried. "You know, she has all the signs of being in extreme terror. Can either of you be helpful on this point? Her heart rate's still way up and we need it to start coming down."

Mitchell cocked his head toward Jimmy. "He's her doctor."

"I'm a neurobiologist," Jimmy said.

"And do you know something I should know?" the resident asked.

"I think she's in some kind of sleep state and is reliving a very bad nightmare."

"Well, we need to wake her up, and then we need to get some serious tranquilizer into her."

Jimmy shook his head. "I hate to see her shocked and drugged in this state. This has happened before, but not so deep or for so long. Can I have a few minutes with her?"

The doctor looked at Mitchell and gestured toward Jimmy. "If he's not the shooter and thinks he can deliver, he can have five minutes, but then she needs to be brought around."

Jimmy gently sat down on the side of the hospital bed. He began the wakeup routine he'd used hundreds of times with Anya. Then he expanded it, talking to her steadily. It didn't matter what he was saying, just that he spoke in the same cadence and tone. He talked about her music, about the wisecracking medical resident, about her keeping him up so late. He chafed her arms and gently moved her head. He found himself talking about the last time they were together, his walking her back to the Ralston Club. He mentioned kissing her, and that it was nice.

He felt her trying to come back. Then her whole body contracted. She sat upright with a harsh intake of breath, her eyes and mouth open. She looked terrified, but in an instant the spasm passed and she recognized and reached for Jimmy. He held her, stroking her arms.

"Jimmy. I was in a dark place. In the woods. I was waiting. Waiting for something terrible to happen. I was going to die, and I couldn't do anything. I couldn't fight and I couldn't run away. I was paralyzed."

"It's all right, Anya. You're in the hospital now."

"I'm in a hospital?" she asked, incredulous.

"Yes. You were shot in the arm. You don't remember?"

"I was shot?" She became panicky and tried to get up.

"Lie down, Anya. You can handle this," he said sharply.

She lay back down. He watched on the monitor while her heartbeat subsided somewhat. Her color was better and her skin felt warmer.

The resident, with Mitchell trailing him, returned to the cubicle. "Looks like the neurodoc knew what the patient needed," he said. "Welcome back, sweetheart."

"I want to go home now." Anya looked around for her clothes.

"No way," said the resident. "You're going upstairs. That arm needs more care, and I want to be sure your doctor friend has actually cured whatever else ails you."

She looked at Jimmy and he nodded encouragingly, trying to be lighthearted. "I'll bring you a big pile of trashy celebrity magazines." He looked over at Mitchell. "By the way, Mitch found you. You owe him a big one."

Anya looked at the detective, confused. "Thank you. I'm grateful."

"I'm glad you're all right, Anya." Then, hating himself, he played the cop. "I'm going to have to speak to you about what happened as soon as possible." He left the cubicle and made arrangements for Anya's hospital room to be guarded. Jimmy stayed until Anya was settled in a private room at the end of a corridor.

Chapter 33

It was well past dawn when Mitchell got back to his house. The door was unlocked and someone was inside.

"Hiya, Flo," he shouted in the direction of the kitchen, where the rattle of crockery could be heard.

"Mitch. I was in the neighborhood so I popped in," Florence said casually.

"I must have been crazy to give you a key."

"Well, I am your nearest living relative. I made coffee."

Mitchell sat down on the sofa and took the coffee gratefully while imparting the news his mother was waiting to hear. "She's okay. Bullet hole in her arm, as strange as always, but okay."

"Who could shoot such a pretty girl?" Florence replied.

Mitchell thought about the day ahead of him, trying to make sense of what had happened. "I gotta go right after I change, Flo. I have a date with Marilyn Monroe."

"You have interesting taste in women on the whole, Mitch. Anyway, there's a nice egg and bacon sandwich in the kitchen for you."

Florence left. After showering and changing his clothes, Mitchell wrapped the egg sandwich in a napkin and ate it on the way to the station. Everyone was waiting for him: search officers left over from the night before wanting to hear particulars on Anya's rescue, the next shift coming on duty, reporters who had been assigned to cover the story. Making his way to the front of the room, he filled in the top-line details.

Marilyn had been brought to the station and put in a holding cell for the remainder of the night. This morning she was waiting for him in an interrogation room, with all the coffee and donuts she could manage. Her heavy makeup had smeared and shifted during the night. She knew she was in need of extensive repairs, and she slid on her huge sunglasses to cover her face.

"Good morning, Marilyn," Mitchell said, entering the room.

Marilyn swallowed the remains of a cherry Danish. "How's Annie?" she asked.

"She's still in the hospital. But she's not too bad, Marilyn."

"Thank the good lord."

"And thank you, Marilyn. But now you have to tell me how you came to be living in a bump on the backside of the South Street Theatre."

"I saw a cat disappear in the wall and bingo! There was this space just going to waste. You know how I hate the shelters, detective."

"How long did Anya know you were living there, and why didn't she turn you in?"

"Almost since she come, detective. Her office is on the other side of my place." She made it sound like they were suburban neighbors. "Annie heard the cat through the wall and found me. I was sure I was a goner, but she didn't do nothing. Just told me not to burn the Theatre down."

"She left you food?"

"Yes. I told you. Very kind of her. She's a good hostess."

"It's not like she invited you to dine in her home, Marilyn. You were trespassing. Squatting. She was abetting."

Marilyn answered petulantly. "I'm just saying."

"And you mentioned money?"

"That was after Norma come. Annie knew it was hard enough for me to take care of myself, let alone Norma."

"I take it Norma's the other woman from last night?"

"Yeah. Norma Jean. The black girl," she said, as if to emphasize her own whiteness.

"Where's Norma now, Marilyn?"

"Lord. I don't know. She ran right after you went for help. Back where she come from, I guess."

"Where's that?"

"Who knows, detective?" She sounded evasive. "But that girl sure helped with Annie."

Mitchell looked at his watch. "I've got to go talk to Annie, Marilyn. I don't think the Theatre will want to press charges, but you can't live there anymore. Will you stay here for a few hours if I make arrangements for a nice lunch?"

Marilyn looked uncertain. "Not in a cell?"

"No cell. And burgers and double fries for lunch. What do you say?"

"Okay, Detective Mitchell. I'll hang for the burger and fries."

Mitchell called an officer through the intercom, gave instructions, and then left for Memorial Hospital. On the way there his cell phone rang. "Detective, the lady bum didn't wait for lunch. She walked out right after you did."

At the hospital Mitchell nodded to the officer on duty outside Anya's room. He took a breath, straightened his collar, and then stuck his head inside the door. "Anya. It's Detective Mitchell."

"Come in. You can open the curtain."

He slid the privacy curtain along the metal ring that surrounded the bed, revealing a very young-looking Anya. She had been thoroughly scrubbed and her hair brushed out like a child's. Her arm was wrapped in a light dressing, supported by a canvas sling. The hospital bed was in a semi-upright position, and a magazine lay on the coverlet.

"I hope I didn't wake you."

She smiled at him. "I was just resting. My parents are on the way from Ithaca. I wish they didn't have to know about this whole thing. I hate to give them such a scare."

"It's a bad deal for parents when their kid gets hurt, but all kids get hurt."

She pushed the magazine aside. "Thank you again for finding me. I guess the 'Detective Mitchell' means you're here on business, not just to say hello."

He motioned toward the chair with a questioning look. She nodded and he sat down. "You were shot and I have to catch the shooter."

"I didn't see anything or anybody."

"You have no idea who shot you or why?"

"God, no. I'm still amazed it happened."

"What were you doing on the stage?"

"I can't remember. I don't remember much after Peter Thayer dropped me off."

"Your buddy Jim thinks you were in some kind of walking blackout."

"I was aware and upset that something didn't fit – something wasn't right. I thought it had to do with my show. I took my boards to the stage. I tried to put everything together, but nothing worked. I remember finally throwing myself down on the stage in frustration."

"That hissy-fit may have saved your life. You were hard to miss on the lighted stage, but if you dropped down unexpectedly at just the right moment, a well-aimed bullet just wings you. The second one, in the dark, knocks out the lights."

Anya said nothing.

"What did Thayer say when he called you that afternoon?"

She frowned. "He was worried about me. I was very short with him, I'm afraid. He offered to come to the Theatre, but I told him no."

"He was picked up outside the Theatre right after you were

shot. Can you think of any reason Thayer would shoot you?"

Anya made a face. "Oh, please. Peter can be a pest but he's harmless."

"Thayer may not be who or what you think he is."

"What do you mean?"

"He's got baggage. Defrocked priest, a wife and a kid, for starters."

Anya turned to look at him. "What? Peter? I can't believe that."

"He's lied to a lot of people about a lot of things."

She couldn't quite wrap her brain around the information. "I'm shocked to hear this."

"Maybe you're too trusting." He was afraid he sounded judgmental.

"Maybe," she said softly, not looking at him.

He turned the page of his notepad. "Let's go back before yesterday, Anya. Let's talk about our mutual celebrity acquaintance Marilyn Monroe."

Anya lowered her eyes guiltily.

"You knew that a homeless woman was living illegally in the Theatre. Not only did you not report it, but you apparently provided her with regular square meals."

Anya's voice was pained. "I don't want Marilyn to be in any trouble. It's all my fault. I somehow decided not to say anything, and it seemed a simple thing to pick up an extra sandwich."

"She could have burned down the entire Theatre with one cigarette."

"I admit that's a very good argument for how stupid it was not to rat her out. But she promised not to smoke or use candles, and I told myself it was just temporary. That she'd move on, or I'd eventually clue someone in about her."

"Is that why you started leaving her money?"

"What? I wouldn't have given her money, detective. Really."

"She said you started with the cash when the other girl

showed up."

"What are you talking about?"

"The little black girl. Norma Jean. Marilyn's roomie."

"I don't know her. All I know is that I shared some lunches with the one who calls herself Marilyn Monroe. Norma Jean? Wasn't that Marilyn Monroe's real name?"

Mitchell left it. "Let's forget about that for now. Let's go farther back." He stood up and walked to the window. There was a blank brick wall about ten feet away. He looked at the wall while he formulated his next words. "The morning after the murders at the Rose Restaurant, you were there at the scene. Down in the gully. I saw you and had you delivered to your friends. That decision may come back to haunt me. Anya, could you have been at the restaurant much earlier, nearer to the time of the crime? Could you have seen something?"

"You're thinking that's why someone shot me. But that's impossible. I simply wasn't there."

"Then maybe someone got the idea that you could somehow reveal the Rose killer through your dreams of the old Sayre murders."

"Detective, that's wrong on so many levels. It doesn't work that way. And only Jimmy and Celia and you knew I was doing the dream analysis. They don't discuss their work."

Mitchell leveled his infinitely clear blue eyes on Anya. "People always talk, even when they shouldn't. They share a secret with a friend they think they can trust. Or they say something by accident. They overhear something and make up the rest, then pass it on, like that old kids' game 'Telephone.' As a cop I can tell you most cases wouldn't be solved without people flapping their gums. Sooner or later, someone always says something to somebody." He paused, watching her, then continued. "And as for dreaming what you don't know, isn't that the scientific hypothesis that your work with the Russian scientist is based on? Isn't that what Celia and Jim Lang have been so excited about?"

"Celia is very excited, probably too excited, but not so much Jimmy. He's more careful."

"Whatever. It doesn't matter. My point is that someone may think you know more than you do and is nervous about that, maybe even wants to silence you, just to be sure. You say you weren't on the scene until morning, hours after the Rose murders. But think back to when you first realized you'd left your bed that night. What was on your mind?"

She closed her eyes. "I knew someone was in trouble. I felt under tremendous pressure to get somewhere, to do something. Once I was outside and had been walking fast for awhile, I wasn't sure where I was. I kept stumbling, almost falling. I couldn't see anything. It was . . . " She stopped and opened her eyes.

"Finish your sentence . . . it was dark? Were you stumbling around and didn't know where you were because it was dark outside? Is that what you just remembered?"

She answered slowly. "Yes."

"So it's possible you were at the Rose Restaurant earlier, sometime in the night?"

"I don't know," she said uncertainly. "But I don't remember a thing about it. I couldn't see anybody if it was dark anyway."

"There would have been some safety lighting in the parking lot of the restaurant."

The officer on guard outside the door interrupted them, startling them both. Mitchell exploded. "What is it, Murphy? You've got a damn bad sense of timing."

"Sorry, detective. But the desk guy called and said the woman's parents are coming down the hall with some other people."

Mitchell looked up and saw Jimmy and Celia with an older couple – Anya's parents. There was a fifth person, a tallish, vigorous-looking man with a neatly trimmed beard, standing apart from the rest of them. "Find out who the fifth wheel is."

Mitchell heard the door lock as the officer went to vet the arrivals.

A minute later Murphy was back. He motioned Mitchell outside the room. "It's a Dr. Yuri Lubov from Cornell University – he works with the other two. He's got a driver's license and other ID."

"Okay. Let them come down. I'm going to stay in the room with them."

Everyone crowded into Anya's small hospital room. Jimmy and Celia hung back while the Gregorys rushed toward the bed. Both parents kissed and hugged Anya, fussing in English and Russian. Anya's mother, a slightly plump, nervous woman, was in tears. She sat down on the bed and held Anya gently, asking repeatedly, "Anya, Anya, you are all right?" Anya kept saying she was fine, trying to calm her mother.

Anya's father, a big-chested man with white hair, took her hand and squeezed it emotionally. "Anya. Why do you come here to this place? I don't want it. Your Aunt Ceci don't want it. And Dr. Lubov needs you at home for his work. Now look what happens."

The trim, bearded man had said nothing. He abruptly motioned the others to get out of the way with a quick movement of his hand. He picked up Anya's chart from the end of the hospital bed and read through it as if he were the attending physician. Peering over Anya's head, he watched the monitors behind her. Then he lifted her wounded arm and looked at it, as if he could see through the bandages. She winced slightly.

Lubov turned to Celia. He spoke with quiet contempt in his voice. "What is going on here? Anya is shot and you don't foresee anything? How could you let this happen?"

Celia involuntarily stepped back from his attack. "I did everything I could to protect Anya, Yuri. I never saw this coming. I would have done anything to prevent it. I was with Anya every day." She seemed to be searching for something – anything — to deflect his attack. "Yuri, the dreams were so good. Anya has initiated dreams substantiated by the historical record. I was so excited for her and you."

"Don't prattle, Celia. Jimmy will provide the science," he said cruelly. "You've gotten above yourself. You were here to take care of Anya, and you have failed." Celia's face crumbled and she took another step away from him.

Anya's mother quickly turned toward Lubov and spoke urgently. "Please, Yuri. I'm sure Celia did everything she could."

"I sent her to protect Anya, not stand by and watch her get shot."

Jimmy stepped toward the older man, his face stiff. "This is outrageous, Yuri. You owe Celia an apology. And everyone else in this room. Especially Anya."

The older man wheeled on Jimmy. "You, Lang. You would do better by Anya if you weren't so interested in Celia. The two of you can't be trusted together to do your job."

Jimmy balled his fists. "This is your fault, not Celia's. You're the one who didn't foresee the consequences of keeping Anya in a lab like a rat, exploiting her, not letting her grow up and be independent. It doesn't take a genius to see that it might cause problems when she finally tries to break away."

Lubov stood stock still. "You think I have exploited Anya?"

"Yes. I do. And you've taken gross advantage of Celia for years."

Anya's father had moved between the two men. "Come, Dr. Lang. Dr. Lubov has saved Anya from things you don't understand."

"He's saved her from living a normal life," Jimmy retorted.

Lubov moved around Anya's father to face Jimmy. "You know nothing, Lang. You know nothing of the dangers to Anya and how hard I have worked to keep her safe."

Jimmy stepped closer to Lubov. "She's lucky she's not dead, and no thanks to you."

Lubov's face flushed. "You have caused all of this. You encouraged Anya to work on her own, get a job, move away from me. Celia can't stop you even though she sleeps with you. Now my daughter is lying in a hospital bed, like her poor mother. This is what I have always feared. From the day she was born."

A profound quiet fell over the hospital room. Jimmy moved instinctively closer to Anya's bedside. Finally Anya broke the silence. "Mom. Daddy. What is Dr. Lubov saying?"

Before anyone could answer, Lubov rushed past Jimmy, bumping him off-balance purposely as he threw open the door and strode through it.

Anya's mother went to her, holding her close and rocking her, whispering, "Shh, shh, shh, shh."

Jimmy looked at Celia, now crouched in a chair, staring at the floor. "You've always known this?" he asked.

She turned away without answering. "I see," he said under his breath.

Frank Gregory, groping for words, ran his hands through his white hair. "Anya, your mother and me, we always loved you as if you were . . . " He couldn't finish and walked to the window.

"Frank, let me." The older woman spoke to her husband's back. She picked up a handful of tissues from a box on the bedside table and wiped Anya's eyes. She took her hand. "I will speak to you as your mother, because I will always be your mother. Daddy and I will always be your parents, regardless of what I tell you now.

"Dr. Lubov is my brother. He left the Soviet Union before us. We followed him. Yuri was always a brilliant boy, with great promise. I don't understand his theories about things we cannot see, but he has won many awards. He is a genius.

"In America, Yuri met a beautiful Russian girl, Alena. He married her. But Alena had terrible problems because she couldn't understand or control the things that came to her in her dreams. She was so kind and sweet, but so troubled. She would seem better for a while, and then Yuri, or the police, would find her outside in the night, wandering the streets, following the voices in her head.

"Yuri and Alena had a child. You, Anya. But it did Alena no good. She tried very hard because she loved you so much, but the dreams got worse. She lost the sense of what was real and what was a dream. I was taking care of you most of the time. Then one night Alena woke up in the night and walked to a waterfall in the park. Someone who saw her on the way said she looked asleep with her eyes open. She was found beneath the falls the next morning."

Lydia Gregory looked at Anya. "Yuri – your father – was distraught. He was unable to take care of you. He thought it best for everybody if we would care for you as our own child. We were unable to have children and we adored you, Anya. It seemed the best solution." She got up to bring Frank Gregory to Anya's bedside. "We talked often over the years about telling you the truth, Anya. But we put it off. And we never did tell you. That was wrong. I hope you can forgive us."

Anya was shaking and crying silently. Her mother squeezed her hand. "Don't think too harshly of Yuri Lubov, Anya. He loves you very, very much. He was always there to check on your progress and to try and protect you from . . . "

" . . . from what I inherited from my mother." Anya finished the sentence and was surprised that the stark truth didn't really rattle her.

Jimmy took Celia's arm and helped her from the chair. Mitchell followed them as they slipped out of the room to let Anya be alone with her parents.

Chapter 34

On the way back to the hotel neither Celia or Jimmy spoke. She went directly to her room. He wandered into the hotel bar. He was nursing his third scotch when his cell phone rang. He listened a moment and then said, "I'm in the hotel bar, Mitch."

In a few minutes Mitchell slid into the booth opposite him. He motioned to the waitress and ordered a beer for himself and another scotch for Jimmy.

"Did these people plan to screw up Anya as much as possible or did it just happen?" he asked, taking his first drink of the beer.

Jimmy shook his head. "I had no idea. I've met the Gregorys many times. They are a close couple and great parents to Anya. Lubov has always been remote and arrogant. A completely cerebral being, a pain in the ass to work with or know in any capacity. He has no friends among his colleagues, except Celia, and I thought he had no family. He lives in a world of things too small or too big to embrace."

"And he chose to pass Anya off to his sister and never let her know where she came from?"

"Apparently."

"And Celia?"

267

Jimmy started on the new scotch. "Lubov hired her when she was just out of grad school, to run his lab. She worshipped him from day one. Celia is incredibly organized and capable. She did everything for him. One of her most important duties was Anya. She handled all Anya's emotional needs and the Gregorys' concerns."

"Celia and Lubov. Are they lovers?"

"You know, I've never been sure about that. I'm still not, despite what she says. But Celia sees herself as Lubov's life partner. Whatever he wanted, she would have unhesitantly given him. Managing all his needs and mothering Anya crowded out everything else."

"Including you."

Jimmy twisted the drink straw between his fingers. "I fell in love with Celia. In the beginning I thought she could feel the same way about me. But Lubov is supremely selfish, especially when he saw what was happening between Celia and me. He demanded even more of her time and energy. We went along like that for years. She'd suddenly show up and be with me, but she'd never stay. It was great when she was there, but she always went back to Lubov."

"Was Celia happy with the situation?"

"I think she lived in a fantasy world where one day Lubov would turn to her and finally declare his love. Maybe she believed he would claim Anya, and the three of them would live happily ever after."

"After today, I guess that ship has sailed," Mitchell commented, raising his beer.

"I've seen Lubov treat Celia disrespectfully, but never with such targeted cruelty. I don't know how she'll get beyond it."

"Maybe you're thinking the gorgeous redhead will finally see what she's been missing with Dr. Jim all these years, and finally throw the mad scientist under the bus."

"That's a laugh," said Jimmy, semi-annoyed. "And I'm betting you have some fantasies of your own. About Anya."

Mitchell sat back in the booth. "I've got too much on my mind to have time for fantasy, Jim. I've got a murder and a disappearance to solve. And now a shooting. Personally, I think Anya is more important than a woman who chose a Russian cold fish to waste her life on."

"All you say is sadly true, detective. And believe me, I'm just as nervous about your unsolved crimes as you are. Anya won't be safe until you find the nut that took a shot at her. What a crazy thing to do. It doesn't make sense."

"I agree with you. It doesn't make any rational sense."

"Are you making any headway?" Jimmy asked.

Mitchell finished his beer and signaled for a new round of drinks. "I have two professional questions for you, Dr. Jim." He held up two fingers. "Give me straight-up, short answers. First question – can someone actually dream about things that have happened in the past, about which they have no knowledge? And second question – can something that happened in the past affect the present?"

"Hypothetically, yes and yes. Is that short enough for you?"

Mitchell shifted. "Let me be less hypothetical. Do you think Anya has tapped into the Sayre murders through her dreams? And can these old murders be connected in some way to the murders at the Rose Restaurant and to Anya getting shot?"

Jimmy spoke as carefully as he could after the considerable amount of alcohol he'd consumed. "I have seen people like Anya, especially those whose senses are connected in multiple, fluid ways like hers are, uncannily come into possession of information they have no apparent way of knowing. The mechanism is usually dreams, when consciousness is shut down and the brain is wide open and defenseless."

"You're a scientist. What could cause that?"

Jimmy shrugged. "Lubov thinks that the past doesn't die; that what happens in the past persists, perhaps in tiny dimensions made of dark energy and matter. Or maybe time itself is an illusion. Maybe the universe is static and that all possibilities already exist. Time only *seems* to move forward."

"Slow down, Jim. You're losing me. But are you saying Anya ran into a ravine following the music playing in her head, and something that happened in that place a long time ago was waiting to wriggle into her brain?"

Jimmy responded carefully. "All I'm saying is that it's a fact that Anya heard non-existent music and followed it to a specific place where she had some strange, sense-defying experiences. Why this happened is anyone's guess at the moment."

Mitchell pushed on. "And my second question. It is possible that the Sayre murders are connected with the Rose murders?"

Jimmy raised his drink and appeared to be assessing its level carefully. "The two events are connected just by dint of the inherent possibility. If a connection can be imagined to exist by someone, no matter how tiny the odds, it can exist. The immutable laws of probability demand no less."

"This is more Lubov high theory? Or just Jimspeak after three scotches?"

Jimmy put down his glass. "Look, Mitch. Phebe is a long-dead-and-gone victim who lived out her short life as a slave and met a particularly brutal end. But if someone thinks she is a restless ghost reaching out from the grave, or thinks that someone else might think so, it could influence his or her actions, thereby connecting the two events."

There was a long silence. Mitchell put down his beer. "Here's what I think, Jim. I think I'm going to leave the heavy scientific theorizing to you and Lubov. Cosmic connections or not, I have to figure out whodunnit. It's what I do. I'm a detective."

"So have you detected anything, Mitch?" Jimmy said, really feeling the drinks.

"Well, I'm glad you asked, Jim. I think I have. I've detected a problem with Anya's story of the night of the murders."

"You mean the following morning."

"No. Here's the thing. It's quite possible Anya was on the scene at the Rose Restaurant not afterwards, but at the time of the murders."

"And you think this because . . . ?"

"I don't just think it. Anya has remembered that she had trouble getting to the Rose that night. She stumbled around and almost lost her way. She was the one who reached the conclusion that this occurred because it was dark. So I went to the Ralston Club and asked a few questions. There's a handyman there who barters his skills for room and board. He's an old guy who spends a lot of time sitting on the porch when he's not being handy, just keeping an eye on things, or maybe imagining he's lord of the manor. I don't know. But he was on the porch when Anya came back from dinner with you and Celia the night of the murders. And he was sitting there when she left the Ralston Club a short time later."

Jimmy began to think that he might have been set up. He grappled with the effect of the drinks. "She could have gone out for a quick walk before bed."

"Mr. Fixit was around for another hour. No Anya."

Jimmy didn't reply. Mitchell leaned across the table. "I have another question for you, doc. Could Anya have arrived at the Rose sometime after midnight, hung around for five hours or so and not remember anything about it?"

"What do you think she was doing, detective? Murdering the Sullivans?"

"I'm asking you, the scientist, to give me a hypothesis. Let's say Anya did go to the Rose earlier. Let's say she saw something. And let's stipulate that at some point she went into the ravine behind the Rose, because that's where I spotted her that morning. What could have happened to all those hours that Anya can't remember? What's your theory, doc?"

Jimmy's brain had cleared some of the scotch through sheer

concentration, and he was listening to Mitchell carefully now. "I can't imagine Anya was in the woods all that time in a conscious state and then forgot."

"She was maybe unconscious, you're saying? She had no injuries."

"No. I'm thinking about sleep. And all that goes with it for Anya."

"Weird dreams. You think she fell asleep and dreamed for hours but doesn't remember any of it? You claim that Anya's the world champion of dream recall. She'd remember."

Jimmy shifted in his seat. "There's something called dream-in-dream. I've read about cases of it. I may have seen it once or twice. Someone dreams they are dreaming. Then they 'wake up' in that dream and dream again. The content of the deeper secondary dream is then suppressed; it's closed to them. It seems to them as if they have not dreamed and therefore not slept."

"She would have no sense of the passage of time, then? She would just be puzzled about why she was out behind the Rose Restaurant at dawn."

"Exactly."

"Okay, Jim. How do we get Anya to remember that buried dream?"

"In the first place, I'm not conceding that she was out there all night or that she dreamed anything. And if she did, I can't get her to go back when she has no memory of where she's been."

"There's no way?"

Jimmy picked up his empty glass, then put it down carefully in front of him. "Unless – I'd have to make some calls."

"Unless what, Jim?"

"I was thinking about hypnosis. Bypass the unrecognized dream repository and go to the source in the brain's memory storage. I saw something about it in a study."

"Get on it, Jim. Because Anya may have seen or done something that night that made someone very nervous. I don't want them to finish what they started."

Chapter 35

Marilyn had walked out of the police station the moment her handler's back was turned. No way they could hold her legally without charges, she knew. And she had some things to do, even though the burger and fries had been tempting.

She headed along South Street into Morristown. The Episcopal Church near the Green ran a soup kitchen and managed a small temporary shelter where homeless people could go to avoid being swept up by the police. Marilyn had told Norma Jean that if they ever were separated, she should either go there to wait for her, or go to the public library.

Marilyn went into the side door of the church and headed for the restroom. She kept her sunglasses on until the previous occupant exited, then went in and locked the door. She washed the dregs of yesterday's makeup off, then dug into her bag and lined up her cosmetics on the narrow glass shelf. She noted that she was running low on Lightest Ivory Bisque (Opaque Coverage) *Guaranteed to Hide Imperfections*. After smoothing a heavy coat of the thick foundation from her forehead to her neck, she applied Revlon Fire and Ice bright red lipstick to her wide mouth and dabbed some in little circles on her cheeks. She finished with dark eyebrow pencil and black mascara. She left the bathroom feeling more like herself.

She went down the hallway that led to the dining area. There was a pile of sandwiches being offered, and Marilyn took two under the watchful eye of the kitchen manager. She poured a cup of coffee and put an extra empty paper cup in her purse. The sandwiches turned out to be bologna on white with a slice of government surplus cheese, which had gone stale, its shiny fake orange color almost glowing through the loose wax paper. She sat at one of the long tables and took a bite, thinking it was a mystery why the soup kitchen didn't use cling wrap, or Ziploc bags. The dry sandwich put her in mind of the lunch Detective Mitchell had promised. She was sorry to have deceived him, sorrier still to miss the burger, but she needed to catch up with Norma Jean.

No Norma at the church. After finishing her sandwiches, Marilyn ambled onto the street, walking briskly toward the Morristown Library. In the back parking lot, Marilyn encountered two women walking to their cars with bulging bags of books. She approached them and held the empty coffee cup toward them, saying something about food. Marilyn was a well-known figure around town and most people couldn't resist a good look at her. That provided an opportunity to achieve the crucial eye contact that made it difficult for them to ignore her panhandling. The women each put a few dollars into the cup. She thanked them. That takes care of the Ivory Bisque, she thought.

She kept at it in the parking lot until she'd covered the next few meals. She didn't push her luck, however. She didn't want someone to complain or call the police. She slipped into the back door of the library.

Up in the stacks on the second floor was Norma Jean, sitting by herself, thumbing through a magazine, her black hair spilling on either side of her face, her eyes hidden behind sunglasses. She looked relieved when Marilyn sat down beside her.

"You get something to eat, honey?" Marilyn asked.

"Yes. At the church. The detective let you go?"

"Sure. He had to, unless the Theatre presses charges, which they won't. They'll just board up our place." The large woman sighed. "Too bad. That was a good place for us."

The other woman looked worried. "What are we going to do?"

Marilyn got right to it. "You told me you got some money hidden somewheres, Norma. I hope you didn't just say that because you thought I'd throw you out. I wouldn't. I promised."

"You kept your word, Marilyn. But I don't know how to get the money." There was a quaver in the smaller woman's voice.

Marilyn ignored that difficulty for the time being. "I been thinking it's time to leave Morristown, Norma. We could go together. You need someone to take care of you."

"Where would we go?"

"I know people in Orange, in Newark, but I don't want to go to those places. Not so nice to the homeless there, no stale cheese sandwiches. We could get ourselves south. It's gonna be cold here soon. How much money you got hidden?"

"He gave me money every time he . . ." The smaller woman's voice trailed off.

"Jumped on you?"

"Yes. There's around a thousand dollars, maybe."

"You got a thousand dollars?" Marilyn asked incredulously. "Let's get it and go south."

"We can't get it. I hid it where I can't get to it now."

"Where?" Marilyn demanded.

"I don't want to talk about it." The younger woman slid lower into her chair.

This conversation went on for some time, getting nowhere. Finally Marilyn let it lay. They stayed at the library until dusk, then walked to the Green for dinner: two hotdogs with everything for three dollars from a vendor's cart. They shared a soda and sat on a bench on the Green to eat. Night began to fall. "We'd better find a place for the night," Marilyn said, throwing her napkin into the provided container.

"What about the church shelter?"

"Naw. Detective Mitchell will look for me there. Let's go down by the old tracks."

Marilyn had some emergency things in a waterproof suitcase that she kept hidden behind a brick wall at the far end of the Presbyterian graveyard. They picked up the suitcase on the way to the Hollow, a local name for the low area beneath the plateau that Morristown proper occupied. The Hollow followed the course of the Whippany River as it left Speedwell Lake and meandered through the woods toward the Ford Mansion Museum, which once served as George Washington's headquarters. In the woods along the river were inconspicuous temporary camps where the homeless gathered for the night until the cold drove them out of town or into the shelters.

The two women spent an uncomfortable night on a damp, dirty mattress with several other men and women doing the same nearby. Norma Jean was frightened, and Marilyn heard her whimpering softly during the night. She pulled an old blanket up under the younger woman's chin. Marilyn hoped that sleeping rough would soften Norma up about the money.

The next day they hit the church restroom facilities and partook of the lunch du jour again – chicken loaf sliced thin on white bread with mayo. Loose wax paper again; sandwich dry as yesterday's. They talked on and off about their situation, Marilyn subtly making the point that there weren't many options for them without Norma's cash.

After a while Norma stopped talking. She looked thoughtful, then nervous. She asked Marilyn for some change and went to make a phone call. When she returned she said, "I think we can get the money."

Marilyn smiled broadly. "How, honey?"

"Someone is taking a big chance. But he wants to help. He can help me get to the money."

"When?"

"He has to check on a few things. I have to call him back at 3:00. I'm nervous about this, Marilyn."

Marilyn rolled her eyes inwardly. With this girl's record with men, it would be a cold day in hell before she fell over one she could trust. But it was a chance at an unimaginable thousand bucks. "I'll be there with you, honey," Marilyn said reassuringly.

Norma knew she was expected to be alone, but she wouldn't have had the nerve to do it without Marilyn. They spent part of the afternoon sitting in the park, sharing a half-gallon of Rocky Road ice cream ($2.50, on sale for half-price at the A&P). "We'll have a big steak dinner after we get your money," Marilyn laughed. "Or whatever we want."

After the ice cream they went back to the library. Marilyn absent-mindedly turned the pages of celebrity magazines and dozed on and off while Norma nervously watched the big clock. An elderly librarian occasionally cast a disapproving look in their direction, but Marilyn knew they wouldn't be hassled. A few years back an enterprising hobo got a lawyer to bring suit against the library for denying him access to the reading tables and restrooms because his appearance and smell offended other patrons. He won the case, and today the public library welcomed all members of the public.

When it was 3:00, Norma went to make her phone call. "He says get there at 8:00," she informed Marilyn when she returned to the table.

"No problem," said Marilyn. "I think we can fit it into our busy schedule."

Chapter 36

That morning Jimmy had arrived at Anya's bedside with a large white orchid plant. He leaned over and kissed her on the cheek, smiling through the remnants of a headache from yesterday's session in the bar with Mitchell. "How's it going, kid?" he asked lightly.

"Aside from nursing a bullet wound and finding out I'm not who I thought I was, it's going okay." She smiled enough to put Jimmy's mind at ease. "That's a beautiful orchid. Thank you."

He put the large pot on the table near several other flower arrangements. There were red roses from Mitchell — an impolitic but probably unconscious choice on the detective's part. He pulled up a chair and sat down. "Anya," he started, then didn't know exactly what to say. "Anya, I never knew that Lubov was your father."

"I know that, Jimmy. You were the only one who ever encouraged me to accept myself for the quirky weirdo I am and get on with my life."

"I've always been fond of weirdos," he smiled and then continued more seriously. "But maybe I should have spoken up sooner and louder."

"I wouldn't have heard what you were trying to say until

now." A silence fell between them. "You know, I always knew how you felt about Celia, Jimmy."

"Yeah. I should have been giving myself the big pep talk about moving on."

"Celia hasn't called me or come to visit."

"She's afraid you hate her. She thinks she's lost everything – Lubov's respect, your trust."

"And you? She doesn't want to lose you."

"I doubt she cares all that much." Jimmy took off his jacket. "Remember the night you and I had a drink in the hotel bar after dinner? We talked a lot about change. We talked about Celia, and about you and me. Celia repeated some of that conversation to me the next day, and I thought you'd told her. I was surprised, and disappointed, I guess. But Celia told me she saw us in the bar. She slipped into the next booth and listened to us talking. She realized things were changing. It frightened her."

"I would never have repeated our conversation, Jimmy."

"I should have realized that."

"Jimmy. Tell Celia I don't hate her. I love her. Just as I love my parents. The people who raised me."

"I'll tell her. How are your parents holding up?"

"I think they're relieved that the truth finally came out. But they're frantic about my current situation. I'm stuck here until the police figure out what happened."

Jimmy nodded. "But you feel as good as you look?" Her slight frame rested under a light hospital blanket. Someone, probably Lydia Gregory, had brought her a silk robe with flowers on a green background. Water lilies, he thought, like the Monet paintings. She was wearing lipstick and her cheeks had a healthier color. Her long hair hung loose about her shoulders, framing her heart-shaped face.

"I'm good, Jimmy. Maybe better than I've been in a long while. Ever since Dr. Lubov's bomb-throwing, I've been thinking about the woman who was my birth mother. I need to find out much more about who she was and her medical background. Obviously I've inherited a fair amount of her idiosyncrasies. The synesthesia. The cracks in the wall between dreaming and reality." She touched the back of Jimmy's hand. "But I think your theory has merit. If I stopped picking at them, maybe the cracks would heal."

"And Lubov?"

Her face darkened. "He chose for me not to know him. That's good enough for me."

The talk of the future reminded Jimmy that he had come here with an agenda. He'd been on the internet and the telephone with several experts on exotic dream states. He had thought about it all night. "Listen, Anya. Detective Mitchell is outside. You can't be safe until the police nail whoever it was that went after you, and he needs some help from you."

"What kind of help can I give him?"

"He's sure you were at the Red Rose Restaurant in the time-frame of the killings. I know you can't remember anything. But I've been on the phone with the doctor who's had the most experience with something known as dream-in-dream. It could be the answer to what happened to you during those five hours."

She listened closely while Jimmy explained the phenomenon and the science involved in reaching walled-off dream content through hypnosis. She said "I'll do it" almost immediately.

"Do you want to ask your parents or Dr. Lubov for their opinions?"

"Dr. Lubov, never. And I don't want to confuse or worry my parents any more than they already are. So let's just get it done, the sooner the better, Jimmy."

"We can do it here. I'll bring minimal monitoring and recording equipment."

"And tell Celia I want her to be here. Just like always."

"All right. Let's get Mitch in here to plan this thing, and then I'll go get my stuff."

* * * * *

Mark West had been alone in his and Michael's townhouse for days. Michael was out of town on a case. With no job to go to, West immersed himself in his decades-long hobby: the old Sayre farmhouse and all that had happened there. His color-coded folders were spread over the tables and floors of the townhouse. Everything had become mixed up in his mind. Images of 175 years ago melded with the present and seemed just as real and immediate.

When the call came, it had seemed unreal, from some far-away place in time and space. He felt as if he had wandered through his life for nearly fifty years just so he would be prepared for the call. In a way, both of them had reached out to him. The two timeframes slid together in his mind, and he was ready. He would help the one and redeem the memory of the other.

Despite his euphoria, West hadn't lost touch with common sense. He understood his responsibilities under the law. He picked up his phone and did what he knew was right. Yet, in his heightened mental state, he was glad Michael was out of town.

Then he received a second call. He listened carefully and was convinced that he was being offered a far better way to help her; to show her his concern. He could spare her the trauma of a police encounter and explain his decision to her directly, to be part of the rescue. As for the police – he'd inform them afterward, when she was in safe hands.

So when she called him back, he changed the plan.

Chapter 37

Jimmy had set up various monitors in a corner of Anya's hospital room. He was waiting for Detective Mitchell to arrive when the officer on guard duty knocked. "I've ID'ed a redhead at the desk. Celia Ormand. She says she's expected."

"Send her down." To Anya he said, "Celia's coming. I'll see you in a little bit."

Celia passed Jimmy at Anya's door as he was leaving. He reached out and touched her hand in encouragement.

Celia, in minimum makeup and a simple white sweater and black pants, looked younger and somehow more real than her usual highly polished self. She stopped in the center of the hospital room, her eyes on Anya, waiting for a signal.

"Hi, Aunt Ceci," Anya said, in the same affectionate, matter-of-fact tone she always used.

Celia went to her. "I'm so sorry, Anya. About so many things."

"Don't be. It doesn't matter all that much in the end."

"But it does. You think I only cared for you because of Dr. Lubov. It's not true. You and Jimmy have always been so important to me. I love you both. Even though Jimmy doesn't believe that. My relationship with Dr. Lubov is something else."

"Please don't try to explain, Aunt Ceci. I'm a big girl. I know life is complicated. You don't owe me answers."

Celia began to cry. Anya reached her hand out and touched the red hair. "Come on, Aunt Ceci. Help me do my thing one more time."

When Jimmy and Mitchell arrived together, Celia was getting Anya set up in the hospital bed. Jimmy walked over to the monitors, talking as he went, trying not to make Celia feel uncomfortable. "Anya, I'm going to use some hypnotic techniques to get to the part of your memory that is sealed off. Mitch has a list of questions he wants me to ask you. If he thinks of something else, he'll pass me a note. Celia, you'll keep an eye on Anya's vital signs on the monitors. And Anya, you should be aware that under hypnosis you will not only recall unpleasant things, you may relive them quite realistically."

"I'm ready." She closed her eyes.

Jimmy led Anya through the pre-hypnotic stages of relaxation and pleasant drowsiness, then down into a deep trance-like sleep. After a few minutes, he brought her up to a lighter hypnotic state. "Anya, can you hear me?"

Her eyes still closed, she semi-mumbled, "Yes."

"Anya, remember the evening of September 23rd. You, Celia, and I spent a very pleasant day in Morristown. We went to a street fair and then had dinner at the Red Rose Restaurant. We thought you'd finished with your dream episode concerning the Sayre murders, and we were all glad about that. Celia and I dropped you off at the Ralston Club afterward. Do you remember this?"

Anya smiled. "Yes. It was so much fun. We were together again and happy."

"Yes. What did you do after we dropped you off at the Ralston Club?"

"I read for awhile. I worked on my show. I got tired and went to bed."

"You fell asleep?"

"No. I thought I would, but I didn't. I got up again and listened to music. It turned out to be *The Moonlight Sonata*."

"Turned out to be?"

"It sort of selected itself."

"And then you went to bed and slept?"

"Yes."

"Did you dream?"

Anya chuckled. "I always dream."

"What did you dream?"

"I dreamed I was on stage at the Theatre. But I had forgotten to dress. I was in my bra and panties, but no one seemed to notice. And when I went to play my violin, the strings were all broken." She related the dream with much amusement, giggling throughout.

Jimmy smiled at Anya's performance anxiety dream. "And what did you dream next?" he asked.

"Nothing."

"Nothing at all? Try to remember. Go to when you went back into deep sleep after your first dream."

"I'm just sleeping. No REM. No dreams."

"All right, Anya. You're sleeping, but can you see yourself?"

After a moment she said, "Yes. I'm lying on the bed in my pajamas."

"I'm going to count to ten. You will close your eyes as if you were going to sleep again. You will dream about yourself lying on the bed, asleep, as you just described. When I reach ten, you will be able to experience what your sleeping self is dreaming."

Anya closed her eyes as Jimmy counted. When he reached eight, he could see her eyes moving beneath their lids as if she were watching something. Celia said quietly, "She's in REM."

"Okay, Anya. Good. What are you dreaming?"

Anya's brow wrinkled. "Someone is crying. On the outside and the inside. I can't see her, but she is suffering and helpless.

She can't move." Anya became distressed and her arms stiffened.

"It's all right, Anya. You can relax and still tell me about it."

"Someone is waiting for something terrible to happen. She can't get away. She has nowhere to go." Anya became silent, watching the pictures in her head. Suddenly she said, "I've got to help her." She made a movement as if to get off the hospital bed.

Jimmy put his hand gently on her shoulder. "Just relax and tell me what you're doing in your dream, Anya."

"I'm getting out of bed. Where's my shoes and jacket? Oh, here they are. I'm going to find her."

"Find who?"

"The one who needs help."

Jimmy looked at the note Mitchell had passed him. "Does anyone see you leave the Ralston Club?"

"Umm. There's a man in a chair on the porch. He's watching me, but we don't speak. I'm walking in the street now." Nearly a minute elapsed before she spoke again. "Now I'm in the woods. It's so dark. I keep tripping on roots. Oh, I almost fell."

"Keep going, Anya."

"I'm out of the woods, but I have to start climbing." Anya's legs tensed as if she were pulling herself up an incline. "I'm climbing up the bank. I'm behind a building now." Her voice caught in alarm. "Wait. Stop. Stop."

"Why are you stopping?"

"There's a car coming. I don't want anyone to see me. I'm going to hide in the doorway."

Anya suddenly stiffened and her foot jerked violently. "Oh. Oh, god."

"What is it, Anya?"

"I've stepped on something."

"What did you step on?"

"It's a person. He's lying on the ground. He doesn't move. Oh, god. He's dead."

"Keep talking, Anya. What are you doing now?"

Silence. Then, in a small voice, "I'm hiding."

"Where are you hiding?"

"I'm down below the bank again. No one can see me here."

"What do you see?"

"A car. Someone is getting out. There is someone else inside the car."

"Can you see who these people are?"

"No, the lights are in my eyes."

"What is the person who got out of the car doing?"

"He's walking to the door of the building. Wait. He's stumbling on the dead man. He's bending down to look. He's holding the man's wrist."

Anya stopped talking. After a couple of minutes, Jimmy prompted her. "What is the person doing now?"

"Nothing."

"Nothing?"

"He's just standing there, looking back at the car. He's thinking. He's thinking now is his chance. He's pushing on the door of the building. I see elephants. Oh, no. He's going in the building."

"What are you worried about, Anya?"

Anya began to speak quickly, jerkily. "I'm running to the car. Get out! Get out! Run!"

"Are you talking to the other person in the car?"

"Yes. But she won't listen. I can't leave, she says. He told me to wait. I have to do what he says."

"What's happening now?"

"I'm saying Get out of here. You're in danger. She won't get out. I pull the door open before she can lock it, and I drag her out of the car. She runs toward the building. Then she sees the man on the ground. She says I did this. It's my fault. She's crying. I make her run with me. I can't see anything, we're running so fast."

Anya was breathing hard. A light layer of perspiration had broken out on her forehead.

"Where are you running?"

"To a hiding place."

"Who is it that you're running with, Anya?"

"It's the girl from the restaurant. It's Lily." She started to gasp for breath.

"Rest, Anya. Rest." It was quiet in the room for several minutes before Jimmy continued. Anya's eyes were still moving under their lids. "Anya? Where are you now?"

"I'm so sleepy. But there is still someone in danger. I don't know what to do. There is someone still trapped. Wait. I hear it."

"Hear what?"

"*The Moonlight Sonata.* I'm at the music place."

"Where's that, Anya?"

"By the big tree."

"You are back at the restaurant?"

She seemed confused. "Restaurant? No. I'm down in the woods behind the farmhouse."

"Okay. What do you see?"

"It's cold and damp. I can smell the dark colors. There are blacks, and browns, and purples. And red. Blood-red. All swirling and moving. The music is so loud now. Someone is here. But I can't find her. I can't help her. I'm too late. Too late. I feel her here but can't reach her. I'm so sleepy."

Mitchell passed another note to Jimmy.

"Anya. Go back. When the man was going in the building – the man with the elephants – can you see his face? Try hard to see."

"I can't see. It's too dark."

Jimmy was about to move on when Anya suddenly was propelled backward by a sharp intake of breath. "No, wait. He's turning to look back at the car. At Lily. The light is shining in his face."

"Who is it?"

Anya's speech had begun to slur. "It's Sebastian Bennett." Her head dropped to one side. "I'm so sleepy."

"She's in deep sleep, Jimmy," Celia whispered.

"That's it, then. She's come to the end. I'm going to bring her out of it."

Mitchell already had his hand on the doorknob.

Chapter 38

When it was dark, Marilyn and Norma left the Green and walked away from town on South Street. They turned on James Street and soon found a barely discernible overgrown path that ran next to a 1950s housing development. The path led into some light woods that soon grew thick and tangled with undergrowth interspersed among larger trees.

Neither of them could see much ahead of them, and there was a good deal of stumbling around.

"I've changed my mind. I don't want to do this," Norma said, whispering. "I'm all scratched up."

"That's nothin', girl. My eye almost got poked out," Marilyn whispered.

"Maybe we should just go back, Marilyn."

"You're so bullshit scared about this, Norma Jean," Marilyn said impatiently. "You're the one who don't want to be seen, that's why we're in these goddamn woods. We need that money, or we're sleeping down by the tracks."

"Okay, okay, Marilyn." The smaller woman's voice sounded a little more determined.

The woods dropped lower in front of them and a bank on their left grew higher. After a good deal more tripping on rocks and roots, Marilyn guessed they were just about behind the Red Rose Restaurant. "All right. Now we got to climb out of here," she said. They moved diagonally to lessen the pitch, Marilyn holding Norma's hand, the larger woman's muscular legs pulling both of them upwards.

When they reached the top they shook out their clothing and smoothed the bits of branches and bark from their hair, then cautiously moved toward the back door of the restaurant. The security lights in the parking lot weren't on, and it was very dark.

The door to the back of the restaurant was open a crack, as he had promised it would be. Maybe this will work out all right, Norma thought. Maybe I can just get away from this place. Somewhere nobody knows me. I swear I'll never let another man touch me again.

In her hospital room, alone now that Jimmy and Celia had left her, Anya tried to sleep. She had missed the hospital's scheduled dinner, but Celia had brought her some soup and a sandwich from the in-house restaurant. She'd eaten the soup but not the sandwich. She opened it up now and picked at the crust.

Unable to settle down, she got out of bed and straightened things as well as she could with one arm in a sling. Her cell phone was on top of the swivel shelf-table that straddled the bed. Next to it was a sheet of paper with a cell phone number written by Detective Mitchell.

She picked up her phone and dialed the number. He answered instantly. "Are you all right, Anya?"

"I'm afraid for Lily, detective."

He'd rather have not spoken with her until it was all over, but she sounded very shaky.

Trying to calm her, he said, "I have good news."

"You've found Bennett?" she asked quickly.

"No. Not yet. I'm out at Sunnyside now. But Bennett and Jillian Tremont were scheduled to attend a medical convention.

Some people saw his car pull out of here this morning. We've put out an APB."

"You've got to stop him."

"We'll have him soon."

She didn't respond. He tried to reassure her further. "Anya, I have every reason to believe Lily's fine. I can't say anything else."

"How do you know?"

"I can't say."

"Please don't be late, detective."

"Get some sleep, Anya." Right after he hung up the news came through that Bennett's Mercedes had been spotted in the parking lot at Newark's Liberty Airport.

Marilyn was excited. "Come on, honey. Let's get that money. I can smell it now."

They went through the door and into the back hall, passing by the kitchen area, moving further into the restaurant. It was dark except for a few automatic low-voltage safety lights near floor level. Norma took the lead, heading for the little private lounge. They stumbled into the room, and Norma pulled the sofa away from the wall and felt underneath it. Her small package was still there, duct-taped to the back leg of the sofa.

Marilyn couldn't contain herself. "It's there? Yes! We're gonna have that steak! Norma Jean, we're gonna get the hell out of this town!" Marilyn took the money and put it into her ample bosom.

Norma stood still. "Wait, Marilyn. Hush. I heard something."

"Oh no you didn't, honey."

They headed back toward the kitchen area. As they entered the hallway, they heard a smooth, sonorous voice. "Not what I expected tonight – two of you. But we'll sort everything out." He turned on a small but powerful flashlight and indicated that they should go into the kitchen. He moved toward a bar-height counter used for food tastings, smiling nervously. Then he dropped the smile and raised the small gun he was holding. "Both of you, please. In front of the refrigerator."

Marilyn took the smaller woman's arm. "Norma Jean. Who the hell's this? This is the guy that's gonna help you out?"

Norma's eyes were fixed on the man with the gun. "No. He's not my friend. It's Dr. Bennett."

"The creep who abuses you at the place that's supposed to help you?" Marilyn was indignant.

The smaller woman nodded her head slightly, her eyes wide, breathing shallowly through her open mouth.

"So your so-called friend tells this bum you're coming here tonight?"

"No. Mark wouldn't."

"Yeah. Sure. You really know how to pick 'em," Marilyn scoffed.

Bennett turned the gun in Marilyn's direction. "Shut up, Big Momma. Go sit down by the ovens." He held the gun on Marilyn while she backed away. There was an old radiator nearby, and he strapped her tightly to it with electrical cords. He turned to the smaller woman. "Take off the silly wig and go over to the sink and wash your face," he ordered.

The woman moved into the shadows and turned on the water. When she came back, a cascade of long blonde hair fell around her shoulders, framing her pale features and big turquoise eyes. Bennett smiled at her fondly. "Now, there's my pretty Lily. We're going away together, aren't we? You'll have anything you want." He moved closer to her and ran his hand along her pale-skinned arm. She pulled away violently.

Bennett's edgy smile disappeared again. "Where did you go that night, Lily? It made me quite anxious and angry when I got back to the car. I told you to wait."

Marilyn yelled from her place at the radiator. "She ran away, you creep."

Bennett spoke in Marilyn's direction. "Lily wouldn't run away from me. She would wait just as I asked her to." He turned back to Lily. "Something happened. What happened while I was chatting with Maureen Sullivan, little one?" He looked into her eyes, waiting for an answer.

Marilyn answered for her. "She got away from you. That's what happened, you asshole."

Bennett slowly got up from his seat and walked over to Marilyn. He kicked her twice, once in the stomach before she had time to cover up, and she retched. Then he picked up a skillet and struck her on the head. Lily heard her groan, and then there was quiet.

He walked back to the trembling Lily. "I thought Anya Gregory might be able to lead me to you, Lily, but she didn't. But I found you anyway, didn't I?" Bennett looked at his watch. "We need to move along. There's another party booked here for 10:00."

He was leading her through the door to a small office when she noticed a pool of blood spreading out from behind the counter. She scampered away from him and followed the blood to its point of origin. Mark West's body lay crumpled on the floor near the restaurant's disabled alarm system.

Lily stared at West's still body and then closed her eyes. She wanted to go to him, to try to help him, but the small bloody hole in his forehead told her he was beyond help. She stifled her outcry. Long experience had taught her to be still, to retreat, to accept, to survive for the moment.

Bennett spoke to Lily quietly. "That upsets you, I'm sure. But it had to be done. I couldn't have you in the hands of the police, and West was the only one who could lead me to you. The poor man thought he was going to be your hero."

When Lily didn't answer, he laughed bitterly. "I only wanted to solve my problem with you, Lily. I didn't want all this. But you told Maureen Sullivan about me. And now you've dragged two more people into it. Poor besotted Mark West and your big black friend over there. But nothing can be done now. The die is cast. I need you to go into the office."

Lily walked slowly into the dark office. She sat down on the chair, waiting as she'd been told. She tried to think back to the only time she'd felt safe, before her father died. When her mother began to date again, it had started. Men came and went. They'd be very kind to her at first. But she found that most of them were just biding their time until they could contrive a situation to get her alone. That's why she ran off with Brandon on her sixteenth birthday, believing his promises to protect her. That had been a terrible mistake, and she'd been making mistakes ever since.

She heard him coming toward the office. He was whistling under his breath. Why did men whistle like that? Brandon used to do that, too, when he was excited.

Bennett came into the office and sat down on Maureen Sullivan's daybed, holding the gun loosely. "Well, Lily. I'm sorry it's come to this. I'll admit you fooled me, in a lot of ways. I didn't think you had it in you." He patted the seat next to him. "By the way, did you find what you came here for? I suspect it was my money. Big Momma probably has it already." He shook his head at her slowly, cocking his eyebrow and reaching out to touch her blond curls. "You're too trusting, Lily. Remember how we talked about that in therapy?"

Lily stared ahead, hardly breathing.

Bennett seemed unable to stop talking, perhaps wanting to postpone the inevitable for a few moments. "Everyone knows your friend West had an unhealthy fixation on you, Lily. He had you all mixed up in his weird historical dramas. People will think Maureen Sullivan found out about his perverted thing for you. He had to silence Maureen. Too bad for Maureen. And people will think West met you here tonight to finally get you all to himself. When that didn't work out, he just couldn't bear it. Shot himself. Too bad for West."

Then Bennett gently turned her toward him. "And unfortunately, Lily, too bad for you," he said sadly. He removed his long white scarf, hand-painted with Asian elephants. "Take off your clothes. We need to set the scene for the end of Mark West's story."

She didn't move. "Come here, little one," he said, and pulled her toward him. He put the gun down on Maureen Sullivan's desk and started to undress her.

Chapter 39

Mitchell looked at his watch. It was just before 8:00 p.m., and they were tying things up at Bennett's house in Sunnyside.

He'd been distracted ever since he got Anya's call. It was still two hours before the police operation. It wasn't all that complicated. Mark West had heard from Lily and informed the police. West was told to get her to the Rose Restaurant at 10:00. According to the registration forms they'd found, Bennett was now on his way to a conference. Lily would be safely in police custody in a couple of hours.

He was still on edge when Anya's second call came through. "Everything's under control here, Anya. I wish you wouldn't worry."

"You're going to be too late," she kept saying. He could hear the frustration in her voice.

"Too late for what?" he asked. But she'd hung up.

Mitchell sat with his phone in his hand for a moment. Then he signaled to his lieutenant. "I'm heading over to the Rose right now. I'll see you there later."

On the way into Morristown, Mitchell's cell phone rang again. It was the duty officer from Anya's guard detail at the hospital. His voice was both excited and annoyed. "Detective,

Andrews here. The Gregory woman just tried to walk out of the hospital. She's really upset. I had to tussle with her in the hallway to prevent her from leaving."

"Christ. What's she doing now?"

"She's back in her room with a bunch of nurses. She keeps saying you're going to be late. They're talking about giving her something to calm her down."

"See if you can get her to talk to me."

Mitchell waited while the officer went into the room and said something to the nurses. Then Anya was on the phone. He could hear her breathing hard. He spoke urgently. "Listen, Anya. You can't leave the hospital. I'm going to get Lily right now. I'll be there within minutes. I won't be late, Anya. You're going to have to trust me."

He heard her soft voice on the other end of the line. "You're on your way?"

"Yes. I'm almost there. If you don't calm down, they're going to have to give you something. Do you understand? You don't want that."

She sounded alarmed. "No."

"Then trust me. I'll call you."

The officer got back on the line, speaking in a low voice. "I think she's buying whatever you said, detective."

I just hope I can guarantee that sale, he thought. He was now frankly uneasy. He stepped on the accelerator and was soon driving into the bank parking lot next to the Red Rose Restaurant. It was dark behind the stores that fronted South Street and nearly pitch-black in back of the restaurant. The security lights were automated and should have been on, but they weren't. He opened the door to his car and walked through a flowerbed between the bank property and the restaurant.

The door should be locked; Mark West was to arrive around 9:45 to unlock it, turn off the security, and then go back home. But from where Mitchell stood, the door appeared to be slightly ajar. The heavy old wood was hanging unevenly, and the red light that indicated an engaged alarm was not on. His heart started to beat fast. Would West have come to the restaurant this early? He had been told to strictly follow instructions.

Mitchell turned off his flashlight and moved toward the door. He pushed on the handle and slipped inside. Everything was still. He moved along the back corridor that led to the kitchen, feeling his way along the walls. He swept his powerful flashlight into the kitchen's interior. Near the dining counter he saw the swath of sticky blood leading to Mark West. No one else was in the kitchen now, but West's body made it obvious that hadn't been the case a very short time ago. He felt a sudden chill. He was too late for Mark West, just as Anya has prophesied.

What had West been doing in the restaurant this early? Could someone beside him have known Lily was coming? His next thought hit him like a sudden clap of thunder. Could Lily have shown up early, too? Given West's corpse, that last possibility was ominous.

Apparently someone else had found out that Lily would be at the restaurant tonight. That person had got West to depart from his police instructions, used him to gain entrance to the restaurant and to shut off the alarm, and then promptly killed him.

Sebastian Bennett's car might have shown up at the airport, but Bennett hadn't been in it.

Mitchell retreated into the corridor and called for backup. He remembered what he'd promised Anya: that Lily would soon be safe in his care. *Trust me*, he'd said. He had a moment of bitter self-loathing such as he'd never experienced before.

He heard the backup unit arrive and went out to the parking lot to fill them in. There was no longer any reason for stealth, and Mitchell ordered a full-out search. More units arrived, and soon the restaurant was ablaze with light as policemen went room to room, floor to floor.

Mitchell had finished searching the second floor when he noticed a small door leading off the landing. He motioned for the officer with him to get back, and he pulled open the door quietly. A narrow staircase led upward, probably to an old attic, he thought.

There were no lights. He silently made his way up the stairs by flashlight. At the top of the staircase was indeed an attic, with boxes and trunks filled with long-forgotten stuff strewn everywhere. There was no ventilation, and the smell of recent death was unmistakable.

Mitchell had to look no further than the first row of boxes. Behind them he saw the well-cared-for leather of Sebastian Bennett's hand-sewn tasseled French loafers. A few more steps and Mitchell saw that Bennett was lying on his back, one arm behind his neck, his head facing straight ahead, eyes open. His legs were incongruously crossed at the ankles.

Mitchell walked over to examine the body. Bennett's untouched face looked as if he was leisurely watching a sports event on television, except the set would have to have been mounted on the ceiling. He looked surprised, as if the losing team had suddenly and unexpectedly scored the winning touchdown. In his chest were three holes left by bullets from a high-powered, small-caliber handgun. There wasn't much blood on his shirt, where the bullets went in. There must be a huge puddle underneath him.

"Call down and tell them we've got another body, Murphy," Mitchell said.

"This isn't what we were planning on tonight, Detective Mitchell," the young officer remarked as he made the call.

Mitchell ignored the comment. "I want every inch of this place gone over again. "Every inch. She could still be here, dead or alive." Murphy relayed the instructions to the informal command post downstairs. Mitchell began to move each item in the attic methodically from one side to the other, dreading every time he uncovered a niche big enough for a small woman's body.

At the back, lying under the eave, he came upon the rotted frame of an ancient wooden bed under a small, high window. He shifted it away from the wall. When he swiped some of the accumulated dirt from the window, he saw that he was at the back of the old house, looking down on the restaurant's parking lot. The lot was now flooded with light from police vehicles, and someone had found the switch for the outdoor security lights. At the back of the lot, he could clearly see a section of jagged wire fencing. Tangled on the wire was something white and shiny.

He left the attic and bolted down the two staircases to the main floor and raced along the corridor toward the kitchen. "Everybody. Behind the parking lot, over the fence." He led the small pack outside to the broken fence. A platinum blonde wig was dangling on the twisted wire.

He could hear stumbling noises in the gully below him. "Get some spots over here," he shouted. Then he went down the embankment the hard way, straight down with minimal maneuvering around the roots and prickly vegetation, following the thrashing sounds in front of him. Finally someone aimed a searchlight in his direction. Others went over the fence several hundred feet to the west to approach from the other side.

Mitchell suddenly saw the two women, far in front of him, trying to locate the small path that had led them into the ravine. "Marilyn. Lily. Stop where you are," he yelled.

They kept going, moving faster.

"Marilyn, it's Detective Mitchell. Stop now."

He saw the big woman pull up slightly, talking to the other woman. Then they started to run again.

"Marilyn. You can't get away, and you're both going to end up hurt. You need to get rid of the gun. Throw it where I can see it."

He heard Marilyn's voice from below. "We'd rather die than

go to prison."

He cursed under his breath. These two pick now to go all Thelma and Louise on him? He tried to make his voice sound patient. "Wait, Marilyn. You promised Annie one thing – that you'd take care of Lily. Annie's counting on you."

"I *am* taking care of her."

"You're going to get both of you hurt," he said roughly. "Listen. You won't go to prison. It was self-defense."

"Tell that to a white judge and jury," Marilyn said defiantly, but they were winding down, he could tell. They had stopped moving. "Self-defense?" Marilyn asked slowly.

"Yes. You saved Lily from Dr. Bennett. Throw the gun away."

He sensed her hesitation and then heard the gun hit the ground a few dozen feet below him. He scampered down to retrieve it, then shouted in the direction of the bank. "Okay. I've got the gun and the girl. Also Marilyn Monroe." Just then he saw the lights of the officers coming along the path from the opposite direction. "Everything's under control," he yelled, fearful that at the last moment he could still lose Lily to an overzealous cop and have to explain to Anya. He'd rather share a jail cell with Marilyn, whoever Marilyn really was, for the rest of his life.

Chapter 40

"Damn it, for chrissakes be careful. That hurts," Marilyn said to Mitchell as he and the other officers got her and Lily up to the parking lot of the Rose. When he had a chance to look at them in the searchlight, he quickly called for ambulances. He put Marilyn and Lily into separate police units to wait.

Marilyn had extensive bruising on her face, and her head was bleeding profusely. She was also bent over, clutching her stomach, in considerable pain. He got an emergency kit from one of the police cars and held a thick pad to her scalp. "Take it easy, Marilyn, you'll be at the hospital in a few minutes. What the hell went on here tonight?"

"I thought I was stupid about men. Except for Joe, of course. But Norma got me beat every time. They rape her, they try to kill her. Even her so-called friend gave her up."

"Mark West did the right thing."

"Sure he did. That's why he's dead, and it's only a miracle Lily ain't dead, too. Not to mention me," she said accusingly. "You and your lot don't know what the hell's going on."

Mitchell was stung. She was obviously right.

"Bennett was waiting for you?"

"For Lily anyways. Wasn't expecting me. He had a gun. He

307

killed Lily's so-called friend."

"What happened to Bennett?"

"I don't know. Lily says she shot him. I hope so. I hope she shot him real good."

"Are you sure that's what happened, Marilyn?"

Just then two emergency vehicles pulled into the parking lot. While he was waiting for the women to be evaluated by the EMTs, he called Anya. She answered on the first ring. "Is Lily all right?" she asked without saying hello.

"Yes, she's with me now. So is Marilyn. They're going to the hospital for patching up. I'll call you later."

Mitchell followed the ambulances to the hospital. The women were kept apart in the emergency area. He didn't want them to have the opportunity to correlate their stories. Marilyn's bloody head wound was not life threatening, and there was only mild internal injury from the kick she sustained. "You might pee blood for a few days, but you're a lucky lady, Miss Monroe," the ER doctor told her. Lily had superficial bruises and scratches, which were cleaned and dressed. The two women were put into separate cells in the county jail as the sun was coming up. He was finishing his paperwork when word came that Jillian Tremont had been pulled off a flight to Scotland by airport police.

He was ready to interrogate Marilyn by 9:00 a.m. She smelled of strong soap and was dressed in clean grey prison garb. With her was a young, nervous woman, the assigned charity lawyer.

Mitchell wouldn't have known Marilyn without her makeup and wig. She was a large black woman who now looked smaller in the ill-fitting jumpsuit. She had a thick patch over the stitches in her head. Her short black hair frizzed around her face. She was an ordinary-looking woman, older than he'd thought, someone who looked like she should be babysitting grandkids.

At the moment she was also a very angry black woman. "You

can't leave me be for a little sleep after all I been through? I can hardly move I'm so sore. That bastard worked me over good."

Mitchell pushed a plate of donuts toward her and offered her coffee.

"I'll take the coffee. Screw the police donuts. I'm sick of them," she said.

"I'm sorry, Marilyn. Nobody expected you to be there."

"I wouldn't have let Norma Jean go alone."

"You should have told me who Norma was right away. You knew everybody was looking for Lily. You could be charged with interference."

"Everybody's looking for Lily all right. Her maniac ex-husband, his lyin' friend, that insane bastard doctor, the police."

"We could have protected her."

Marilyn's face turned dark. She had abandoned her alter ego. "Yeah, then why *didn't* you protect her? Somebody *did* tell you where she was, and you *still* couldn't protect her. And now *he's* dead. Lily and me both know what happens when you need help in this world. The police don't listen to you. They hand you over to the one you need protection *from*."

He couldn't argue with Marilyn's charges.

Marilyn ended her tirade quietly. "I tried to do what I promised Annie."

"You did. You saved Lily from Bennett."

"Well, I would have, but I was tied up and knocked unconscious."

"Start at the beginning, Marilyn."

Marilyn told Mitchell how Lily had finally worked up the nerve to call Mark West; how he made arrangements to leave the door open for her at 8:00.

"Are you sure about the time, Marilyn? It was supposed to be 10:00."

"Man, you guys couldn't find your own wachamacallits." She rolled her eyes and slumped in her chair.

Mitchell ignored the dramatics. "Why did Lily want to get in the restaurant?"

Marilyn answered his question as if she was talking to a particularly slow-witted fellow hobo. "Because she wanted to get her money. A thousand bucks from that so-called doctor creep. You can figure out what for. She hid it in the restaurant. Now how come you didn't know that?"

"And you got there by 8:00?"

"Yeah. The door was open, so we went in. We got the money. By the way, detective. Where is that cash? You see it gets back to Lily. She earned it the hard way."

"It's evidence for the moment, Marilyn. Go on."

"The doctor was waiting for us. I didn't know him. Lily looks like she's gob-smacked. He says he's taking Lily away with him, gonna give her everything. Right. When I heard that I knew we was both dead. He ties me up under the window, knocks me in the head with a damn fryin' pan. Then he goes off with Lily. He was a cruel bastard. Lily was a scared little whipped puppy. She must have known what he had in mind, but she went along anyways." Marilyn lowered her eyes. "I was like that once. You probably don't believe it 'cause I'm a big woman, but it can happen to anybody."

"I know that, Marilyn. What happened next?"

"I thought I'd get my bullet right then. But I guess he thought he could do me on the way out. He took Lily into a little office. I could hear Bennett talking. Then all of a sudden, Lily flies out of the office, practically naked, running like a deer. He's after her, cursing. They run out, and that's all I know until she comes back to the kitchen."

"It doesn't sound like you were exactly unconscious, Marilyn."

"Well, I was in and out."

"What happened when Lily came back?"

"She said she shot Bennett. She still had the gun. She untied me, got her clothes, and we ran."

He couldn't, for the life of him, see Lily shooting her abuser. It wasn't her nature or her history. "Are you sure you didn't get loose, Marilyn, and help Lily? Got ahold of the gun somehow? It wouldn't be a bad thing if you had to stop Dr. Bennett to save Lily."

"The fancy white doctor shot by the crazy black lady bum. Tell that to the judge."

That was all Marilyn was saying.

Chapter 41

Since the first day she became hostess, Lily had been a topic of conversation among policemen who frequented the Red Rose Restaurant. There'd been the usual sort of macho lewd talk about a particularly attractive woman, but with something slightly uneasy underlying the comments. Now, as Lily was led into the interrogation room, Mitchell could see why.

Lily wasn't really a woman. She was still that pretty girl you always dreamed about when you were a teenager. Small, so she could look up at you with those enormous eyes. A perfect little figure, a tiny girlish waist that you could enclose with your two hands, but with spectacular development above. Blue eyes with long dark lashes, rosy cheeks set off by clear light skin, all framed by what else? Long, wavy, naturally blonde hair. Any boy, any man, would salivate to be seen with her, to be with her.

She had the kind of looks that could have helped her get anything she wanted: the popular high school jock, a rich husband, maybe even some version of stardom. Mitchell had no idea how bright she was, but she had certainly squandered her unique attributes. Instead of wielding her power to her own advantage, she had been the victim of that power. Men of all ages noticed her; many would have felt privileged to treat her like a queen.

313

Yet she invariably ended up with the wrong men, the worst men.

How could that be? Learned fear, and the unthinking obedience required to avoid further punishment is what psychiatrists would answer, thought Mitchell. Helplessness was an abused person's basic technique to survive. It soon becomes a habit, and it's like catnip to potential abusers.

She had entered the interrogation room with a court-appointed lawyer, a tired-looking older man. Mitchell motioned for both of them to sit down. "Did you eat breakfast? Have a donut, coffee."

The lawyer helped himself. Lily looked fragile and exhausted. She didn't seem to notice her surroundings; she was lost somewhere inside her head. But when Mitchell spoke, the big eyes cleared, and she focused intently on him. When she shook her head, a blond curl tumbled over her high forehead. She let it stay there.

"I want to know everything about last night, Lily. From beginning to end."

The lawyer responded for her quickly. "Mrs. Doone knows the truth is the only thing that's going to help her. She's going to tell you everything."

Mitchell nodded and turned to his notes. "You were living at Sunnyside because your husband had a long history of beating you up. You were in upstate New York when all that happened. How did you end up here in Morristown?"

"It was because of Father Thayer."

"Father Thayer? Peter Thayer?" Mitchell asked incredulously.

"Yes. He was at the church in my town. He noticed what was going on with Brandon. A lot of people suspected what was happening, but Father Thayer was the only one to try to do anything about it."

"Did Thayer always behave as a clergyman toward you?"

A small frown appeared on her forehead. "I know what

you're thinking. Father Thayer had a reputation. But he never
. . . tried anything with me. After he left town he didn't forget
me. He got me a place at Sunnyside and helped me get away
from Brandon. I was supposed to be starting a new life."

"Supposed to be?"

"Dr. Bennett was a good doctor at the beginning. He was
helping me understand how I ended up in Sunnyside. But he
began to get personal with me. He insisted on my appointments
being at his house."

"Did anybody notice this interest in you?"

"It was about then that Miss Hildebrant got me the job at
the Red Rose Restaurant. I don't think Dr. Bennett liked that.
He wanted me to stay away from other people." Tears suddenly
welled in her eyes, magnifying their size and color. "I'm so sorry
about what happened to the Sullivans."

"Richard Sullivan never bothered you in any way?"

"Oh, no. Both the Sullivans were wonderful to me." The
tears spilled over, and Mitchell handed her a box of tissues. "But
then Dr. Bennett started."

"You mean, sexually."

"Yes." She was silent for a moment. "He played the piano
for me. He played beautifully, but it made me nervous. After the
first time – the sex, I mean – I could tell he was, well, not really
sorry afterward, but regretful. He paid me every time, maybe
so I wouldn't tell, I don't know. I hid the money at the restaurant
because I knew he could get in my cabin."

"You didn't tell anyone or try to stop him?"

"Who would believe me? He was the great doctor. I'm the
crazy patient with man troubles."

"What about Peter Thayer?"

"I wanted to say something to him, but I couldn't. After all
he'd done for me, I felt the thing with Dr. Bennett was somehow
my own fault. And I didn't want to ruin anything for Father
Thayer. He had his own past that he was trying to escape."

"I understand, Lily. It wasn't your fault. What happened next?"

"I was pregnant. Dr. Bennett told me not to worry, that he'd take care of everything. But then Lenny Paco showed up at the restaurant."

"Your husband's friend."

"Yes," she said bitterly. "I knew Brandon had sent him. At Sunnyside you're supposed to tell if anyone from your past shows up. But with things like they were with Dr. Bennett, what could I do? Lenny watched me all the time. There was talk going around the restaurant because I was sick in the mornings, and some awful rumors about Richard Sullivan got started. And then Lenny told Brandon I was pregnant by Richard."

"Your husband showed up at the restaurant?"

"Yes. One night after work. He dragged me into his car and forced me. Of course, he's my husband, so I guess it's not rape. He threatened to cut my face if I didn't tell him who I was pregnant by." She put her face in her hands and cried again. "I let him think it was Richard Sullivan. I was too scared to say anything else."

"It *is* rape, husband or no."

She shrugged, as if the distinction made little difference.

"You're not pregnant now."

"No. Dr. Bennett arranged an abortion. I went to the appointment like he told me to, and that was the end of that."

"All this must have been terrible, with no one to talk to."

"There was no one. I sort of knew that Mark West liked me. But he was just too nice. I couldn't drag him into it. I wish to god that I had never called him to help me get the money. Poor Mark. I'm so sorry about Mark. Sorry about everything." She chewed her lip so hard Mitchell thought it might bleed.

"In the end, you did tell someone about Dr. Bennett, didn't you, Lily?" he asked quietly.

"Yes. I shouldn't have, but I did."

"Maureen Sullivan."

"Yes. She was so kind to me. She gave me the job of hostess and helped me get the hang of it. She knew something was wrong. One day she sat me down after work and asked me if I was in trouble. I told her everything. Dr. Bennett, the abortion, Brandon."

"What did she do?"

"She was furious. She said she was going to call the police. But I was frightened about that and asked her to wait until the next day. She wanted me to stay there that night, but I didn't. I asked her not to say anything to Richard. I went back to Sunnyside. I knew Dr. Bennett was always away on the weekends. He stayed in town with the woman who owns Sunnyside, Miss Hildebrant, or they went away weekends. I was going to pick up my things and run away."

"But Bennett was there at Sunnyside?"

A sudden shudder ran over her small shoulders. "Waiting for me. I think Maureen was so angry she called him anyway. He was waiting in my cabin, out-of-his-mind crazy. He put me in his car and we drove back to the Rose. He told me Maureen would understand he loved me and keep our secret. But I knew he was going to tell Maureen I was just a nut case – that it was common for patients, especially my type of patient, to make up stories about their therapists."

"What happened after the two of you got to the restaurant?"

She shook her head. "Everything got confusing. Dr. Bennett told me to wait in the car until he came out for me. He headed for the back door of the restaurant. I watched him trip on something in the parking lot and lean over. Then the back door opened. It was Maureen. He went inside with her."

"What happened next?"

"I was sitting there in the car. I couldn't move or even think. And suddenly – the strangest thing happened. A woman came up to the car. A young woman with long, dark hair flying around

317

her face. I didn't recognize her in the dark, and at first I thought I was seeing things. She banged on the window until I was afraid Dr. Bennett would hear and come out. When I lowered the window, she told me I was in danger. She pulled the car door open, and I ran toward the restaurant to get away from her." Her eyes filled with tears again. "I saw Richard Sullivan on the ground. And then the woman was there, dragging me away from the building. I finally just went with her. We ran through town until we came to the Theatre on South Street. She led me down the alley and knocked on a window. Marilyn was there. The woman told Marilyn to keep me hidden no matter what. 'No matter what,' she kept repeating."

"Did you figure out who the young woman with the black hair was?"

"When I saw her in the light I remembered her from the restaurant with her friends."

"So you were with Marilyn all the time we were looking for you."

She put her chin out and said defensively, "We are friends. Marilyn has had lots of troubles with men, but she learned to take care of herself. She's teaching me."

"What did you think happened to Richard and Maureen Sullivan?"

"I didn't know. First the papers said an illegal immigrant killed them. Then that Brandon had killed Richard. I didn't know what to believe. But what could I do? Nothing would bring them back."

"Did you think that Dr. Bennett might have been involved?"

"All I knew for sure is that he would be looking for me, and he'd want to hurt me for running away. Marilyn said we had to do what Annie said. That I had to keep hidden. Marilyn went into town and got me a big wig and sunglasses, and some dark makeup, so we could move around outside."

Mitchell shook his head at this bit of simple ingenuity. "Let's move on. Eventually you called Mark West to help you get your money from the restaurant."

She was overcome with guilt, talking rapidly, offering excuses. "I never would have asked him if we weren't desperate. We had lost the place in the Theatre. We were sleeping outdoors. We had to get money to leave Morristown. I never thought Mark would call Dr. Bennett."

"Mark West called the police. It was the right thing to do. He wanted to help you. I told him to get you to the Rose Restaurant at 10:00. He would never have done anything to put you in danger. But he was tricked. Bennett probably convinced him it would be better for you if you got picked up by your doctor rather than the police."

She looked completely confused. "But how did Dr. Bennett know the police would be at the restaurant at 10:00? How did he know to call Mark?"

"I have a good idea about that." Mitchell's voice was clipped and angry, but he didn't answer her question.

"Right now we have to talk about what happened to Dr. Bennett, Lily. What I think happened is that your good friend Marilyn got loose and surprised Bennett, got the gun somehow. I think Marilyn wants me to think it was you who did the shooting, because you have a very compelling excuse."

Lily looked angry for the first time in the interview. "No. Marilyn didn't kill Dr. Bennett. I did."

"Tell me about it."

"Dr. Bennett sent me to the office. "I knew what he was going to do to me. I tried not to think about anything. It was like every time before, but somehow I knew this was different. I felt I was close to death. To tell you the truth, I really didn't care all that much. I just sat there, waiting."

"And?"

"And he came in and began talking to me. He had some terrible plan to blame Mark West for everything. I let him start to undress me. I didn't know what else to do. He took off his scarf and put it around my neck. I just sat there. It was easier that way. I just let my mind slip away."

"What happened next?"

"I heard Marilyn in the kitchen. She was screaming to me. Something about 'don't let him,' and 'fight back.' I came back to myself, to what was happening. Dr. Bennett had put the gun down to undress me. When I heard Marilyn, I rolled away from him and ran. He didn't expect it. I just ran as fast as I could.

"I thought I could get away and hide somewhere, but he kept coming. I ran up the stairs to the second floor and then up the old stairs to the attic and hid. But he knew where I was. I was trapped. At the bottom of the stairs he started talking again about how he loved me. And you know what, detective?"

"What?"

"I almost went to him. It would have been so easy to just do what he wanted." She stopped for a moment, thinking back. "But this time I didn't. I waited until he was in the attic, real close, and I shot him. I hadn't even realized I'd picked up the gun in the office when I ran. But there it was in my hand, and I aimed it and pulled the trigger. He spun around and almost fell on me. I shot him two more times after he fell down. I used all the bullets in the gun." She said it like she was reporting the weather.

"What did you do afterward?"

"I went back to the kitchen and untied Marilyn. I got my clothes and we ran."

He looked at her — tiny, neat, quiet — almost gentle. Sitting there playing with a silver ring on her finger, lost in thought. If she and Marilyn were telling the truth, this habitually helpless girl-woman had coolly fired the bullets meant for herself into her tormentor.

After Lily had been returned to her cell, he pushed the intercom for the duty officer. "Send Officer Hadley in," he said.

The blonde police officer came in. He indicated for her to sit down. "Hadley. I have a question for you. I suggest you answer it very carefully."

"Sure, Mitch," she said nervously.

"How did Sebastian Bennett find out we were going to pick up Lily at the Rose Restaurant last night?"

Hadley bristled. "Just because I work closely with Dr. Bennett at Sunnyside doesn't mean I'd ever confide police business, Mitch."

Mitchell spoke slowly and deliberately. "You've been keeping Bennett updated on this case from the beginning. Don't even try to lie about it. I'll have your telephone records by this afternoon."

She considered the effort involved and the probable outcome of stonewalling him. Everybody knew that she, as the police liaison to Sunnyside, was close to Bennett. She had been proud of that. She spoke with Bennett often. She was always so flattered to get his calls. Many of her fellow officers had certainly overheard her talking with Bennett.

Her career was over. Lying could get her in real trouble. "I'm sorry, Mitch. Dr. Bennett was so concerned about Lily. I just wanted to offer him some comfort. I thought . . . "

"Never mind what you thought. You let him know the minute we heard from Mark West, didn't you?"

"I didn't want him to worry any longer than necessary. I didn't really tell him anything directly. Just that she was safe and would be picked up soon."

"And he was so grateful at this news. So he talked you a little further in, right? Pressed you for details?"

"I didn't mean to go so far."

"You realize that if it had worked out the way Bennett planned, it would have been your signature on Lily's death warrant? And Marilyn's. As it is, you bear responsibility for Mark West's death."

Hadley's face drained of blood. She turned her face away and hoped she wasn't going to throw up. "I'm sorry. I was incredibly stupid. You'll have my resignation."

"Today." He left the room and slammed the door.

After his interview with Hadley, Mitchell went to the hospital. Sitting in a chair by Anya's bed, he filled her in on some of the details of last night. Most of it would be in tomorrow's newspapers.

She was quiet for a moment before speaking. "I'm so relieved and grateful that Marilyn and Lily are all right. I knew something terrible was going to happen. I was frantic to stop it. I didn't know what to do except call you and then try to get out of here. I'm sickened by the whole terrible story and flabbergasted to learn of my part in it. I don't know what else to say."

"I'm sorry I didn't get there in time for Mark West."

"Nobody could have foreseen that. Not even weird little me."

He silently thanked her for her generosity. Then she said, "I have no memory of that night – of going to the restaurant and seeing Bennett with Lily – or dragging her out of the car and stashing her with Marilyn."

"Strange as it sounds, when you put Lily's life in the hands of a deluded street person, you did her the biggest favor of her life." In whatever dimension she dreams in, Mitchell thought, how did she know to do that? He had a million more questions but didn't want to follow up on any of them at the moment. Maybe not ever.

It was as if she knew what he was thinking. "Thank you for not pressing me for answers I don't have." He reached out and touched her small hand where it lay on the bleached white hospital coverlet. She didn't pull away. Her green eyes were opaque and she spoke without looking at him. "On a conscious level, I never sensed anything about Bennett. I thought he was just interested in me as a scientific phenomenon. He picked up on my synesthesia right away. But then, after the Rose murders, he

322

started pressing me about Lily. He thought I knew something and he wouldn't let up, and I couldn't understand why. That's what I was trying subconsciously to figure out that afternoon. I thought it was something about my show."

"I just hope I never have to try and explain any of this in a court of law." He smiled a little, something he didn't do often.

She smiled back. But then she remembered where she was – in the hospital with a bullet wound. "So Sebastian Bennett tried to shoot me because he was sure I knew something?"

Mitchell leaned forward. "Bennett was getting increasingly squirrelly about Lily and thought you knew something, that's true. But if he wanted to kill you, he wouldn't take a shot at you inside the Theatre auditorium. That potshot was a high-risk, irrational act. That's not his style."

"Bennett didn't shoot me?" she said, grabbing his hand. "Don't tell me I'm still a target."

He took both her hands in his. "Take it easy. We've got the gun that shot you. A groundskeeper found it under a tombstone at St. Peter's. The gun is registered to Peter Thayer."

"Not Peter," she blurted.

"No. His wife."

"Peter's wife shot me?"

"Thayer left her and his kid a year ago. Thayer sends her money but she's desperate to get him back. Last week she came here to beg him to come home. She watched him with you, and she could tell how he felt about you. She knew all the signs only too well. She followed him, trying to decide what to do. On the day you were shot, she saw him go up to your room for a considerable time. When you two came downstairs, he couldn't take his hands off you, she says. She followed you to the Theatre and slipped into the dark auditorium, just to sit and think. No one saw her.

"Then all of a sudden the lights went on and you came on-stage, standing in the bright spotlights, right in front of her. She felt the gun in her pocket. She says it was like she'd been given the answer to all her problems. She slipped down the aisle to get closer, took two shots from the sound booth, then walked out the front door while everybody was running around trying to get the lights on."

EPILOGUE

When I want you – in my arms
When I want you – and all your charms,
Whenever I want you all I have to do is dream,
Dream, dream.

The Everly Brothers: Phil and Don

Chapter 42

Anya was released from the hospital the next morning. Jimmy came to pick her up. "Where's Celia?" Anya asked.

Jimmy fidgeted with the small suitcase that contained Anya's belongings. "She's gone back to Ithaca."

"Without saying anything to me?"

"Anya, why don't you just give it some time?"

"I still can't believe how everything has changed."

"As we've discussed, nothing stays the same."

Anya was standing by the bed, lightly touching the dressing on her upper arm. "But I've still got you, right, Jimmy?"

Jimmy put down the suitcase. "Yes, you still have me." He put his arms around her, and she looked up at him. He lowered his head and kissed her. The kiss took awhile, and when it was over, they were awkward about separating but smiling with pleasure.

Anya finally broke away, fumbling for her sweater. Jimmy helped her pull it over her bandaged arm. He picked up her bag. "Where to, Anya? Are you hungry?" he asked, still grinning. He felt incredibly excited.

"First I'd like to have a long, long shower. Then I want to rest in my own bed. Then maybe you could pick me up for dinner. I'd like some really good food," she said, holding his hand in both of hers.

"I would love to buy you a great dinner," Jimmy answered, feeling totally dislocated after a single kiss – somewhere between an unbelievably fired-up adolescent on the verge of his first romance and a man who had spent the last few years becoming the world's biggest cynic about love.

At the Ralston Club, Jimmy left her at the door of her apartment with a short kiss on the tip of her nose, which slid to her mouth and briefly reprised the kiss at the hospital. Inside her room, she put down her bag, stripped off her clothes, and headed for the bathroom. She shampooed her long hair three times before getting out of the shower.

After a peaceful dreamless nap she got up and poured a glass of white wine. She began to get ready for dinner. She chose her most dramatic dress, black clingy jersey to mid-calf, and low at the neck to show off an interesting jade necklace Jimmy had once given her for a birthday – her twenty-first, she remembered. It set off the green in her eyes, and she'd always liked it. She also put on long, beaded chandelier earrings and her favorite, but seldom-worn, green snakeskin high heels. She pulled her hair up at the sides, away from her face, emphasizing her striking widow's peak, and secured it with a jeweled oriental hair ornament. Her thick hair flowed from the ornament down her back.

Jimmy's reaction to her, the way he looked at her when he came to pick her up, was different from anything that had passed between them in their long history together. He couldn't take his eyes off her as she walked down the stairs to his car. He waited to close her car door until she was settled in the front seat. When he got in his side, she tucked one leg under the other and turned her body toward him, her eyes clear and shining.

She was rested and relaxed for the first time in weeks, eager for the evening to start. They headed to a newly refurbished restaurant in a high-rise hotel just outside of Morristown. Jimmy ordered an expansive dinner, including a special tasting menu of appetizers. He laughed at how hungry she was, how she enjoyed each dish, including the wines. They held hands between courses.

By the time they'd finished dessert, it was nearly eleven. They went into the hotel's dimly lit bar. She sat close against him in the booth, and he leaned down to kiss her at regular intervals. Jimmy had held back on the wine and drinks and was now in a delicious state of uncertainty and anticipation. "What next, Anya?" he finally asked, calling for the bar bill.

She didn't answer for a long minute, not looking at him, smiling to herself. "Jimmy," she said, shaking her head, giggling. "I don't know what's next."

"I didn't mean metaphorically or in the long term," he said, kissing her neck. "I was talking about tonight."

She looked at him, still smiling but dead serious. "I adore you, Jimmy. But I have to work into this with you. Tonight I'd like to do a little more cuddling, and more of this kissing, which you do very well, but then I need to go home by myself, if you aren't too insulted. I'm mentally exhausted."

Jimmy was immensely disappointed, but he was also willing to wait. He pulled her closer to him. "Let's get out of here then, before the bartender asks us to get a room."

He parked down the block from the Ralston Club, and they kissed quite a bit more before he walked her up the steps, his arm around her, her head on his arm.

"Sweet dreams, Anya," he said, watching as she ran lightly up the stairs in her green high-heeled shoes.

Chapter 43

This long, beautiful fall is still hanging on, thought Florence Mitchell, humming to herself as she prepared dinner in her neat little townhouse near the Green. She was glad. She loved the change of seasons but preferred winter to take its time setting in and to be truncated by an early spring. She looked at her watch and then picked up the phone. "Yeah, Flo?" Detective Mitchell answered.

"Just reminding you, Mitch, dear. Dinner at 7:00? You remember?"

"Yes. I'll be there, for godsakes. I gotta go. I'm working."

"And don't forget to wear a nice shirt. And bring a good wine."

"Got the wine. Screw the shirt. Good-bye, Flo." He hung up. Her only sister was coming into town from Pennsylvania. He wouldn't disappoint Flo. He never had, despite their unique style of communication. And he didn't mind his aunt, although when the two sisters got going on history – they both worked for local museums – that would be his cue to slip away.

He pulled up to his mother's at 7:00, in a fresh shirt and carrying two bottles of wine. Florence was at the door waiting, and behind her, in a deep pink skirt and white fitted blouse, gracefully balancing a plate of appetizers, was Anya Gregory.

Mitchell hung back on the threshold. "What's she doing here, Flo?" he said urgently, under his breath.

"I ran into Anya at the market and we decided we'd like to get together, the two of us, you know, just to talk," she said, smiling disingenuously.

"Where's Aunt Cathy?" he asked.

"Oh, she couldn't make it after all."

Mitchell rolled his eyes and thrust the wine at his mother and went inside. "Hello, Detective Mitchell," Anya called from the sofa.

He'd gone to the hospital the day she was released to see if he could take her home. He'd seen Jimmy kiss her in the hospital room. He'd followed them to the Ralston Club, then put an officer he knew well on a discreet off-duty stakeout with instructions to call him if Anya left the Club later.

Mitchell had caught up to Anya and Jimmy at the hotel restaurant, taking his buddy's place in a spot where he could observe but not be seen. After watching them all over each other at dinner, he'd returned to town and gotten drunk. After that, he refused to speak of Anya to his mother or anyone. He didn't look for her and hadn't seen her.

Mitchell didn't return her greeting and didn't sit down. "I don't even want to know what Flo told you to get you here," he said, talking to a spot slightly above her head. "And please god don't call me Detective Mitchell if we have to eat dinner together."

Anya smiled, amused. "Okay, Mitch. But all your mom told me to get me here was that she was making tiramisu for dessert."

"Florence is too damn clever for her own good." His mother returned to the living room with the opened wine and two glasses. "Nice wine," Florence said, looking at the label and ignoring his glowering look. "I'll leave the bottle on the table.

Help yourselves while I finish dinner."

Mitchell sat down opposite Anya on the other side of the coffee table and poured the wine.

Anya spoke into the awkward silence. "I hope it's okay that I came, Mitch. I haven't seen you around town. You never called."

"Been busy. Thought you'd be back in Ithaca by now."

"Without saying good-bye? Of course I wouldn't do that. I owe you a tremendous debt. You put up with a lot of stuff you didn't understand and you somehow managed to find me when I was really in a tight spot." She paused. "You told me to trust you, and I did."

Her statement infuriated him. "You don't have to be grateful to me. Screw grateful, Anya. I was just doing my damn job," he said intensely, refilling his wine glass.

"Your mother should have washed your mouth out with soap when you were little," she said, a little hurt.

Mitchell drank wine. "Sorry. I can be an unpleasant bastard. But you know that."

"Just be nice for Florence's sake, Mitch. She's got a great dinner cooking out there. Don't make me sorry I came."

"Okay. Nice talk." He scanned her as she sat lightly on his mother's sofa, one leg tucked underneath her, her green eyes watching him. "You look healthy enough. How's the arm?"

"I'm fine. There's just a little dimple from the bullet."

Mitchell tried to put out of his mind an image of him tracing his tongue around the small, reddish hollow that he could see just above her elbow.

She asked him about Marilyn's and Lily's pending cases.

"You've been to see them, I heard," he responded, hesitating to talk out of class.

"Yes. I'm going to have to testify. But you know that," she mocked him lightly. "And Jillian Tremont. Do you think she will support Lily's case?"

"I don't comment on the legal aspect of cases. I hand over the evidence and let the lawyers take it from there."

"Mitch, this is a social occasion, not a Law and Order episode. We can make small talk, can't we?" she said, frustrated. "You can trust me," she added.

"Can I?" he asked, which was a mean thing to say, he thought immediately. He relented. "Tremont will testify that she knew Bennett was abusing Lily. It was his pattern. But they had skimmed a small fortune from Sunnyside operations, and it was past time for them to abscond, so she thought it really didn't matter. Young women were Bennett's weakness, but Tremont usually didn't care, as long as it didn't jeopardize their scam of the moment."

"Why hadn't they gone?"

"Tremont says Bennett decided that Sonia Hildebrant's money and resources were worth a longer-term effort on his part. He could marry her and settle down for awhile and make the most of a very generous piggybank. Tremont was jealous and angry about that. They'd been together a long time. But Bennett promised her big money to move on without him."

"But Bennett's decision left the problem of Lily."

"Yes. Once he decided to put all his chips on Sonja, Lily had to go. But then Lily spilled the beans to Maureen Sullivan. Things just spun out of control after that. Instead of having to make just one little girl that nobody would miss disappear, he now had to silence Maureen, and quickly. Then Lily took off, thanks to you. He had to use Mark West to get to her, so West had to go."

"And then Marilyn shows up with Lily at the restaurant. Another unexpected situation."

"By that time he might have been so committed to his marriage scheme that one more body didn't make much difference. Although things had become so unraveled he might have just run for it in the end. Who knows?"

She shivered. "The thought occurs to me that Sonja's days would have been numbered if she'd married Bennett."

"I think you could have bet on that."

"How did she ever get involved with someone like him in the first place?"

Mitchell shrugged. "Bennett reeled her in at some big psychiatry conference in Switzerland. He's a clinical psychologist. His resume was heavily padded, but Sonja fell for him and didn't look too close. After he was over here, he sent for Jillian, who was a very good therapist and could run that side of Sunnyside while Bennett was busy jiggering Sonja's operating and construction accounts."

"Jillian was nervous about Bennett. I could tell. She grilled me about him and Lily the day I was at Sunnyside."

"The game had changed. She saw the end of things approaching. She knew that Bennett was ruthless."

Anya leaned back on the sofa. "I can't get Lily out of my mind. She's the perfect victim. The first time I saw her, I could sense her desperation."

"There are lots of girls like Lily," Mitchell said harshly. "Irresistible bait to the worst kind of men. Huge sex appeal, but so innocent and defenseless. A fatal combination. Like a sweet little doe, waiting to be gobbled up by the wolf."

"It's a terrible thing to be so vulnerable."

"She may be vulnerable, but she's alive, and a whole lot of people who were around her are dead. Maureen and Richard Sullivan, Mark West, Bennett himself. Pretty nearly Marilyn. All because of their connection to Lily Doone. And Brandon Doone will be behind bars for life or pretty near. Lily's final revenge."

"Lily was a victim most of her life, but you're right. She's also a survivor." Before she could stop herself, she added, "Unlike Phebe."

He looked at her sharply. "I suppose I'll never understand

how you knew that Lily was in danger, the first time on the night of the murders or the night Bennett got his."

She shrugged. "I don't have an answer for you. Beyond there being a lot of similarities and coincidences between what happened at the Rose Restaurant now and in the past, I just don't know."

"You've seen Michael Williams's articles in the paper?" he asked.

"You mean how Phebe got justice 175 years later through Lily?" Anya frowned. "Marlee Quinn and your mother are worried about Michael. He seems to be pouring all his grief about losing Mark into the Sayre murders. Taking up Mark's obsession."

"He's been warned not to bring your name into it, Anya."

"By you, I take it. Thanks." She put her hand to her throat where she was wearing the necklace Mitchell had found in the ravine. Jimmy had had it restored and reset with an emerald, to signal her new freedom from the past. She no longer felt an aversion to the necklace.

"I hate to say it, but your friend Celia pushed a lot of buttons with Mark West and Michael Williams."

"Celia's life was coming apart and she was trying to hold on. She didn't realize that she was feeding Mark's overwrought theories about what happened in the past and that Mark was returning the favor by encouraging what she wanted to believe about my dream episode. The two of them got tangled up where their obsessions met. It was a disaster."

"People want to believe what they want to believe. That's why scam artists can always count on pretty good odds," Mitchell remarked. "Don't let Michael Williams be a pest, even if you feel sorry for him," he added.

Anya looked up and saw Florence smiling at them. She announced dinner.

After dinner, Florence eschewed help in the kitchen. "You

can take Anya home when she's ready, Mitch. Or out for an after-dinner drink, maybe," she said hopefully.

"We're both busy people, Flo," Mitchell said brusquely in response to her attempted manipulation.

They walked to Mitchell's car. He held the door for her. They rode in silence to the Ralston Club, where Mitchell pulled up to the curb on the opposite side of the street. He shut off the car but didn't get out, and she stayed in her seat.

After a minute or two, he started the engine again. He drove toward the Morristown Green, then around it, passing the place where Antoine Le Blanc had once kicked spasmodically at the end of a rope on a pleasant September day. After turning off the Green at Washington Street, they soon passed the Morris County courthouse, where Le Blanc had been tried and sentenced. Mitchell turned onto Western Avenue and then Ann Street, where he quickly veered right at a sign that read *Fort Nonsense: National Park Service*. An apocryphal, if enduring, historical tale held that George Washington had ordered a lookout post built at the highest point of Morristown simply to keep idle soldiers busy, hence the whimsical place-name.

They drove upward along a curved, snaking road that switchbacked up the steep hill. Anya was surprised she had never noticed a hill this high only two blocks from the Morristown Green. The hill's topography, bare at the time of Washington's sojourn in Morristown, was now completely obscured by modern development and dense tree cover.

At the top of the hill were parking spaces for visitors. Mitchell parked and came around to get her. The paths that wandered throughout the hilltop shimmered in white moonlight. She could just discern post-mounted signage that interpreted the site at intervals.

They walked to the eastern edge of the hill. Below them was Morristown's Green, a dark square surrounded by the lights of dozens of shops, banks, townhouses and restaurants. Intersecting the sides and corners of the Green were many roads leading in all directions, linking a myriad of towns and villages, just as they had done in colonial times. And there was South Street, the road that connected Samuel Sayre's farm, where three people had been cruelly murdered, to Morristown's Green, where an equally brutal revenge had been legally administered.

Mitchell took off his jacket and draped it around Anya's shoulders. He led her to a bench near an enclosed information kiosk. They sat down. "Fuck," Mitchell said under his breath, followed by a quick "sorry about that" when he realized she'd heard him.

"I was hoping you wouldn't open this conversation with one of your favorite words," she replied.

"What conversation? We're having a conversation here?"

"A conversation about all the stuff you want to know. That's why you brought me up here, yes?"

"I meant to dump you at your place and get on with my life."

"Well, you didn't. Why not?"

He leaned against the back of the bench. "You've driven me crazy since the moment I first laid eyes on you."

"Do you wish you'd never met me?"

"Maybe."

"Ask me something you want to know."

"Okay. What's up with you, Anya? I was sure you'd be back where you came from by now."

Anya leaned forward. "That was my first thought. That I'd be better off at home, with my parents, where my little oddities were known and accepted. Where I'd be taken care of. I'd tried to break away on my own and had to call for help. I thought maybe I should just go back with my tail between my legs."

"Like Lubov and Celia Ormand wanted you to."

She nodded her head, a bit sad at the mention of her biological father's name. She had not yet spoken to him, although she knew that she would eventually do so.

"Mitch, I've had some long talks with Sonja Hildebrandt. We've sort of become friends."

"After being Queen of Morristown, she's in a real messy spot."

"She was indeed going to marry Bennett. She'd given him complete authority at Sunnyside. He had gotten a lot of her and other people's money. She intends to give everybody who wants to pull their support their money back. But she's determined to go on with Sunnyside."

"Sonja Hildebrant is used to having what she wants. If she wanted a women's shelter, she got it. If she needed an attractive doctor to run it, she bought one."

"She only wanted to do good."

"She took stupid shortcuts. You don't put people in sensitive positions without checking them out. Bennett was a career swindler at best and a serial killer to boot. And Peter Thayer was an unwise choice as spiritual advisor to young women."

Anya sighed. "She did the same thing with me, you know. She hired me on instinct without knowing anything about me." When he didn't comment, she continued. "I thought I'd *so* be out of a job at the Theatre. But Sonja told me the board wants me to stay on. They don't see me directly to blame for anything. Except maybe not informing them of Marilyn Monroe's squat at the back of the Theatre," she finished sheepishly.

Mitchell was unsure of what she was saying. "Are you saying you're staying here in Morristown?"

"Yes, I am. For a while anyway. I want to have an independent life. There are some new medications that may be able to block my vulnerability during dreaming. It's the opposite approach to actively pursuing complex, troubling dreams and maybe inadvertently giving them a life of their own. Jimmy is doing the research to decide what might be worth trying."

At the mention of Jimmy's name, Anya felt him pull away. "What else do you want to know?" she asked.

"Is Jim Lang going to be in Morristown?" He wanted to add "with you" but couldn't bring himself to say the words.

"If you want to know if Jimmy and I are together, you should just ask. I want everything to be out in the open. I don't want to run into you in town and not be able to talk to you. Or don't you care one way or the other?"

He didn't hold back. "Of course I care. Look at me – I'm an idiot. Still totally hung up on you."

Anya couldn't see him in the shadows. She reached up and touched his face lightly. He reflexively took her hand and held it.

Anya didn't take her hand back. "You know, you just disappeared. You never called. I hadn't seen you around town. I had to call your mother."

"*You* called Flo?"

"Yes, but that's not important, Mitch. Here's what I think you want to know. I'm not going to rush into anything with Jimmy. He's in Ithaca running his lab, and he'll probably be through here on his way in and out of New York doing this research for me. Jimmy is a lovely man, but he's coming off years of a corrosive relationship. He needs time to think about a lot of things.

"Bottom line is I don't know what's going to happen. But I've been thinking of you a lot, Mitch. You *are* a surly bastard. And if you ever hope to meet my parents again, you better clean up your language." Her lips turned up in her crooked smile. "But I'd like to see you, if you want. If you can take it for what it is. I'm in a very strange place now, between one stage of my life and the next. There's a huge gulf separating those two places. I'm afraid I might fall on my way across it, but I want to try."

Mitchell was quiet, but she could hear him breathing faster.

Anya poked him playfully. "So?"

"I'm thinking."

"About maybe getting hurt?" she asked.

"Yeah." She didn't reply. They watched as another car made its way up the long road to the top of the hill. Then he turned to her. "Screw it. What the hell." He put his hand on her arm and gently pulled it toward him. He leaned over and found the dimple where the bullet had gone in. He kissed it several times and then brought his head up. He kissed her face in several key spots until he settled his mouth on hers. Her skin was so sensitive to his touch that she could feel the narrow indentation above his upper lip.

Neither of them heard the officer approaching until they were caught in the yellow circle of the flashlight. "Excuse me. The park closes at sunset. I'm going to have to write a ticket. Go over to your car and get your license and registration, sir. I'll follow you."

Mitchell broke away from Anya and looked up. "Murphy. I can't believe this. You really do have the worst sense of timing in the entire fu . . . reaking world."

"Jeez. Sorry, Mitch. How could I know? God. Sorry." Murphy turned and hurried back to his black-and-white.

The police car pulled hastily away. He apologized for the language, but he wasn't really sorry, and she really didn't care. They laughed together for the first time. He kissed her again.

Then they were silent, looking at the sky where the full moon was rising, filling the hilltop with dazzling, icy white moonlight. He felt an unfamiliar private smile tugging at the tightness of the old cleft scar. He wanted that sensation to last forever, but he was willing to settle for as long as possible.

POSTSCRIPT

We are all equal in the presence of death.

Beyond the question of Antoine Le Blanc's guilt, the fairness of his conviction, and the brutality of his execution, the Sayre case lives on, fanned by the crosscurrents of history, social justice, and simple morbid curiosity. In addition to perennial retellings in all manner of print, the case has been featured on television, presented as a dramatic play, and even today a retired judge gives historical talks on the trial in the very courtroom in which Le Blanc was condemned 175 years ago. In fact, what is left of the hanging apparatus used to deliver Le Blanc from this life is still stored in the attic of Morristown's courthouse.

The next few pages describe the final fate of the principals of the tragedy. I have also included some photographs, surviving archival records, and artifact images from this extraordinary event.

After Antoine Le Blanc's body was removed from the scaffold, it was taken to a room in the courthouse where several dozen observers, including a seven-year-old boy, assembled to witness the next phase of Le Blanc's punishment.

A highly respected physicist, Professor Joseph Henry of The

College of New Jersey (later Princeton University), had traveled to Morristown with several colleagues to perform a series of experiments that involved applying a crude battery device to Le Blanc's exposed muscle tissue. At the time it was not well understood that a battery creates electricity by generating a chemical reaction between certain substances in a solution, a process that occurs naturally in the human body. Whether the witnessing doctors actually thought that a newly dead body might be reanimated by electricity is not known.

At any rate, incisions were made in Le Blanc's legs, arms and neck in order to lay bare the major muscles. The leads of a large, primitive battery were connected to certain muscle groups. When the battery was activated by adding the electrolytic solution, it was meant to transmit a jolt of electricity that would cause life-like contractions of various body parts.

Unfortunately, during the preparations, one of the doctors nicked Le Blanc's carotid artery. While this messy mishap was being cleaned up, the output of Professor Henry's battery was mostly dissipated. (It was Henry's greatest regret that he did not have his four assistants wait longer before filling the battery with acid to start the chemical reaction.)

After the marginally successful experiments with the weak battery, the corpse was flayed. The hide was transported to the Atno Tannery a few blocks from Morristown's Green, to be processed by tanner Silas Mills. The resulting leather was made into various useful mementos, like wallets and book covers. Later, it was claimed that only leather items signed by Sheriff George Ludlow were genuine chunks of Le Blanc.

Le Blanc's bones, early rumor had it, were cleaned of blood and tissue and then articulated (strung together). The skeleton was reported to have taken up residence in the medical office of Dr. Isaac Canfield, a local doctor and witness at the trial and aftermath. However, in 1893, during excavation for an extension to the county clerk's office, a three-foot-long wooden box was dug up. The box contained a label identifying the human bones within it as those of Antoine Le Blanc. A full set of bones was present in the box (some of the longer bones had been sawn in half to fit), with the exception of a skull.

The lack of a skull among these bones is interesting. There are two existing plaster-like "death masks" that were purportedly cast directly from Antoine Le Blanc's visage after his death. These death masks are indeed contemporaneous to the time of Le Blanc's demise, based on evidence of an identification tag written in early nineteenth-century script. The claim that the masks are ancient fakes rests on the observation that the cast shows no apparent neck trauma due to the hanging. However, the death mask is quite short-necked, and the casting medium could have been applied so as to conceal evidence of hanging.

The final disposition of the box of bones and the whereabouts of the missing skull remain twin mysteries.

Judge Samuel Sayre Jr. (the title of judge reflected his former position as justice of the peace in nearby Roxbury before he moved to his ancestral home in Morristown) and his wife Sarah were laid to rest in the Morristown Presbyterian Church burying ground. Their shared gravestone is located in sector 31, near the front of the cemetery. Virtually all of the engraving, rendered in soft limestone, has eroded away. However, the memoirs of Edwin A. Ely, written in the late 1880s, record the full engravature, which can be read near the photo of the Sayres' gravestone in the pages that follow.

Judge Sayre's two daughters by his first wife, Mary and Harriet, were supremely fortunate to have been away from home on the dark rainy night of May 11, 1833. Mary, then 26 years old, was on an extended visit to relatives in Sussex County, and Harriet, 23, was at school in New Haven, Connecticut. Chillingly, Le Blanc's confession included the information that he had flirted with a plan to wait for Mary's return because she had a gold watch that he fancied. Both sisters married within a few years of the tragedy. Mary lived almost into the next century, but Harriet died young, in 1849.

Phebe, at her death only 18 years old, was buried in the pauper's section of the Presbyterian burying ground. There she slept in peace for nearly a century and a half, until 1971, when her bones were washed out of their resting place during a rainstorm. Phebe's section of the graveyard had suffered undermining during the construction of a highrise business complex called *1776 On The Green*, which was erected less than a stone's throw from her plot. Phebe's bones and those of others were reburied at the back of the burying ground. The author could find no trace of a memorial to these lost souls, although there is a marble stone near the Memorial Garden that remembers the many anonymous burials in the historic graveyard, including hundreds of Revolutionary War soldiers buried in mass unmarked graves.

And what of Phebe's 19-year-old brother Martin, who played a brief but pivotal role in both the nonfiction and fictional threads of the narrative? Born into slavery, his existence confirmed by his surviving slave birth record, Martin theoretically would have been eligible for emancipation under New Jersey law within six years had he not run away. It was the loss of Martin's labor that caused Judge Sayre to travel to a seedy boarding house in New York in the late spring of 1833 to hire, by the very worst of luck, the man who soon would be convicted of killing him.

Where did Martin go after his escape? Did he ever know what happened to his owners and his sister Phebe? Did he successfully secure his freedom somewhere far from Morristown? Did he leave descendants who were destined to be free American citizens? Martin is an enigmatic ghost in this tragedy, his name a footnote in the annals of crime only because he chose to take his chances and escape from bondage in the crucial time-frame of the sinister Frenchman Antoine Le Blanc's ill-fated arrival in America.

The old Sayre homestead, built by Samuel Sayre's ancestor in 1749, passed out of the hands of the family in the years after the murders. It remained a private home for many decades. By 1940 it had become the Old Turnpike Inn, serving overnight guests. In the 1950s, it was Winchester's Turnpike Inn, and then the Wedgewood Inn in 1960. The Wedgewood Inn was a leading caterer of private parties as well as an upscale restaurant until 1980.

During the following decades, the old Sayre homestead would house a series of restaurant/nightlife venues, among them Society Hill, Argyles, Phoebe's, and finally, Jimmy's Haunt. Then, in 2007, the 258-year-old building at 217 South Street was torn down to make way for yet another of modern Morristown's ubiquitous banks.

Virginia Vogt
June 2012

DEATH AND AFTERMATH

(Photographs and images)

Crime and punishment grow out of one stem.

— *Ralph Waldo Emerson*

THE SCENE OF THE CRIME

One hundred years later

From the collections of the North Jersey History Center/Morristown and Morris Township Library

The Sayre family homestead was built in 1749 by a direct ancestor of Judge Samuel Sayre. On the evening of May 11, 1833, the judge and his wife were bludgeoned to death in the stable, a few feet from the house. Phebe, a young black "serving girl," was killed in her bed with an axe. At the time of this picture (1940) the Sayre homestead at 217 South Street had been converted to a boarding house called the Old Turnpike Inn. Later the building would become the Wedgewood Inn, followed by a series of short-lived hospitality-related businesses, ending as Jimmy's Haunt in 2006. The following year the historic site was demolished to make way for a bank.

350

THE
EXECUTION

OF

Antoine Le Blanc,

Will take place on Morristown Green, about noon this day. All persons, except those belonging to the troop, going on horse-back, or in wagons, or carriages of any kind, are notified and requested to leave their horses and carriages at some convenient place out of town, and to go the place of execution on foot. This arrangement becomes necessary, and all well-disposed persons will yield to it, when it is known, that the horses cannot be accommodated in the town, and that horses, wagons &c., would create confusion, if not danger; and would greatly interfere with the spectators on that occasion.

Friday, Sept. 6th 1833.   GEORGE H. LUDLOW, Sheriff.

PRINTED AT THE JERSEYMAN OFFICE, MORRISTOWN, N. J.

B Howell Frank Howell & M Howell went to see him hung by the neck

Courtesy of the Morris County Heritage Commission/Morris County Freeholders

Le Blanc was captured the day the murders were discovered and (after a week-long trial and about twenty minutes' jury deliberation) was sentenced to be hanged on September 6, 1833. It is estimated that more than twelve thousand men, women, and children witnessed the hanging amidst a generally celebratory atmosphere. Sheriff Ludlow, by posting his "broadside" (above), did his best to deliver a well-ordered and safe spectacle of death for his community.

351

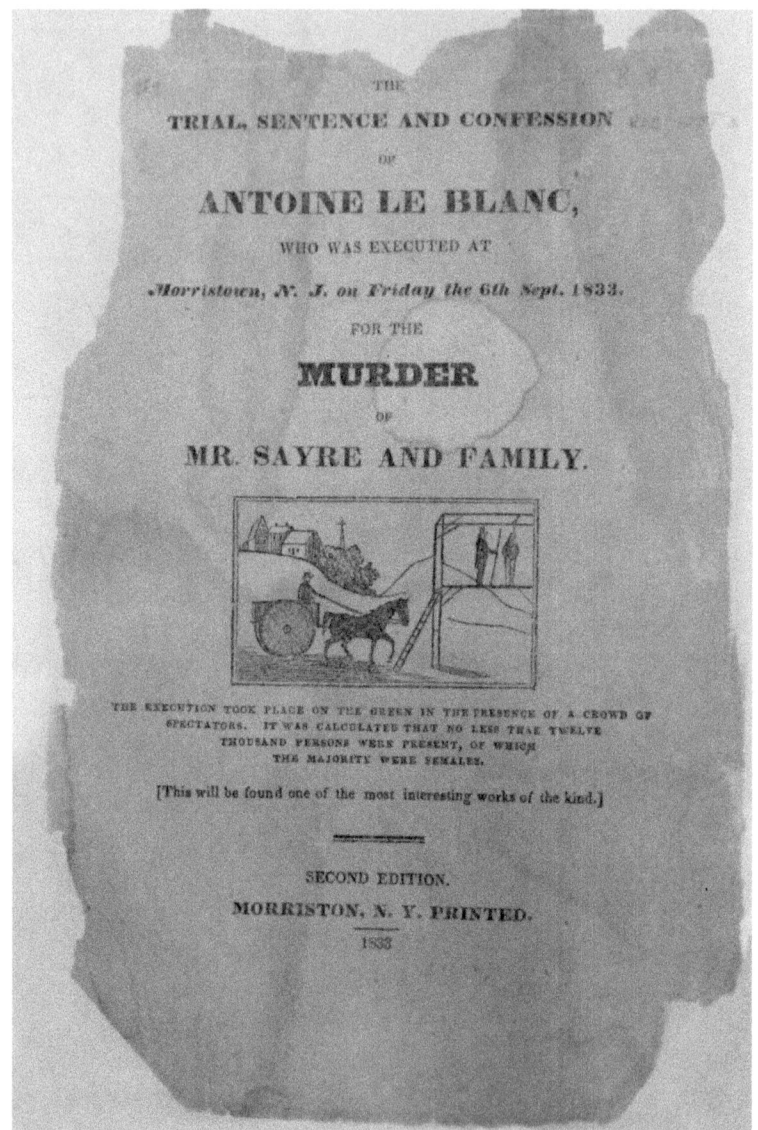

The cover of one of the souvenir "hanging" booklets that recounted the trial, sentence, and confession of Antoine Le Blanc.

A NEW WAY TO DIE

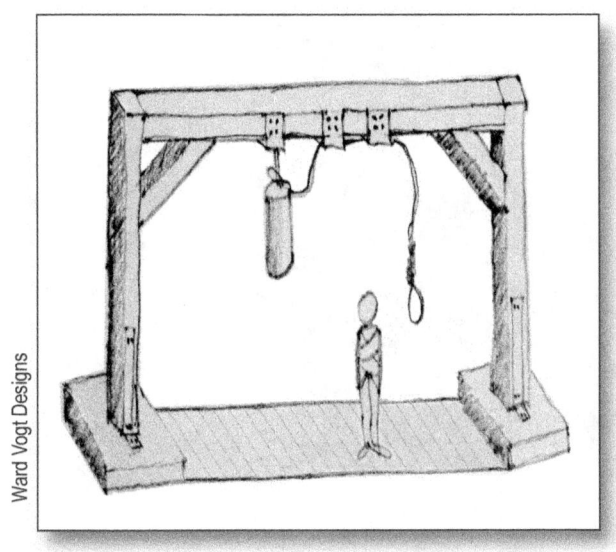

Ward Vogt Designs

The souvenir booklet of the hanging (at left) inaccurately represents the doomsday apparatus used to execute Le Blanc. Stephen Vail, the owner of Speedwell Ironworks just north of Morristown, devised a method that counterbalanced Le Blanc's weight against a heavy piece of iron. When the iron was released, he was catapulted upward rather than dropping through a trap door. The method proved to be ineffi-cient, however, and Le Blanc kicked and struggled for several minutes, to the apparent delight of at least some of the crowd.

353

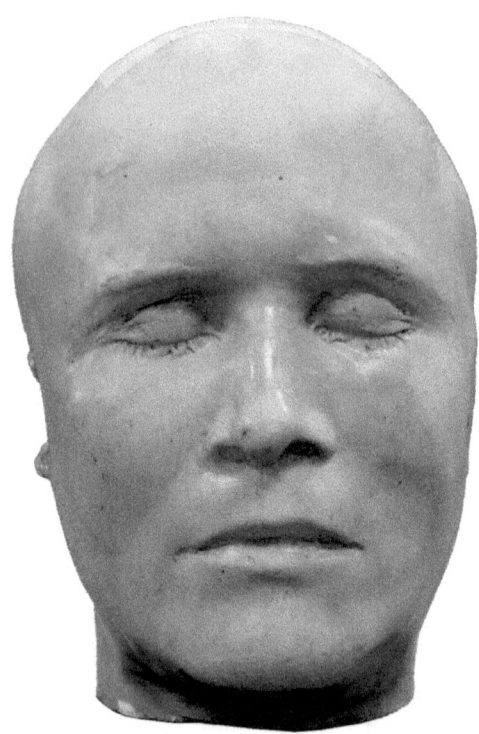

LE BLANC'S "DEATH MASK"

Genuine?

The neck appears to have no marks of trauma despite the brutal hanging. However, the neck was cast rather short, and any neck wounds could have been concealed by the casting medium.

From the collections of the North Jersey History Center/ Morristown and Morris Township Library

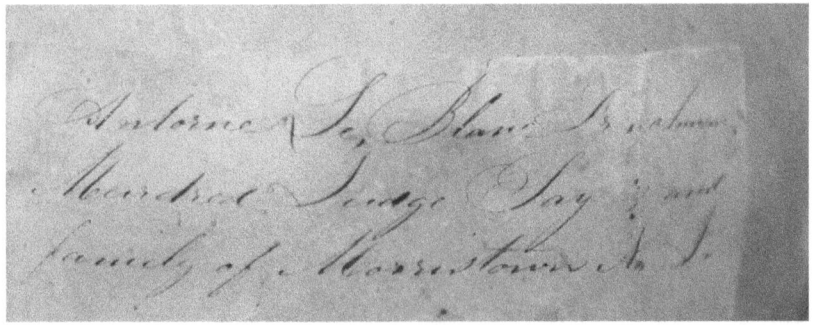

This identifying tag on the top of the mask is written in authentic early nineteenth-century script. It reads: *Antoine Le Blanc, Frenchman, Murdered Judge Sayre and family of Morristown, N.J.*

Triple Slaying In 1833

But its long history was not all a happy one. It was back on May 12, 1833, that a crazed Swiss, Antoine LeBlanc, went on a rampage and killed his employer, Samuel Sayre, Sayre's wife and the maid. LeBlanc was later caught and sentenced to death.

LeBlanc lured Sayre to the stable at the rear of the main house and then slew him with a shovel. He then lured Mrs. Sayre to the stable on the pretense that her husband was ill. She too died from shovel blows and knife wounds.

He then went into the house and killed the maid with an axe. LeBlanc, a sailor, and guest at the inn run by the Sayre's at the time, fled to the New Jersey meadows where he was caught, and brought back to Morristown.

Here he was sentenced to death and was hanged publicly on the Green. Legend says his skin was used to make pocketbooks.

Wallet made of human skin allegedly that of
Antoine Le Blanc

From the collections of the North Jersey History Center/ Morristown and Morris Township Library

The smudge at the upper left of the wallet is likely Sheriff Ludlow's signature, which was claimed to be a guarantee of the item's authenticity.

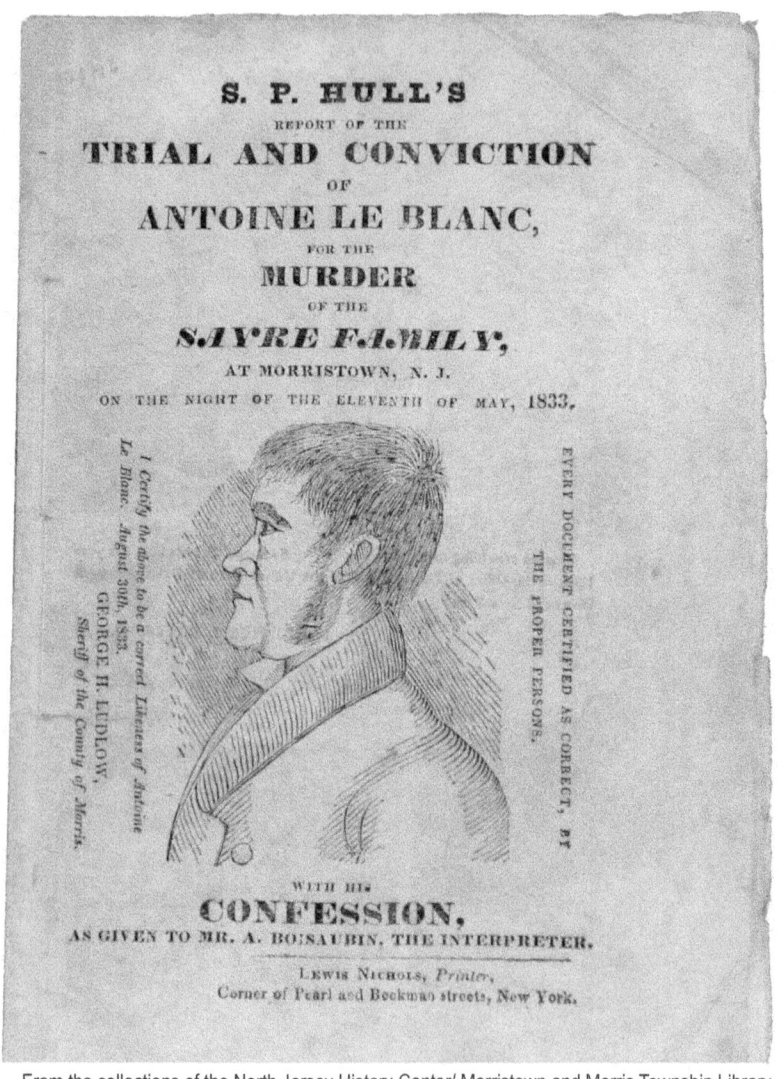

From the collections of the North Jersey History Center/ Morristown and Morris Township Library

"I Certify the above to be a correct Likeness of Antoine Le Blanc." So swore George H. Ludlow, sheriff of Morris County, in another version of the widely circulated "confession."

ANTOINE LE BLANC'S "DEATH MASK"

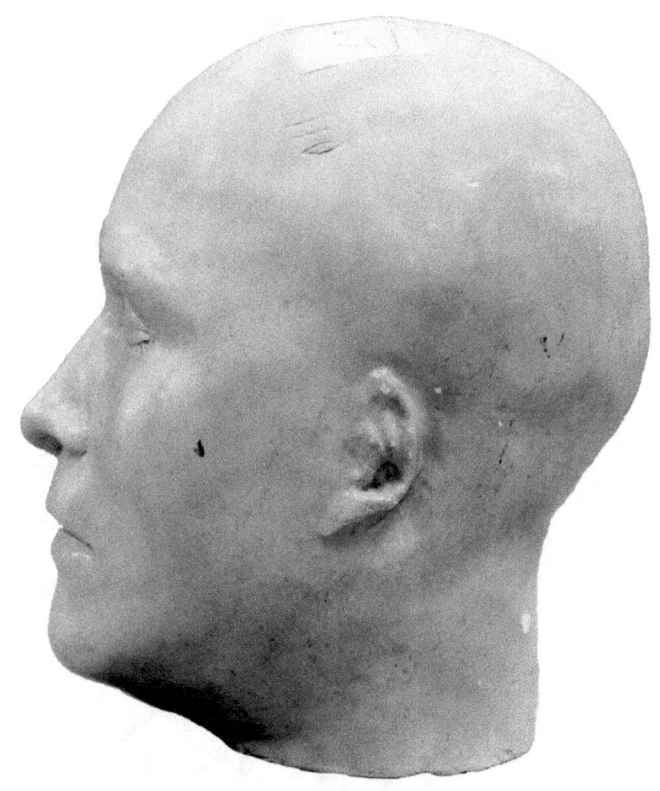

From the collections of the North Jersey History Center/ Morristown and Morris Township Library

There are two known Le Blanc "death masks" made of painted plaster-like material, created by person or persons unknown. The detail and overall artistic merit are quite fine.

357

PHEBE'S BIRTH CERTIFICATE

"I certify that my negro female slave named "Jude" was delivered of a female black child named Phebe at my house in the township of Roxbury in the County of Morris on the 8th day of August A.D. 1815 -- Witness my hand this 20th day of Jan'y 1818." (signed) Samuel Sayre

Samuel Sayre was required to register Phebe's birth because of the gradual emancipation legislation of 1804, although he did not do so until three years after the birth. Slave owners often named the babies born to their slaves. Slaves seldom were given last names, unless that of their master.

Phebe was 18 years old at the time of her murder in 1833. Theoretically, she would have been freed from servitude in three years, at the age of 21.

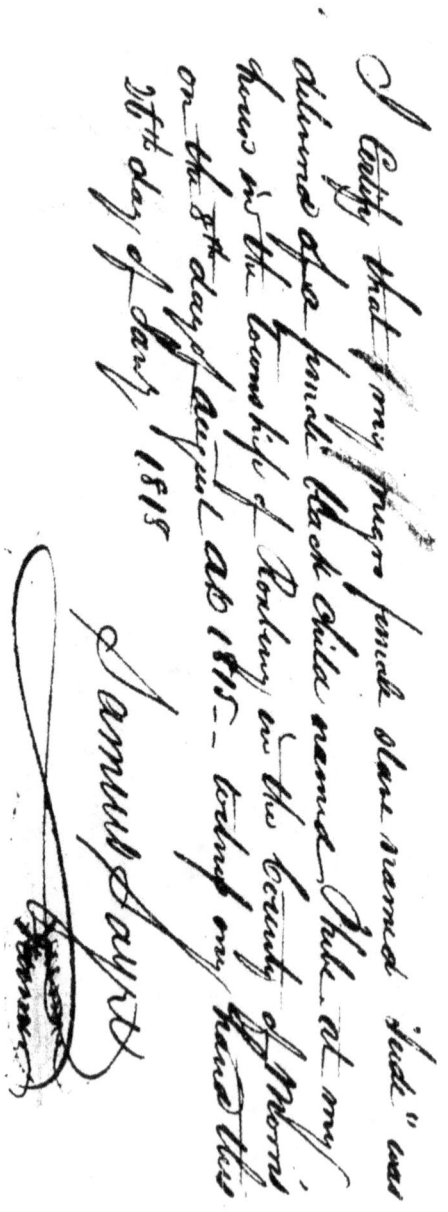

Courtesy of the Morris County Clerk's Office

MARTIN'S BIRTH
CERTIFICATE

"I do hereby certify that my negro slave named Jude was delivered of a male child which I have named Martin at my house in Roxbury, Morris County, on the fourteenth day of July last, given under my hand at Morris Town this first day of Novem'r 1814."
(signed) Samuel Sayre Jun'r

Martin was born just a year before Phebe, on July 14, to the same mother, Jude. The fathers of slave babies were rarely identified on slave birth certificates. At the time of his escape, Martin was 19 years old and six years away from legally gaining his freedom at the age of 25.

Instead, Martin chose to run away. It was Martin's departure that sent Samuel Sayre to New York looking for replacement labor from the large pool of newly arrived immigrants there. To his great misfortune, Sayre selected Antoine Le Blanc.

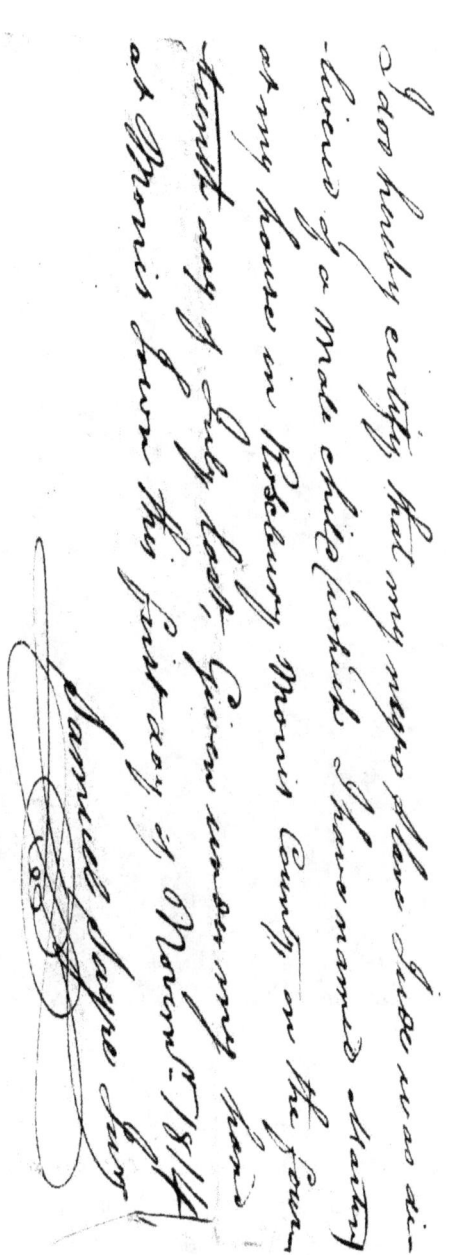

Courtesy of the Morris County Clerk's Office

359

THE SAYRE TOMBSTONE

Sacred
to the Memory of
SAMUEL SAYRE
Aged 62 years,
and of his wife
SALLY
Aged 58 years,
who were interred
Monday, May 13
1833.

Courtesy of the Presbyterian
Church on the Green
Photograph by Ward Vogt

This tombstone in Morristown's Presbyterian Church on the Green's burying ground marks the final resting place of Judge Samuel Sayre and his wife Sarah (whom he called Sally). An old memoir written in the 1880s, *The Personal Memories of Edwin Ely,* records the original engraved text, which today has completely weathered away.

"We are all equal in death."

The Memorial Garden of the Presbyterian Church on the Green

The 18-year-old Phebe was buried without ceremony in the Presbyterian cemetery in a pauper's grave. Her bones were washed out of their resting place in a 1970 storm and then were reburied, along with others, at the back of the graveyard in an unmarked site.

Today, nearly 180 years after her death, Phebe still lies in the old church burying ground at the heart of Morristown. She sleeps eternally in the company of the highborn, common citizens, fellow slaves, and a large population of anonymous dead, including many hundreds of Revolutionary soldiers and eighteenth-century smallpox victims – all now united in death, regardless of their status in life.

AFTERWORD

If you have any questions about *Death By Moonlight*, please feel free to contact the author through the author's email address:

virginia_vogt@yahoo.com

You can order additional copies of the book through the author's Facebook page:

Cost: $18 plus $4 shipping for a total of $22.

If you would like to order a quantity of books for use by a book club, please call the author to make arrangements:

973-539-6622

Death By Moonlight is available in hard copy or as an ebook at:

Amazon.com

To order directly by mail, send a check for $22 ($18 plus $4 shipping) to:

Lucky Publishers
3 Martin Lane
Morristown, NJ 07960

You may also order the book from your local bookstore.

www.ingramcontent.com/pod-product-compliance
Lightning Source LLC
Chambersburg PA
CBHW050029030726
47506CB00001B/183